THE SIDE OF THE ANGELS

THE SIDE
OF THE ANGELS

*

JOHN ROWAN WILSON

THE
COMPANION BOOK CLUB
LONDON

This edition is published by The
Hamlyn Publishing Group Ltd. and is issued
by arrangement with
William Collins, Sons & Co. Ltd.

Made and printed in Great Britain
for the Companion Book Club
by Odhams (Watford) Ltd.
S.469.UBG

'Is man an ape or an angel? Now I am on the side of the angels.'

BENJAMIN DISRAELI

'. . . Man has just made his greatest discovery since his first use of fire, and the splitting of the atom—I refer to the cracking of the genetic code. It was a quarter of a century after Rutherford's first announcement of the splitting of the atom went unnoticed by the Press that the enormity of the discovery burst upon the world with the Hiroshima bomb. The same will be the story of the genetic code. Before the end of the century, scientists will tamper with the genetic formulae of many species, including man, in a roulette hitherto reserved for the gods and the devil; man will deliberately create new kinds of being—no doubt in due course his own superior and master.'

PROFESSOR S. WARREN CAREY,
Medical Journal of Australia,
24th June, 1967

PART ONE

CHAPTER ONE

IN THESE DAYS OF AUTUMN each morning was a little greyer, a little colder than the last. The sun rose slowly behind the enormous mountains in the east, shedding a thin light over the river and the vast expanse of rolling plain through which it made its way to an inland sea a thousand miles to the south. The city lay in the middle of the plain, its factories and tower blocks huddled together as if in mutual protection from the impersonal forces of the wilderness. Its streets were wide and geometric, far too large for the meagre traffic which passed through them—they marched broadly to the edges of the desert and then petered out suddenly, giving place to the narrow ill-paved track which had been there for centuries, long before the city had been built. It was like a settlement in the middle of the sea, kept alive by the railway which passed through it and the airfield into which the jets lumbered each day from every point of the compass.

The autumn was short in this part of the world. Soon the clouds would darken further, the rainstorms which blew up so quickly would change to sleet and the sodden fields would acquire a thin covering of ice. And a few weeks later still, the snow. Then the stillness would close in on the city, the whole vast steppe would be hushed and silent. Only the river, wide and powerful and fast-flowing, would resist the powers of the cold. Eventually the river itself would falter. Blocks of ice, borne sluggishly downstream, would catch in the reeds and remain. One morning the river itself would be still and silent. The dark Asiatic winter would have taken charge of the land.

The postman pedalled his rusty bicycle slowly out of the city, his satchel on his back, his collar turned up against the cold. He glanced up at the mountains, saw the coming winter there, and shivered. His cycle creaked as it moved off the main road on to the track leading down towards a small group of wooden villas which looked on to the river. The road was bad, and after a while he dismounted resentfully from his bicycle and began to push it. He had always disliked this part of his morning round.

7

He looked at the houses with disgust. These dachas by the river were yet another of the bourgeois fashions which were sweeping the country. And occupied by foreigners, most of them, lecturers at the University or scientists from the new Research Centre just south of the town. People who went around with their noses in the air, speaking their own languages, paying visits abroad to congresses, wearing foreign clothes. They seduced the local girls with their money and their talk of travel and their sophisticated ways. There had been nothing but trouble since they came.

He stopped at one of the smaller houses. The garden was unkempt and there were no gates on the stone posts. The driveway was rutted and the potholes which lay along it were filled with muddy water from a rainstorm during the night. The postman propped his bicycle against the gatepost and plodded up the path, his boots squelching in the mud. There was only a single letter to be delivered. The usual foreign name. He pushed it through the letter-box and made his way back down the drive. Standing at the side of the dacha, with a wooden canopy over it to protect it from the weather, was a Moskvich saloon. It was many years old and there was rust under the paintwork; an old blanket was thrown over its radiator. The postman spat on the rutted driveway. Private cars, no less. And how long was it since the State had given him a new bicycle? There would be a reckoning, one of these days.

Through a haze of early morning sleep Karas was aware of the unfamiliar sound. He searched his memory to identify it, but it was only when he heard the postman's boots clumping back down the drive that he realized that it was a letter dropping through his box. He frowned. Nobody ever wrote to him here; all his correspondence came to him at the laboratories.

He slipped quickly out of bed, hardly disturbing the sleeping girl who lay at his side, and went to the window. He pushed back the curtain and saw the postman spit on the driveway before getting on his bicycle. He knew what the man was thinking and his spine tingled a little with something which was not entirely fear—it was more a kind of restless unease. In this country one never felt entirely secure—acceptance was always conditional. You were useful to them because you gave them a prestige they badly needed, and they paid you back with privileges and extra comforts. By

8

their standards you were well-paid, you had preference in housing and in buying a car, the restriction on your movements was much less than the rest of the population had to put up with. At the same time you were never truly part of the community—you lived the life of a privileged outcast. The peasants and the workmen hated you for your standard of living, the bureaucrats feared and distrusted you for the foreign influence which had filled your formative years. They knew that there were areas in your mind that they could never touch, memories against which they were constantly compared. It was as if you carried within you a vast intangible library of subversive material which could never be destroyed so long as you were alive to read it.

A hard and dangerous life had taught Karas the necessity of establishing a pattern of habit and predictability. He glanced at the sleeping girl in the bed. It didn't necessarily have to be a particularly virtuous or reputable pattern. If authority thought it knew your weakness, it was less likely to suspect you of other more dangerous vices. A man could amuse himself without incurring suspicion or censure, so long as he kept on doing so in the same way. Looked at from this angle, his relations with Anya, and with the others who had preceded her, could be regarded as a precaution as well as an indulgence.

He looked at the bed to see if he had awakened her. She was still asleep, lying across the bed with an abandon that suggested that sleep itself was to her a deeply sensual experience. He walked quietly out of the bedroom on his bare feet.

The pine floor of the bungalow creaked beneath his feet as he entered the hall. It was still not fully light and he almost tripped over a frayed patch in the carpet. There was a smell of dust and of the cabbage cooked for last night's dinner. At the end of the hall he could just see the front door—dingy and brown-painted, with a frosted glass panel set into the upper half in a hopeless attempt to let in more light.

Lying in the wire basket behind the letter-box was a single letter. The sight of it increased the feeling of unease that had started the moment he had heard it fall through the box. In the ordered life he led, something so greatly out of the ordinary carried a threatening quality. Why should anyone want to write to him here?

He picked up the envelope and recognized the writing

instantly. Max. That made it even more mysterious. Max Bremer was his oldest friend and close colleague at the laboratory—he was the head of the Molecular Genetics section in which Karas worked. He would be seeing Max in less than a couple of hours in the ordinary course of events. Karas was overcome with the feeling that something must have gone dreadfully wrong. He tore open the envelope and began to read.

Dear Peter,

This is a hard letter to write, almost as difficult as the act itself. But both are necessary. I have thought about this for a long time and have often been tempted to discuss it with you. But there was always an instinct which held me back, and now I know it was a correct one. There are certain decisions that a man must take entirely alone.

By the time you receive this letter I shall be dead. While I hope you may regret this, I don't think you will be conventionally shocked by it. We have often talked in an abstract way of suicide, and we were always both agreed that a man has the right to take his leave of the world at his own discretion. There is really little to keep me here. Sophia may miss me for a while, but she is self-sufficient and I think she will soon adjust herself. I am sure that she, like you, will understand why I must do this. But for the beginning at least, she will need consolation and support. Could I ask you to help her in whatever way you can?

I cannot give you a single reason for my decision. It has been on my mind for a long time. As you know, I have attacks of depression which come suddenly upon me from nowhere, leaving me apathetic and bewildered. It is a kind of nightmare in which the dead weight of the world seems to be crushing down on me. Perhaps it would have been better if I could have gone back to Vienna. In this place, particularly when the winter is closing in, one feels lost in the impersonal vastness of the country, alone, friendless, and forgotten.

But there is more than that. For some months past I have been tormented by the knowledge that my work has reached a point beyond which I cannot and dare not take it. Often I wondered whether to talk to you about it but I was afraid that you might think that I had lost my judgement. And if the conclusion I had come to was right, it was not a responsibility I could reasonably ask someone else to share.

I know that I am too tired and lacking in strength to face this problem, yet I cannot bring myself, in the last instance, to destroy knowledge. I therefore bequeath it to you, to your ingenuity and your strength, which I have always so much admired. With your natural instinct for the ways of the world, you may find the answer in a way I never could.

My notes are attached. I think you will be able to understand them. They are yours now. I ask only one thing, in the name of our friendship; that you do not knowingly hand them over to anyone who might use them for harm rather than good. I beg of you in particular to make no decision on impulse. But, knowing you as I do, I am sure this is an unnecessary request.

Ever yours,
Max.

Under the signature, as an afterthought, he had written, 'I shall miss our games of chess on Friday evenings.'

Karas felt a sickness in his stomach and the beginning of tears in his eyes. He folded up the letter and put it in his pocket. Attached to it were half a dozen sheets of exercise paper, covered with notes and figures in Max's spidery, rather childish handwriting. He sat down and read through them. When he had come to the end he frowned and read them again. Then he put the letter and the notes back into the envelope and stood for a while in thought. What had happened was something too large for rapid assessment. The emotions aroused in him by Max's letter and the notes which had accompanied it were beyond any of the rules which he had developed for the management of his life. He knew at that moment that something had happened to him which would have immeasurable, unpredictable consequences. The existence he had planned so carefully was destroyed at a stroke, leaving in front of him a vast abyss of danger and uncertainty.

It was very silent in the house. He went to the bedroom door and listened. Anya was still asleep. She had heard nothing. He entered the room and she stirred in the bed. The springs creaked as she sat up. She said sleepily, 'What is it?'

'Nothing. You can go back to sleep.' He took off his

dressing-gown and pyjama jacket and began to run water into the wash basin.

'What are you doing?'

'I have to go to the laboratory.'

'But it's early.'

'I have an experiment that needs setting up.' Through the semi-darkness he could feel her disbelief. He added apologetically, 'I forgot to tell you about it last night.'

'Why are you in the dark? Why don't you draw the curtains?'

'I didn't want to wake you.'

'I shan't go to sleep again now.'

He turned off the tap and went over to the window to draw the curtains. The dawn was just breaking. It was very still outside; the sky was a dull red merging into black. There were patterns of frost on the leaves in the overgrown garden; beyond lay the river, heavy, metallic, and choked with the autumn rains. Far to the east, over the mountains, rose a bank of enormous black clouds. He turned back to where the morning light revealed to him the small, sparsely-furnished bedroom, the threadbare rugs and the cheap pine furniture. There was an old flyblown photograph of Lenin on one wall which had been there when he first rented the bungalow. He had never quite plucked up the courage to take it down—after all, there was always the cleaning woman. It might possibly be noticed and reported.

'It's getting colder,' said Anya. She slipped her arms into her pyjama jacket and buttoned it across her large pink breasts. Then she swept her blonde hair back from her forehead and began to fix it with hairpins. She was only nineteen and she had a remote, slightly enigmatic beauty which remained intact whatever the circumstances or the time of day. Even now, without powder or lipstick, her skin slightly greasy and her slanting brown eyes clouded and heavy with sleep, she was still desirable. Yet, as Karas looked at her, the pleasure they had taken together seemed primitive and tasteless. Like so much of his life, it carried the flavour of calculation. He saw himself as Max might have seen him, as a man who had sacrificed too much of himself to caution and self-indulgence. A man of ambition, who stilled his intellect with games of chess and his flesh with young girls, whose work was stamped with competence to the exclusion of brilliance. He was suddenly disgusted with the effectiveness of his adaptation to his environment.

Turning back to the basin, he splashed his face with soap and water, dried it hurriedly, and began to put on his clothes. He took care to remember to take Max's letter from his dressing-gown and put it into an inside pocket of his jacket. For a moment he thought that Anya had noticed this and was about to make some comment on it. But fortunately she was distracted by her own problems.

She said, 'Are you going in the car?'

'Yes.'

'How am I to get to the University? I have a lecture at ten o'clock.'

'There's a bicycle outside. You can borrow that.' Before she could argue he was disappearing through the door. 'I'll see you this evening.'

Outside there was an icy wind. Nothing like it would be in a few months, but still a bitter reminder of the recurrent agony of the Siberian winter. He turned up the fur collar of his quilted coat and ran for the wooden shelter where the sturdy little car huddled against the weather. It started, as noisy as ever but reliable, and he drove through the deserted pine-woods towards the city. After a few miles the track gave way to a wide metalled strip, and the pines to block after block of apartment buildings and shops and building sites. Over to the north was the University, a complex of pretentious neo-classic buildings which housed and taught several thousand students from all over the Republic. Here it was that Anya spent her days, in the study of economics, politics, and social science.

Karas turned left and drove south on the new highway towards the Scientific Centre. The buildings here were of a more recent period than the main University block and showed distinct signs of Western cultural penetration. On the way to the laboratories there were a series of tower apartment blocks, functional and featureless in a style which would have attracted no special attention in San Francisco, Amsterdam or Tokio. Here were housed those members of the Centre who had not managed, like Karas, to emphasize their individuality by renting accommodation outside the town. He stopped the car at one of the blocks and went inside. He pressed the button for the lift but there was no response; presumably, as so often, it was out of order. Karas cursed and began to run up the stairs.

Max's flat was on the fifth floor and by the time he

reached it he was flustered and out of breath. He pressed the bell and waited. Through the thin door he heard movement in the flat and the sound of voices. Then the door was opened.

The man who stood facing him was someone he had never met. He was thick-set, with a flat expressionless face, thin ginger hair, and large hands covered with freckles. His clothes smelled of sweat and tobacco smoke. Karas said, 'Who are you?'

'Police.' The man spoke roughly, in a thick provincial accent. In his small eyes Karas saw the mindless brutality of his calling, allied to the traditional peasant hatred of the new élite.

'What's the trouble? Why are you here?'

The man did not answer. Instead he motioned Karas into the flat with a jerk of his arm. Karas entered the tiny hall which led into the living-room. He glanced quickly round him. Everything in the flat was as he had remembered it, yet he noticed that the arrangement was subtly changed. It was still tidy, but not with the tidiness of a man who lived there and enjoyed his life. The newspapers were neatly piled together on a table, the books were all on the shelves, and Max's desk was, for the first time, empty and polished and free of tobacco ash. Through the door of the bedroom Karas heard the movement of feet and the systematic opening and closing of drawers. The flat was being searched.

The plain-clothes policeman showed him into the living-room and closed the door behind him. At first he thought the room was empty, but as he turned round he saw a small portly figure standing motionless at the window and staring down into the courtyard of the apartment building. It was Suvorin, the Director of the laboratory.

Suvorin turned away from the window and looked at Karas through his steel-rimmed spectacles, saying nothing. He was a man in his middle fifties who somehow contrived to be small without delicacy and plump without bene-volence. While the cheeks were podgy and the eyes a faded innocuous blue, there was something in the set of his mouth, a drooping of the corners and a narrowness of the lips, which spoke of a lifetime of anxiety and discontent. Deep carved lines stretched from his nose almost to the side of his ample jowls. His white hair was worn rather long, and distributed a perpetual dusting of dandruff on to the shoulders of his dark blue suit.

14

Karas said, 'What's happened? What's the trouble?'

Suvorin clasped his stubby hands together behind his back. When he spoke, his harsh voice held funereal overtones. 'You haven't heard?'

'No.'

The small eyes regarded him gloomily. He said, 'This is a very tragic affair. Max has killed himself.'

Though he knew what the news must be, there was an extra pain in the confirmation of it. Max, his only friend, who had laughed with him and trusted him, who had despaired and yet who had never quite been able to bring himself to ask him for help while he was alive. In his heart Karas knew that he had failed Max, failed him through the caution and calculation which had made him unapproachable for a man with an agony to share. He fancied now that he remembered occasions when Max had tried to confide in him and he had failed to respond, because one always tried as a matter of policy to avoid such personal obligations and entanglements. In this country, he had reasoned, one had troubles enough without looking for more.

Sick with a sense of shame and failure, he sat down and put his hand to his forehead, shielding his grief from Suvorin's eyes. 'Poor Max,' he said softly. Suvorin said nothing. Karas asked, 'How did he do it?'

'Sleeping tablets.'

'And Sophia—?' Sophia was Max's wife.

'She'd gone away for the night, to visit her mother. She wasn't due back until this afternoon.'

'How did you hear about it?'

'He must have tried to get out of bed or something. There was a thump and the people in the flat below heard it. They tried to rouse him but they couldn't. So they called the police.' Suvorin glanced momentarily at the door, beyond which the search was still proceeding. 'He died half an hour later in hospital.'

'Were you able to speak to him?'

Suvorin shook his head. 'He did the job properly,' he said. 'He knew what he was about.' He spoke resentfully, as if Max had somehow been guilty of sharp practice in disposing of his life without seeking permission. Karas said coldly, 'What are the police doing here now?'

'It's routine. Technically, suicide's an offence. They have to investigate it.'

'It seems hardly necessary to take the flat to pieces.'

15

'That's up to them. The law has its own rules.' He dismissed the subject with a wave of his hand. Then he gave Karas a searching glance through his spectacles. 'Have you any idea why he did it?'

It was the question Karas had been dreading. Now, he knew, was the time for him to produce Max's letter, to explain what he was doing at the flat, to hand the whole matter over to the authorities. As an employee of the laboratory he had no right to have secrets. His work, with all its implications, was the property of the Centre. It was Karas's duty as a scientist and a citizen to hand it over to Suvorin now.

To withhold the letter would be foolish and dangerous, but Max's words rang in his head, controlling his tongue, holding him back from speech. He had failed Max in life by his caution and indifference. Was he to betray him again now? 'No,' he said. 'I don't know why he did it.'

'You were his closest friend,' said Suvorin.

'Perhaps.'

'You visited him a lot.'

'We used to play chess together.' It had started as an occasional evening and eventually came to be a regular thing. Every Friday he would come to the flat at about seven o'clock. The three of them would drink a glass of wine together; Sophia would go into the kitchen and make a simple meal—cold meat, with a salad, ice cream, some bread and cheese. Then he and Max would settle down with the chessmen. Max was a competent player but never quite as good as Karas. Since boyhood Karas had shown exceptional talent for the game. He had a capacity to visualize situations in a three-dimensional way, assessing not only how they stood at the moment but the various permutations which might develop in the future. He had a dash and opportunism that Max, a careful conventional player, could never hope to match. Fortunately Max was just good enough to stimulate Karas to give of his best. And he had never minded losing.

'Did he ever mention the possibility of doing anything like this?'

'No. Of course, he had these attacks of depression—'

'Yes. We all knew that,' Suvorin broke in curtly. His answer was curiously abrupt, as if for some reason Karas was under cross-questioning and had failed to give a satisfactory answer. He had the feeling that Suvorin was accusing him of something, probably of failing to anticipate Max's action and thereby preventing it. Yet it was difficult to be sure—Suvorin was not an easy man to understand. He lived his life in a cloud of distrust; of his superiors, his colleagues, his subordinates. Perhaps his suspicious manner was no more than force of habit and bore little relation to the situation in hand.

Karas tried to move the conversation into another area. 'Does Sophia know?' he asked.

'Not yet. They're trying to get in touch with her.'

'It will be a terrible shock,' said Karas. It was what one always said on these occasions. But it occurred to him as he spoke that he really knew very little about Sophia. He had met her often, it was true, on his visits to the flat, but she had never encouraged familiarity. She was a dark woman, a few years younger than Max, with a severe, rather humourless face and a small-boned, neat body. She moved quickly and gracefully and was by no means unattractive in a lean, desiccated way. She was said to be devoted to Max, but on what evidence Karas was never entirely sure. Max, for his part, was always kind and amiable with her, if a little remote. He hardly spoke about her at all to others. In their presence, one never felt that atmosphere of contact and tension, either of love or hate, which springs between people who live together in close emotional contact. Superficially, they might have been brother and sister. With each other they were polite, considerate, and apparently totally sexless.

Suvorin shook his head in disapproval. 'How a man can bring himself to do such a thing I don't know.' He turned to Karas. 'Can *you* understand it?'

'Well, I'm not a depressive—'

Suvorin said irritably, 'It's pure selfishness, that's what it is. He wasn't thinking of her or anyone else. He was thinking of himself.'

Karas felt the bulk of Max's letter in his breast pocket. 'The dead weight of the world is crushing down on me . . .' But even if he could have shown the letter to Suvorin, he knew it would have been impossible to make him understand. 'I don't suppose he enjoyed doing it,' he said.

'It's a question of responsibility,' said Suvorin querulously. Responsibility towards whom, wondered Karas. It seemed implausible that Suvorin should be very concerned about Sophia, in whom he had never shown very much interest when Max was alive. Yet he evidently felt a sense of grievance. Why? Perhaps he was thinking of the administrative problems which would be created at the laboratory. It was by no means unlikely. Suvorin's egocentricity was so absolute that it had a kind of innocence to it, like that of a child. It was not that he chose to see everything that happened entirely from the point of view of his own interest and convenience—he had simply no consciousness that any other point of view existed.

Over small matters Karas had often found this amusing. But today it left a sour taste in his mouth. In a few weeks, he thought bitterly, Max would be forgotten; or perhaps recalled occasionally as an embarrassing incident, an interruption to the work. The man was gone—the kind, gentle, civilized person, with his passion for chess and his deprecating sense of humour. Max, the good loser, had played his final losing game.

Karas felt a sudden desire to get away—there was nothing to stay for now. He said, 'If there's something I can do—'

His words hung in the air. Suvorin was looking out of the window, brooding. He said, 'What brought you here?'

'Just now?' said Karas, and then wondered why he had said it. It sounded far too much like an effort to gain time. He went on hurriedly, 'I'd arranged to pick Max up and drive him to the lab.'

'So early?'

'We both wanted to make an early start.'

Suvorin did not reply. In the silence between them the story began to sound a little implausible. Karas felt uneasy. Finally Suvorin's dry, rasping voice broke the silence. 'You're sure he didn't write anything to you?'

Karas's stomach turned over. But he replied quickly and easily, 'No,' he said. 'Nothing at all.' As soon as he had spoken he was conscious of the magnitude of what he had done. To omit to mention the letter was, of course, an offence; but to deny it was something far more serious. Even if he changed his mind later and decided to hand it over to Suvorin, he would still have to explain his present denial. He knew enough of Suvorin, and of the system under which they both lived, to realize that such an act would never be completely forgiven.

Suvorin was standing with his back to him, immobile, looking out of the window. It was impossible to form an estimate of whether he believed the denial or not. Karas forced himself to remain silent—he must not betray himself by any nervousness in his manner. If only he had been wise enough to stay away from the flat! He might have gained a few hours of time, a little freedom of action. He might never have been asked the fatal question at all. The whole delicate fabric of his life, which he had worked so hard and so long to develop, had been irrevocably breached by this one hurried act. He felt hopelessly naked and exposed. He knew in that moment that he would never feel entirely safe again.

CHAPTER TWO

The policeman let him out of the flat without speaking. As he walked down the stairs he noticed a cleaning woman working away across one of the lower landings with her scrubbing brush. She looked up momentarily as he passed, wringing out a cloth into her bucket. Her face was pasty with bad food, her mouth set in a grim, resentful line. She stared at him sullenly as he passed by.

He got back into his car and drove along the wide empty road towards the town. He felt the bulk of the letter in his breast pocket, like a bomb which at any moment might explode and destroy him. He glanced at himself in the driving mirror, afraid for a moment that he might be already betraying himself with some obscure sign of guilt —a line round the eyes or a twitch of the jaw—but he was reassured. The long, dark, rather battered face which he had carried around with him for the last thirty-five years was as impassive as ever.

Yet the change within him was vast and immeasurable. All through his life he had struggled to preserve his independence. He had tried at all costs to evade any attempts to possess him. In his personal relationships he had looked always for an amiable friendly indifference. It was not perfect, but in a hostile world it was as much as one might reasonably ask, or give. It was this kind of relationship which he had thought he had found with Max. They had talked each morning at the laboratory; on Friday evenings when the chess was finished, they had discussed their work, music, art, books. There had been long, easy silences. And gradually something more had come into their relationship —a form of affection that went beyond anything that was ever expressed in words between them. Each had respected the other's privacy, his difference in attitude and psychological make-up. The relationship had been valuable to both of them. It had made life worth living in this vast, arid, foreign land. At the same time there had been no possession. They had made no demands on each other.

Now, in death, Max had possessed him. He had a right to resent it—it was contrary to their unspoken agreement. The one friend who had claimed to demand nothing had ended by demanding everything, and with a few sheets of paper had turned him into an outlaw. Yet somehow resentment would not come. He thought of Max's naked corpse lying in the mortuary, the tall, spare frame making ridges and hillocks under the white sheet, and he could feel only pity. By an act of such immense finality, Max had removed himself from all ordinary obligations.

Yet the letter remained an illegal object which he had lied about and concealed from his superiors. There had been suspicion in Suvorin's voice when he had asked him why he went to the flat so early, whether he had received a letter. Had the old man really been convinced by his answers? It was impossible to be sure. It was an outrage, of course, that he, a scientist of distinction, should be feeling guilt and fear for keeping to himself the contents of a private letter. But indignation was useless. If the world was mad, one must live within its madness. The fact was that he would never feel secure so long as the letter remained in his pocket.

He turned left on the by-pass which had been built between the University and the Research Centre so that motor traffic could avoid the town. There was a stretch of open country, with occasional small tracks going off to the left into the pine forests. He looked through the driving mirror—there was no one else on the road. He took the next turning on the left and drove rapidly down a side road into the woods.

As always, the surface deteriorated sharply as soon as one moved away from the main road. The little car crashed and jerked through the ruts and potholes; a pheasant rose in panic from the forest as he passed through. After a while, when he felt certain of being unobserved, he stopped the car and took Max's letter from his breast pocket. He read it through again and then opened up the folded sheets of the scientific notes which had accompanied it.

He went through them again several times. Then he took each sheet in turn, put his hands over his ears to shut out all sound, bent his head, and concentrated totally on what was written on the paper. It was a trick he had been able to perform ever since he was a schoolboy with pages of print, or arrangements of cards or chessmen. It was like the click of a camera shutter—the image was imprinted on his memory, vividly and ineradicably. He did the same with each sheet. When he had come to the end he opened the car door and looked carefully around him. The road was still deserted. He took out a box of matches and set fire to the letter and the notes. When it was all burnt he dropped the ashes on the ground and carefully crushed them into dust with his feet.

Around the Research Centre there was a barbed wire fence twelve feet high. At night the wires of which it was constructed were electrified and fierce dogs were released to roam through the park which surrounded the buildings. All day armed policemen, their shoulders straining at the dun-coloured material of their baggy uniforms, stood at the two gates checking the papers of everyone who entered. Karas stopped his car and showed his pass. The policeman glanced at it and then looked up, as he did every day, at Karas. He did not smile or give any sign of recognition. After a moment's hesitation he snapped the passport shut and motioned to his companion to open the gate.

The laboratories were a collection of modern brick constructions, each four stories high and separated by concrete paths and a few arid lawns. Karas drove past the buildings for Immunology and Virus Research and parked his car by a smaller and newer building which carried a plaque saying 'Department of Molecular Biology'. Just inside the entrance a porter sat at his desk reading yesterday's newspaper. On the wall opposite to him there was a board listing the senior research staff—starting with Max as director, then himself, then Samsonov and Pilic, the two juniors. He pushed the indicator on the board to show that he was in. None of the others had arrived yet.

In the laboratory he changed his jacket for a white coat, and tried to forget his anxiety in work. One of the advantages of research was that there was always something to do, no matter what mood one was in. There was the excitement of creation, if the creative impulse was there. If not, there was a vast amount of quite satisfying routine work involved in checking and developing previous observations. But today even the routine defied concentration. He found his mind wandering and made several mistakes in simple calculations. At around ten o'clock he gave up the effort and retired gloomily to his office. His laboratory technician brought him a glass of tea from the canteen. As usual, they were out of lemons. The tea was half-cold and far too sweet. He was sipping it distastefully when the telephone rang. When he took off the receiver he heard Suvorin's voice on the other end of the line.

'Peter?'

'Yes.'

'I'm holding an emergency meeting of department heads to discuss the present situation. I'd like you to attend in Max's place. Can you manage that?'

'Yes, of course.'

'Good. It's in the main conference room in the Administration building. We'll see you there in ten minutes' time.'

Karas finished his tea and left the department for the Administration building. As he walked along the avenue leading up to it he was joined by Leskov, the head of the biochemistry department. Leskov was a large man in his middle fifties with a shiny bald dome fringed on either side with a bush of black hair. He was wearing a grey suit which looked as if he had put on weight since he had bought it.

'Terrible news,' said Leskov.

He spoke in a booming, organ-pipe voice, like a man intoning an obituary notice. Karas wondered why it was that Leskov, no matter how friendly he was, always succeeded in exasperating him. He nodded stiffly in reply.

Leskov went on, 'Alexei told me you were at the flat.'

All the senior staff were in the habit of referring to Suvorin, among themselves, by his first name. But somehow Leskov managed to infuse into this familiarity the implication of a special relationship. Karas said, 'I called there to pick him up.'

Leskov raised his bushy eyebrows. 'At half past seven?'

'Yes.'

Evidently Leskov had heard all about the details of the affair from Suvorin. Karas wondered, as so often before, what was the precise relationship between the two men. Most of the time Suvorin made no secret of his contempt for Leskov, and indeed had a tendency to make fun of him openly in a rather embarrassing manner. He liked to mock Leskov's slowness, his lack of creative talent, and his plodding, pedestrian mind. Sometimes, when he was in one of the sudden savage moods that occasionally took possession of him, he would go out of his way to humiliate Leskov in front of the others. Leskov would flush and become more foolish and clumsy than ever. Yet, a day or two later, all this would be forgotten and Leskov would be offered marks of unusual favour. Affairs of secrecy and importance would be discussed with him, while Max, who as Deputy Director was really concerned with these matters, would be ignored.

'I suppose,' Leskov said, 'you've no idea what made him do it.'

He replied firmly, 'None at all.'

'You were very close—'

'Not really.'

Leskov's scepticism was unconcealed. And justified, of course. Yet what could one say? The truth was that theirs had been a type of relationship which was impossible to describe within the context of life in the Centre. A relationship of ease and good humour. Never suspicious or watchful, having no significance at all except in personal terms. How could one describe it to such a man as this?

They walked together in silence for a while. As they reached the door of the Administration building Leskov said, 'He will be greatly missed.'

'Yes.'

'Yes indeed.' Leskov spoke as if Karas had in some way been disagreeing with him. He coughed nervously. There was an obvious tension about his manner which could not be explained simply by grief at Max's death. Plainly he had some additional preoccupation of his own in regard to the meeting they were about to attend. It was not very difficult for Karas to guess what it was. The job of Deputy Director of the Centre would now be vacant, and Leskov was a strong candidate. Already, even in this moment of tragedy, adjustments were being made, ambitions expanded, plans modified. It was only to be expected. As if to confirm his suspicion, Leskov added, with a faint note of anticipation in his voice, 'We shall all have to work very hard to take his place.'

Suvorin sat in his office, listening to the sounds of their footsteps as they walked down the corridor to the conference room. Fedorov, Karas, Leskov, Zabergan—he knew the step of each one, as he knew their voices, the way they dressed, the smallest change of expression on their faces. They were his only family, just as the laboratories were his only home.

Suvorin was a widower and he lived by himself in an apartment just above the office in which he now sat. It was an arrangement that suited him. His wife, with whom he had had little in common, had died ten years ago. He had no children and his only near relatives lived over a thousand miles away in the north. When he had been married, he had always resented the time he had been compelled to spend away from his work, and after his wife's death he had been secretly relieved to move out of his flat and into his present quarters. All his anxieties and fears, his triumphs and defeats, were centred round his small scientific empire. He thought of nothing else and he associated with no one who was not connected in some way or another with his work.

His office adjoined the conference room. He heard the department heads go in and seat themselves. Then he entered through the side door and walked to his chair at the head of the table. At his right was an empty chair where Max would have ordinarily sat—then Leskov and Fedorov. On his left was Karas, and below him Zabergan, the microbiologist, a small quiet neat man, with a scar on the left side of his face and an artificial hand which he had acquired in the late stages of the last war. He was a man of great kindness and courtesy, yet it sometimes seemed that the war had removed from Zabergan some component of his personality as well as mutilating his body. Loyalty had assumed in him an obsessive, almost military quality which seemed strange and inappropriate in a scientist. With loyalty he stilled all criticisms and solved all problems. He was a reassuring subordinate. But in matters of any complexity his contribution was necessarily limited.

Suvorin's gaze took in the four familiar faces with an instant recognition, not only of their physical features but of their characters and their relationship towards him. Zabergan, dutiful, upright, unambitious, conventional in thought and morals, old-fashioned in his devotion to friends, family, and the country. Fedorov the intellectual, concealing beneath a caustic tongue and an affectation of cynicism a deep dissatisfaction with his own work. Suvorin knew that Fedorov had only one ambition—to be a truly creative original scientist—and was tormented by the knowledge that creativity had always tended to escape him. Leskov was a natural bureaucrat—a careful, reliable, humourless workhorse, limited in talent but unlimited in ambition. He felt he knew these three totally, without reservations. Only Karas still escaped him—Karas, with his sharp, analytical brain, his detached amiability and his quiet but determined independent spirit. So far, Suvorin knew his independence only as an inference from his manner and the expression on his face. He did not resent it as such. He knew that it was an indispensable component of great ability. But he knew too that there was a limit to the amount of freedom which would be allowed to it. His job as Director was to leave such men enough independence to do the good work on which the Centre depended and yet maintain the degree of administrative control which the system regarded as necessary. This was a tight-rope which would be difficult for both of them to walk, and only time and experience could tell whether they would succeed.

Two brilliant men out of five—himself and Karas. And the other three were able, intelligent, and reliable. It was not a bad score as scientific institutes went. And yesterday had been better, with three first-rate men out of six. At least, that was what he had thought. But now he wondered about Max. Was it possible that he had been finished for some time and that nobody had noticed it? It was true that he had done fine work in his day, but scientists sometimes went off quite suddenly and it often took several years to find out that their gifts had deserted them. But this again was part of his job as Director—to have his finger on the pulse of his little kingdom. Now he felt uneasy. It was apparent that he had not known Max at all. That was bad enough, but the inference from it was even more frightening. What about the others? Could it be that they too had secrets from him?

He looked at the four faces. Zabergan, unconscious of his scrutiny, was proceeding, with his customary slow deliberation, to light a pipe with his disabled hand. Fedorov was doodling abstractedly on a piece of scrap paper. Leskov met his eyes and smiled nervously. Karas looked back at him, the expression on his face silently asking the reason for this prologue to the meeting. The long heavy features held nothing more than his usual detached, slightly ironical expression, but Suvorin was nevertheless a little discon-

certed. Alone of the whole group, Karas made him feel
vulnerable. He made him feel as the others never did, that
he too was being judged in the same way as he judged others.
And behind this a disturbing question nagged in Suvorin's
mind. Why had Karas called at Max's flat?

Suvorin glanced back at the notes he had brought in
with him and began to speak. The others settled back in
their seats and prepared themselves for the kind of monologue with which the years had made them only too familiar.
It was Suvorin's custom to open every staff meeting with a
long and rather rambling speech, disjointed in form and
repetitive in content, in which he displayed for the benefit
of his department heads the status of his current thought.
In the process he displayed it also to himself, since it was
his custom to do most of his thinking aloud and he was
frequently unaware of what he really thought until he had
heard what he said. Karas had always been fascinated by
these displays. From the ill-assorted mixture of speculation,
grievances and prejudices, the alternating moods of pug-
nacity and humour, spite and generosity, bombast and
doubt, it was possible to form a picture of the workings of
Suvorin's mind. At these moments he resembled one of
those experimental animals in which a loop of stomach
brought out to the surface demonstrates to the observer the
inner workings of its body. With Suvorin it was as if his
mechanism of thought, and the pitch and sway of his
emotions, were similarly exposed to the public view.

Suvorin began on a heavy, sepulchral note. 'You all know,'
he said, 'the great tragedy which has overtaken our institute.'
He paused, his eyes resting on Max's empty chair. 'A dreadful thing. Dreadful.' His voice began to change, as the
inevitable distractions crowded into his mind. He began to
talk, not so much to his audience as to himself. 'I was
completely taken by surprise. He said nothing to me,
nothing at all. I had no indication of what he intended to
do. If he had only spoken to me, I would have done anything I could to help him. If he had problems in his work,
we could have worked them out. It's a most extraordinary
thing. I can't understand it.' His voice rose a little in resentment. 'It wasn't an impulse. It was planned. He sent his
wife away. He knew he was going to do it. It wasn't as if
he had any trouble with money. Or domestic matters.' It
was like an indictment. 'He was completely free here to do
as he wished, to run his own department. I left him to

himself. I didn't interfere.' Suvorin became querulous and defensive. 'I took the view that he would be happy if I left him to himself. Now I think perhaps I was wrong. Perhaps I should have taken more of a detailed interest in his department.' A threatening, hectoring note began to appear. He looked around aggressively. 'Perhaps in future I should do that with *all* departments—'

Karas looked at the others. He knew them so well that he could recognize the signs of anxiety in each one at this last remark. Zabergan puffed more energetically at his pipe, Leskov wriggled nervously in his seat, and Fedorov seemed to retreat even farther into his secret unhappy world. It was impossible to know whether Suvorin made such indirect threats of interference as a deliberate attempt to cause alarm, or whether he was merely speculating aloud as to what was the best method of carrying out the obligations of his own job. This kind of resolution to take a more direct interest in the routine matters of the departments was by no means new—it came up about once a year, whenever something happened which worried Suvorin and made him think that he was losing touch. Like most of his attitudes, Suvorin's system of administration oscillated between two incompatible extremes. On the one hand there was his genuine theoretical belief that scientists should be left alone to get on with their work, but fighting against this were all his personal inclinations towards domination and inter-ference. When he did decide to interfere it was always very painful for the head of that particular department. Suvorin's practical scientific experience was now ten years behind him, but he was reluctant to admit the implications of this. It was not easy to break it to him tactfully that his knowledge was out of date and his personal participation the reverse of helpful. The experiment usually ended in a quarrel between him and the department head and a delay in work of several months while disagreements were sorted out.

To the relief of everyone, Suvorin did not pursue this particular point. He became distracted by another idea and his mind wandered off at a tangent. Every now and then in his monologue he would come back to the subject of Max. It was plain, when he spoke of Max, that he did so with genuine affection and regret. It was known by everyone that he had loved and admired Max as a man, and respected him as a scientist. At times indeed, tears would come into his eyes and he would have to take his glasses off and polish

27

them. Then he would veer away again to his worries about the Centre, dragging up minor anxieties which they had heard many times before. It was beginning to look like one of those quite pointless meetings which he sometimes called, for no other reason than a craving for an audience and a fear of being alone.

Then, quite suddenly, his manner changed. He stopped in the middle of some particularly inconclusive piece of reminiscence and looked around at them all as if they had been collectively responsible for trying to divert him from his main purpose.

'But I didn't call this meeting simply to talk about Max,' he said severely. 'The work of the Centre has to go on.' He paused and then said with great solemnity, 'I'm afraid that Max's death has plunged us into a very serious crisis.'

He paused for effect and looked straight at Karas. Karas was aware that some suitable reaction was expected of him but he found it hard to produce one. Suvorin had a tendency to make these announcements of crisis periodically. Usually they boiled down to nothing very much. Suvorin, nettled by his lack of reaction, went on irritably, 'Yes, I really mean that, Peter, whatever you think. It's a very serious crisis indeed.'

He turned irritably to the others. 'Max, as you know, had considerable administrative responsibilities as Deputy Director. Presumably due to his illness, it turns out that these have been completely neglected in the last four months. There's a mountain of paper work waiting to be done.'

He paused. 'I'm sure we're all going to pull together in this very difficult time. I'll try to take over some of the administration myself but I already have more than I can conveniently handle—there's a limit to how much I can do.' He turned to Leskov. 'Nicholas, I'd like you to help me with this and ultimately take it over completely. You'll be Deputy Director as from now.'

Leskov's body was shaken with a tremor of gratification and relief. He opened his mouth to speak, and Karas wondered for a moment if he was going so far to forget himself as to make a speech of thanks. Fortunately, by the time he had recovered sufficiently to say anything, Suvorin had already turned his attention elsewhere.

He was speaking more slowly now, frowning slightly as he looked at the notes in front of him on the table. 'Now we come to matters specifically connected with Max's department. As you know, he was down to represent us at the International Symposium on Molecular Genetics in Geneva six weeks from now. For the prestige of the Centre, it's vital that we should be represented, even though Max is no longer available.' He said to Karas, 'Peter, I want you to go in his place. I also want you to take acting charge of the department. Get everything straightened out, supervise the work of the juniors, and get the place on a proper working footing. Can you do that?'

'I think so,' said Karas. He spoke with confidence. The commission was no surprise to him. He was the only person in the department with sufficient seniority to take Max's place. The very fact that he had been invited to the meeting had made it clear what was likely to happen. Like Leskov, he was a logical benefactor from the death of his friend.

He waited for the conference to be wound up—surely that must be the end of the business they had been called to discuss. But Suvorin stayed in his seat. The anxious frown remained on his face. 'All these,' he said, 'are routine matters. When I spoke of a crisis, I was not referring to them. Our real problem is in regard to Max's own research work. And here,' he said heavily, 'I'm presented with a situation totally outside my experience. I'm not sure at the moment how we are going to be able to handle it.' He paused, as if in doubt whether to go into further detail, and then decided against it. He took off his glasses and turned his pale blue eyes on Karas. 'I'll come over and talk to you about that tomorrow morning.'

CHAPTER THREE

AFTER THE MEETING Karas went back to his laboratory. His anxiety about his own position, which had faded a little after he had destroyed Max's letter, now returned to him with redoubled force. He racked his brains in an effort to guess what unpleasant surprise Suvorin might have in store for him. But it was impossible—he could make no sense of it. He would simply have to wait until tomorrow. There was at least one reassuring feature. If he had been under any serious suspicion Suvorin would hardly have put him in charge of the department.

He tried to put the matter to the back of his mind. Fortunately there was enough work to keep him busy. As soon as he began to investigate the organization of the department, it became apparent how much it had been neglected in the last few months. He called in Samsonov and Pilic and tried to get a picture of the work they had been doing. Both of them seemed relieved rather than resentful at the thought of receiving some supervision. As the discussion proceeded, Karas felt the pleasure of using his natural talent for organization. He found himself moving quickly towards solutions of problems which Max had been fumbling with ineffectually for months.

He lunched off sandwiches at his laboratory bench and then worked hard through the afternoon. He could not repress a feeling of guilt when he realized that this was his most enjoyable day's work since he had come to the Centre. Yet he knew that Max himself would have been the first to understand. Sometimes, when some administrative confusion had occurred, he would say wryly to Karas, 'Really you should be looking after this kind of thing, not me.' Karas had suspected then that Max was right; now he was certain. In a few weeks he would have the whole place straight—the department would begin to make sense as an entity. He would show Suvorin what could be done. Then he would go to Geneva. There, too, he was confident of making an impression. He was a forceful speaker and an accomplished linguist. His German and English were almost perfect. With a little luck he might make a reputation for himself outside the Centre. Important figures would be there—academicians, members of the Central Scientific Committee. If only he could work his way safely through this present situation, the possibilities were limitless.

It was after six o'clock when he left the laboratory. He drove to the gate, showed his pass, and was let out into the road. Then he turned right and drove along the by-pass towards his house. On his right he saw the block where Max had lived. He stopped the car at the roadside and counted up the floors. There was a light in the corner flat on the fifth floor. Sophia must be at home.

He realized now that all day he had been putting off the thought of his responsibilities towards Sophia. It was not simply that it was bound to be a difficult situation, in which he would have to play a gentle, sympathetic role which did not come easily to him. The fact was that he had never felt entirely relaxed with Max's wife. She had always seemed to him rather solemn and humourless. She was too intellectual for his taste, too intense and withdrawn. Nor had he ever felt that she had any great liking for him. She was correct and polite, but had responded coolly to his attempts at friendship. He had the feeling that he was tolerated for Max's sake but that in her heart she disapproved of him.

Just the same, Max had asked him to look after her. And she must be desolate at the present time. He could not think of any friends she might have except himself. Apart from a half-time job giving lectures in German literature at the University, her life had been entirely dedicated to Max. The Friday evenings they all spent together were, apart from an occasional concert, their only entertainment. Like himself, the Bremers were cut off by their foreignness from what little in the way of social activity the city had to offer. He would do what he could for her. It was the least he owed to Max.

He parked the car and climbed the stairs. As he passed by the lower landings he heard family noises through the thin doors. A child cried, a radio blared the noise of an accordion band. A greyhaired woman was coming down the stairs carrying a shopping bag. She looked at Karas briefly as he walked past her.

He rang the bell of the apartment and the door opened almost immediately. She stood there in front of him, a slight, neat figure in a white blouse and a black pleated skirt. Her black hair was drawn back from her forehead and the austere, classical lines of her face were accentuated by her pallor. She smiled at him tentatively; grief made her look young and vulnerable. He realized for the first time that she was probably no older than himself.

She looked at him gratefully. 'I was hoping you'd come.'

'I didn't know whether you'd be back. Then I saw the light in your window . . .'

'Come in and sit down.'

He came into the flat and she closed the door behind him. She said, 'It's lonely here now. And a little frightening. I badly needed someone to talk to.'

He said awkwardly, 'It must be dreadful for you.' It sounded inadequate and he added apologetically, 'I know there's nothing anyone can say—nothing that can really help, that is . . .'

31

'You're here. That's the main thing.'

She showed him into the living-room. 'Stay here and I'll make some tea.'

A few minutes later she returned with a tray on which there were two glasses of tea and saucers containing slices of lemon and sugar. As he stirred the sugar into the hot liquid he said to her, 'Do you want to talk about Max? Or would you sooner not?'

'I don't know. Better not, I think.' Her soft, gentle voice had always been at variance with the severity of her appearance, and at times it was difficult to hear what she said. She looked around the room as if somehow there might be something hostile concealed there. 'They searched the flat,' she said.

'Yes, I know.' She raised her eyebrows and he added in explanation, 'I was here this morning.'

Her surprise remained. 'Why?'

'To pick him up. I was driving him to the laboratories.' Before she could question him further, he went on, 'Suvorin was here too.'

'Yes.' She got up and walked restlessly to the window. There was a photograph of Max on a small card table. The pose was rather old-fashioned and it had been crudely touched up. The photographer had accentuated the black eyes and hair, the oval face, and the look of romantic melancholy. It showed a side of Max, but left out so much. It said nothing about the lanky, round-shouldered grace of movement, the constant half-smile on his lips, the elusiveness, and the remote kindness. Sophia said, as if to herself, 'He sent me away, you know. He didn't want me.'

'He didn't want anybody.' Suicide was, after all, a private affair. Were there no circumstances, he wondered, in which a woman could realize that a man might wish to be alone? Was it necessary for her to feel needed, even in the moment of self-destruction? 'You would have felt you had to try to stop him.'

'I suppose so.'

'If he'd already made up his mind—' Max was never a man who liked to argue. He was easily influenced and tended to agree for the moment, particularly with people he liked or admired or who were stronger and more positive than he. His agreement was more courtesy than lack of conviction. When it really mattered, he would always swing back in time to what he really believed. 'You would have argued him out of it. He knew that.' She stirred the lemon in her glass, crushing it carefully to squeeze out the bitter juice. He said, 'It had happened before, hadn't it?'

She nodded. 'One has to try.' She added defensively, 'Well, that's so, isn't it? You can't just let them go ahead. He had phases—sometimes he got better and then he'd thank me for stopping him doing it. I hoped one day he'd feel all right and he wouldn't want to do it any more.'

'Yes, I understand,' he said. Her hands were trembling. Karas said, 'You mustn't reproach yourself.'

'I failed him.'

Now the tears came. Perhaps it was better for her to cry —at least, that was what people always said. He waited for her to stop sobbing. Then he said, 'You didn't fail him. It was his own affair. Nothing to do with anybody else. If he didn't want to go on, he had the right—'

'Oh, you don't understand.' She said sadly, without bitterness, 'You never loved anyone, not really.' She looked at him through her tears, challenging him. 'That's true, isn't it?'

Perhaps she was right, he thought. Certainly it was true of women. He had used them for pleasure and companionship, he had laughed with them and amused them and made love to them, but that was all. He did not feel ashamed of it. He could not, after all, command his own emotions. He said, 'I was very fond of Max.'

'In your own way perhaps. But it doesn't really mean anything to you. You don't know what it means. You're just a body and a brain.'

He felt slightly embarrassed at the turn the conversation had taken. He never felt at ease talking about himself. 'You're wrong,' he said. 'I cared very deeply for him.' Then he spoiled it by saying, 'We all did.'

'You all did?' Her lips twisted but the smile had no humour in it. 'All of you—Suvorin as well? Did he care deeply too?'

'Yes, I think he did.' Suddenly her eyes made him uneasy. She seemed to be asking him where he stood in relation to Suvorin. He had a fear that he might have sounded sanctimonious and sycophantic, like Leskov. He qualified it rapidly. 'So far as one can know—'

'I know.' The tears had gone now. He was shaken by the bitterness that appeared on her quiet face. 'Suvorin cares for nobody.' She repeated, 'Nobody.' She waited for him to speak but he said nothing. 'He plays with you all, I suppose you must have realized that. He flatters you in turn, he makes promises. He uses what you can give him. That's all. There's nothing else.'

He was startled and dismayed. It had never occurred to him that this quiet, prim woman who made coffee and cakes and discussed Mozart in her bluestocking way, had all the time been swayed by such violent emotions. The whole picture he had of Max's tepid, gentle homelife began to break up before his eyes. 'I don't think that's true,' he said.

She did not seem to hear him. The grievances, dammed up over the years, had taken possession of her.

'Max helped him to build up the Centre. He couldn't have done it on his own. You've no idea what it was like in those days. Max worked day and night, he never stopped. But when the people from the Central Committee came down, there was always some very good reason why he couldn't see them. He accused Max of intriguing with the Central Committee to take over his job.' She gave a melancholy smile. 'Max! Can you imagine him? But there was no convincing Suvorin. He never trusted Max after that, he tormented him from that moment onwards. He said his work was no good, he was lazy, that he had run out of ideas . . .' She leaned forward and said intensely to Karas, 'Admit it! Haven't you heard him say that?'

Karas said unhappily, 'He's an unstable man. We all know that. He's probably said the same kind of thing about almost everyone at the Centre.'

She hardly seemed to hear him. 'Poor Max,' she said. 'It hurt him so bitterly. He couldn't understand it, you see. Because he was so loyal. Even right to the end. It drove me mad—I even got to the state of despising him for it. It was as if he had begun to think that Suvorin was right, that perhaps he *was* no good.' She paused. 'Don't you understand what I'm trying to say?'

'That's not why he killed himself,' said Karas. 'Depression isn't like that. Not Max's sort, anyway. It comes from inside.'

She looked round the small dingy room, at the tidy bookshelves and the gimcrack furniture. 'When I think of Suvorin here this morning. In my home. With policemen—'

'They weren't his policemen.'

'Do you think he couldn't have turned them away if he'd wanted?'

'I don't know.' That was the kind of thing one never knew. It depended on all kinds of things—what sort of police they were and what they were there for, how things stood in one year or another.

'Police,' she said with disgust. 'Going through our home, our possessions, our private correspondence. And he sat there and watched them, just as he once sat there when he used to come and visit us as a friend—accepting our hospitality—' She stood up. 'You're not drinking your tea. You don't like it perhaps?'

'It's not that.'

'I forgot. I remember now what you prefer.' She opened the cupboard and looked inside. 'Yes, they've left us this. I'm surprised.' She took out a bottle of whisky and tore the cap off. Then she put down two glasses and half filled each of them with whisky. 'This is very special. It was given to us by an English friend who came to visit.' She looked anxiously at the glass. 'Is that enough?'

'Almost too much. It needs water.'

She brought a jug of water and poured some into the glasses. Then she lifted her own. Before she drank, she said ironically, 'To this kind, beautiful country.' She took a swallow and then put the glass down. 'I don't really like whisky much.'

'It's an acquired taste.'

'Like so much of our lives here.' It was as if she had handed him a code word to which she expected an answer. But he said nothing. She went on, 'Do you think we shall ever acquire it, Peter?'

He hesitated. It was an unexpected and slightly alarming situation. He had expected her to be unhappy and depressed, but this wild, desperate resentment came as a complete surprise to him. Max's death had broken open that hidden box in which she, like all of them, kept those thoughts which were too dangerous to utter. They all had their reservations about the country and the system and the Centre itself. But it was foolish to put them into words, even to friends. One tried to manage one's life as well as possible without getting involved in matters where a man could do no good to others and much harm to himself. It was not a heroic position, but this was not a time or a country for heroes. While Sophia was in this frame of mind she was a menace not only to herself but to anyone who associated with her. The convention was always the same. When anyone said anything tactless, one simply pretended not to hear. He put down his glass and looked at his watch. 'I think it's time I was leaving.'

She ignored him. 'Has it ever occurred to you how different everything might have been? We could have lived in London, Paris, New York—anywhere in the world. Everyone wants scientists now. If we didn't like one city, if the climate didn't suit us or the people were unkind—we could pack up and go somewhere else . . .' Her voice faded away, lost in the substance of her dreams. 'Did you ever go to Vienna, Peter?'

'Only as a boy.'

'We lived there, Max and I. It was during the war, of course, and the Nazis were there and it was horrible in all kinds of ways, but there was still quite a lot left of the old days. Things which perhaps to you don't seem very important, like stuffy little restaurants with flat-footed waiters and men reading newspapers in those bamboo holders they used to have. And the way people used to talk about politics and music and any old thing, getting terribly excited about it, quite pointlessly. And furniture that had been in the family for I don't know how many generations. It might not have been especially beautiful or valuable but there was a continuity about it. We didn't know how much it mattered to us until we lost it.' Her voice was soft and nostalgic and he felt himself being dangerously touched. It was useless to think like this, useless and foolhardy. Yet the cry of his European past was like some forbidden sensual pleasure gripping him beyond the bounds of prudence. He could not stop himself listening. 'We brought a few things with us when we came here. Some books and pictures and that vase over there.' She pointed to a vase full of flowers. It was tall and elegant with a delicate blue design on the porcelain. 'I don't know whether it has any value but my father loved it and I loved my father. It's all I have left of him.' She added, 'Of my own people.'

'It's beautiful,' said Karas.

The temptation to softness and humanity was like a seduction. Then, as if taking pity on him, she drew back. 'You don't have to say that,' she said. 'You don't have to say anything. I know how it is with you, Peter. You've got a future here and there's no sense in spoiling it by thinking of things which are dead and gone anyway. You have your work and your chess. Good conversation—' She hesitated

36

for a moment as if wondering whether she dared say something. Then she added, with an affectation of lightness, 'And
your girls, of course . . .'

He frowned, baffled and disturbed by her changes of
mood. He said defensively, 'That's my life. After all, what
else is there?'

'I know. I think you're very sensible.' She finished her
whisky at a gulp. 'You've solved all your problems. Not like
Max. He envied you, you know.'

'Did he?'

'Yes. He was so worried and undecided. He admired your
certainty, your drive. He relied on you a lot.'

He knew it was true. And yet, to him, what he had to
offer seemed cheap and threadbare compared to Max's
simple goodness. She said, 'I sometimes think you were the
only person who could really have done anything for him.'

'Done what?' he asked.

'There was something he needed that I couldn't give him.
But you could have done. He stretched out to you—didn't
you ever feel that?'

There came back to him a sentence in Max's letter. 'Often
I wondered whether to talk to you about it.' Karas pictured
Max trying to screw himself up to the point of a confidence,
then repelled by a word, a laugh, a brash, insensitive phrase.
He knew now that there must have been many such
occasions. The truth was that he had developed a talent for
shutting away awkward facts, for fending off attempts by
others to involve him in their own affairs. But, after all,
once you began, where did you finish? A man couldn't take
responsibility for the whole world. He said, 'What are you
saying? That I let him down?'

'We all let him down.'

There was a falseness in what she said and he seized on
it with relief. 'That's melodrama. I was fond of Max, you
know that, but he wasn't Jesus Christ. He was a man and he
had his weaknesses. Because he was gentle and vulnerable
and kind, he made everyone feel they owed him something.'

'Didn't they?'

'Something, yes. But he owed something to others too.
To you. Even to me perhaps. You never think about it
because you believe I can look after myself.' He added,
'Max had to solve his own problems in the end, like the
rest of us. Why should I be asked to accept any special
obligation?'

He had unconsciously expected her to pursue the argument, but she did not. She stood looking at him with an expression of puzzlement on her face. In the silence the echo of his last words seemed to acquire a violence he had not intended. Eventually she said, 'I've never seen you so emotional as this.'

His anger left him. 'I'm sorry. I was upset. I thought you were rather unfair.'

'You don't like to be involved, do you?' He did not reply. After a pause she said, 'Was there anything special worrying you?'

'What do you mean?'

'I don't know. I just wondered.' She looked up and took his glass. 'Some more whisky?'

'I should be going.'

She ignored him and poured another drink. She went out into the kitchen to add water to the glass. When she came back she said, 'Do you know, Max didn't even leave me a note. Nothing at all.' Karas could think of nothing to say. She went on, 'That's not like him—to have left nothing behind.' Karas sipped at his whisky. She looked at him steadily. 'He didn't write anything to you, Peter, did he?'

He had been waiting for the question and he answered without hesitation. 'No, I'm afraid not.'

'You could tell me, you know.'

'Yes, I know that. But he didn't.'

'I expect Suvorin asked you the same question, didn't he?'

'Yes, he did, as a matter of fact.'

She looked at him intently. 'What is it, Peter? Are you keeping something from me?'

He was exasperated. Why couldn't she leave him alone? 'Nothing whatever. Why should I?'

She smiled at him, with a curious intimacy. 'I don't know the meaning of what happens to your face or the changes in your voice—not yet anyway. But I know there's something you don't want to tell me.' Karas tried to conceal his consternation. It was alarming to think that his face and voice might be constantly betraying him. Until today he had not cared how closely people might study him, since he had had no secrets from anyone. He thought back nostalgically to the days of his innocence, before Max's letter had corrupted him and made him into a conspirator. Sophia seemed to divine his anxiety. She said gently, 'Don't worry too much. I don't think Suvorin is quite as observant as I am.'

He felt a great desire to get away, before she disturbed him further. He swallowed his whisky. 'I really must go—'

'That's all right.' She made no attempt to keep him. But there was a plea in her voice as she added, 'You'll come to see me again soon? It's very lonely here.'

'Yes, of course. I'll do anything I can. You know that.'

'Yes, I do.' Softly, using all the overtones of her voice, she said, 'I'm sorry if I said anything to upset you. You've been very kind.'

The conventional phrases fell awkwardly from both of them. They somehow seemed to call attention to the temporary atmosphere of intimacy which they replaced, and he kissed her cheek. He had done this as a routine for years, but now for some reason it faintly embarrassed him. Her hand touched his for a moment. She said, 'Before you go, Peter, could I give you one piece of advice?'

'Of course.' He looked at her questioningly.

'Be careful with Suvorin.'

He frowned. 'I think you're prejudiced against him. He's really quite a nice old man—'

She said, 'Think that if you like. But try to be careful.'

As Karas left the apartment block the cleaning woman was busy with a brush on the steps. He smiled at her and she looked blankly back out of a tired, stupid face. It was a long day, he thought, for whatever work she was doing. He drove back to the dacha and made himself a meal of cold meat, potato salad, and beer. He tried to think about the implications of what had happened but he felt too tired and a little frightened. Resentful also, so far as one could ever sustain resentment against Max. There was a voice inside him which asked why, if Max wanted to kill himself, couldn't he have just done so and left other people in peace, without throwing his problems in their laps? If only Max had discussed the matter with him before he died . . .

But then he wondered what he would have done in those circumstances. He realized as soon as he contemplated the idea what an impossible situation would have been created. As soon as Max had explained his problem, the two of them would have become part of the conspiracy, and Max was no conspirator. No, there was no use in being angry with Max. He always won, because you knew in your heart that he was better than you, and your anger against him was always turned ultimately into shame. Who could win against a man who showed no resistance, had no vanity, offered no reproach?

The telephone rang. It was Anya. He could hear the anxiety in her voice, eager for a note of affection from him, a reassurance that his unexpected behaviour that morning hadn't been anything to do with her. Until the moment he heard her voice he had forgotten her, but now he felt a desire for her company. He said, 'Are you free now? Can you come and see me?'

She made a pretence of considering it. 'I had promised to go dancing—'

'Oh, in that case—'

'But I think I can get out of it,' she said hurriedly.

'All right then. I'll pick you up at the students' club. I'll be over in twenty minutes.'

When they got back to the bungalow Anya took off her coat and gloves and rubbed her hands together for warmth. Her face was bright and flushed, and when he kissed her mouth it was cold to his lips.

'It's getting cold,' she said happily. 'There were snow-flakes this morning. In a few weeks they'll be ski-ing in the mountains.'

'I suppose so.' Anya was a leading member of the University ski team. The first time he had ever seen her she had been hurtling down one of the competition slopes, her body poised like that of a bird in flight, her white teeth biting her lower lip with child-like concentration. She made love, he had found, in the same kind of way, as if it were yet another physical skill in which she was determined to excel.

He went into the bedroom and lit the oil stove. Then he came back to the living-room and they sat together on the old battered sofa. He held her in his arms while she chattered on about the other students and the lecturers and an amateur dramatic show in which she had been given a minor part. He tried to pay attention to what she was saying, but his mind wandered constantly back to his preoccupations. After half an hour he took her by the hand and led her into the bedroom.

As always, she stripped off her clothes immediately and then stood for a moment inspecting herself in the wardrobe mirror. Carefully, she smoothed away a wrinkle on her flank

40

which had been left by her girdle, in the way a sculptor might smooth a piece of marble with a silk handkerchief. Then she turned to Karas, who was lying on the bed.

'Do you like me?'

'Yes. Come here.'

She lay on the bed beside him and he kissed her. Then he moved away from her and began to touch her breasts. As he ran his hand down towards the lower part of her body he stopped at a small brown birthmark just above the pubic hair. He traced the outline of it with his finger. He felt her muscles go tense and she moved away from him.

'Why do you do that?' she asked.

'Why not? I like it.'

'It's ugly.'

'It's an imperfection,' he said. 'Without it your body would be too perfect. It would be boring.'

She said impatiently, 'I don't understand that.'

'I don't know that I do myself. But it's true.'

The baffled, impatient frown on her face reminded him that she was nineteen and he was thirty-five, she was a packaged product of a shining new race while he carried in his blood the brilliance and the weariness and the pain of a thousand years of ancient civilization. She might for a moment find him attractive and interesting, but he was part of a world that would be used for what it could give and then never replaced. Sophia's memories of Vienna, which had brought a lump to his throat an hour or two ago, would have been greeted by Anya with incomprehension, even derision.

But one should not expect too much of anyone. He looked down at her legs. They were strong, graceful and beautifully proportioned, with none of the awkward bulges of the professional athlete. There were no imperfections there. Her eyes followed his and she said complacently, 'Are they boring too?'

'No. They're magnificent.'

She gave him a proud, happy smile. 'It's a question of exercises. I do them all the summer when there is no ski-ing.' She was very earnest about it. 'Shall I show them to you?'

'Later,' he said. 'Later.'

When it was over she said, 'It was good?'

'Yes.'

'Very good?'

'Very good.'

She persisted. 'I am exciting to you?'

'You know you are.'

'I don't know.' She seemed vaguely dissatisfied. 'Tonight it was different. I don't know quite how.' She sighed and then said, 'Sometimes I think you don't really love me at all.'

He had never said he loved her. It was something he always avoided saying, no matter how great the temptation. He said, truthfully, 'I love your mouth and your energy, your sweetness, your physical perfection—' Surely it was a great deal. The sad thing was that when you put it in words it somehow seemed so little. He tried to think of something else. She said, quite seriously, 'And my intelligence? I'm third of all the students in my section.'

'Yes, of course.' There didn't seem much more to say. He kissed her affectionately and she clung to him for a while. Then he gently disengaged himself, got out of bed and put on a dressing-gown. He looked out of the window at the tangled woodland behind the bungalow and the great yellow river beyond. The snow had partly melted but it would be back again in a day or two.

Anya said, 'What's worrying you?'

'Nothing.'

'I think there's something.' She came and stood beside him and put her hand in his. It occurred to him that she had never once asked him why he had left her so abruptly that morning. Yet she must have been in an agony of curiosity. At what age was it that they learned that it was wiser not to ask questions?

He said, 'Last night my best friend killed himself.'

'Oh,' she said. It was almost a groan. Life was so important to her that its voluntary renunciation seemed utterly appalling and against nature. 'Poor Peter! How terrible for you!'

'Worse for him.'

She shook her head in a baffled way. 'I don't understand. How could a person do such a thing? What was it? What made him do it?'

It was impossible to try and explain. The context in which Max lived—the depression, the fear, the indecision, the responsibility—were meaningless to her. It was another language, another world. He said, 'I don't know.' He gazed out at the drab black trees, the melting snows, the vast

42

indifferent river and the mountains lowering across the plain. 'Perhaps he felt the winter coming on.'

She looked at him in astonishment. 'The winter? But that is the most wonderful season here.'

'Yes, of course.' How could a man kill himself when the ski-ing was only just a few weeks off? He turned and kissed her tenderly on the mouth, with great gentleness and affection as you might caress a child or an animal. A child would do what it could, it would give you all the understanding and affection in its power, but only a fool would expect from it more than it was able to understand. She clung to him and sighed happily. She was at peace now, her body warm and loved, her eyes closed against his shoulder. But his own eyes were open and there was an ache in his heart for something he could not define. Into his head came a phrase which Sophia had used, but which seemed to hold within it the inexpressible yearning of his heart. 'My own people,' she had said. He repeated it to himself as he warmed his hands on the soft, loving, but never entirely satisfying flesh of his mistress.

CHAPTER FOUR

THE NEXT MORNING, Karas had just finished going through his mail when he heard Suvorin's steps in the corridor leading to his office. It was a slow, ponderous, old man's step, and the thick rubber soles of his shoes made a squeaking sound against the linoleum of the corridor. Imperceptibly, over the years, that sound had become a part of the lives of all the senior officials, and Karas tensed involuntarily when he heard it. The footsteps stopped at the door of his office. Suvorin did not knock—he never knocked. His practice when he made visits on his juniors was to walk straight into the office and begin talking immediately.

He closed the door behind him and sank into the chair opposite Karas; he was carrying a brown file full of papers which he put down to one side of him on the floor. He seemed set for a long stay.

'You haven't moved out of here yet?' Karas looked at him questioningly. Suvorin explained, 'I meant into Max's office. You ought to do that as soon as possible.'

43

Karas had been wondering about this. It was rather a delicate matter, and he did not wish to seem too eager to take over. 'I'll do it today,' he said.

'The sooner the better. It's important to make it plain that you're in charge and that you intend to pull things together. There may be difficulties at first but I'm ready to help you in any way I can. Don't hesitate to come to me if you're in trouble.' His tone was a little perfunctory. He added, as if to make sure the offer was not taken too literally, 'Of course this is all going to mean a great deal more work for me too.'

He halted, and Karas made the kind of sympathetic noise which the situation seemed to demand.

'Oh yes. You've no idea what I have to put up with—no idea at all. It's all very well for you young men. You can get on with your research, spend your time on the kind of work you really care about.' He waved a hand, in a gesture which seemed to take in not only the room in which they were sitting but the whole complex of the laboratories. 'You want for nothing. Money, facilities, expensive equipment. Have you ever thought of the administrative drudgery I have to go through to get it for you?' He repeated melodramatically, 'Drudgery. That's what it is.'

Karas nodded politely. He could tell this was mere preamble. When Suvorin had something important to say, he never liked to speak about it immediately. His method was to ramble on for a while about minor issues and then suddenly to introduce into the conversation the problem that was really on his mind.

'You should see my mail,' Suvorin went on. 'Inquiries, forms, requests for pointless information. There's no time to do any useful work any more. Everything's too big now. The Central Committee has lost control. The Secretariat—' He shrugged contemptuously. 'They're just a pack of clerks. What do they know about science? All they care about is power. They want to keep control of everything I do. They won't delegate, that's the trouble.' Karas was very near to smiling. Suvorin's own idea of delegation was to forget totally about certain departments while he spent his time meddling in the affairs of others. 'It's disastrous,' he went on. 'Disastrous. In this country we have some of the finest scientists in the world. We should be ahead of the Americans. But there's no trust—no loyalty.' If there was really no loyalty, Karas thought, Suvorin himself would have been

44

in trouble years ago. His sense of grievance led him into grave indiscretions. If his superiors had ever got to know what he said about them in the privacy of the laboratories, he would have been disgraced many times over. But it had never happened and never would. Whatever they might think of him on occasions, they were Suvorin's men. It was out of the question that they should betray him.

Karas glanced out of the window, suppressing a yawn. An old gardener was walking slowly along the path trying to brush the leaves into a heap. Each time he did so the gusty mountain wind blew them away again, scattering them along the paths and the flower beds. The old man seemed quite unperturbed at the repetitiveness and futility of his task. A few emaciated birch saplings which had been planted to add variety to the lawns were bent almost at right angles, torn by the violent wind which blew from the mountains. Out there, the air would be cold and savage, threatening winter. In the office it was stale and enervating. It seemed to him as if he and Suvorin were suspended in some time-less, motionless atmosphere, like two grains of dust. The harsh querulous voice droned on. Sometimes on these occasions Karas found that his whole body ached from the battering of the stale repetitious phrases. Suvorin had a limited repertoire of these monologues. Often they were mere reiterations of old grievances—the dominance of the Central Committee, the stupidity of the Secretariat, his failure to be elected to the Council of the Academy of Sciences. Karas had long since stopped wondering how reasonable or well-founded these grievances were. At one time he had thought it worth while speculating whether there was real hostility to Suvorin in high places, or whether the whole situation was a delusion developed out of the twisted recesses of his own personality. He had wondered how much Suvorin's aggression gave rise to the hostile responses from others who so embittered him. But now he had heard the stories and complaints so often that fatigue had set in. He no longer cared whether Suvorin was right or wrong, aggressor or victim.

As a kind of protective reflex, he had learned to switch off his attention in the way a man might switch off a hearing-aid, while at the same time keeping his ears open for any switch to a topic of immediate significance. In the middle of a story about a squabble which had taken place years ago over a building licence, he heard Suvorin say:

45

'It was a very unpleasant business. They got at Max behind my back. They went to him and asked him if he could manage without the new building. And Max—' Suvorin's lips tightened. 'Well, we mustn't speak ill of the dead, they say.' He looked at Karas as if hoping that Karas might encourage him to do so. After a pause he went on, 'But the truth is that he let me down.' He shook his head gloomily. 'I hadn't expected such disloyalty from him.'

'Max wasn't disloyal,' protested Karas. 'He might have been a little too agreeable—'

Suvorin did not seem to hear him. 'I don't blame him, really,' he said in a magnanimous tone. He paused for a moment and then added, 'It was his wife who was at the root of it all.'

'Sophia?'

'Yes. She was a bad influence on him. Max should have told her years ago to mind her own business. But he was too weak. I warned him at one time. I said, "Stop her intriguing, Max. She'll be the end of you one of these days." But he did nothing, of course. Well . . .' Suvorin went no further. He seemed to imply that in warning Max against his wife he had somehow done everything for Max that could have been expected of him.

This was something quite new to Karas. At the Centre, women were not generally supposed to take any active part in affairs. 'Why should she make trouble?' he asked.

Suvorin laughed shortly. 'My dear Peter—why do women make trouble? Boredom, I suppose. Ambition for their husbands.' His voice took on a rougher note. 'And she never really accepted our life here. She resented me. She had no real loyalty to our country or our political system. She said nothing, but I could always tell. She longed to be back in the West.'

So Suvorin knew, thought Karas. In this country you didn't actually need to say anything. In the course of time you gave out an atmosphere which they had grown to recognize. It was not enough to be silent and discreet. Sophia had never said anything outside her own house that might be construed as a criticism of the régime, while Suvorin himself railed every day about the indolence of the bureaucracy and the stupidity of the Government. Yet in the last analysis Suvorin had faith and Sophia had none. And in this world it was by faith alone that men were saved.

A tremor of apprehension passed over him. If faith were

all, how would he himself be judged? Would his abilities count for anything if ever it became said of him, as evidently it had been of Max, that he was disloyal? And was it possible ever to give the degree of loyalty they required, without abandoning for ever his own pride and his own individuality?

Suvorin was watching him closely. 'I'm well aware,' he said, 'that you may feel certain personal obligations towards Max. I do myself. But the good of the Centre comes first.' He spoke as if this was a matter beyond argument. When Karas made no reply he stood up and said with sudden anger, 'Come in here and I'll show you something.'

He led Karas into Max's office. It was over a week since Karas had been there and he was startled by the change. Normally, Max had been an untidy worker. Books and journals had been scattered here and there, cupboards were full of piles of old reprints. He cultivated bulbs on shelves and fed the pigeons who came in and dropped messes down the inside of the window. But now everything was changed. The room was still dusty, but all the clutter had gone. Only a few rings in the dust showed where most of them had been. It was as if someone had deliberately tried to eradicate all traces of Max's presence.

'Who did this?' Karas asked.

Suvorin looked at him coldly through his steel-rimmed spectacles. There was rage in his eyes. 'He did. He destroyed every note, every record of his work, every dish and jar and bottle of culture medium. He cleaned the place out. What do you make of that?'

Karas said in perplexity, 'It's astonishing.'

Suvorin pulled open a filing cabinet to demonstrate its emptiness. 'He left nothing—nothing. He knew very well that these records weren't his property. They belonged to the State. He must have known what a crime it was to destroy them.' There was genuine agony in Suvorin's voice at the realization that Max was beyond punishment for this outrage. He went on, 'It's an alarming situation. Very alarming indeed. I shall have to put in a report about this whole affair to the Secretariat. They'll want to know everything. It's a serious matter when a man of his seniority commits suicide. They'll want a complete medical report, possible reasons why he did it, an account of his personal relations, his work record over the last year. Every detail. And what have I got to go on?' He said resentfully, 'He never visited

47

a doctor, his wife is unco-operative, he confided in nobody and left no records.' The violence died out of his voice, and he said, looking closely at Karas. 'At least, that's what I'm asked to believe.'

'It's possible, surely.'

'Possible.' Suvorin repeated the word dubiously. 'I wonder.' After a moment's thought he seemed to throw his speculation aside, for the present. 'Well, no use crying over spilt milk. What we have to do now is to get things straight again.' He paused and then said, in a challenging tone, 'Haven't we?'

Karas nodded cautiously. Suvorin was obviously working up to something but it was not yet quite clear what it was. A moment later it was made clear to him. The tone of Suvorin's voice became brisker and more decisive. The softening-up process was over. 'Now, Peter, what I want you to do is this. As the new head of the department, I'd like you to prepare me a detailed analysis of its achievements during the last six months, with particular reference to work done by Max himself. All right?'

'It may be a little difficult,' said Karas, 'since Max destroyed all the records.'

Suvorin suddenly became jocular. It was a rather fearsome, determined jocularity which he had developed for avoiding awkward issues. 'Ah, but you're a young man of initiative, Peter. You should enjoy a difficult job.' His teeth were bared in one of his wolfish, unconvincing smiles. 'I'm sure you'll be able to manage this. I'll look forward to receiving your report in a week's time.'

He sidled quickly out of the door before Karas could argue or protest. When he had gone, Karas sat and thought over their conversation. Looking back, it was now plain to him that every part of it had been carefully planned beforehand by Suvorin. The reminder of the necessity for loyalty, the warning against Sophia, the touch of flattery, the shadow of a threat. And the final demand—a report on work done in the department for which no official records existed. A report which could only be written by a man who had received some private communication on the subject . . . Karas realized that he was being given a chance to save himself. He had the opportunity to search the laboratories, to claim to have found some notes left by Max in some out-of-the-way place which the search had missed. He knew, as surely as if Suvorin had told him in words, that if he did this his offence would be forgiven, and he would be allowed a chance to show his ability as a department head. This was his chance to show loyalty, to show faith. Suvorin liked and admired him, he knew. If he could get over this particular hurdle, the possibilities were limitless. But if he refused it, what would be his future then?

He felt a great weariness at the thought of the test which had been put to him. Could it be that this was merely the beginning of something, that success depended on a series of compromises of this kind? He looked around the barren office, stripped of Max's personality and ready for his own occupation. In a few months, he knew, Max would be almost forgotten. This was the post he had secretly longed for, which had come to him by an unlooked-for stroke of fortune ten years earlier than he could reasonably have expected it. But now—where was the joy in it? He had a vision of years ahead of reports and personal battles, of conflicts of loyalty, of struggles for advantage for himself or his department. He felt a perverse longing for the simple straightforward life of his laboratory. There, at least, there was neither corruption nor compromise.

He left Max's room and went back to his own. As he walked towards his desk he noticed a brown cardboard folder on the floor by the visitor's chair. He remembered now that Suvorin had dropped it there when he had first come into the room. Presumably he had forgotten it—he often left things behind in other people's offices. As Karas picked it up, some papers slipped out on to the floor. He was about to put them back in the folder when he saw his own name in the writing on the top sheet of the pile. He hesitated for a moment. The correct thing was to return it to the folder instantly without reading it, but he was overcome with an irresistible desire to know what Suvorin had been writing about him. A week ago it would not have mattered so much. He would have been curious, but he would have resisted the temptation. Now he could no longer do so. Quickly and furtively, he opened the folder and read. The typed sheet was a draft letter to the Secretary of the Central Committee. The first paragraph was taken up with routine matters connected with Max's death. The second paragraph referred to himself.

'Because of the urgent need for continuity I have appointed Dr. Peter Karas to be acting Administrative Head of the Department. I have made it plain to him that this appointment is on a provisional basis and makes no permanent commitment. Much will depend on his performance in the next few months. I regret to say that Dr. Bremer left the Department in a very unsatisfactory state. Presumably as a consequence of the mental instability which led to his death, he destroyed all records of his own scientific work. However, I am confident that it will be possible to uncover information on this subject, and I have set Dr. Karas on to this as a task of first priority. His initiative in this respect will provide the crucial test of his future value to us in a more responsible capacity.'

Karas had just finished reading when he heard the familiar squeak of rubber-soled shoes in the corridor. He slipped the letter back in the folder and dropped it back on to the floor. When Suvorin opened the door he was sitting behind the desk.

Suvorin halted for a moment just inside the door and looked at him without speaking. Then he said, 'I think I left a file behind.'

Karas got up and looked down at Suvorin's chair. 'So you did.' He picked up the file from the floor and handed it over. To himself, his performance felt stiff and unconvincing. Suvorin looked at him intently through his spectacles. It occurred to Karas that Suvorin not only knew that he had opened the file and read the letter, but that the file had been deliberately left there for that purpose. He felt the blood running into his cheeks. Suvorin gave a satisfied little nod and left the room.

The workers at the Centre ate their meals in a huge cafeteria in the Administration. Off this there was a smaller dining-room with a circular table reserved for heads of departments. The food was the same but their rank gave them the privilege of waitress service and some degree of privacy. The administration of the cafeteria was in the charge of Pavlov, the dining-room superintendent, a thick-set man with sleek black hair and baggy sallow cheeks. As Karas entered, Pavlov hurried up to him.

'Dr. Karas, my congratulations!'

Karas looked at him with surprise and some distaste. He had never liked Pavlov, who was commonly suspected of selling part of the Centre's meat ration on the black market. 'What is it?'

'I have received notification from Dr. Suvorin's office that you are now a department head. You are consequently entitled to use the special dining-room.' Karas nodded and strode with his long legs through the crowd in the cafeteria. Pavlov hurried beside him. 'If there is any way in which I can help you—'

Karas nodded again and left him to go into the smaller room. Leskov, Zabergan, and Fedorov were already seated at the table. Suvorin was not there, but Karas knew that he only rarely appeared in the dining-room. It was his practice to eat alone in his private quarters.

Leskov rose from his seat. He had obviously been prepared for this occasion. He said ceremoniously, 'This is our first opportunity to congratulate you on your new appointment. I'm sure I speak for all of us when I wish you great success.'

'Thank you,' said Karas. He could see that he was expected to be rather moved by the solemnity of the occasion. It was kind of them, of course, to be so friendly about it, but he found this formality irksome and a little ridiculous. Surely they were taking the whole thing too seriously.

'If there is any assistance we can give you,' said Leskov, 'we shall of course be only too pleased.'

Zabergan and Fedorov murmured their agreement. How difficult it was, thought Karas, to make personal contact with any of them. After five years at the Centre he knew virtually nothing about what they thought of their country, the Centre, or each other. They seemed content to act the part of the two-dimensional characters which Suvorin had created within his own imagination. He had decided that Leskov was plodding and conscientious, Zabergan loyal and unimaginative, Fedorov a brilliant but impractical intellectual. Obviously there must be a great deal more to them than that. Behind their public facades there must be complex, contradictory natures, loves and hates and jealousies and fears. But concealment had become a way of life with them. He would never know them now.

They were likeable, harmless men, Karas reminded himself. They were civilized in their interests and had the same values and cultural standards as himself. They had all loved and respected Max. As far as he himself was concerned, though he had never been intimate with any of them, they liked him and wished him well. He should be grateful to them for that.

Why, then, should he feel so lost, so utterly cut off? There was something about their conversation which gave it the taste of dust in his mouth. As he sat there at the table and listened, his exasperation increased with each minute that passed. The conversation was intelligent, calm, reasoned, tolerant, but in the end it meant nothing—caution and calculation had stolen the life from it. They spoke of the University and its intrigues against Suvorin, the Central Committee and its obstinacy in not allowing Suvorin a freer hand, the Academy and its incomprehensible refusal to recognize Suvorin at his true value. There was not an opinion voiced that was not Suvorin's, not an enemy or a friend that was not his enemy or friend. Could there be anything so sickly and wearisome, thought Karas, as total loyalty? Was there anything so futile, such a betrayal of man's true nature, as intelligence without courage?

Leskov was describing, in his ponderous way, some complex manoeuvres in relation to the building up of a new steroid chemistry section in a rival part of the University. 'Alexei's determined to stop it,' he said severely. 'And quite right too. It's a deliberate attempt to take funds from our own group.'

The triviality of it exasperated Karas. Science he could understand, administration he could understand, but this petty squabbling about grants degraded their whole occupation. 'I find it hard to believe that,' he said.

Leskov looked at him in astonishment. 'It's a fact,' he said. 'Alexei told me only this morning—'

'He was probably exaggerating. You know how he does.' It was really too stupid for men of their distinction to sit here talking as if Suvorin were completely beyond human criticism. 'These men are scientists like us. When it comes down to it, they're probably just interested in steroid chemistry.'

He instinctively looked round the table in the hope of some sympathetic response from one of the others. Zabergan avoided his eye. Fedorov, deep in contemplation over a plateful of goulash, did not seem to have heard the conversation at all. Leskov was regarding him severely across the table, and it occurred to Karas that his first appearance in the special dining-room was hardly the time to acquire a reputation for unconventional behaviour. It wasn't as if it really mattered one way or the other. He said propitiatingly to Leskov, 'Of course, I know nothing about it. You may well be right.'

The conversation throughout the rest of the meal was

desultory and innocuous. Afterwards they separated and returned to their departments. As Karas walked across the campus, he found Leskov at his elbow. By the set expression on his face, it was obvious that he had something important to say.

'I just wanted to tell you,' he said in his intense nasal voice, 'that I was very sincere when I welcomed your promotion. I've always thought that you had great potentialities.'

'Thank you very much.'

'Soon after you came here, I said so to Alexei. I told him that you had great imagination and originality.' Leskov breathed hard, fighting to talk against the gusty wind. 'It's sometimes necessary to tell him these things. He's a very busy man and has great problems on his mind. He doesn't have very much time to study the character of others.' As if afraid that Karas might interpret his remarks as criticism, Leskov went on hurriedly, 'It's simply because he's so busy. When he wants to be, he's a very shrewd judge of character.'

Karas said nothing. Leskov must have had some reason for talking to him like this. He waited for it to emerge.

Leskov plodded on. 'You obviously can't know Alexei as well as we who have worked in close contact with him for years. I know that he's very anxious that you should succeed in your new responsibilities. He's not a man who likes to interfere in the private lives of others, but he does notice things.' Leskov paused, and the silence between the two men became heavy. Karas felt his muscles grow tense. He had a feeling that something was going to be said that he was not going to like. Leskov said, 'I hope you'll forgive me if I speak personally.'

'What is it?' said Karas.

Leskov paused. 'There are two things really. The first concerns our conversation at lunch. I know that it didn't seem important to you and that you had no intention of being disloyal, but—' He hesitated. 'As a department head, one has certain special responsibilities. Alexei needs all of us behind him in his struggle with the University.'

'I see,' said Karas. He felt anger rising within him, but he knew that he must control it. 'And what was the other?'

Leskov took a breath before replying. Then he spoke rapidly and with considerable embarrassment. 'It concerns Sophia Bremer. I know she's a great friend of yours and you feel a duty towards her at the present. But I really think you'd be wise not to see her just for the moment.'

CHAPTER FIVE

DURING THE DAYS THAT FOLLOWED Karas sometimes wondered why he had not reacted more violently and spontaneously to the impertinence of Leskov's advice. It was perfectly outrageous that Leskov (or rather Suvorin, who had obviously been behind the conversation) should take it upon himself to tell him not to see the wife of his best and oldest friend.

But he had remained silent. Why? In the first place he had been utterly taken aback. And Leskov had wisely walked away almost immediately, giving him no time to think of a suitable reply. Yet Karas knew in his heart that there was more to it than that. An important decision still remained to be made, one that a prudent and careful man should not make on impulse. In everything that happened now in the laboratories, he was being offered an unspoken choice. Was he with Suvorin, utterly and totally, or was he not? If he was, there would be great rewards. He could prove his loyalty by keeping away from Sophia, and by the nature of the report he wrote on Max's work. He had been offered provisional membership of an exclusive club. Was he prepared to pay the entrance fee?

The others had paid it in their time, and the result was all too evident. Yet what was the penalty of refusal? To revert to his former status, as a junior research worker with no further chance of advancement? That might be bearable if it was the only way of preserving his integrity. The only trouble was that to anyone familiar with the extremism of Suvorin's nature, such a moderate punishment seemed unlikely. To anyone who refused his love, Suvorin had only one alternative gift to offer—his hatred.

Karas delayed, hoping indecisively that something might happen to offer him a compromise in his dilemma. Somehow he could not bring himself to take the decisive step that might lead to the total destruction of his career. It seemed fantastic that he should be called on to make such a sacrifice just to give a little temporary consolation to a woman who had never been more to him than the rather colourless wife of an old friend. And at the same time he could picture Sophia, alone in her tiny flat, without friends or visitors, a foreigner in a country which she detested, with no one to turn to but himself. Max's wife, who had pleaded for his help, who waited all day in vain for a knock on the door, a ring on the telephone. . . .

He tried to force the picture out of his mind. He worked late at the laboratories each night, as if trying to convince himself that he had no time for anything but his work. He made a start on the report which Suvorin had demanded. He questioned Barov, Max's technician, about the destruction of Max's papers, but Barov was either unusually ignorant of what his master had been doing or impenetrably discreet. He was able to contribute nothing of real value.

Each day Suvorin came into his room and talked, sometimes for several hours. He was still almost embarrassingly friendly. He confided in Karas all kinds of details of his early struggles, his suspicions of the Secretariat and the Central Committee, his present battles with the University. He did not mention either Max or the report again. Yet somehow he managed to make it plain to Karas that he was being tested for his fitness to carry his new responsibilities. Karas was convinced that the brown file which had been dropped in his room had been left there deliberately for him to read. Suvorin had not seemed angry when he had betrayed his confusion—on the contrary, he had seemed rather pleased. It was if the knowledge that Karas was capable of an action of that kind had in some way made him appear more suitable for the position he was to occupy. No doubt, too, Suvorin had been delighted at his own cleverness in the springing of his little trap. As the days went by, Karas noticed that Leskov too had developed an increasing self-satisfaction. Presumably they were all aware that he was not seeing Sophia.

Karas felt that he could have borne the situation more easily if it had not been for the indulgent, self-satisfied way in which his compliance with authority was being received. The attitude of both Suvorin and Leskov served to emphasize the fact that he had given in to authority and made it impossible for him to sustain the pretence that he was omitting to visit Sophia simply because of the amount of extra work he had to do. For some reason they would not allow him to save his face. With an elephantine lack of sensitivity they insisted on reminding him of his humiliation. Their approval was more painful than any insult to which they could have subjected him.

He saw no one outside the laboratories. In the evening he

would go back to the bungalow and sit in his chair, brooding, until it was time to go to bed. He could not concentrate on a book, and when he got to bed he was unable to sleep. The solitary routine of his life had not seemed so bad before, when he had been free of serious problems. He had eaten and slept and worked and satisfied his sensual appetites—it had not been perfect but had been acceptable. But now his sense of isolation became almost unbearable.

It was the solitude, in the end, which forced his decision. He sat in his tiny living-room, gazing wretchedly out of the window at the overgrown garden or watching the squalls of icy rain slashing like a whip across the flank of the great river. Suddenly he knew that he could bear it no longer. He picked up the telephone and dialled the number of the women's hostel where Anya lived. After a long delay she was found and brought to the phone. He said, 'It's Peter here.'

'Oh.' She seemed surprised and not entirely pleased. 'I wondered what had happened to you. It's been over a week—'

'Yes, I know. I'm sorry. I've been terribly busy. I've been at the laboratories every night. I was going to ring you—'

She interrupted him. 'It's all right. I've been busy too. I couldn't have seen you anyway.'

There was none of the eagerness in her voice that he had come to expect. He said, 'I wondered if you were free this evening.'

'No. I'm afraid not.'

Disappointment struck him with an almost physical intensity. 'Well, perhaps tomorrow—'

'No. I'm sorry.' Before he could speak again she said, 'Peter, I wanted to tell you this anyway. I'm not going to see you again.'

He was totally disconcerted. He had thought sometimes of winding up the affair himself, but it had never occurred to him that she might take the initiative. 'But why—?'

'You know why. You don't really care, you never did.' She added, 'Anyway, there's somebody else.'

'Oh.' She was right, of course, it had been an affair of convenience for both of them. If the convenience was gone, there was no more to be said. But he made one last struggle. 'If we could meet once more, to say goodbye—'

'No. We can do that now. It's better.' She said gently, 'Goodbye, Peter.'

'Goodbye.' He heard a click and the line went dead. So that was the end of Anya, sweet, simple, beautiful Anya who loved the winter and the ski-ing and the love-making. She would marry some bright, keen young student of engineering or oriental languages and they would have children as strong and healthy and patriotic and beautifully ignorant of the world as themselves. He would remain in her memory as an exotic transitory incident of student days.

What life held for her was plain enough, but what was there for him? In an agony of loneliness he picked up the telephone again and dialled Max's number. After a few rings there was a click and he waited tensely for Sophia to reply. But a strange female voice spoke.

'What number are you dialling?'

He gave the number.

'That number has been discontinued.' Before he could ring off, the operator said rapidly, 'Who is calling?'

He hesitated, wondering whether to ring off now. But the operator would be able to trace the call. He said, 'My name is Karas, Dr. Peter Karas.'

The line went dead. So that was that, he thought. Suvorin would know in the morning, if not earlier. He might as well go and see her now.

When he rang the bell of the flat Sophia answered the door almost immediately. She was wearing a neat, severely tailored black dress which was rather more formal than he would ordinarily have expected—he realized that in her restrained, unobtrusive way, she was in mourning. She greeted him courteously but without fuss. She did not seem in the least surprised to see him.

He said awkwardly, 'I'm pleased to find you in. I wasn't sure—'

She said, closing the door behind her, 'I'm in most of the time.'

Her tone asked, without self-pity, where he would expect her to go. He felt more than ever ashamed at leaving her alone for so long. 'I tried to telephone you,' he said. 'Evidently it isn't functioning.'

'They cut it off as soon as Max died,' she said indifferently. 'It was really what I expected. I have no priority any more.'

'I suppose not.'

He sat down and, without asking him first, she brought out the bottle of whisky. He protested, 'There's no need—'

'Of course you must have something. Otherwise I shall feel like a bad hostess.' She poured the whisky and water. 'You see, I know how to make it now.' She poured a small glass of cherry liqueur for herself. 'I will take something too, so that you will not feel lonely.' She lifted the glass to her lips. '*Prosit.*'

'*Prosit.*'

With every movement, he thought, with every word, even her way of drinking out of a glass, she emphasized her fidelity to a world now at least a thousand miles and twenty-five years away. She wore her clothes and her few pieces of jewellery in a way he could not easily define, but could never be anything else but European. She had presumably made the black dress herself—it had a style which you never saw here, which took him back to the cafés in the crowded streets around the Opera, where the girls sipped coffee in front of Sacher's or paraded around the pavements of the Ringstrasse pretending to be indifferent to the eyes that watched them. Her pride in her European origin was so deeply ingrained that it was like a challenge to everything around her—the dingy apartment with its peeling paint, the pretentious neo-classic buildings crouching in the corner of this vast wilderness. She cared for nothing there, accepted nothing, was impressed by nothing. It was easy to understand the reason for Suvorin's resentment and suspicion of her.

She put down her glass and smiled at him. Her gratitude warmed him more than the drink. She said, with one of her unexpected flashes of affection, 'It's so good to see you, Peter.'

'I'm sorry I couldn't come earlier,' he said. 'I've been very busy.'

'It's good of you to have come at all.' She paused. 'I don't suppose it was easy for you.'

There was something oppressive in the way everyone seemed to know all about his affairs and to be watching his every response to the pressure of events. He said rather curtly, 'What do you mean?'

'Life here is very predictable,' she said. 'It's bound to be, isn't it, since everyone has to work according to rules. Surprises are really only produced by people acting as individuals. And we don't believe in that any more.' Like so many of her remarks, this was more than a statement of fact—it was a challenge. As on his previous visit he had the uneasy feeling that she needed him for something more than friendship or sympathy—that he was the only link she had left with the only world she cared about. 'You see,' she went on, 'I've been here longer than you. I've seen this before with others. The time comes when you're given the choice—to be a person or—' she hesitated and then said with a kind of contemptuous pity, '—a thing.'

It was foolish to pretend that he did not know what she meant. But he could not bring himself to agree with her. 'The others?' he said.

'Yes. Your colleagues. There's nothing wrong with them. Not really. They just don't exist any more, do they? Leskov —well, perhaps he never existed. Zabergan—he's a sweet, kind man. Faithful until death. They got him through loyalty. He loves Suvorin, you know that? He'd do anything for him. Loyalty like that can be a vice, a sickness,' she added softly. 'If you believe in God, it can be a sin.' She looked up at him with a faint smile. 'You see, I feel these things strongly. I'm an emotional woman.'

'What about Fedorov?'

'He knows nothing and feels nothing. He despises Suvorin's intellect but his own mind will always give him a good reason for doing what Suvorin wants. He gave in very easily.'

'And Max?' The terrible question was between them—it had to be asked.

She said, 'Max was a strange, complicated man. I thought sometimes that he was hopelessly lost, fading away helplessly like a mist. Then for a while he would appear again. But in the end—' She frowned, stopped abruptly. 'I don't want to talk about Max.' She stood up and said, 'It's dinner-time. I'll make you something to eat.'

'No. Please don't trouble—'

'You live alone in that bungalow. I don't suppose you've had a proper meal for a week.'

She made determinedly for the kitchen. He said, 'Let me help you.'

'No.' Her tone was decisive. 'There are plenty of books on the shelves. Read something. I won't be long.'

He took a book from one of the shelves and read while she prepared a meal. There was spaghetti with a meat sauce, some cheese and a bottle of red wine. When the meal was ready he put down his book and sat at the table.

'What were you reading?' she asked.

'Thomas Mann. *Buddenbrooks*. It's a favourite of mine.'

She did not reply, but simply sat there staring at her plate. He was embarrassed to see that tears had come into her eyes. He asked awkwardly, 'Do you know it?'

She nodded. After a short silence she said, 'Such a sad, beautiful, cruel world. Shall we ever see it again, Peter?'

There was a terrible danger in this nostalgia. He knew in his heart how destructive it could be and had fought it all his life. He spoke almost brutally. 'No,' he said. 'That world has gone for ever. It doesn't exist anywhere, you must understand that. It isn't just in this place that the grace and beauty has been lost. . . .'

She pressed her hand on his with sudden urgency, digging her long nails into his flesh. He feared for a moment that she was going to break down, but the physical contact seemed to give her strength. At length she said, 'At least you're here, Peter. That's very important to me. You don't know what it means.'

In spite of the obvious claim it made on him, he could not resist a surge of happiness and pride. He was glad now that he had come to visit her, no matter what the cost might be. He was a man, not a thing, he thought, defiantly, and he would act as a man. The remembrance of his own feeling of desolation as he sat by himself in the bungalow gave him an understanding for what she must be enduring. Alone, without Max, hated and despised, robbed of her friends, even of the small comfort of her telephone. He said gently, 'It's bound to be hard for a while.'

She looked at him with a slight frown as if there was something he had not fully understood. She seemed to contemplate the possibility of explaining it to him and then discard it. She took her hand abruptly from his and dabbed the tears from her cheeks. 'Why did you come?' she asked. Before he could reply, she said, 'You were warned against me, I know that, yet you still came. I suppose I should say to you that you shouldn't have taken the risk, because it was dangerous for you. But I won't. I think it was better for you as well as for me that you came.'

'It wasn't such a serious risk.' Karas tried to speak lightly. After all, he told himself, what could Suvorin do? He could be angry, but then he was always being angry with someone or other. At the worst it would mean some momentary unpleasantness, some temporary loss of favour.

She seemed to read his thoughts. 'You mustn't pretend it

isn't important,' she said. 'One incident is nothing in itself, perhaps, but it may be regarded as a test. Suvorin thinks well of you, he wants you, but he wants you to be his. He'll soon tire of you if he finds you don't really belong to him.'

'Suvorin told me he valued my independence and initiative,' said Karas. 'He could hardly expect subservience as well. That would be illogical.'

'You think he's a logical man?' She added reflectively, 'With men like Suvorin it is always the same. He's intelligent enough to recognize quality in another man. But at the same time he wants to own it. If he cannot, his admiration turns to hate. If he finds that he *can* own it—' She shrugged her shoulders. 'Well then, it isn't quality any more, is it? So he despises it.'

Karas smiled uneasily. 'So I can't win?'

'Of course not.' She looked at him with pity. 'You're not intended to win. Only Suvorin wins.'

Karas thought of Suvorin's bitter unhappy face, the tirades of resentment against the Central Committee, the Academy, the University, the petty battles for influence. 'Perhaps not even he,' he said.

She thought for a moment. 'Yes, you're right, of course. When there is no true freedom there can be no escape from fear. No matter how high you go there is always someone about to destroy you, someone below to intrigue against you. Even at the very top itself. Perhaps they are the most terrified of all.'

They had finished eating and she got up to clear away the dishes. As she walked into the kitchen she said casually over her shoulder, 'Tell me—now that Max is dead—who will go to Geneva?'

He knew, without having been told in so many words, that the news was confidential. But his mind rebelled against this pointless, habitual secrecy. 'I shall,' he said.

'What will you be able to say, if the research programme is in such confusion?'

'Oh, it's not that kind of conference. It's a general discussion. Projecting future trends in molecular biology. You know the kind of thing.'

She came back with a bowl of fruit and some cheese. 'And what are they?' When he looked puzzled she said, 'These future trends you talk about. Are they very important?'

'I think so.'

'You sounded unusually solemn when you said that.'

'Did I?' He took an apple and smoothed it between his hands, polishing the pink surface with an almost sensual affection. 'Of course, one shouldn't get too pretentious about these things, but the fact is that every major branch of science has its moment of supremacy, a moment when it trembles on the brink of something huge and dark and unknown and rather terrifying. At one time it was like that with astronomy, and recently with atomic physics. Now—' He looked down with something approaching awe at the piece of fruit in his hands. 'Look at that,' he said to Sophia. 'What do you see?'

'An apple,' she said. 'What else?'

'A miracle,' he said, correcting her. 'The miracle is that it's an apple like a hundred million others, yet at the same time if you drop it on the ground it will make a tree, different from any other apple-tree that ever was and ever will be. Infinite uniformity, together with infinite individuality. And both these qualities contained in code in an infinitesimal molecule within the seed that gives rise to it. That's what molecular biology is about. We know some things about the code already. When we break it completely we shall know something about the nature of life.' He bounced the fruit in his hand and looked up smiling at her. 'Don't you think that's a little frightening?'

To his surprise she did not smile back. There was an abstracted expression on her face. 'Yes,' she said slowly. 'Yes, I do.'

'Cheer up,' he said reassuringly. 'I didn't really mean you should be frightened.'

There was a short silence as he peeled the apple, cut it neatly into quarters, removed the core and began to eat it. She watched him for a while and then said, 'Will you tell me something, Peter? I'd like you to be absolutely truthful.'

'About what?'

'About Max. How good was he—as a scientist?'

Karas hesitated for a moment, trying to think of the best way of putting it into words. 'He was pretty good, I would say. Better than Suvorin or Leskov, or even Zabergan. I hate to say it, but probably better than me too—he was more methodical. He had a capacity for exploring the full implications of any idea he had.' She was about to speak but he went on quickly, 'That's my estimate of his potential. It doesn't necessarily mean a lot in terms of what he might have done. There's so much chance involved. For every

62

problem there are a few clues and you have to do what you can with them. But there's nothing to tell you whether any particular problem is soluble with the methods available at any particular time. Most of them aren't, when you come down to it. Most great scientists are only great because they happened to strike the right approach to a problem at the right time.'

She looked at him closely. 'And you don't think Max did?'

Karas shrugged. 'Nobody knows what he was doing. He destroyed all his records.'

'Everything?'

'Yes. He was very thorough. There's nothing left.'

'And he didn't tell you anything?'

'No. I told you before—' He stopped and looked at her sharply. 'Did he say anything to you?'

'Not exactly. But I know he worried a lot. Particularly towards the end.'

'Naturally. It was his illness. You must remember that. Everything looked threatening to him.'

'Yes, I know. But just the same—' She thought for a moment and then said, 'This business of the code you were talking about. This collection of atoms which make up life. Since you know what they are, would it be possible to change them?'

'Theoretically,' said Karas. 'As soon as the code was worked out, people started talking about that. But it would be technically very difficult.'

'What would it mean, if you did?'

'Well, nobody knows, of course. Macfarlane Burnet has suggested that it might be possible to make completely new viruses, ones to which there was no immunity because they'd never existed before. Another man in America suggested something similar.' He waved his hand dismissively. 'They're both brilliant men but one mustn't take it too seriously. Scientists like to throw out ideas. And Burnet's an Australian with an odd sense of humour.' He said, 'Believe me, it's wild talk. There's nothing in it.'

'I see.' She seemed to lose interest in the subject. For a while they talked of other things. At ten o'clock he said, 'I think I ought to go. I don't want to destroy your reputation completely.' As he put on his coat he said, 'I'll call in again soon. I can't be sure which evening.'

'It doesn't matter. I'm always in.'

He hesitated before leaving the flat. Then the desire to share his anxieties was too much for him. He said, 'Suvorin has asked me to write a report. About Max. What he was working on. He says he feels sure I can find out.'

She came towards him. She said, with great intensity, 'Don't tell him anything, Peter. For God's sake. Nothing. Whatever you know, don't tell him. If Max wanted it destroyed, you owe this to him. Please.'

He turned away from her, as if unconsciously seeking a release from the pressure she tried to put on him. He walked away towards the window and looked out of it. From the height of the apartment he could see the whole city spread out in front of him—the small group of squat buildings which constituted the Research Centre, the grandiose tower blocks of the University, the smoking chimneys of the industrial complex over to the west. Beyond that was the prairie, endlessly vast, with countless millions of stars swinging eternally above it through the heavens. At the other end of the scale, infinitesimally small, was the molecule of life, a lock for which the key might at any moment be fashioned. Suddenly a great heaviness and fatigue came over him. He said, 'There's nothing for me to report. He told me nothing.'

CHAPTER SIX

IT WAS APPARENT to Karas the very next day that Suvorin knew of his visit to the flat. There was something in his manner, a brooding withdrawal, a hint of menace, that could not be mistaken. There had been defiance, his eyes said as they looked coldly at Karas, a deliberate disregard of instructions. A serious matter. It had been noted and would be considered at leisure. In the meantime he said nothing and took no action.

Karas wondered how the information was passed to him. Was it the telephone operator? Or, more likely, the cleaner who hung around the stairs in the flats? Many of them were known to be police spies. But the mechanism was unimportant. It was the consequences that mattered.

He had never been out of favour before and the experience was unpleasant. It brought home to him how much he and all the others at the Centre were dependent on Suvorin's liking and support. The hierarchy was such that they never met anyone senior to Suvorin—all contacts with higher authority had to be made through Suvorin as Director, all the information which went to the Central Committee came from Suvorin personally. Suvorin could at any time destroy his career with a stroke of the pen.

He was reminded, too, of his especially vulnerable position as a foreigner. The common people hated the Germans, as they called them all impartially, no matter what their nationality. They were cut off from the University scientists by rivalries and feuds which dated back to the original setting-up of the Centre. The authorities in the capital were known to distrust them. Without Suvorin to fight for them and speak for them they were outcasts.

Since nothing was said, he was not able to defend himself. It was impossible to contest an accusation which was never openly made. Suvorin did not even go so far as to ostracize him. He still came in to see him, but his visits were less frequent and he talked less. Sometimes, indeed, he hardly spoke at all. He formed a habit of walking into Karas's office and then walking silently over to the window, from which he would stare at the chill wind-swept campus and the stunted row of trees which lined the main walk between the various laboratory blocks. When Karas attempted to start a conversation Suvorin would grunt abstractedly but make no real response. Occasionally vague, gloomy statements would escape his lips and he would launch himself on one of his habitual attacks on the University or the Central Committee. But somehow it was not said in the same way. Suvorin's manner was subtly changed. Before, when he had ranted on about these matters, it had seemed to be part of a determined effort to involve Karas in his obsessional pre-occupations. But now, if Karas made an intervention he did not seem to hear it. He appeared to be talking to himself.

Karas began to notice a change in the behaviour of the other department heads. It was not that they adopted a hostile attitude towards him. If anything, their politeness and consideration were rather more marked than before. It was as if they knew he was in trouble and were, in their own timid, withdrawn way, sorry for him. But they could do nothing for him, that went without saying, and if Suvorin were present they took pains to avoid talking to him for fear of being regarded, however unreasonably, as his ally. And in their sympathy there was a faint flavour of relief at the knowledge that Suvorin's hostility was not for the moment fixed on any one of them.

At times he was tempted to give way. What, after all, was Sophia's friendship to him, that he should sacrifice for it his peace of mind and the career to which he had given his life? At these times a touch of warmth or humour or true understanding might well have been enough to win him over. If any of them had been able to forget their loyalty to Suvorin even on one isolated occasion—then, Karas thought, he might have been lost. In that moment of relief at finding a man of his own kind that he could talk to, he might well have abandoned Sophia and disclosed the contents of Max's letter, eager to share the responsibility he had so reluctantly accepted.

But in his more perceptive moments he knew that it could never happen. He was crying out for a language that they had long ago forgotten to speak—if indeed they had ever spoken it. And since, in his present isolation, that language was the thing which he craved above all others, he had little choice but to go to the only place where he could find it.

Each night he climbed the stairs to Sophia's apartment. The lift remained out of order. Sometimes other tenants in the block would pass him on the stairs but they said nothing to him. The charwoman gazed at him out of unforgetting eyes as he passed by. He would knock on the door and Sophia would open to him immediately. An eager smile would appear on her face as she opened the door. What did she do with herself, he sometimes wondered, during the rest of the day? The flat was so small that there could be little enough housework. He could not help picturing the long, melancholy hours of her day; her morning lecture at the University, then a visit to the food store, a frugal lunch, an afternoon spent reading or listening to the radio, watching the clock as it moved round to six o'clock—waiting for the sound of his step on the threadbare linoleum of the landing.

Each evening she had a meal waiting for him, usually with some small delicacy—a pot of caviare, a tin of crab, some fruit that she had queued for at the small free market in the town. The whisky was finished now, but there was always wine or vodka for him to drink. She had rearranged the furniture of the flat and put some new covers on the chairs. Every now and then she was able to buy flowers and for a few days the living-room would be bright with their colour. In Max's time it had always had an austere, dusty look. When Karas commented on the change Sophia flushed with pleasure.

'I tried to make it cheerful for you,' she said. 'I keep thinking of that threadbare place of yours down by the river, without anyone to look after it. I don't wonder you were miserable there.'

She spoke with slight complacency. He was about to protest that he had not really been miserable in those days —the arrangement had worked very well until the upheaval in his life caused by Max's death. But she had tried so hard to give him pleasure that it seemed cruel to rob her of the illusion. 'It wasn't so bad,' he said.

'Max and I often used to say how wretched it must be. You looked so uncared for.'

'Did I really?'

She nodded. She was sewing up a rent in the lining of one of his jackets while he sat in the easy-chair opposite to her with a glass of plum brandy at his elbow. 'Seriously, Peter, those girls were no good for you.'

He said lazily, 'They were nice girls. I know you won't believe me, but they were.'

'I know you thought it was very daring,' she said, 'but it was really rather adolescent, you know.'

There seemed no obvious answer to this. Fortunately she did not expect one. She snipped her thread with a pair of scissors and held the jacket up for inspection. 'All right now?'

'Fine. Thank you very much.'

As he was putting on the jacket Sophia said, with a somewhat exaggerated casualness, 'Do you ever see her now?'

'Who?'

'That last girl of yours. Anya something.'

He buttoned the jacket carefully. 'Of course. Didn't you know? She sleeps every night at the bungalow.'

Her eyes blazed for a moment, and then she recovered herself. She laughed artificially. 'Oh, I see, it is a joke.' When she was angry her Austrian accent became more pronounced. She added, 'Not so very funny, I think.'

He grinned at her. 'Would it matter to you?'

'I'm fond of you, Peter. I admire you as a person. I wouldn't want you to make yourself look foolish.'

She was very solemn and German tonight, he thought. He himself had drunk several glasses of vodka and one of plum brandy—he felt mellow and slightly irresponsible. 'You're concerned about my reputation?'

He could tell by the flush which came up on her face that she had taken the implication of his question. She said defiantly, 'Yes, naturally.' Anticipating his next remark, she said, 'Your visits here are different. We are old friends.'

'Yes, of course.' The desire to tease her left him. Somehow it was all too easy—there was no real fun in it. He said, 'Tell me about Max. How you married him and everything. Were you very much in love with him at that time?'

She said sadly, 'Everyone was in love with him. He was kind and considerate and amusing and intelligent. He wasn't very good-looking but he was interesting—you know? It didn't matter if he wasn't exactly handsome. All the girls were crazy for him. He had such a great sense of fun.'

Karas frowned. 'I can see all the rest. But I never thought of him as having much sense of fun.'

'No,' she said, 'I can understand that. It was a sad thing. That side of him got lost somehow. Not because of anything special that happened, I think. It was just—something of youth. It went away as he grew older. Something left him —I don't know what it was. Life, strength, vitality. . . .'

'Did it change your feeling for him?'

She nodded gravely. 'Oh yes. It would be foolish to pretend. I still loved him, but in a different way. I was never sure of him, somehow, because he was not sure of himself. He became—fragile. You know what I mean?'

'I think so.'

'Because of this we lost contact. We didn't talk in the same way. He was unable to face so many things. Then— on that last night'—her voice broke—'he couldn't face me either. He sent me away.'

'I can see that was terrible for you,' he said sympathetically. 'But you must see how it was. He had to do it.'

She stood up suddenly and turned away from him. It occurred to him that she was near to tears. He moved towards her with some vague idea of consoling her, but because of his haste, and perhaps also the effect of the vodka, he moved clumsily. He brushed against the small three-legged table which stood beside him and caught his glass with his sleeve. As he snatched at it to prevent it falling, his foot caught against an electric wire. The vase which Sophia and Max had brought from Vienna was jerked off the table and smashed to pieces on the floor.

He looked down at it in consternation, sobered instantly by the realization of what he had done. Sophia gave a cry of agony, like that of a woman who sees her child destroyed before her eyes. She fell down on her knees and gathered the pieces of pottery to her as if by touching them she could in some way restore them to what they had once been. Then, realizing the hopelessness of it, she dropped them on the floor beside her. Still on her knees, amid the wreckage of her only treasure, she sobbed like a child. In the vague undefined hope of doing something to comfort her, Karas knelt down beside her and put his arm round her shoulders.

'I'm sorry,' he said, 'so very sorry—' She went on sobbing, with painful, gasping cries. She seemed unconscious of his presence. 'Please, Sophia,' he said desperately. 'I'll do anything I can to put it right. But please don't cry like that.'

For a little while she said nothing. Then she spoke, in a low, almost incoherent voice. 'It was all I had,' she said. 'All that was left—of my father and our old house in Vienna —and the only time when I was ever happy—'

'Please—please, Sophia, I know how you feel, really I do. But please don't be so unhappy—'

'I've lost everything now,' she moaned. 'My country, my friends, my husband. I just had that one thing to remind me that it wasn't always like this. Now everything has gone.' Her voice rose almost to a pitch of hysteria. 'It's as if the best part of my life had never happened. There's nothing left of it.'

He said gently, 'You have me.'

His arm was round her shoulders, his fingers pressed against the woollen fabric of her dress. Even in this moment of her grief and his own guilt, he was conscious of her warmth, and the faint smell of the powder on her body. It occurred to him that the first touch of a woman was always something so new and important that no other situation or emotion could completely suppress it. She moved slightly and he could tell that she too, for all her unhappiness, was conscious of his arm and his closeness to her. Beneath all the other emotions between them, sex ran like a deep current, forcing its way ever nearer to the surface. Her sobs died down, but still the tears rolled down her face. She took a handkerchief from her belt and began to mop her eyes.

'That was silly,' she said, recovering herself. 'You mustn't take any notice of it.' She blew her nose and put the handkerchief back in place. The crisis was over. Now was the time for her to stand up, or for him to take his arm from her shoulders. But neither of them moved. He thought how strange was the situation in which he now found himself. He could not even say definitely whether she was physically attractive to him. Seen casually in the street, he would not have looked twice at her. Yet somehow, ever since the day of Max's suicide, emotions had developed between them— resentment, protectiveness, jealousy, affection. Each time he had visited the flat their intimacy had imperceptibly increased, and the unspoken implications behind it had become stronger. Now he had touched her and the affair had become overt—he was in some way committed. And she, when she had stayed within the shelter of his arm, had become committed too.

They stayed immobile for a little while. Then, as if changing the position for comfort, she moved a little closer to him and he kissed her. She made no resistance to him. After a while he drew away from her and looked at her face. It wore, not the peaceful, contented face of a woman who had just received a declaration of love, but an intensity of desire which startled him.

'I always wanted you,' she said. 'Surely you knew that?' He shook his head. 'Yes, always—always, even when Max was alive.' Her long fingers touched the side of his face. 'I want you now.'

CHAPTER SEVEN

IT WAS A STRANGE AFFAIR. It was as if they had become married before they were, in any true sense, lovers. The prosaic content of their relationship, which would ordinarily have been built up on the basis of passion, had in this case preceded it. With them sensuality was like an extra ritual grafted on to the quiet evenings together, the food and drink, the discussions about books and music and the affairs of their daily lives.

It was surprising to Karas to see how quickly the ritual had developed and how rigid it became. It was now tacitly accepted that he should call at the flat each evening after work. If he desired to change the arrangement he had to reckon with the expression of disappointment which imme-diately appeared on her face. He was experienced enough with women to realize the implications of the way in which the affair was developing. At one point he decided that he must emphasize his independence, even at the cost of being cruel to her. Deliberately, he stayed away for three nights. But he found the loneliness intolerable. All the pleasure he had formerly taken in his work had gone. His apprehension about his position at the laboratory was always with him. The city, at its worst in these chill, damp days, depressed him utterly. It was as if the whole civilized world had died, far away across the boundless steppe, and left him interred in a concrete tomb with no companions except those who hated and distrusted him.

He went back to Sophia, who welcomed him with only a slight trace of complacency, and they resumed the affair as before. Each evening he would drink for a while as she prepared the dinner, then they would eat and afterwards talk over their coffee. A silence would fall and he would go over and kiss her. At a certain point she would free herself from his arms and go through into the bedroom. He was expected to wait. She did not like to undress in front of him or for him to see her naked. In due course he would hear the creaking of springs through the thin bedroom door and would know she was in bed. Then he would go through to join her.

The curtains were always drawn. In the darkness she would lie beneath the sheets, saying nothing while he undressed preparatory to joining her. Her body was thin and dark, with breasts which were little more than folds of the skin. Her skin was dry and lacking in elasticity, and her belly was concave, with the bones of her pelvis rising in sharp angular ridges around it. She made love willingly and competently, but in the way an intelligent person will take care of a minor, necessary activity of life. To her the physical relationship was no more than an incident—a pleasurable incident which she passionately desired, yet always secondary to her affection for him and her unending interest in the workings of his mind and heart. He knew that if he had become impotent the next day it would not have impaired her devotion to him in the least. He was flattered and touched by the realization of how much she cared for him. Yet he knew he did not love her and never would.

It was after they had made love that she really came to life. Unlike Anya, who either fell immediately asleep or else

71

lay there gossiping idly until the impulse came over her to make love again, Sophia would sit up in bed, draw a bedjacket round her to ensure that he could not catch so much as a glimpse of her body, and light a cigarette. Then she would talk, her eyes bright, her voice crisp, her mind sharp and analytical. It was as if, to her, sex was a stimulant rather than a soporific—a drug which had the temporary effect of removing the distractions of the body from consideration and leaving her with those aspects of life which she truly cared about.

It was a new experience for him, to have a love affair with a woman who had a mind as well as an attractive body. While he had always known that she was intelligent and well-read, his social contact with her in the old days with Max had never led him to realize how exceptional she was. It had always been obvious that she was the more forceful partner in the marriage, but it was clear to Karas now that she had deliberately played down her own abilities so far as she could. When he taxed her with this, she said indifferently, 'Yes, I suppose so. What else could I do?'

'Most people like to shine in company.'

'I never cared very much about that. And there were special problems involved in living with Max. He was like a delicate piece of china or glass around the place. Like the old vase, you know—the one that got broken. I could have broken Max as easily as that. So I had to be careful always. To keep in the background, not to damage his self-confidence. It was very tiring sometimes.'

It was obvious that she took a deep pleasure in having an intimate relationship with a man whose strength could stand up to her own. It was satisfying to Karas too, in spite of the somewhat prosaic aspect of their physical relationship. It was indeed the only anodyne he had which would soothe for at least a time the state of constant anxiety in which he lived. In the little flat, as they lay together in the darkened room, he could temporarily forget the troubles which surrounded him.

Running like a thread through all her thoughts were certain master themes. Her longing for Vienna, her alienation from the Centre and all it stood for, her hatred of Suvorin. He tried to steer her away from these obsessions, not only because they had the effect of reminding him of his own problems, but because they contained the seeds of danger to herself. If she persisted in her hostility to Suvorin,

72

what was her future—who would speak for her in the cold, hard days to come? Without a husband she was hopelessly vulnerable.

He tried to point this out to her. 'We all have these thoughts sometimes,' he said. 'But we have to go on living here. And we can't change the way things are. We have to put up with the disadvantages. It's a mistake to talk too much about them—even to think too much about them.'

There was never any question of her missing the implication in what he said. 'I suppose they've told you I'm disloyal.'

It was pointless to deny it but he softened it a little. 'They're uneasy about you. They suspect you of independent views.'

'They're quite right,' she said defiantly.

'Yes, I know. That's one of the things which make you so dear to me.' He spoke tenderly, yet, as always, he avoided the word 'love'. She noticed it and her lips moved in a wry, sad smile. 'Just the same, you must think of the future. You want to hold on to your flat and your job. Who else can help you but Suvorin?'

'Do you think he ever would?' she said sceptically.

He thought. 'Yes, I think so.' She was about to speak but he interrupted her. 'No, let me say something. I know his faults, we all do. He's capricious and dictatorial. He's a little unbalanced about anything which he regards as a threat to his own authority. He can be spiteful and malicious. Yet there's a sort of generosity in him. He has a genuine affection for the people who work for him. He knows scientists and understands their problems to an extent I've never seen in anyone else. He treated Max badly, I agree, but he really cared for him and I know that in his heart he feels miserable and unhappy about his death. A lot of his suspicion of you may be due to the feeling that you distrust him.'

She shook her head. 'It's no good,' she said. 'What you say may even be true, but I could never bring myself to talk to him. The fact is, I can't stand the sight of him and it would be bound to show in my face.' She said bitterly, 'This country. This damnable country.'

'There are men like Suvorin everywhere.'

'Of course. But in other places you can get away from them. That's the difference.' There was nothing to say to that, and he remained silent. Eventually, in a quieter, more reflective voice, she asked, 'Peter, supposing you didn't live here, where would you choose to live?'

'I don't know.' It's a question he had often secretly asked himself, as presumably they all had. 'Not Germany or Austria. And not America, really, either. It's a good place for science but somehow I feel that they'd be tied up with a lot of things I don't like here—size, competitiveness, this fever all the time to be the biggest and the best. I'd like to get away from all that.'

'Then where?'

'It's hard to know. England perhaps.' He was pensive. 'My father once went there when he was a boy. He used to talk about it a lot. He was a timid, serious man and he liked the quiet of it—everyone was very slow and formal and polite, he said. They made a religion of not interfering with each other. And he talked a lot about the parks in London—great big meadows, he said they were. Every Sunday the band played and the children sailed their boats on the lake. Nobody bothered anyone, nobody got excited. It was a country, he said, where a man had a right to own himself. That attracted me.' He shrugged away the picture. 'It's probably all changed now.'

'Supposing you were offered the chance—'

He became irritable. 'We mustn't talk like this. It's just dreams—nonsense. It does no good and it can be dangerous. I'm very well treated at the Centre. We have a good life, far better than the ordinary people. As scientists we are respected and we have great privileges. As for Suvorin,' he said, 'he's just a man who's been spoilt by too much of his own way. I don't think we should take his moods too seriously. And when all's said and done, he's given up his life to the Centre.'

She said, 'The Centre's a projection of his own ambitions. He's given his life for himself.' She added implacably, 'And the lives of others too.'

He shook his head. 'I can see I shall never convince you.'

'No,' she said with decision. 'You never will.'

He was suddenly weary of the whole situation in which he found himself. For years he had tried to isolate himself from controversy, to mind his own business and get on with his work. Now, through no fault of his own, he was implicated in the kind of conflict he detested, a prize to be disputed between two implacable enemies. Suvorin and Sophia were each, in their own way, fanatics, prepared in the pursuit of a principle to cast aside all consideration of peace and comfort. Was he to lose everything because

74

neither of them was prepared to make the least concession? What on earth was the necessity for him to choose between them in this fashion?

'It's all very well to talk like that,' he said, 'but we have to think of the future. Whether we like Suvorin or not, we have to find a way of living with him.'

She looked at him pensively. 'You think you have a future with Suvorin?'

'It's possible, yes. Of course,' he said, 'I'm out of favour just at the moment—'

'Because of me, you mean?'

'Well—partly, yes.'

'And if I was to be more agreeable to him—more loyal—it might be easier for you?'

She did not say it scornfully, but as if seriously trying to understand the position. Yet he felt ill at ease. 'Would that be so dreadful?'

'No, I suppose not. I can see how difficult it is for you, Peter,' she said. 'Believe me, I understand. And I love you, you know that—I don't want you to lose your career.' Her voice took on a new intensity. 'But it's not just me, can't you see? It's your own freedom and independence. I'm just a test, to prove that you really belong to him, heart and soul. And I'm not the only test. What about this report you have to write for him?'

He said uneasily, 'I'll do the best I can. He can't expect information that isn't available.'

'Can't he?' She was merciless. 'Don't fool yourself, Peter. If you don't give him what he wants, nothing I can do will ever make any difference. That's the thing that matters. That's what he's waiting for.'

As he thought about it after he had left her, he knew that what she had said was right. Until the report was written and handed in he was like a man living under a suspended sentence. Nor could he feel that there was any hope of permanence in his affair with Sophia. The shadow of Suvorin lay constantly over it. It was merely a matter of time before he took steps to bring it to an end.

When it finally happened, it was in a way he had not anticipated. He called at the flat one dark Friday when there was sleet in the air and the winter seemed only a few days away. To his surprise she met him at the door. She was wearing her coat and hat ready to go out.

'I was just going down to the post-box,' she said. 'I wondered if you'd go with me.'

'Of course.' There was a hurried artificial quality in her manner which told him that something had gone wrong. She did not speak until they were in the street outside the flats. Then she said, 'I'm sorry about this. I wanted to get you outside before you said anything.'

'What's the trouble?' His mouth turned dry and he realized with shame that he was afraid. 'What's happened?'

'I have a friend in the next apartment. This morning when I came back from shopping, she told me two electricians had been around—checking on some faulty wiring, they said. That's plausible enough. The wiring is terrible and the fuses are always blowing. But she told me that she heard them moving in my flat for at least half an hour. And she said they didn't look at all like electricians.'

'I see.' They walked in silence. The street went straight as an arrow for over a mile, leading down towards the town. Its width was absurdly excessive for the few cars which passed along it; an occasional tram, bulging with people, rattled its way into or away from the city. As they drew nearer the town it became more populated. Men in cloth caps and thick-hipped women in shawls and shapeless coats strolled heavily up and down the pavements. A few shops were open, a bookstore crammed with students, a men's outfitters displaying suits which looked second-hand even before they were bought. The women queued as always at the food shop for those special delicacies which fluctuated wildly in their availability from day to day or month to month, nobody knew why. As they passed by a crowd of people buying kvass from a barrel in a side street, Karas was conscious of the faint earthy smell which one always associated with the working people—a smell which spoke of overcrowding and the lack of baths, of poor facilities for dry cleaning, and a culture which regarded talcum powder and deodorants as decadent and reactionary. It spoke too of a kind of honest realization that human beings, like all living animals, had their distinctive odour and might as well accept the fact. Once one got used to it, it was by no means unpleasant.

Eventually they came to some wrought-iron metal gates; the notice fixed to them said 'Krupskaya Park of Rest and Culture'. Inside there were asphalt paths arranged in a geometrical pattern between flower beds and rows of shrubs.

There were the inevitable pieces of sculpture—Krupskaya herself, Lenin of course, and one or two local dignitaries. There was a small pavilion for exhibitions near the entrance, but it was closed. Apart from a young couple holding hands as they walked, and a few old people sitting derelict on the benches, they had the park to themselves.

He said, 'So you thought we might be overheard?'

'Yes. I didn't want you to say anything indiscreet.'

'We could go to the bungalow. . . .'

'My poor Peter,' she said, gripping his arm. 'You are out all day. I don't know whether they have microphones fixed in the bungalow now. But once we went there—'

'You're rather taking it for granted that it's happened in your flat. You can't be sure—'

'One doesn't have to be sure. Once you accept it as plausible, that's it. And you do, don't you?'

It was no use deluding himself. Everyone knew it was done. 'Yes, I suppose so.'

They walked around the drab paths of the park, muffled up in their overcoats, the leaves blowing round their shoes. The day was drawing to its close. In half an hour it would be dark. They were quite alone. She said, 'Of course, you realize it can't go on for very long like this?'

'What do you mean?'

'We can't spend the rest of our lives walking in parks. And the pressure has hardly begun yet. Suvorin is determined to make you do what he wants. He'll find a way of parting us. There's only a little time left in which I can still help you.'

'Help me?'

She did not answer immediately. They walked for a while. Then she said, 'There's only one thing for you to do. You must get away from here.'

He made a gesture of impatience. 'That's out of the question. We all know—'

She interrupted him. 'Wait a moment. There's something I have to tell you.' A woman with a shopping bag came towards them out of the gathering dusk. Sophia waited for her to pass before she went on. 'When Max was at the international meeting in Leipzig last year he met a man at a reception. His name was Hoffman. He was a naturalized American but he was Austrian by birth. Max and he had one or two mutual acquaintances in Vienna. Hoffman suggested that they should correspond on scientific matters,

send each other books and reprints and so on. Max agreed.
Then, quite casually, Hoffman asked Max if he had ever
thought of returning to Vienna to work. Max of course
said no. Hoffman didn't pursue the matter, but just before
he left he said that if ever Max changed his mind he was
to put a certain sentence in one of the letters that accompanied the books to be sent. Then everything would be
arranged at the next international meeting he attended.
That was Geneva.' She waited, as if expecting Karas to say
something. When he remained silent, she said, 'Someone
ought to write to Hoffman and tell him Max is dead.'

He looked at her but her face was hidden by the collar
of her thick cloth coat. 'Me, for instance?' he said.

'Yes.'

He pondered. The implication in her words was clear. It
was a fascinating and rather frightening suggestion. One
sentence in a letter and he could be free of Suvorin and
the Centre, of this dead city and this dreadful oppressive
winter. A life without fear or uncertainty or the necessity
to bend before authority. He could drink French wine, buy
the books he wanted, travel where he pleased, say whatever
came into his head. They would take him in place of Max,
he had no doubt of that. They wanted scientists, everybody
did nowadays. He thought of his father and his memories
of that one visit to London—the autumn there would be
mild and gentle. No looming black mountains or vast
heaving rivers, just the breeze rippling the ponds, the swans
flying, the leaves turning from green to brown to yellow
and then dropping from the chestnuts on to the soft green
grass. . . .

He said, 'Who is this man Hoffman?'

'Nobody of importance. Max thought he was just an agent
—a posting-box for somebody else.'

'Who?'

'He didn't know. They were interrupted. Then Max had
to leave. He never saw Hoffman again.'

He was struck by the risk she was taking for his sake. 'You
realize how dangerous this conversation is?'

'I'm in your hands,' she said simply.

His mind was busy exploring the possibilities which had
been opened up in front of him. One heard, of course, of
this kind of thing happening, but he had never visualized
it happening to himself. 'Do you think Max would have
done it?'

'I don't know. He used to think about it, but he couldn't make up his mind. In the end he just couldn't face it.'

'Face what?'

'The worry and tension of getting away. The risk of being caught.' She said with sad affection, 'He wasn't exactly a man of action, you know. And even if he had got away he'd have had to start all over again. He couldn't face that either.'

'And you would have been prepared to stay behind alone?'

'Yes. Why not? After all, his life was no good to him as it was. And mine has never been much. Surely it was better that he should try to get away than do what he did.'

They made another circuit of the gravel path. He found himself looking behind bushes to be sure that they contained no eavesdroppers. He was overcome with the squalid furtiveness of it all. Was this what his great ambitions as a scientist had come to—conspiracy against his adopted country, coded letters, fear of the police? 'No,' he said in a spasm of revulsion. 'It's absurd. It's crazy. Anyway, the way things are, I'll probably never get to Geneva.'

'Oh yes,' she said with conviction. 'You can get there.' She paused. 'If you want to, that is.'

'Even if Suvorin doesn't like my report?'

'You could make him like it.'

'What do you mean?'

'You could make something up. Something that sounds interesting and plausible. It would take months for him to find out that it wasn't true. By that time you'd have gone.'

He shook his head. The idea of such a forgery appalled him. It was against all his training, all the ethics of his calling. 'No, I really couldn't do that.' He pushed the temptation away from his mind. It had been attractive for a moment but it was too squalid to consider. Suvorin, after all, had been kind to him and had trusted him. At the Centre they were a closely-knit group. Whatever they thought of each other personally, they had all had one thing in common—their scientific integrity. It was what he had managed to live by for all these years. 'No,' he said. 'It's out of the question. Anyway, this is my home and my country. I accepted it voluntarily and I must stick to it. I can beat this present trouble—I'm sure I can. I don't want to go.'

She thought for a moment and then seemed to accept his refusal. 'All right,' she said. 'I understand.'

He had the feeling that behind her acquiescence there was a conviction that her defeat was only temporary, that in the end he would change his mind. He said seriously, 'I mean it, Sophia, I really do. I know you love me and want to do the best for me and I'm grateful to you. But this isn't the right way for me. I know it isn't.'

'All right, *liebchen*.' She looked at him with great tenderness and squeezed his arm through the thick coat. 'You know, you're very sweet and kind and loyal. And strong also. It's not simply that I love you. I have a great respect for you.'

He pressed his hand in hers. Strangely enough, in this cold, unfriendly park, wrapped in their heavy winter coats, they achieved a closeness and warmth which they had never known in the moments of greatest sexual intimacy. They walked along for a little while happy in their mutual affection and trust. Then she said, 'The park will be closing soon. We must go back to the flat and have dinner.'

CHAPTER EIGHT

IN THE FOLLOWING DAYS a new pattern became built into their routine. When he visited her they would start off with a walk in the park and then go back to the flat. As soon as they entered the flat their conversation became cautious and guarded; they spoke only of general matters. But as time went by they found it increasingly difficult. It was really impossible, Karas found, to keep the conversation entirely neutral on all occasions. Opinions would slip out inadvertently. To forget the possibility of the invisible eavesdropper was dangerous. But to remember it constantly led to an intolerable artificiality. It was almost worse than not being together at all.

The only part of the old intimacy that remained to them was in that first half-hour in the park when they talked without fear of being overheard. But this, they both knew, could not last for long. Soon the snow would fall, the paths would be covered with drifts and the park would be closed. And that would be the end.

During these short, precious interludes of privacy they spoke of many things, but she never again mentioned Hoffman or the Geneva conference. Sometimes Karas, in moments of depression, was tempted to raise the subject again, but he fought off the temptation. His pride revolted from the idea of running away—he must stay where he was and fight it out. Yet he was overcome by gratitude at her selflessness in offering him the opportunity. For if he left she would lose not only her lover but her only friend. In a cold and hostile foreign country, she would be totally alone.

Meanwhile he worked on his report. Surely, he thought, if he used all his ingenuity he could present something which would be at least acceptable to Suvorin. Together with Barov, Max's technician, he rooted through the small amount of information which had survived Max's final orgy of destruction, looking for anything which could in any way be magnified to read like a useful piece of research. He dragged in work which had been carried out before the six-month period which the report was supposed to cover, and credited Max with some work which he himself had carried out. In the end, he surprised himself by what he was able to accumulate. The report was not an impressive one—it could never have been that in the circumstances— but it was by no means so indecently sparse as he had at one time feared. Indeed, if one read it cursorily, or in an indulgent frame of mind, it could seem like quite a passable record of achievement.

His optimism was encouraged by the fact that when he sent the report through to Suvorin's office there was no immediate reaction. Several days went by and he heard nothing. Suvorin did not visit him. Then, on the Friday morning, he heard the familiar squeaking of the rubber-soled shoes on the linoleum outside his office. Suvorin opened the door, ponderous and deliberate as ever, and sat down in Karas's armchair. He was carrying the usual brown folder full of papers. His face was sombre, and his fingers were locked tightly together, a habit he had when he was about to embark on something unpleasant. The drawn look about his mouth drew attention to the curious pale yellow colour of his complexion. Karas began to wonder how he could ever have been so complacent as to imagine that he might get through this affair without trouble.

Suvorin was in no hurry to speak. He looked out of the window for several minutes before he said, in a tight voice, 'I've read your report.' He paused, as if waiting for some response to this announcement. But Karas remained silent. 'I'm afraid I have to tell you that it's quite unacceptable.'

It was the opening shot of a battle which both of them had anticipated. As Suvorin had started with his rehearsed opening, Karas responded with his prepared reply.

'In what way?'

'In every way,' said Suvorin. 'It's the most unsatisfactory departmental report I've ever received. It's an insult to my intelligence.'

Karas recognized the early stages of a process with which all the departmental heads had become familiar. Argument, to Suvorin, was not an intellectual exercise but an act of will. He instinctively preferred to operate on the kind of emotional ground where he was most at home. When confronted with any form of disagreement, his method was to work himself into a rage and avoid all detailed discussion of issues.

Karas struggled to keep his temper under control. 'If you'd tell me precisely what you object to—'

'Oh, I haven't time to go into all that detail,' said Suvorin contemptuously. He was whipping himself up. Each remark was slightly more aggressive than the last. 'In any case you know perfectly well what I mean.'

'Of course,' said Karas coldly, 'if you're determined not to discuss it—'

Suvorin seized on the remark. It was plain that he had been hoping to provoke Karas into some kind of personal discourtesy. 'I shall discuss what I please!' he shouted. 'I'm head of this Centre. Remember that, young man. I will not be told what to do by anybody, you included. Is that clear?'

'Of course it's clear. But what on earth—'

'If you put in an unsatisfactory report, you must be told about it. You're no different from any other scientific worker here. You must accept discipline. Oh,' said Suvorin savagely, 'I know you don't like it. I know you have your own ideas about what should be done. You're not prepared to accept the advice of those more experienced than yourself. You're not prepared to play with the team. You wish to be an individualist. Isn't that so?'

Individualist, in the way it was used by Suvorin was a supremely loaded word. Karas said, 'No. Not in that sense. But surely some individual thought is necessary for a scientist?'

Suvorin did not appear to hear him. 'I blame myself,' he said bitterly. 'Yes, I must take some of the blame. I advanced you too quickly. It went to your head. The result is that you think you can do as you please and say what you please. You look down on your colleagues. You won't take advice—'

Karas was gradually becoming maddened by the elusive nature of the attacks being made on him. He could see that, in spite of Suvorin's ranting and apparent loss of control, he was nevertheless quite determined to avoid any mention either of Sophia or of his real objection to the substance of the report. This carried a possible implication that Suvorin's position was not quite as strong as he liked to make out. Karas decided to take a chance and counter-attack.

'What you're giving me isn't advice,' he snapped. 'It isn't even criticism, in the ordinary sense of the word. It's just personal abuse.'

Suvorin looked at him aghast. He was like a man confronted with a totally new experience. He said, in a constricted voice, 'Don't dare to speak to me like that.'

'I can't see that you leave me any alternative. You won't explain exactly what you're complaining about—'

'I don't have to explain myself to you!' shouted Suvorin. 'I am Director here—not you. You must do as I tell you. Do you understand that? Do you accept that?'

Karas felt his self-control beginning to crack. 'This isn't the army,' he said. 'I'm a scientist, not a recruit. If you aren't satisfied with me I shall go elsewhere—'

'Elsewhere? What are you talking about? This is rubbish. Nonsense. You are employed by the Centre—'

Karas had not really known what he had meant. He had just been wildly trying to find some way of achieving a sensation of independence. He said doggedly, 'There are other Centres. I could apply for a transfer.'

To his surprise he realized that he had scored a hit. Suvorin's eyes became cautious. Why? It occurred to Karas that while the application for a transfer would almost certainly be refused, the very fact that it had been made would damage Suvorin in the eyes of the Central Committee. He held a grenade in his hand, and if he cared to take the pin out he could blow them both to pieces. But what was he to do with his new-found knowledge? He sat tongue-tied, wondering how his discovery could be turned to best advantage. Then, to his astonishment, Suvorin stood up abruptly and walked over to look at a picture on the wall of the office. He spoke in an ordinary conversational tone. 'I like this picture,' he said. 'You have good taste. Where did you get it?'

'It belonged to Max,' said Karas. Surely, he thought,

Suvorin must have seen it a hundred times before in this very office.

'It's very beautifully painted,' said Suvorin sententiously. It was obvious he knew nothing at all about painting. 'If I have a criticism, I would say the perspective of the bridge is not quite accurate.'

'Perhaps the artist didn't care so much for perspective.'

'Every artist cares for perspective,' said Suvorin in a schoolmasterish voice. 'It's simply a failure of technique. But the trees are very good.' He swung round on Karas as if he had at last plucked up the courage to look him in the face. 'I wish to apologize.'

Karas was taken aback. 'There's really no need—' he said awkwardly.

'Yes.' Suvorin was as determined in self-abasement as he had previously been in aggression. The effect was, if anything, more embarrassing. 'There's every need. I handled the situation very badly. The only excuse I can offer is that I am extremely harassed and overworked at the present time. You have no conception of the anxieties of my job—none whatever. There are endless problems. . . .' He shook his head hopelessly as he contemplated the enormity of his task. 'And now you.' In a sad, paternal voice he said, 'You're not making life easy for me, Peter.'

'In what way?'

Suvorin ignored the question. 'Oh no, you're not. You must have realized the hopes I had in you. After all, I can't last for ever. I shall have to retire in a few years. I can tell you confidentially that this worries me a great deal. Not for myself—I can't wait for the day when I get away from this treadmill. A little country house, some fishing. . . .' A dreamy look came into his eyes. Karas could almost have laughed at the absurdity of the dream. Suvorin had no life away from the laboratories. He had no friends, no social circle of any kind. He would not have been able to fish for an hour without going mad with impatience because the fish had failed to bite. But the pleasure of retirement was one of his dreams, his favourite fantasy. He dragged himself away from it with difficulty. 'I need someone to succeed me here. Someone of quality. It's a great worry to me. Max would never have done, even if he had lived. Leskov has no imagination, Fedorov has no interest in administration. Zabergan's too obliging. He'd be clay in the hands of the University—' He sighed. To how many of them, Karas wondered, had Suvorin at one time or another promised the succession. Now it was evidently to be his turn. 'I've never made a secret of the fact that I thought you had certain exceptional qualities.'

Karas made a vague noise expressing gratitude. This sudden reversal of attitude was bewildering. He waited for some indication as to what it meant. Suvorin ploughed on. 'I still think you have those qualities. What I forgot—and I blame myself for this—is that you are still relatively young and inexperienced. You need somebody to help you. Now I haven't the time, as you know, much as I should like to. So I've been discussing your report with Leskov. I know you think he's a bit dull, but he's very good at this kind of thing. He said he'd be only too pleased to help you to get it right. You two could work together on it and I'm sure you'd come up in the end with the information I want.' He opened his folder and quickly plucked out Karas's report. Stapled on to it was a green typed sheet. 'Leskov's been good enough to make some comments on it already. Very sensible ones, I think—'

He handed the report to Karas, who dropped it on the desk without looking at it. He was trembling with anger and he held his hands deliberately under the desk to conceal the fact. 'I'm afraid I can't do that,' he said.

Suvorin frowned. 'What do you mean?'

'I can't do it. This report concerns the department of which I'm in charge. It contains all the information available. If you have any complaints about it I'm very happy to hear them, and I can't believe you're so busy you can't spare an hour to discuss them with me. But Leskov knows absolutely nothing about molecular biology. I should be wasting time talking to him.'

Suvorin's façade of tolerant paternalism suddenly cracked. His pale eyes flashed with rage. 'I've had enough of this arrogance of yours!' he said. 'Let me remind you of a few things. You are a guest in our country. We welcomed you here and gave you advancement and special privileges. In the Centre you have been accepted as one of us. We were friendly to you and we expected friendship in return. Instead of which we're rewarded with impudence and defiance. You keep secrets from us—' Karas tried to protest but he waved it aside. 'No, don't deny it, I know it's true. You think you have no obligations towards me or the Centre or this country. You prefer to associate with people you have been repeatedly advised against—very well. But let me tell you one thing, my tolerance isn't inexhaustible and in the last resort, we must decide who our friends are. Whoever isn't with us is against us. Think that over.' Before Karas could say anything he stood up abruptly and walked to the door. As he left he said, with great intensity, 'And whatever happens in the future, remember I tried to help you. Always remember that.'

The next morning, when Karas entered the department he noticed something intangibly different about it. It was curiously quiet and dead. Instead of the usual smell of tobacco from Barov's pipe there was a clammy odour of polish and disinfectant. He went through into the main laboratory. It was empty. When he returned to his office he saw an envelope on his desk. In it was a note from Barov.

Dear Doctor,
    So sorry to leave you, but I was notified on coming in this morning that I was to transfer immediately to Dr. Fedorov's department. Don't wish to let you down but nothing I can do about this. Sure you will understand.
                                            Barov.

Karas sat at his desk for quite a long time. Then he picked up the telephone and dialled Suvorin's internal number. A secretary answered.

'I'd like to speak to the Director.'

'I'm sorry, Dr. Karas. The Director isn't available. Can I give him a message?'

Karas hesitated. 'No, don't bother.'

'Shall I ask him to ring back?'

'Yes, please.'

He put down the telephone. Suvorin would not ring back. Nor was he ever available on the telephone unless he wanted to be. Karas picked up the telephone again and dialled Fedorov's number. There was no real point in it—this was not Fedorov's doing. Still, perhaps at least he could embarrass him. Once again a female voice answered the telephone. 'I'm sorry, Dr. Fedorov's in the middle of an experiment. He can't be disturbed. . . .'

It was useless, he knew. He forced his mind back to his work but it was hard to concentrate. He wandered round the laboratories and spoke in a casual way to one or two of the junior research workers. Was it his imagination or were they, in some indefinable way, less respectful, more offhand in their reactions to him? He fancied that when he left them they were a little relieved. It was plain to him that the word had gone round. The mild disfavour which had shadowed him for the last few weeks had turned into something far more serious. He had seen this kind of thing happen before. He knew that the removal of Barov was not an accidental or an isolated event—it was the first shot in a campaign which had been planned against him by a powerful and implacable enemy. He could not guess the form the campaign would take, but his knowledge of Suvorin told him it would be carried through to the finish. It could end only in his capitulation or his total disgrace.

He came back to the office and sat for almost an hour at his desk staring out of the window. He thought back to the days, only a few weeks ago, when Max had been alive and everything had seemed set for a lifetime. When he had been safe and contented with his work, his mistresses, his games of chess; when Suvorin had been a remote, eccentric, friendly figure and Sophia a woman who made coffee and little Viennese cakes and talked about Brahms. Now the pattern of all their lives had been wrecked beyond repair. How much longer, he thought, would he be allowed to occupy this room and sit at this desk? What future would Suvorin allow him? And what would happen to Sophia, friendless and alone in a remote and hostile country? What would happen to the department, to old Barov, torn without a moment's notice from the job which had been the mainspring of his life for twenty years? Had Max ever thought, he wondered, of the chain of events he was setting in motion as a consequence of his act?

Lunch-time arrived. Somehow it seemed very important that he should go to the dining-room for lunch and sit with the others at the communal table, facing out their embarrassment and disapproval. As he walked across the campus to the main block he saw a small figure coming out of the building to his left. It was Zabergan. He deliberately looked away so as to give the bacteriologist a chance to avoid him if he wanted to, but Zabergan hurried so as to fall in beside him as he walked up the main avenue—it was almost as if he were anxious to join him. His lips smiled nervously under the thin black moustache. He at least seemed in no way changed. They chatted about trivialities as they walked along to the communal dining-hall.

Together they traversed the vast cafeteria towards the private dining-room for department heads. Ordinarily there was something pleasant about the kind of attention one attracted, but today Karas hurried awkwardly through. As usual Pavlov, the dining-room superintendent, was standing by the door of the private room. As Karas was about to go through the door he sidled rapidly in front of him, barring his way.

'Please excuse me, Dr. Karas—'

'Yes, what is it?' Karas frowned at him. There was something in Pavlov's tone which warned him of trouble.

'I must apologize for an error. Over the past few weeks. . . .' He seemed to have difficulty going on. Karas noticed beads of perspiration on his large shiny forehead. 'I was under the impression that you had taken over Dr. Bremer's department on a permanent basis. It has only just been brought to my attention that the appointment is no more than provisional. In these circumstances—' He looked at Karas and then at Zabergan rather desperately, as if hoping that one of them might help him. He said very quickly, 'The private dining-room is only for the use of permanent heads of departments.'

Karas flushed. 'Nonsense! I've never heard of such rubbish—'

'No, Doctor.' Pavlov was gathering courage. 'It's not nonsense. It's the rule of the Centre. It is not I who made it. It is my function only to see that it is observed—'

Karas was tempted to simply push him to one side, but Pavlov had wedged himself in the doorway. Looking over his shoulder it was possible to see the others eating at the round table. The argument must have been audible to them all but none of them looked up from their food. As Leskov turned to one side to help himself to vegetables, Karas saw to his surprise that for once Suvorin himself was eating with them. He said to Pavlov, 'Get out of my way. I'll discuss this with the Director.'

Pavlov shook his head. 'I'm sorry, Doctor. I have orders. I must not let you in.'

Karas felt a tug at his sleeve. Zabergan said, in a voice filled with commiseration, 'Come, Peter. We can eat out here.'

Karas was outraged by Zabergan's pity. He said bitterly, 'This is nothing to do with you. Why don't you go in and join the others?'

88

'No, we'll stay together.' Zabergan led him gently away from the doorway. 'After all, the food's the same, isn't it? We can get a table by ourselves. There's one over there.' Karas realized bitterly that there was nothing he could do. Suvorin was in a position to inflict upon him any ingenious humiliation he happened to choose. He allowed himself to be guided to a small table for two. 'You sit here and keep it for me,' said Zabergan. 'I'll get some food.' Before Karas could protest he had left him there and gone to join the queue at the service counter. As Karas sat and waited for him he could feel eyes watching him from all sides. The scene at the door of the private dining-room had been observed and overheard. It would be common property throughout the Centre within an hour or two.

Zabergan returned with two plates of beef stew and vegetables. As they began to eat he said, 'I can't imagine how that happened.'

'Can't you?'

'No,' said Zabergan, as if unconscious of the irony in Karas's voice. 'Of course, I can see that if there is such a rule, Pavlov must do his duty, but surely it would have been possible to notify you in some other way.'

'You think it's just a question of rules?'

'Well—' Zabergan looked uncomfortable. 'I suppose so, yes. If that's what he says—'

Karas had been feeling gratitude towards Zabergan. He at least had had the decency not to scuttle off into the private dining-room and leave his friend alone. But now his gratitude turned to irritation. There was a limit to the credulity any man was entitled to show. Moreover, the depths of his own humiliation was now only just beginning to come home to him. It was like a wound which feels only numb for the first few minutes and then the real pain appears. 'You don't think Suvorin had anything to do with it?'

Zabergan did not reply immediately. He put down his knife and fork and his left arm, the one with the artificial hand, began to tap the table. It was a habit he had acquired at times of great tension or agitation. 'Peter, I'd like to talk to you about Suvorin. I've known him for many years. He has his faults, I'm aware of that, but he's a great man, just the same. I think he deserves our loyalty.' He stopped, as if waiting for Karas to say something but Karas did not speak. Zabergan went on, 'You must remember he has done wonders for the Centre. He has built it up until it's one of the best in the country, perhaps in the world. And against all kinds of opposition. He's had to fight all the way. Perhaps it's made him a little hard and intolerant, but believe me, underneath it, he's a kind man. When I think what he did for me when I came out of the army, disabled as I am—' He paused, momentarily overcome by emotion, and then went on, 'You may think he's being a little hard on you just now, Peter, but remember we've all been through it one time or another. You're very well thought of here, people sympathize with you more than they may be able to say at the moment.'

'I see.'

'The main thing to remember is that there's no use in making an issue of it. Suvorin's the Director, after all. We all have to give way to him when the time comes. And usually he's right, you know, in the long run.' Karas looked at Zabergan in despair. He did not know what he thought of him. Horror, pity, disgust? He did not know. What had Sophia said about him. Something like loyalty being a perversion, a sickness. Karas pushed his plate aside. He said, 'Why don't you go through and join the others?'

Zabergan looked at him, puzzled. 'Sorry—I don't understand.'

'I think you do. Go back and tell them what happened. They're waiting for you.' He felt the need to strike out at somebody, to inflict pain comparable to what he himself was suffering. Zabergan, for all his kindness and vulnerability, was one of them—he was Suvorin's lackey, he was part of the conspiracy against him. Karas said savagely, 'Surely, you don't think I was taken in by this pantomime. It was all arranged, wasn't it? I was to be humiliated. You were with me. You watched me as I came out of the lab so that we both came over here together. And when I was shut out you'd stick by me like a good friend. The only one I had left. And when I began to feel sentimental about you, you'd tell me what to think about Suvorin. Isn't that right?'

'No—no—' The hurt in Zabergan's soft brown eyes was appalling. He was like a dog who had made overtures of friendliness and been brutally kicked. 'That's not true. We all like you, Peter. We want you to be happy here. We value your work. If only you'd trust us—' As his agitation grew, his artificial arm moved more jerkily than ever. 'Suvorin is on your side. He wants to help you. Believe me—'

Karas had to fight the urge to give in, to be readmitted

to the safety and comradeship which was being offered to him. He was seized by a fear that if he stayed with Zabergan any longer the temptation would be more than he could bear—he would collapse into the same servitude as the others. He got up violently from the table, sending his chair crashing to the floor. 'I don't want to hear any more,' he said harshly. Pointing to the private dining-room, he cried, searching for the words that would hurt and wound, 'I'm leaving now. Go to your master. Tell him you did everything he told you but it didn't work. And don't be frightened, he'll know you did your best. He won't punish you. After all,' he added, 'he's a kind man, isn't he?'

He left the table and made his way across the cafeteria. He had spoken loudly and his voice had silenced the clatter of plates and crockery from the tables around them. The people sitting at the tables looked at him in fascinated interest as he passed by—their conversation would be material for speculation and gossip throughout the whole Centre. Karas passed by them without looking. He was unconscious of their gaze or of the buzz of conversation which arose after he had passed by. All he heard as he walked away across the restaurant was a sound which he knew he would never forget throughout the rest of his life—the rhythmic tapping of an artificial hand on a wooden table.

In the Park of Rest and Culture the bushes were as tidy as ever, the sparse scrubby grass as carefully protected. In the gathering twilight there were only a few listless couples walking the paths. An old man was eating messily out of a paper bag and throwing scraps to a mongrel which crouched expectantly at his side. The paths and lawns were powdered with fine snow.

Karas described his encounter with Zabergan. Even to think of it in retrospect made him tremble with agitation. 'So I left him in there,' he concluded. 'He didn't even watch me leave. I turned back to look at him as I left the dining-room and he was staring straight in front of him, still tapping that artificial hand of his on the table. It was dreadful—dreadful.'

'You're sure it was all planned by Suvorin?'

'I was at the time,' said Karas miserably. 'But now—' His voice rose in desperation. 'How can one ever be certain about a thing like that? The thing that torments me now is that he might have just been trying to be kind to me.'

'That's the trouble,' she said, with the compassion of deep experience. 'One never does know. For as long as you know Zabergan, you'll never be sure whether he was being honest with you or not. You mustn't blame yourself, or him. He's a good man—everybody knows that. But he has to survive. You bend or you're broken.' She said without emotion, 'That's the rule.'

'For everyone?'

'For everyone. There are some who are unfortunate. They find, when it comes to the point, that they can't bend. Something within them makes it impossible.'

He knew she was speaking of him. 'You think I'm one of those?'

'Yes.' As she said it, he knew that she was right. It seemed strange now that for so long he had gone on in the complacent conviction that he could somehow make his peace with the system, getting what he wanted out of it without fighting or without selling himself. He had always hoped that if he avoided looking for trouble he would somehow manage to escape it. Now trouble had found him and his way of life was in ruins. It was plain to him for the first time that theories and plans were useless in this kind of situation. The moment came that showed beyond doubt what kind of man you were. The implications of it frightened him, yet there was an excitement in having discovered himself, and a kind of pride he had never known before.

He said, 'Then you were right the other evening. There's nothing for me here.' The decision he was about to make was enormous. It was a leap in the dark, a destruction of his whole life and his whole previous self. And strangely enough, it was they, the ones who wanted so badly for him to conform, who had driven him towards his destiny. They had driven him to Sophia, to these secret treasonable conversations in this prosaic dreary little park. At no step had they left him any alternative, any middle ground between treachery to them and a betrayal of his own honour.

He looked at Sophia and knew that this was the last time they would meet as lovers. They would never sleep together again. All that was over. Now there was only conspiracy, conspiracy so dangerous and terrifying that it excluded every other kind of relationship. He said, 'Tell me more about the arrangements for Geneva.'

PART TWO

CHAPTER ONE

EVEN IN THE MEDITERRANEAN it was possible to feel the approach of winter. As Weldon went down the steps of the heavy stone house into the street he buttoned his overcoat around him and pushed his fingers deep into his yellow hogskin gloves. At five o'clock it was already turning dark; though the lights of the city glittered gaily enough, there was a definite feeling that Rome, like all the rest of Europe, was drawing like a snail into its shell for the winter ahead. Weldon looked forward to getting away—there were few countries more depressing than Italy in bad weather. Where next? Perhaps a day or two in Paris—he had a standing invitation to visit Duclos at the Pasteur Institute. Then London again and back to the States in time for Christmas. Blanche always got angry if he failed to go home for Christmas.

He hailed a taxi and directed the driver to the Hassler Hotel. Along the Via Veneto the lights were glittering and the crowds were pouring in and out of the shops and department stores. He thought back over the interview of the last two hours. It was his practice never to make judgements while a man was actually talking to him. It was easy to be influenced by so many irrelevant things—charm of manner, fluency of exposition, a general atmosphere of distinction and success. It was only afterwards, in the chill darkness of the taxi or the impersonal seclusion of the hotel room, that one could make a valid estimate of what a man really had to sell.

He paid off the taxi and walked into the hotel lobby. The doorman touched his cap and Weldon paid him back with a polite, distant smile. He took the lift up to his room and took off his overcoat. It was a black vicuna which he had bought in Vienna two years ago. Almost every article he wore was a souvenir of his incessant travels—the suit from Savile Row, the Brooks Brothers' shirt, the hat from a little shop near the Place Vendôme. He went into the bathroom and washed his hands and face. Afterwards he stood for a moment looking at himself in the mirror. As always, he found his own appearance reassuring. The long, oval face, with the sallow complexion and the gentle, sensitive mouth, the sleek black hair, still untouched by grey—somehow it all added up to a kind of apparent distinction which he knew only too well to be lacking in any real basis. He had many years ago lost any illusions about his own intrinsic qualities, but it was encouraging to know that his outward appearance had the capacity to impress.

He sat in his armchair and smoked a cigarette. He felt tired, but it was too early for a drink. Leading his kind of life it was only too easy to get into bad habits. Carrera—what was one to make of him? A good record of publications, an Associate Professorship, nothing in his record to suggest the charlatan or the crank. He didn't even claim that he had discovered a cure for schizophrenia—just a promising line of research which was being blocked by higher authorities out of jealousy and personal animosity. And yet . . . as the man's personal brilliance and plausibility began to fade from his memory, the facts that remained were somehow insufficient to convince. What actual concrete evidence had been produced? Was it really credible that nowhere in Italy could he find proper appreciation, if the work was all he claimed? Wasn't it a little strange that he should be so ready, indeed eager, to give up everything and transport himself to America to put himself at the service of a purely commercial organization?

As he sat down at the writing-desk to draft his report, Weldon knew in his heart that this was just another fake. It was hard to know exactly where the flaw was, but ISIS would find it in due course. There was a whole routine procedure—Forms of Disclosure, asking for full details under pledge of secrecy, endless inquiries about methods and results, ending, as so often, in one final inquiry which remained unanswered, simply because no satisfactory answer existed. Only then would the file be closed. ISIS was infinitely patient. It cared nothing for time or money. It investigated every lead and showed neither disappointment nor anger when the vast majority of them led nowhere. The few, the very few, that led to success were more than sufficient to pay for a hundred failures.

They would guess, of course, from his report, that Carrera was almost certainly a fake. He would not be so foolish as to commit himself directly, but they would read between the lines. And they trusted his judgement, not only because

94

of his experience but because he was supposed to have an instinct about such matters. Perhaps, thought Weldon, with a melancholy self-knowledge, it was because he was a little bit of a fake himself. A man had an instinct for his own kind.

He had arranged to dine with Menotti, the main ISIS distributor in Italy. Menotti was a tall, heavy, bald-headed man who held not only the ISIS agency but many others as well. Weldon envied Menotti not only his wealth and power, but his independence. By comparison with ISIS he was tiny, but in his own small world he was a king and recognized as such. Little happened of any importance in Rome without Menotti's knowledge.

The two men sat over dinner gazing out through the glass walls of the restaurant at the people moving up and down the Spanish Steps. When Weldon had finished describing his visit to Carrera, Menotti said, 'An interesting job, yours. I often wish I was a scientist.'

Could it be, thought Weldon in astonishment, that a man he so greatly envied could possibly be so foolish as to envy him? 'Personally,' he said dryly, 'I often wish I was a business man.'

'Up to the minute with all the latest advances. Travelling. Meeting all those brilliant men. Very satisfying, I would say.'

Weldon gave his vague, non-committal smile, the small change of a man who lived a life of transient superficial contacts. In his world you accepted what you were given in the way of compliments; it was a mistake to sell yourself short. If his job was a mixture of reporting, specialized detective work, and something at times perilously close to industrial espionage, he was not under any obligation to reveal the fact. To Menotti, evidently, he was a scientist and somewhat enviable as a consequence. There was something slightly warming in the discovery.

Weldon finished his lamb cutlets and refused dessert. Menotti called for coffee and lit a cigar. 'I was waiting until you'd finished dinner to tell you this,' he said. 'Mulholland called from London while you were out. He'd like you to go back tomorrow on the morning plane.'

Mulholland was the manager of the ISIS London office. For the last year he had been fighting a running battle to detach Weldon from the New York office administration and bring him under his own control. He made no secret of his desire to cut Weldon down and to rob him of status. So far he had been unsuccessful, but he was determined and persistent and Weldon was afraid of him.

He could tell by the way Menotti looked at the end of his cigar that the message had been not so much a request as an order delivered with all Mulholland's customary boorishness. He felt rising within him the usual mixture of anger and apprehension which he always associated with his dealings with Mulholland. Yet there was no change in his soft, rather languid voice.

'That may not be possible,' he said gently.

'He said it was a message from Mr. Henderson.'

Menotti was still not looking at him. Weldon was suddenly aware that Menotti was sorry for him, that all that stuff about envying his life as a scientist was just a method of building him up, so as to compensate for the knowledge that he was at the beck and call of a lout like Mulholland. Menotti knew too that if the message was from Henderson, there was really nothing further to be said. 'I booked you a seat on tomorrow's plane just in case,' he said.

Weldon made a pretence of considering the matter. 'I suppose I could just manage it.'

The face-saving ritual was automatic. Beneath it his mind was gnawing away nervously at the implications of the summons. Henderson. What could the old man possibly want with him? To Weldon, Henderson was no more than a name printed on stationery, a photograph in a company report. Henderson was one of the great men of ISIS, so important that he was unknown, a remote, incomprehensible god-like figure. It was almost a shock to realize that he might be encountered in the flesh.

'Did Mulholland say what it was all about?' he asked.

'No,' said Menotti. 'Just that it was urgent.'

It occurred to Weldon that perhaps this was the end. Perhaps it was a sign that Mulholland had won, that the position he had defended for so long had been taken at last. He felt a momentary flash of something close to panic. Menotti saw it in his eyes and was shocked. He said anxiously, in his soft Italian voice, 'How are things in ISIS for you now?'

Weldon's first impulse was to bluff, to say everything was fine. But Menotti was an old friend—and he probably knew the truth anyway. 'Not so good,' he admitted.

Menotti sat in pensive silence, looking out over the city, puffing at his cigar. Over the years he had grown fond of

96

Weldon. He was seized by a momentary temptation to offer to help in some way, to use what influence he had among the rulers of ISIS, to offer him an alternative job with his own organization. Friendship and affection struggled with his businessman's calculation and the inherent caution of his race. The connection with ISIS was a very profitable one for him. It might be dangerous to tamper with it by getting mixed up in any internal squabbles. By helping Weldon he had everything to lose and nothing whatever to gain. Nobody could expect a man to take action under conditions of that kind. He said, with genuine regret, 'I wish I could do something to help.'

Weldon paid the hotel bill, slightly over-tipped the hall porter, and climbed into the car which was to take him to the airport. It was one of Menotti's cars, and that meant five dollars saved off the expense account which would pay for a present for Nicky when he went home to the States. He liked to buy presents for the children, though, truth to tell, it was usually a rather disappointing experience when he handed them over. Nicky and Mary Ann didn't seem to like any of the things which had appealed to him when he was young—most of their toys were founded on variations of esoteric cults, stemming from television programmes he never saw. Nicky wanted to disguise himself as a space-traveller or Batman, and Mary Ann was involved in a status race with her school-mates in connection with a series of teenage dolls which possessed practically every physiological function except a tendency to burst into tears half-way through the middle of every calendar month.

Perhaps it was the inevitable result of being an Englishman living in America. The children really belonged to Blanche, not to him. Good, sound Americans in their T-shirts and jeans, they no doubt found him as baffling as he found them. He sometimes wondered what they really thought of this remote stranger, with his exotic accent and European clothes, who descended on them at intervals for a few weeks at a time, and then departed to some corner of the world which to them was no more than a name in a geography lesson.

The driver took his bags out of the car. Two neat yet capacious suitcases in dark fibre, bought in Amsterdam, their combination of practicality and luxury diagnostic of the professional traveller. He never carried hand luggage on a short journey, just one paperback and a copy of *Time* magazine. He handed the Italian coins from his pocket to the driver and walked across the tarmac to the first-class entrance of the plane; behind him the economy class passengers, the fag-end of the year's tourism, struggled under their load of gifts, cigarettes and duty-free schnapps. Once in his seat he refused the free champagne and settled down for a sleep.

In London the air was clouded with a fine drizzle. He took a taxi to the Savoy. London was full and they had no available rooms. However, for Mr. Weldon . . . The assistant manager found a cancellation for him and showed him up to a pleasant room overlooking the river. The depression which had been hanging over him throughout the day lifted temporarily. There was always something reassuring about the Savoy. Surely a man who was known and respected there could never be regarded as a total failure in life?

He had lunch in the Grill and then took a taxi to the Company offices, which occupied a new tower block at the upper end of Charing Cross Road. Inside the entrance was a brass plaque with 'International Syndicate of Industrial Services' engraved upon it in small letters, and above that, in large capitals, the single word ISIS. Mulholland's office was on the top floor. It had been lavishly furnished by an interior decorator who specialized in creating appropriate surroundings for senior executives, and everything inside it had been laboriously chosen to build up an atmosphere of elegance and distinction. Everything, that is, except Mulholland himself, who carried within him a natural deep-seated vulgarity which success was powerless to modify. He was a bony Northern Irishman in his middle-thirties, with a bulbous nose and a coarse doughy complexion, the legacy of several attacks of acne in adolescence. His sandy hair was thinning on top, to reveal an unpleasantly freckled area of scalp. He wore expensive suits of slightly too light a grey and slightly too sharp a cut; his brown leather shoes were heavily polished. He had retained traces of his Belfast accent, but in the course of a varied career he had managed to overlay it with a variety of other intonations, picked up in Sydney, Johannesburg and Kansas City. The result was a voice, and a man, almost without discernible nationality, expressing no tradition or manners except those of his employment, no aspirations apart from his own drive for money and power.

In addition to the interior decorator's contribution to the room, Mulholland had added his own in the shape of various ornaments; African carvings, shrunken heads and similar curiosities which had been brought for him by his subordinates as souvenirs of various business trips. They served the double function of acting as talking points for visitors and of reminding his staff of what was expected of them. When Weldon was shown in he found Mulholland engaged in admiring a new trophy on his desk.

'Take a look at this, Arthur. Ferris brought it back for me from Taiwan. Solid teak. Weighs like lead. Just lift it.'

Weldon lifted it and put it down again. It was a block of smooth pale hardwood about a foot long, concave at the upper end and with an oriental face carved delicately into its surface. 'It's a beautiful piece of carving,' he said.

'Oh sure,' said Mulholland indifferently. 'But that's not the point.' He grinned lewdly. 'It's got a religious significance. Did you know that?'

'No.'

'Look at that upper end. Doesn't it suggest anything to you?' Weldon shook his head. 'It's a phallic symbol. How about that? A foot long and weighs half a stone.' Mulholland guffawed. 'Doesn't it make you envious?'

Weldon knew that Mulholland went in for this kind of talk deliberately in order to embarrass him, perhaps to pay him back for the fact that he had consistently refused to bring back souvenirs himself. He made no attempt to smile, and his disgust must have shown on his face. Mulholland's grin was quickly replaced by a flicker of anger. He said shortly, 'Where the hell were you anyway? You didn't tell anyone where you were going. I had to telephone over half Europe to find you.'

'New York had my itinerary.'

'Did they hell. Henderson had no idea where you might be.'

'They must have got their lines crossed somewhere.'

Weldon spoke indifferently, but he knew he was on dangerous ground. He had, it was true, posted New York a copy of his itinerary, but, in accordance with his usual practice, he had sent it slightly late, so that they would only get it after he had started. He knew in his heart that it was a rather childish thing to do, and also somewhat dangerous. But it was part of the illusion of independence which he had always cultivated.

Mulholland went on, 'Then, when I finally located you, Menotti said you were out on some confidential job.' He took his gold toothpick out of his pocket and dug a piece of meat out of a gap behind one of his lower incisors. 'What were you doing? Knocking it off with one of those Italian chicks?'

It was an old game of Mulholland's to pretend that Weldon was an incorrigible lecher, who spent most of his time abroad in sexual adventures. Usually the allegations were made as a joke, sometimes they carried an edge of seriousness. Weldon was far too experienced to be provoked by them. 'Of course,' he said, with a kind of weary contempt. 'That's how I spend all my time in Europe.'

'Well, I wouldn't be surprised.' The doughy face was alive with malice. 'You really have the best of it, you scientists. Screwing your way around the world. Nobody knows where you are or what you're doing . . .'

There were times, thought Weldon, when it became almost impossible to stay in the same room with Mulholland and retain your self-respect. The alarming thing about him was not so much the type of man he was (almost everyone had encountered individuals of his kind at one time or another, in golf clubs or army messes or propping up the bar on board ship) but his record of achievement within the Company, and the position which he at present occupied. For the fact was that, in the ten years that Weldon had been at the organization, he could not recollect anyone who had achieved such a rapid and unimpeded rise to power as Mulholland. He had done this in spite of the fact that he was known to be stupid and uneducated, an empty braggart and a drunken bully. Indeed his whole personality was in direct contradiction to the image which ISIS endeavoured ceaselessly to project to the world. This image was of a supremely responsible organization, so large that it could hardly be considered as commercial in the ordinary sense of the word. ISIS dealt with Governments on a footing of equality, it disposed of revenues equivalent to those of a small independent state. It drew heavily for its senior staff on university departments, civil servants of distinction and the star graduates of business colleges. And yet, existing parallel with all this, was Mulholland, hiring and firing, boozing and whoring his way to success. Mulholland, to whom responsibility was meaningless and business ethics a joke. Not only did he exist, but he was well-known to the great ones at the head of ISIS. He entertained them on their visits to England and they were apparently not shocked or disgusted by him. On the contrary they spoke of him approvingly as a vigorous aggressive manager, a rough diamond but none the worse for that. When Weldon reflected on the extraordinary contradiction he was sometimes overcome with a kind of panic, founded on a suspicion that perhaps the whole façade of ISIS was nothing but a fake. Could it be that he, and a multitude of others, had been deceiving themselves all these years? Could it be that when it came to the point it was Mulholland who most truly expressed the spirit of the organization?

Mulholland had picked up the Taiwan carving and was transferring it to his mantelpiece. He placed it among the rest of his collection and regarded it appreciatively. 'Really quite a piece.' His face changed. 'Mind you, if Ferris thinks it's going to take my mind off his expense sheet for that Far Eastern trip, he'll have to think again.' He sat down at the desk and tapped with a hairy finger on a piece of paper which lay in front of him. 'I'll tell you something, Arthur. I can read an expense sheet like another man can read a detective's report. I don't need anyone watching my men as long as I can read their sheets. I spent eight years of my life travelling and I know every trick. I know why a man's taken the day off, when he's got drunk with a client, when he's had a woman. Believe me, Arthur, when you write one of these you're writing the story of your life, whether you know it or not.'

There was a sour taste in Weldon's mouth. He could feel the threat in Mulholland's words. Presumably this was one of the treats in store for him if Mulholland ever achieved his object and had him transferred under his control. The expense account was a traditionally vulnerable area for all except the most senior of ISIS employees. The organization paid salaries which were adequate but no more, but it had always been generous with expenses. A man who travelled round for ISIS lived well, often indeed so well that he found his home life rather sordid and suburban by comparison. It was hard to get back from the hotel suites and the geisha parties to a life of lawn mowing and putting the children to bed. The expense account acted as a consolation for irregular hours, incessant travel, and the loss of home life. To have it dissected and analysed by Mulholland would effectively destroy any comfort it might bring.

He felt a powerful desire to get away from the office at all costs. He said sharply, 'You still haven't told me what Henderson wanted.'

Mulholland hesitated. 'It's a special assignment. He wants to brief you personally. He's in Geneva now, at the Richemond Hotel. He wants you to fly over there tomorrow. I've booked you a seat on Swissair.'

'Do you know what it's about?'

Mulholland looked ostentatiously at his watch. It was a large, showy affair which told you the day of the month and several other unnecessary things as well as the time. He said, 'I have an appointment in a few minutes. We can discuss it further over dinner.'

Weldon knew these dinners only too well. They were Mulholland's substitute for a social life. A man almost totally without friends, he spent most of his evenings entertaining his subordinates to protracted meals in expensive restaurants. There was always too much to drink, rich heavy food in cream sauces, brandy and cigars, and endless talk, growing increasingly bombastic throughout the evening, about Mulholland's own achievements. They were to be avoided whenever possible. Weldon struggled to escape.

'I'm afraid I already have a dinner engagement—'

'Stand her up,' said Mulholland brutally. 'Do you good. You can't be on the job every night at your age. Besides this is important. Henderson wanted me to give you some background.'

The use of Henderson's name was an open threat. Looking into Mulholland's eyes, Weldon had a sudden suspicion that Mulholland knew nothing at all about the assignment, that there was nothing to talk about over dinner, and that he had only been dragged back to London instead of being sent straight to Geneva because of Mulholland's desire to establish an ascendancy over him. If this were the case—as it almost certainly was—he could safely defy Mulholland and refuse the dinner invitation. He contemplated the possibility, but only for an instant. He dared not take the chance. Despising himself, he shrugged acceptance. It was just another of the petty humiliations which made up the pattern of his life.

CHAPTER TWO

FALKENBURG'S OFFICE in the Rue de Rivoli was furnished in the French Empire style. *Planet Magazine* liked the head of the bureau to soak himself in the atmosphere of the country. Falkenburg was a conscientious man and he had done the best he could. He had even gone to the extent of cultivating a nervous habit of shrugging his shoulders in what he imagined to be a Gallic way, and making expressive gestures with his fingers every now and then when emphasizing a point. His French features editor, Jennet, on the other hand, was working on a mid-Atlantic pose in the hope of being transferred to head office in New York. He had recently invested in a crew-cut and made various abortive efforts to smoke a pipe. The two men spent a good deal of time trying out their spurious national personalities on each other.

Falkenburg was looking with fascination at a teletype from the New York office. 'John Henderson, for God's sake,' he said. 'I thought he was dead.'

Jennet twitched the side of his face in a way he had picked up from Humphrey Bogart. 'I never heard of him.'

'Oh, he was quite a celebrity in the States at one time. You'll find a big file on him if you care to dig it out. Old-style commercial roughneck. A gambler. Made a million dollars before he was twenty-five by making a corner in nutmeg or some goddam thing. In and out of deals of one sort or another all his life. Actually made the cover of *Time* once just after the war. The last thing we heard of him was some hullabaloo with the Costa Rican Government over mineral concessions. Legal enough as it turned out, but politically tactless. In the end Washington persuaded ISIS to buy him out and make him a vice-president. Since then he seems to have become respectable.' He added in qualification, 'Or so I imagine. One doesn't hear much about him.'

'What does he want?' asked Jennet.

'According to Charlie Schwartz he wants Sarah Manning —on loan for three months. It seems she's his niece or something. Did you know that?'

Jennet shook his head. 'Did you?'

'No. The whole thing's a little mysterious. Doesn't say what he wants her for, but Charlie wants us to co-operate.

He says there may be something good in it for us. Can you spare her?'

'Do I have a choice?'

'Not really.'

'Things are pretty tight staff-wise at the moment,' said Jennet mechanically. He had learnt enough in his five years at *Planet* never to agree without protest to any reduction in the size of his department. 'She's one of my most experienced writers. Can I hire a replacement?'

That meant, thought Falkenburg, that when Sarah came back in three months' time Jennet would have managed to increase his already excessive staff by one. The boy would go far. But after all, why not? 'Okay,' he said, rising to show that the conference was at an end. 'And perhaps you'd ask Sarah to come up and see me.'

Falkenburg was not particularly impressed by the fact that Sarah Manning was related to a multi-millionaire. The *Planet* offices, particularly in the more desirable international centres, were full of such girls—it was considered an amusing job by graduates of the more expensive female colleges. He had met Sarah on a number of occasions and he felt he knew the type only too well. It was not a type he particularly liked or felt at ease with. Tall and ash-blonde, with that curious smooth hygienic look that they brought away with them as a graduation souvenir from Smith or Vassar. The kind who ate their way through men like termites digesting a piece of furniture. They had little respect for business status and in his experience you had to show them who was boss right from the beginning. He took out a pair of heavy reading glasses which he used as a device for preserving a distance between himself and refractory employees.

When Sarah was shown into the office he waved her to a seat without looking up and made a pretence of being lost in scrutiny of some papers. After he had kept her waiting for a suitable time he pushed the memorandum aside and whisked the glasses off his face with a decisive gesture.

'Well now, Sarah,' he said briskly. 'I don't know whether Jennet told you what I wanted to see you about—?'

'No. He said nothing.'

Her voice had a softness about it which was slightly unlike that of a native American, and reminded him more of one of those cosmopolitan women from central or Southern America, brought up in a bilingual society with American overtones. He remembered now that there was some story about her having spent her childhood in an embassy in Venezuela.

'I've just received a cable from Mr. Schwartz in New York about you. He tells me that your uncle, John Henderson, has asked if we will loan you to him for a special assignment for three months. Did you know anything about this?'

'Nothing at all.'

'He hasn't asked you if you'd agree?'

'No.' She gave no impression of surprise. 'But then he wouldn't. He's that kind of man. He just assumes that other people are delighted to do everything he wants. It works most of the time.' She glanced down at the cable. 'I gather it worked with Mr. Schwartz.'

Falkenburg looked at her sharply. She had a strange way, which he remembered from previous occasions, of tilting her head slightly back and half-closing her eyes, while a faint, remote smile played around her lips. It gave the disconcerting impression that she might be harbouring some secret joke at the expense of the person she was talking to. He thought back over what she had said. Had there been a trace of disrespect in her voice, an inference that *Planet* executives like Schwartz and Falkenburg would instinctively fall flat on their faces at the word of this superannuated tycoon? If so, it was impossible to pin down. And her face was impassive, almost demure. 'Naturally,' he said coldly, 'Mr. Schwartz is prepared to help if he can. But he told Henderson that it was up to me to decide whether I could spare you. Before that I wanted to make sure whether you were prepared to go.'

'What *is* the assignment?'

'That's the odd part about it. We don't know. Henderson says it's too confidential to disclose to anyone but you. He insists it's very important. And he wants you urgently.'

'Where is he?'

Falkenburg looked down at the teletype. 'He'll be at the Richemond Hotel in Geneva from tomorrow. He wants you to go there as soon as possible.'

Sarah said, 'And you've all agreed?'

'I spoke to Jennet and he says he thinks he can manage to spare you. Are you willing to go?'

She shrugged her shoulders. 'Why not? It sounds as if it might be interesting.'

'What are you working on now?'

She said with faint distaste, 'That story about the pregnant ballerina.'

'I expect one of the other girls could take that over.'

'Or we could drop it altogether.'

Falkenburg shook his head decisively. It was as he had suspected—the girl was a little too big for her boots. 'It's news,' he said. 'People want to read it. On *Planet Magazine* we never get too big to handle the news.'

Well at least, thought Sarah as she left the office, whatever the job was, it just had to be better than the ballerina; a bitch in anybody's language, who claimed to have chosen the father of her baby on purely eugenic grounds, with the idea of producing another Nijinsky or Pavlova. It was perhaps as good a way as any of bluffing out the fact that she didn't know who the father was, but hardly in Sarah's opinion worth the time and the space that *Planet* was prepared to give to it. It would be nice to get away from Paris and see Uncle John again. It wasn't easy to approve of the old man, but you had to admit that there was something about him you didn't fully appreciate until you associated with the new-wave men like Falkenburg and Jennet.

Or Maurice. Well, that was another good thing about this development. It would force her to take action about Maurice. The whole thing had been drifting on far too long. It had been obvious for months that some decision would have to be taken. Now at last they had reached the point of natural termination.

It was after half past twelve and she had arranged to meet him for lunch. She went to the cloakroom and spent a little time on her appearance—at least she owed it to him to look her best on this last occasion. Then she put on a light raincoat and made her way into the Rue de Rivoli.

She arrived on time at the restaurant. Maurice, as usual, had not arrived. He was always a little late for appointments, never so much as to be grossly impolite, but enough for him to arrive rather breathless and full of excuses and conscious charm. She had sometimes grown irritable with this habit and had tried to teach him a lesson by arriving deliberately late herself. It had never been an entirely successful gambit, and she had always rather despised herself for it afterwards. In any case, she reflected, you could never beat a man on his own ground. When it came to unreliability Maurice was a natural, effortless performer. She could never hope to compete with him.

She ordered a Cinzano and settled down to read *Le Monde*. The restaurant was almost empty and when the waiter had served her he leaned up against the wall, his napkin dangling from a listless hand, and watched her working her way through the newspaper. The waiter's eyes travelled up the long legs to the slight, athletic body, clad in a white blouse and dark brown skirt. How old was she, he wondered. Twenty-five? Not more, surely—as an expert observer he noted the smoothness of her hands, the slight golden down at the nape of the neck. The hips were a little narrow, but the breasts not bad at all considering how tall and thin she was. She was rich, of course, he knew it instinctively, one could never fool a waiter about a thing like that. It was curious that it was so obvious, for there was nothing really smart about her. Her clothes were not couture, they were ready-made and fairly inexpensive and she wore practically no jewellery. Her hair was swept back from her forehead in a simple and rather unfashionable style—she certainly didn't go to the hairdresser more than once a week. Yet somehow she carried an aura of affluence and privilege with her. It was there in the way she carried herself and a certain effortless indifference towards the opinion of others. And there was something, too, about her skin. It sometimes seemed to him that there was a special quality about the skin of the rich, as if they had been wrapped from childhood in some precious oil which kept them free and unviolated by the savageries of the ordinary world.

Yet she would be cold, he assured himself, consoling himself for the fact that she was both desirable to him and totally unattainable. Cold, indifferent, self-centred. Her mouth was wide, he had to concede that, but it meant nothing in an American woman. There was no true sensuality in her face.

He broke off his reverie as he saw Maurice Lapas approaching the door. He admired and respected Mr. Lapas, who was an excellent customer and a very good tipper. What was more, he was a man who knew his way around and had the reputation of getting value for money. One could hardly visualize a man like Lapas wasting his time on one of those transatlantic icebergs. Perhaps there was more in the girl than one saw at first sight.

Lapas walked quickly over to Sarah's table, kissed her on the cheek, and sat down beside her. He was a tall man in his early thirties with a dark aquiline face and a ready smile which he had inherited from his Greek father. His tough shrewdness about money matters, which was purely French, had come to him from his mother's side.

'I'm miserable to be so late,' he said. 'I got stuck with one of those awful agents. He was trying to sell me a book on tribal customs in East Africa by a lascivious American anthropologist. I thought he'd never stop talking.'

'Are you going to buy it?'

'Perhaps,' said Maurice. 'At the moment he's being a little greedy.' Lapas was what is known as an 'adventurous' book publisher. He dealt mainly in avant-garde novels or in sociological works with a vaguely salacious flavour. He was also known to strike an extremely hard bargain with his authors. 'But he knows he'll have to agree to my terms in the end. I have an arrangement with a certain book club which will be good for both of us.'

He gave an artful, but at the same time curiously boyish, smile. This book club, in which he had a controlling interest, was a device in which he took great pride. It distributed semi-pornographic illustrated books to a private subscription list at considerable profit. Maurice's life was taken up with such faintly discreditable devices. He found them more amusing as well as more profitable than conventional business.

'Does the author know you own the book club?'

'Why should he? It's none of his business. Anyway, if he insists on writing a dirty book about Africans—'

He laughed and began to order the meal. It was impossible, Sarah thought, to approve of Maurice, and yet very difficult to dislike him. He had a curious kind of inherent innocence, an almost total lack of shame. She said, genuinely curious, 'Aren't you ever ashamed of yourself?'

'Never.' He was, she could see, speaking quite sincerely. 'I do what I have to. I was born too poor to choose my own way of making a living. I had to take what was open to me. If they offered me the chairmanship of Hachette tomorrow, I'd never touch this kind of book again. But unfortunately they haven't as yet. Anyway, if I didn't do this, somebody else would. I was just the man who saw the opening.'

It was the standard defence of all opportunists. It was not easy to argue against it. Not, at least, if you had been born into wealth—wealth made probably by methods not so very different from those which Maurice had used to drag himself up from poverty to significance. And one had to say this for him—he was totally free from hypocrisy. He made no pretence of being anything but what he was. Though he tried to get the better of his competitors, he was without malice. To him it was all a game, a delightful game of acquisition and possession which he always won.

Was it so priggish of her, she wondered, that she could not accept him without censure and be as amused at his adventures as he was himself? The trouble was that there was no method of description of what was wrong with Maurice that didn't seem hopelessly old-fashioned nowadays. You couldn't call him a heel or a scoundrel without making yourself seem ridiculous. You couldn't criticize a man, in the 1960s, for being short of a sense of honour. Yet that was the real trouble with him.

Behind her air of calm and confidence she sat unhappily, unsure of herself, inhabiting a world where her own standards of behaviour aroused no response. She had a deep fear that perhaps her whole attitude to life was hopelessly wrong—demanding a standard of thought and action from others which no reasonable person could be expected to give. Certainly that was the view which Maurice took of her. Yet the demands were deeply fixed in her own nature. How could she abandon them without abandoning her own personality?

It seemed to her sometimes that if she stayed long enough with Maurice he would eventually destroy her by destroying her belief in her own standards. Certainly there was no chance of ever converting him to her point of view. She envied the fact that, unlike herself, he was obviously never troubled by the slightest shadow of doubt as to the essential rightness of his own behaviour. His cynicism seemed to carry within it all the essential strength which was traditionally supposed to arise from a consciousness of virtue. There was something intimidating about the depth of his self-confidence.

Yet one thing was certain—whether he was right or wrong, whether her own attitude was reasonable or unreasonable, it was impossible for her to marry him. She was fond of him and amused by him, she had even thought for a time that she was in love with him, but in the end all of these things would founder against the barrier of a different standard of conduct. An essential language was missing between them. She could not live for the rest of her life with a man whom she could not trust to tell her the truth. She could not put it to him bluntly in these words—he had never been able to understand what the nature of the barrier was. Perhaps, she thought, to a European, brought up in the world of arranged marriages and liaisons accepted without fuss or complaint, it would be incomprehensible anyway. The best thing was to break it off now, without fuss or recriminations. She said, 'There's something I wanted to tell you. I have to leave Paris tomorrow.'

He frowned, slightly puzzled by the seriousness of her manner. 'On an assignment?'

'In a way.'

'Will you be gone long?'

'I don't know. At least three months. Maybe for good. I don't know.' She paused and then said apologetically, 'I think this is the end for us, Maurice.'

He was obviously startled. Before he could speak she went on hurriedly. 'After all, we both knew it was bound to come, didn't we? We've been through it before—'

It was hard to know how he was taking it. Under the conventional reaction, how genuine was his distress? So much of his life was an act that it was never easy to distinguish his real emotions from the façade with which he covered them. Yet if he was acting, he was doing so with skill. 'This is a terrible shock,' he said. 'I never imagined—' Surely there could be no doubt about his distress? He said eagerly, 'But you'll come back, I'm sure of that. Whatever you say—'

'Not to you, Maurice. I shan't come back to you.'

'I don't understand. Have I done something wrong?'

'No. It's nothing to do with that. Surely you can see it's better for both of us.'

She was oppressed by the banality of her words, the tired repetitive nature of her predicament. Life might force you to live through such situations, but it was too much to expect you to thrash out the details in conversation. She said, 'Let's just accept it.'

He shook his head. She was touched to see that he was genuinely unhappy. Perhaps his toughness and realism was only skin-deep after all. She fought against a wave of tenderness that might destroy her resolution. He said, 'I don't understand. What is it you have against me?'

It was impossible to tell him. Surely he had no right to ask her. 'It's nothing like that—'

'Yes. Yes, it is,' he said miserably. 'You disapprove of me, don't you? My business methods, the way I talk and think, the way I run my life. Always there is this moral attitude between us.' As if determined to torment himself, he added, 'I think in your heart you despise me.'

'No, Maurice, that's not true. Believe me—'

'Yes. I think you do.' He spoke with decision. It was for the first time apparent to her how much sensitivity and insecurity lay beneath his apparent self-confidence. 'You expect too much of everyone. It's not just me. You look down on your work for that magazine. You think the people you write about are worthless and those who read it are morons, who want nothing but trash. That's true, isn't it? You've said so many a time.'

It was true, of course. One said so many things which sounded brutal and uncharitable when repeated. Was she indeed such a prig as his words suggested? Perhaps so. She found herself with nothing to say.

He went on, his English disintegrating under the strength of his emotions. 'Always you disapprove,' he said. 'Of everybody, of everything. And of me—you disapprove most of all.'

It came to her that he had always loved her more than she had ever suspected—had always believed in his heart that she would eventually change her mind and agree to marry him. His obvious pain was such that she could not be angry with him even when he was insulting her. She pushed away a plate of untasted food. 'I'm sorry, darling, I'm sorry.'

But it was too late to stop the flood of his resentment. He said stubbornly, 'You don't want a man—you want a hero. I'm not a hero so I'm not good enough for you. Well let me tell you this, there are no heroes, there are only men. If you ever find what you think you want, he will turn out to be a man, too, but he'll break you in the process. I warn you of that.'

She did not reply. Possibly, she thought, he was right. Possibly people like Maurice and Falkenburg and the rest of them were all the world had to offer. But you couldn't accept that simply because they said so. Anxious to placate him, she pressed his hand. 'Don't be angry with me, Maurice.' Under the influence of her touch he seemed to recover himself. The flash of violence died down. The hurt, humiliated boy was replaced once more by the successful business man, the invulnerable sophisticate. It had been an unusual outburst. Never before had he revealed how easy it was to wound his pride. He forced a smile. 'I'm not really angry. Just a little afraid for you. But of course you're like the rest of us. You do what you have to.' The smile was almost natural now. 'It seems strange for me to be giving advice when I never took it myself.'

'Dear Maurice.' She felt a flood of affection for him. This was the mood she liked best in him—independent and with a touch of gallantry. In this mood he appeared as a whole man who understood himself and made no excuses. He had had to make his own way by whatever means came to hand, he could not afford the luxury of grand gestures, yet within that narrow framework he was kind and generous and amusing. This was the Maurice with whom it had been possible for her, however fleetingly, to have fallen in love. She had seen him at first as a product of a Europe which could not be reasonably judged by the standards of a relatively young and inexperienced American girl; expressing an attitude to life which might even turn out to be the right one, if you understood it well enough. It had taken her six months to understand that while it might indeed be right for Maurice, it could never be right for her.

He was relaxed in his chair now, totally recovered, smoking a cigarette. 'Now tell me why it is you have to go suddenly. What is it about—this new assignment?'

She told him. To her, as she repeated it, the story sounded rather lame and incomplete. She was surprised to find him listening to her with intense seriousness. 'As you see,' she said, 'I don't really know very much about it.'

'It sounds very curious,' he said. 'Very interesting indeed.' He frowned as he thought it over. 'I didn't know you had such eminent relatives.'

'Uncle John isn't really eminent. Just very rich.'

Maurice shook his head. 'I know about him. He's more than that. This affair must be of considerable importance.'

'You think so?'

'Yes. I have a feeling for such things. It's one of my talents as a publisher.' In spite of the vanity behind his words, she knew it was no more than the truth. He went on, 'I hope it turns out well for you. I'm still very fond of you, Sarah.' He paused and then went on seriously, 'But if anything goes wrong, if you have problems, or there's something difficult or unexpected, I want you to know I'm always here to help you. Whatever happens, I'm always your friend.'

She looked at him and was overcome with affection. He really cared for her. He was one of the few people in the world who could offer her something without wanting anything in return. Yet there was a tiny doubt in her mind which she could not repress. Knowing him as well as she did, she could not help wondering whether his solicitude was not in some way affected by his knowledge of the position and importance of Henderson. The agonizing thing was that she could never be sure. Would she ever be rid of these painful uncertainties? Or were they one of the penalties of wealth which she was condemned to carry with her for the rest of her life?

She was suddenly ashamed of her distrust of Maurice. On an impulse she turned her face towards him and kissed him on the lips. The waiter watched them with interest tinged with envy. Perhaps he had been wrong—she was not so cold after all. Mr. Lapas was no fool. He shuffled on his protesting feet towards the cash desk. If he was not mistaken, they would be asking for the bill any minute now.

CHAPTER THREE

HENDERSON sat in the living-room of his hotel suite, picking abstractedly at a late breakfast. O'Keefe, his Director of Public Relations, reclined in an overstuffed armchair opposite to him, talking as usual. He had been talking for some time, and Henderson, who was in an unusually taciturn mood, had switched his mind off and occupied himself with his own thoughts. But the others would be coming soon. He had better start dealing with the matter in hand.

For at least the third time O'Keefe was running through his plan of campaign. 'The villa's all fixed up, ready for occupation. We just need to finalize the documents. They're all made out in your niece's name, waiting for her to sign. So far as the escape is concerned, we have a water-tight arrangement—'

'I know. You told me before.' Henderson sipped his orange juice and put it down. It was stupid to drink orange juice; it always gave him indigestion. That was the trouble with being old, his body had begun to dominate his life. At one time he had been able to drag it round with him from one place to another like a Victorian lady with a paid companion, abusing it, setting it ridiculous and pointless tasks for his own amusement, ignoring it if he felt that way. Now his body was like a servant grown powerful in proportion to his own weakness. Quietly, imperceptibly, it had taken charge, revenging itself for all the humiliations he had heaped on it. And he was powerless to resist.

His body woke him at six o'clock to pass water, it refused to sleep on hard beds, it rejected good tasty food that it had once been only too pleased to get. It wouldn't let him smoke or drink too much. It had protested constantly, in an ill-tempered way, during this particular trip. His body wanted him tucked up comfortably at home, with the sunshine slanting through the blinds of his bedroom and the mist rising from the sierras, instead of by this black unfriendly lake, in an icy November.

In some ways he could hardly blame it. He thought with longing of the sun-baked stillness of the California ranch, the horses nodding their heads in anticipation as he approached their stalls with his pockets full of sugar, the two Rhodesian ridge-backs that thundered out of the yard as they heard the sound of his car on the gravel of the driveway. He poured cream in his coffee and turned his large shaggy head towards the window which framed the grim cloud-capped peaks on the other side of the lake. Only another few days.

O'Keefe would have to take care of the detail. It shouldn't be too difficult, now the plan was set up. He didn't like leaving so much to others, but then he never had. They said in ISIS that he was reluctant to delegate. Well, maybe. A man had to work from his own experience. He had always found that things went better when he took care of them himself. But this was a job that had to be delegated. There wasn't any choice—he was too well known. If they tracked the thing back to him in the early stages that would be the end of it.

O'Keefe had paused only momentarily and then started up again. Henderson regarded him with distaste. A professional ideas man—he had met scores of them in his time. O'Keefe was tall and heavily built, with a handsome face spoiled only by a pair of narrow deep-set eyes and a nose which had been broken at college where he had been a promising amateur boxer. His fair hair was slicked back over his scalp and he was dressed with considerable care by a British tailor. Gold watch, gold cigarette case, signet ring with a bogus family crest. A keen, energetic man, thought Henderson sourly, brimming with sincerity and company loyalty. They turned your stomach but you found yourself using them.

Henderson said, 'Of course this whole thing depends on Hoffman's information. Are you sure he's reliable?'

'Certain,' said O'Keefe positively. He always believed in being positive. 'Don't worry about that.'

'It's a pity we can't use him for the operation.'

'It's impossible. He's tied up with that Moscow job. We couldn't get him off it without blowing the whole works to ISIS. And you don't want that.'

'Christ, no. We should have a discussion lasting six months and then they'd find it was too late to do anything. Just the same—'

'There's no problem,' said O'Keefe. 'Everything's taken care of.'

There was something exasperating to Henderson about O'Keefe's complacency. 'Don't be so cocksure,' he said in his rasping, old-man's voice. 'Nothing's as certain as all that.' He grumbled, 'I've got a lot at stake here.'

O'Keefe showed his teeth in a smile. 'Sure, Mr. Henderson, I appreciate that.'

'I've taken a lot of trouble to set up this operation. It's got to go right.' He glared at O'Keefe under his heavy brows. O'Keefe thought: the old bastard, what did he do to set it up? That was the trouble with this outfit, you were the one who dreamed up the idea, and then some old front-office dead-beat picked it up and claimed it was his. If it came off he took the credit, and if it blew up in his face it was your fault for talking him into it.

'It's a risk,' said Henderson, almost talking to himself. 'I know that. I'm not afraid of risks. The trouble now, with a big organization like this, everyone's scared to take chances. It's like being in the Government. We're going to show them what can be done if you use a bit of creative imagination. Right?'

'Right,' said O'Keefe enthusiastically. He had to play in with Henderson, there was no alternative. He could not have put the idea through on his own, and certainly none of the other vice-presidents would have looked at it.

Probably Henderson himself would have turned it down five years ago. But now he was coming to the end of his power and influence and he knew it. ISIS had more or less written him off, and it was driving him crazy. He needed another big coup—something that would get him back on to the cover of *Time* magazine. Something that would recall the old days when everything he did was news. The old man wanted to go out with a bang.

Well, a bang was what he wanted too, if he was ever going to get ISIS to take real notice of him. The fact was that they needed each other. He said what he knew Henderson liked to hear. 'The trouble is, they've got too many committees over there in New York.'

'Right,' agreed Henderson. Perhaps O'Keefe wasn't quite as stupid as he had thought. 'I've told them about it over and over, but they take no damn' notice.' He added, inconsequentially, 'Do you know I'm the second biggest shareholder in ISIS?'

'Is that right?' O'Keefe tried to sound impressed. But in fact, he knew ISIS was so enormous, the shareholdings so scattered, that no individual holding was of any significance. The corporation nowadays was a kind of independent, self-perpetuating bureaucratic entity, responsible to nobody.

Henderson sucked with gloomy satisfaction at his false teeth. 'I was the fourth biggest until a year ago. Now I'm the second. That counts for something, you know.'

'Oh, sure.'

'All right then,' said Henderson as if he had terminated an argument to his satisfaction. 'Now, what about this fellow Weldon. Why isn't he here?'

'He's due any time.'

'I wanted to see him yesterday,' said Henderson irritably. 'Why does it take three days for him to get from Rome?'

'Well, it seems he went back to London. Mulholland wanted to brief him—'

'Crap!' said Henderson. He snarled at O'Keefe in the absent-minded way of a man cuffing a dog that had forgotten its place. 'This operation has nothing to do with Mulholland. He's just trying to build himself up.' He added offensively, 'He's not the only one. This organization's full of little men trying to promote themselves.' Then he suddenly tired of bullying O'Keefe. He asked in a normal tone of voice, 'You think Weldon's right for the job?'

'Yes.'

'Why?'

'He has the scientific background, the languages. He's tactful. In the job he's been doing he's accustomed to dealing with this kind of person.' There was no point in telling Henderson that Weldon was currently in disfavour, and that there was a big movement in New York either to fire him altogether or else to put him under Mulholland. It would only worry the old man. Weldon was good from O'Keefe's point of view, since he didn't represent competition. The trick was to sell him just enough to Henderson to justify your own judgement in selecting him, but not so much that he began to sound like a plausible competitor for your own position. He added, 'He's not an executive, of course, no real drive, but we don't need that.'

'He's reliable?' asked Henderson querulously.

'Absolutely.'

'If he isn't I'll hold you responsible.'

God, thought O'Keefe, the old swine. The greatest idea I ever had, the best chance to make myself a name, and he stole it from me. Now he tells me I'm responsible if anything goes wrong. Still, it's not finished yet. Anything could happen. He's an old man, he could fall ill. Maybe even die. He doesn't look so good, God knows. O'Keefe said to himself, willing it to happen: he could fall down dead this very minute.

The orange juice regurgitated in Henderson's throat. He felt a pain across his chest. Indigestion? Heart disease? A chill passed across him. It occurred to him that he could fall down dead, this very minute. It could happen.

Why did he think of that suddenly? This damned climate, probably, this rotten foreign food. He should get back to California, to his horses and dogs, his possessions. What would happen to them if he died? It was an agonizing thought that he would have to pass them on to someone else. He knew now why the old kings had their possessions buried with them. Their treasures, their animals, even their wives. It was right. A king's world should not exist without him. He had a sudden, satisfying picture of a vast funeral pyre, the smoke visible for a hundred miles around, the poisoned land, the slaughtered animals . . .

He was aroused from his reverie by a knock on the door. O'Keefe opened it to admit Sarah and a thin dark man with a faint air of melancholy. Henderson knew instantly that this must be Weldon. He looked at him appraisingly, as he had looked over the years at many thousands of men he had hired to do his bidding. Sensitive, he thought, sensitive and a little overbred. He was like the kind of horse that looked fine and sleek and well-proportioned, a real beauty in the paddock, but carried something in its eyes that told you it wasn't a stayer. He had the kind of dark over-smooth handsomeness that looked rather dated now, calling up memories of Scott Fitzgerald and Bob Montgomery. Henderson took note of the tentative smile, the anxious wrinkles around the eyes, the obvious desire to please. The kind of man you bought. Of course, when it came down to it, you bought most men. And not just simply with money. O'Keefe you could have any time you wanted for the smell of an opportunity, the chance to make an impression, the hope of a bigger job. With Weldon's type you played it softer, a little more understanding. That type of man would work for nothing for a few kind words. You didn't even have to promise them anything. If you played it the right way, they made up the promises themselves.

Then he looked at Sarah. As always on the rare occasions when he met her, guilt tugged at his heart. He thought of her mother, his once-pretty sister, Fran, who had married a Harvard man and watched him die of typhoid in Rio. Now she travelled the world with a new husband twenty years younger than herself, who had never worked and was never likely to do so, so long as the money held out. As for Sarah —she seemed contented enough, she was wealthy, but settlements and trusts were not everything. She needed a family, someone of her own blood. He should have done more for her, but there had been so many other things . . . But it was too late now. There was no use worrying.

He kissed Sarah on the cheek and shook hands with Weldon. 'Glad to see you both,' he said. 'Dr. Weldon, Sam O'Keefe has just been telling me great things about you.' Weldon made a vaguely appreciative sound. 'And you, Sarah, you look fine, but you've lost weight. Have they been working you too hard on *Planet*?'

'Not hard enough.'

'They didn't raise any difficulties about you coming here?'

'No.'

'I didn't think they would. They'll be grateful to me when we're through. Now sit down and be comfortable, and I'll tell you what it's all about.'

He paused, savouring the solemnity of the moment. His

biggest independent operation since Costa Rica. It was almost like a religious ceremony, when you finally lit a fuse and let it go. He said to Weldon, 'Do you know of a Dr. Peter Karas?'

Weldon's heart sank. This was the kind of question he detested. People like Henderson always imagined that if you were a scientist you automatically knew every other scientist, of whatever discipline. He searched his memory but the name alone meant nothing to him. In his early days with isis he would have been panicked by a question like this, but over the years he had managed to develop certain protective mechanisms.

'Well,' he said, 'I don't know him personally, of course . . .'

This was usually fairly effective but for some reason it seemed to exasperate Henderson. 'I didn't expect you to be a friend of his,' he said. 'I wanted to know if you'd heard of him.'

Weldon said desperately, 'It's a familiar name . . .'

'What do you mean, familiar? Have you heard of him or haven't you? Do you know what he does? What his work is?' As Weldon remained unhappily silent, he shouted, 'Well, for Christ's sake, do you?'

'Not offhand, I'm afraid, no.'

'Jesus!' Henderson turned to O'Keefe. 'What the hell is this? You told me this fellow Karas was a famous scientist.'

'He is,' said O'Keefe, glaring at Weldon. 'Hoffman says he is. He knows what he's talking about.'

Weldon pursed his lips dubiously. He had never been very impressed by Hoffman, an excitable German physicist who had managed to sell himself to isis as an expert on scientific developments on the other side of the Curtain. Most of his information turned out to be either common knowledge or actually misleading. But this was no time to start an argument. He said, looking as always for some middle ground, 'He could be well known on the other side, without making much impact over here.'

Henderson glowered. 'Hoffman said he was world-famous. Now it seems our own expert's never heard of him.'

Weldon said, searching desperately for clues, 'Who does he work with?' Henderson gloomily picked up a sheet of paper from the table in front of him. The affair was getting off to a bad start. Never a very patient man at the best of times, in old age he found himself becoming increasingly testy and pessimistic. If Hoffman and O'Keefe were trying to make a fool out of him, God help them. He said peevishly, 'Someone called Suvorin. Have you heard of *him*?'

Weldon's face cleared. 'Naturally. He runs one of the best biological units in the Union. And—' At last memory came to his aid. 'Yes, of course. Bremer and Karas. They've done some first-rate work on bacteriophage. On the genetic side, that is. Bremer in particular. He's a really outstanding worker—'

Henderson broke in. 'Was,' he said shortly. 'He's dead.'

'Oh? I hadn't heard that,' said Weldon. He felt no emotion. To him Bremer was no more than a name on a number of scientific papers. He had never known him personally. He could not see why Henderson should invest the news with such significance. 'How did he die?'

'He killed himself, so they say. But that's not the point. The point is that Hoffman met Bremer at a meeting in Leipzig not very long ago. They got talking. Bremer was an Austrian and Hoffman formed the idea that he was getting homesick for the West. So he made an arrangement to swap books and journals with him. And he told him that if he wanted to change his boss he was to put a certain sentence in one of his letters. A few weeks back Hoffman got a letter from this fellow Karas instead. He said Bremer was dead and that he was coming in his place to the Geneva meeting, just over a week from today. He used the code sentence.'

'So you think he wants to come over?'

'Yes.' Henderson paused. 'Do you think he'd be valuable to us?'

'Valuable?' Weldon thought for a moment. ISIS had a vast research programme ranging from explosives and dye-stuffs through fertilizers to drugs. It had a huge biological institute in New Jersey. It had made use of a great many unlikely people in its time. No doubt it would be able to absorb Karas as well as anybody else. Whether he would want to be so absorbed was another matter. 'You realize,' he said, 'that what he does is pretty well pure science? I mean, it hasn't any strategic implications or anything like that.'

'Of course not.' Henderson waved a hand impatiently. 'That's the last thing we want. If it had, we should have to turn him over to Washington.'

'I can't see how it could be much use commercially—'

'Never mind. That's not the point. The point is,' said

Henderson slowly and emphatically, as if explaining something to a backward child, 'that this man is a scientist who wants to carry out his work in an atmosphere of freedom. We're privileged to be able to give him that opportunity. We have a chance to show him—and to show the world—what a free system can do for a scientist that the other people can't.' He looked round the room and said, grandiosely, in his booming voice, 'That's what we're all here for.'

Weldon nodded reverently; there seemed little else to do. Henderson went on in a more prosaic tone. 'Now, this is how it works. We have a big villa on the other side of the lake. O'Keefe has the arrangements all fixed. He'll get in touch with Karas as soon as he arrives. As soon as Karas can arrange to slip out of the hotel, we pick him up and take him to the villa. The whole thing will be kept absolutely secret. This is our show, remember—nobody else's.'

He paused to emphasize this last point. Then he returned to the details. 'He can stay in the villa while we fix him up with a passport and a visa to get him into the States. It shouldn't take too long. Meanwhile, your job, Weldon, will be to get his confidence, talk to him about his work, you know the kind of thing, one scientist to another. Get all the information out of him you can. Then, when we get him over to New York we'll put him under contract to isis as head of a new research section at Falls Ridge. When it's all set up—in our own time—we'll blow the whole story. How about that?'

He looked about him triumphantly. After a long silence, Sarah said, with a puzzled frown, 'You can really do that?'

'Tell me why not.'

'Well, what about the passport?'

'That's all fixed—don't worry about that.'

She was momentarily lost for words. 'But shouldn't this be a Government thing? I mean, how about Washington?'

His smile disappeared, his old grievances sparked up a flame in his mind. 'To hell with Washington. This is my affair. I fixed it, didn't I? This is neutral territory. If I dare to invite some guy to stay at my house, what's wrong with that?'

'I don't know, but . . . Well, why do it this way?'

'Because I want to.' He spoke like a violent, wilful child. 'This is a valuable man. We need him for isis. If Washington get to him, they'll have him in one of these university institutes, we won't be able to touch him. There could be a lot of money in this.' Somehow he was failing to carry conviction. He became disconcerted at the sight of the two respectful but sceptical faces in front of him. He burst out in anger. 'Hell, this is something we can do. We can show those bastards in Washington. We can show the world.'

He glared at Weldon, demanding some kind of response. Weldon nodded appreciatively. This was certainly no time to start an argument. He wondered dispassionately whether Henderson was going mad. It was quite possible. Men in his position did go mad, just like anybody else. But there wasn't anything you could do about it. You had to play along just the same. With what he hoped was the right amount of awe in his voice, he said, 'It's an amazing idea.'

'Sure it is,' said Henderson aggressively, as if Weldon had been contradicting him rather than agreeing with him. 'The best things I ever did, everybody thought they were crazy beforehand. Everything looks crazy to people who are scared.'

Sarah said, 'How about Karas? Do you think he'll accept this?'

'Sure he will. Why shouldn't he? After all, we've got something pretty good to offer him. Scientists are no different from other people. They like good money, a decent home, security, a nice place to work, good facilities. We could give him everything he wants in that line. Over and above that, we make him a national celebrity.' He smiled at her with the persuasiveness that had made him several fortunes over the last forty years. 'And that's where you come in, Sarah. A series of articles for *Planet*. Something more than ordinary reporting. A study in depth. The analysis of a defector. You know what I mean. His background, how he lived there, what made him feel he had to come to the West. Not just the scientific stuff—the human side. People are going to want to know everything about him. His parents, friends, love life, everything. I tell you, Sarah,' he said earnestly, 'there's a Pulitzer Prize in this.'

His drive and enthusiasm were catching, you couldn't deny that, thought Weldon. It was said that he had got where he was over a heap of dead bodies, and it was probably true, but just the same he had dash, he had fire. He put some meaning into the job. When he began talking it was no longer simply a question of piling one year of cautious service on another, playing it for a nice pension and one of those cute little houses for retired people in

St. Petersburg, Florida. For the first time in years Weldon felt something approaching enthusiasm. Perhaps, after all, this could be what he had been waiting for—something exciting, possibly even historic.

Watch it, he said to himself, suddenly scared at the reappearance of emotions he had for so long managed to suppress. Watch it, you've been had this way before. Genuine full-blooded wholehearted enthusiasm was, he knew, a most dangerous commodity in ISIS. The synthetic variety, of course, was welcomed and indeed demanded. You were supposed to give an appearance of keenness, of adventurous thought, of positive thinking. But at the same time you were expected to be prudent—the Company could not afford to be compromised. And flexible. Enthusiasm, in the Company's view, was a reversible process.

Weldon knew the Company by now as he knew the moods and foibles of his own wife—indeed better. Under its grandiose exterior the Company was fickle and undecided. It set much store by research and forward planning, but when the time came for action it had great difficulty in making up its mind. Once a decision had been made, it demanded total loyalty from its servants, no matter how misguided its policy might turn out to be. The Company was touchy and emotional. It desired passionately to be loved, yet was tormented by a suspicion that outside forces all for this morning. You'll be getting more information against it. It was possessive and demanding, careless of the interests and feelings of others and yet bitterly hurt when they struck back at it. Unconscious of the contradictions of its own attitudes, unaware of its own motivation, it nevertheless complained constantly of being misunderstood.

The Company, in a word, was a woman, while Henderson was without question a man. There was, thought Weldon, a rather alarming contradiction here. Yet so far as he was concerned, at this moment of time, Henderson *was* the Company. You had to go along with him. And if you had to go along, you might just as well get the credit of being a keen supporter. 'It sounds like a real breakthrough,' he said. Breakthrough was a favourite word in ISIS.

Henderson said, apparently satisfied, 'Okay then. That's all over the world disapproved of it and were working as we go along. Hoffman's still in Moscow but he's keeping in touch with me. I'll pass on anything that concerns you. I'll be here for a few days, then I have to go back to the

States. We'll meet again in New York.' He stood up and put out his hand to Weldon. 'It's been nice meeting you, boy.' He put his arm round Sarah. 'Sarah and I are going to discuss family matters.'

When the two men had gone, he said, 'Well, my dear, I'm glad to see you're as lovely as ever.' He added, 'A little too thin, mind you. But I suppose that's fashionable.' He sighed. 'I don't see as much of you as I'd like to these days. It must be—what—over a year—?'

'We're both busy,' said Sarah.

'I suppose so. Just the same—' He said, with an unfamiliar note of apology in his voice, 'I sometimes think I haven't done as much for you as I should have done.'

'You mustn't worry about me. I'm quite happy as I am.'

'Do you see your mother at all?'

'No. She writes occasionally from Hong Kong.'

'It's all wrong,' said Henderson gloomily. 'Everyone needs some kind of a family. When your father died, I should have taken over. But—well—you know how it is with me. So much to do—and then there's Nancy—'

Nancy was Henderson's mistress, an ageing ex-actress who spent her time redecorating his various houses in different parts of the U.S.A. As Henderson grew older she became increasingly obsessed with her prospects of inheriting his money and pathologically jealous of his blood relations. She was the one person of whom Henderson seemed to be afraid. 'Look,' said Sarah, taking him by the arm, 'stop worrying about me. I'm all right. It's lovely to see you again. Don't spoil it by feeling guilty.'

'There's my girl.' Relieved of his obligation, Henderson relaxed. 'As soon as I heard of this affair I thought of you. I knew it would appeal to you. It's a great opportunity for a girl at your stage.'

'Yes. It sounds terrific.' She tried to keep the doubt out of her voice.

'But I'm being selfish as well, of course. It'll be good to have you working with me. And I can trust you.' He looked at her earnestly. 'This is a very delicate business. O'Keefe's a useful man but he's out for himself, not for me. He needs watching. You'll be there to look after my interests. So if anything bothers you, don't hesitate to telephone me, either in New York or in California. This house at the other side of the lake will be in your name. It's better that way. I don't want my name to appear and it would be a mistake to involve ISIS at this stage.' He brooded for a moment. 'This fellow Weldon—what do you think of him?'

'I only met him just now in the lift. He seems all right.'

'Well, watch him, will you?' Henderson said anxiously. 'Stay close to him. Try and find out if he's trustworthy. If he isn't, we shall have to replace him, though God knows there isn't much time.' Now that the men were gone, all his anxieties about the project came to the surface. It was a relief to be with someone to whom it was safe to show them. 'This is a hell of a big thing,' he said, 'and I can't handle it directly myself—that's what makes me nervous. I don't even know this fellow Karas. I can't assess his motivation—you'll have to do that for me.' He pulled himself together and said, with a return to his old confidence, 'But I'm not worrying too much. People want the same kind of thing in the end, no matter who they are and where they come from. The chances are he'll turn out to be pretty much like anybody else.'

CHAPTER FOUR

THE VILLA was a heavy stone-built edifice in the Italian style, set high above the road which skirted the south shore of the lake. Facing on to the lake was a terrace, the stones cracked and the balustrade encrusted with moss, and below it a large garden, which led down to the water. At the back, at the end of the long dark tree-lined drive, was the main entrance, with a heavy square portico which had once sheltered the carriages of the wealthy. The house had a palatial air, as if privacy and dignity had been thought more important than mere beauty, or even comfort. It had been built in 1910 for a minor German royalty, destined only to enjoy it for a few short years. Since then it had passed through a series of hands—a film actress, a financier, a timber millionaire. None had inhabited it for long. Somehow it had achieved no emotional hold over its occupants. For years now it had been empty, with only occasional rentals for holidays or conferences.

The downstairs rooms were large and airy, sparsely furnished with the kind of heavy central European furniture which is cheap to buy because no ordinary house can hold it. The floors were polished and covered with oriental rugs, once luxurious but now turning threadbare. There was a heavy staircase and a gallery looking down on the hall. From them led the main bedrooms, filled with the same clumsy furniture as downstairs and dominated by four-poster beds with heavy plush curtains and thick feather mattresses. Out of these led the bathrooms, each of them large enough to do duty for a bedroom in itself. On the floor above lived the small staff of permanent servants, supervised by the Dietrichs, a silent bulky Swiss housekeeper and her husband who looked after the garden.

A suite of rooms on the ground floor was reserved for an office for O'Keefe, a silent automaton of a typist, and a young man introduced by O'Keefe as 'Keith Walker, my personal assistant.' Walker carried an air of slight mystery, partly stemming from the fact that Henderson had never mentioned him in the preliminary briefing, but rather more from a certain elusiveness about his personality. He was always polite and amiable, but in a curiously characterless way. He was neither tall nor short, particularly fat nor particularly thin, and his accent identified him with no particular class or geographical area of the United States. He wore dark grey executive suits, unobtrusive ties and spectacles with library frames. He spoke very little and seemed content to remain as a shadow to O'Keefe. And yet there was something about him which made this picture seem incomplete. Genuinely colourless men, in Weldon's experience, usually made some effort to make themselves interesting. Only a man of secret resources could be content to remain so utterly in the background. What those resources might be in Walker's case, he had no means of guessing.

There was a period of ten days before the meeting was due to start. Henderson had gone back to California, and O'Keefe was occupied with large and complex plans which involved himself and Walker, and a series of bulky, taciturn young men who turned up in a large black Mercedes for conferences in O'Keefe's office. For Weldon and Sarah there was little to do. They explored the gardens and went sailing on the lake, and when the weather was bad they sat in a glass conservatory filled with potted plants and played gin rummy. Weldon sent to New York for books and journals on molecular biology and spent several afternoons skimming through them and making notes. This was a job at which he was an expert—to take a subject at short notice and cram himself with information on the most recent research, so that within a week or two he could converse on something approaching equal terms with men who had been carrying out experimental work in the field for years.

They all sat together for meals at a long table in the dining-room leading on to the terrace—O'Keefe, Weldon, Sarah, and Walker. Walker said little, but O'Keefe talked incessantly.

'What we have to remember about this guy Karas,' he said, 'is that he's been walled up there for over twenty years, ever since he left Hungary as a boy. He's a great scientist, okay. But he's been starved of all means of normal communication. He's never read a truthful newspaper or seen a play or a movie that isn't loaded with propaganda. He's never spoken to anyone who dared to tell him the truth about what's going on in the world. So he's going to be all screwed up. He's going to be like a kid in some ways.' His imagination soared. He said solemnly, 'I see him like one of those guys that were in Jap P.O.W. camps for years during the war, that had so little to eat that their stomachs just couldn't take good rich food when it was handed to them. The hard cold truth is going to hit this fellow like a pound of filet mignon with French fried onions to a man dying of starvation. He just won't be able to digest it all at once. So we've got to be subtle. We've got to feed it to him gradually. See what I mean?'

Weldon nodded apathetically. Both Sarah and he had come to the stage where argument with O'Keefe seemed hardly worth the energy involved. Inanity succeeded inanity, oversimplification was piled on half-truth to such a stupefying degree that it was impossible to know which one to pick out for disagreement. They had also found that if they did contest any of his statements, O'Keefe had his own methods of dealing with conversational rivals. The most usual of these was to lift his voice a number of octaves and talk right through them. As a variant, he would yawn and look out of the window, or cry, 'Yip yip, good boy!' to the housekeeper's spaniel bitch, which detested him.

He lit a cigarette and went on, 'The other thing is this. All his life he's been taking orders. Told what to do in every little thing. Yes sir, No sir, if you want to argue you can go to Siberia. He's not like us—independent and used to free discussion. The whole situation is bound to be strange as hell at first. If we leave him to take too many decisions for himself he'll feel lost. We've got to guide him, give him psychological support until he can stand on his own feet. And most important of all—' He paused and said with great solemnity, '—let's try not to make life too complicated for him. In his own interests, we've got to give him a clear line to follow. If we start disagreeing among ourselves he won't recognize that it's just our normal exercise of free speech. He'll think we don't know where we're going. It'll just confuse him.'

'What you're suggesting,' said Sarah coldly, 'is that we take up the same kind of attitude that he risked his life trying to get away from?'

It was impossible to puncture his complacency. 'Not at all,' he said. 'You misunderstand me. What I'm suggesting is a gradual process of education. As I said before, this guy is a convalescent.' He added firmly, 'We've got to treat him as such.'

Afterwards when O'Keefe and Walker retired to the office, Sarah and Weldon walked in the garden. The weather was cold and clear. The lake and the sky were of a vivid, almost unreal blue, the snow-capped peaks to the north towered sharply above them. Each night there was frost, which turned gradually into drops of moisture in the thin November sun. Weldon said, 'Would you like to be re-educated by O'Keefe?'

Sarah laughed. 'Do you suppose he'll ever come?'

'Karas?'

She nodded.

Weldon said, 'I don't know. I have no picture of him, really. Supposing he does come, why is he coming? It isn't very clear, is it?'

She said, with a trace of irony, 'He's supposed to be choosing freedom.'

'Yes, I know. But I can't really feel it's as simple as that. I've met quite a few of their men at one time or another. Scientists don't do too badly over there. In an area like molecular biology, there's no real political pressure. Most research workers are pretty narrow in their interests, you know. If they have good facilities and a comfortable life, they don't worry about much else.' He saw a dubious expression on her face. 'You don't agree with me?'

'I've no idea one way or the other. The trouble is that we don't know anything about him at all. He's just a shadow to us. So when we talk about him we begin to generalize. My uncle says he'll be pretty much the same as anyone else.

O'Keefe thinks he'll be a kind of sleepwalker, who'll need months of indoctrination before he can lead a normal life at all. You think of him as just a scientist, interested in his work and the next meal and nothing much else. Perhaps you're all just describing the man you want him to be. But when it comes down to it, he's an individual, isn't he? He may be pleasant or unpleasant, simple or calculating, clever or stupid. We just don't know.'

Weldon nodded agreement. 'And he's equally in the dark about us.' He paused. 'What do you suppose he'll make of us when the time comes?'

'God knows.' She looked round the garden and the house and then glanced at Weldon, slight, sensitive, humorous, ineffectual. She thought of Henderson and O'Keefe and of herself, making an effort to see them all with the eyes of a stranger, a man from another planet. For the first time she saw Karas, not as a victim or an object of charity, but as a judge over them all. In the next few days in this villa, not only themselves but a whole civilization would be on trial. It was a disturbing thought. She said uneasily, 'This is the great decision of his life. He's gambling everything on us. And what are we, after all? Can we be sure that we're better than what he left behind?'

'Not personally perhaps. But surely, if we have a better system—'

'Yes. But just the same—' She struggled to express herself. 'Our system ought to do something for people, shouldn't it? When I think of meeting him, together with people like O'Keefe and Walker—it's as if I had to introduce my family to a stranger that I wanted to impress, and I knew in my heart they were vulgar and greedy and deceitful. Even Uncle John—I admire him and I love him because I know him and I know the life that made him what he is. But to someone like this man Karas, who doesn't know that world—' She left the sentence unfinished. After a pause, she added, 'I just hope he isn't expecting too much.'

A few days later, after lunch, when the servants had cleared away the food, O'Keefe said suddenly, 'Karas is in Geneva.' He paused for dramatic effect. 'He arrived yesterday. From now on, the fun's over. We shall really have to get down to work.'

There was a perceptibly critical note in his voice. It occurred to Weldon that O'Keefe had been watching the walks in the garden and the conversation in the conservatory during the long idle afternoons. No doubt he had been watching with some jealousy. After all, Sarah was not only beautiful and rich, she was also a source of influence with Henderson. O'Keefe had himself made one or two tentative approaches to her but quickly abandoned them on receiving no response.

'I think everyone's been fully briefed,' he said. 'Arthur, you're all set up to talk to him when he comes?'

'Yes,' said Weldon.

'And you. Sarah—you've all the information you need?'

He spoke in the manner of a captain of a team, assuming as a matter of habit the maximum possible degree of authority which could be extracted from the situation. 'I shan't interfere with either of you in the performance of your jobs. You're carrying out an expert function which I'm sure you're competent to handle without any guidance from me. However—' He looked fiercely at each of them in turn. 'There has to be one co-ordinating authority in every operation, and in Mr. Henderson's absence that happens to be me. If any problems arise in these special areas I shall expect to be notified. And if there's any help I can give, I want you to know I'm always here, ready and willing.'

Weldon frowned—O'Keefe's attitude disturbed him. According to his remembrance, O'Keefe's job had been confined by Henderson to the escape and the management of the villa; he had been given no authority at all over himself or Sarah. He had an impulse to remind O'Keefe of this, but he recoiled from the tiresome argument which would ensue. It was possible that O'Keefe had genuinely misunderstood his instructions, or that Henderson himself had given incompatible orders to the two of them (a very plausible hypothesis—it was constantly happening in ISIS). An argument would lead nowhere and would simply cause unpleasantness; if it were referred back to Henderson, he would probably treat them as a group of squabbling children and bang their heads together. Weldon knew that a row would upset him for days, while O'Keefe would probably forget all about it in an hour's time. An imaginative, unaggressive man, he thought bitterly, was always at a disadvantage in a situation of this kind. He lost every fight. The small ones seemed too trivial to bother with, the big ones terrified him with the risks involved.

He had forgotten about Sarah, who had no such inhibitions. She reacted sharply, forcing O'Keefe back into his legitimate frame of reference. 'You can leave our end to us,' she said sharply. 'How about yours?'

'My end?'

'The escape,' she said. 'Have you got it properly fixed up?'

O'Keefe frowned. It was obvious that he took exception to her tone, but she was after all the old man's niece. He decided to let it pass. 'I think we can say the staff work's a hundred per cent tied up,' he said ponderously. 'All we are waiting for is the signal to go. Right, Keith?'

Walker said in his thin, humourless voice, 'We're all set for zero.'

'And when,' said Sarah with slight acidity, 'is count-down?'

O'Keefe hesitated. 'I'm not sure I ought to tell you that.'

She gave an indifferent shrug of the shoulders. 'Okay, then forget it. I only asked out of politeness.'

O'Keefe was visibly disconcerted. It was plain to Weldon that he had been secretly looking forward to giving an account of his plan. This was, after all, the great moment of his career. It would no doubt in due course take an honoured place in his repertoire of stories of brilliant coups in the life of a public relations man. Weldon and Sarah had heard many of these during the past week. The rescue of the lost explorer in the Andes, the marriage of a margarine tycoon in a captive balloon, the launching of a prize for the discovery of the first male contraceptive pill. He was proud of them all, but they could hardly compare with the present operation. Finally the temptation was too much for him. 'Well, maybe you ought to know. Of course you realize that this is in absolute confidence.'

'I take it that those thugs in the Mercedes know your plan,' said Sarah tartly. 'I imagine you can trust me as much as them.'

'Oh sure, sure.' O'Keefe retreated quickly. He said to Walker, 'Okay?' Walker nodded assent. 'Well, this is how it goes.' He adopted the tone of a general briefing his troops before battle. 'As I said, the delegation touched down in a special Aeroflot plane at noon yesterday. They're staying at the Schwartzwald Hotel—that's a smallish hotel, some-what old-fashioned, down by the lakeside. They have one wing at the Schwartzwald allocated to them. They registered at the meeting yesterday afternoon, then went to a concert together in the evening. This morning at nine o'clock they left for the Palais des Nations. They stay there all day at the conference, then they attend another reception at their own embassy. Tomorrow another conference, then another reception given by the organizers of the congress. Next morning, 10.35 hours, they take off for home.'

He took a fat green cigar out of his breast pocket and began to peel off the celluloid wrapper. 'That's their programme. Now for ours. The doorman at the Schwartzwald is on our payroll. He was given a note to smuggle to Karas inside his morning paper. We have to be careful because Karas is never alone. He shares a room with another scientist called Varkany. The doorman has reported to us that Karas got the note; so he knows who we are and where we are, and what our plan is to get him away. The plan goes into operation this afternoon.' He looked at his watch with a slightly theatrical gesture. 'In exactly ninety minutes' time.' He paused and turned to Walker. 'Keith, would you get me the map?'

Walker went through to the office and came back with a roll of cartridge paper under his arm. He and O'Keefe spread it out on the dining-room table, weighting the corners with ornaments from the sideboard. It was a detailed scale plan of the Palais des Nations. Walker handed O'Keefe a pointer and he began to explain, tapping the plan with his stick. 'Here,' he said, 'are the small committee rooms, where the various sub-groups of the conference spend the first part of the afternoon. At 15.30 they leave these smaller rooms and all collect together for a plenary session in the large hall. There's always a certain amount of confusion at this point. There's a bottleneck here at the entrance of the hall, which will be made worse by the fact that somebody'—he smiled craftily—'has by an oversight forgotten to unlock one of the available entrances and misplaced the key. Karas will be momentarily separated from the others in the crush. My men will form a barrier round him and he'll be rushed down a narrow side staircase—here—the top of which will be instantly blocked by a waitress dropping a whole tray of coffee cups. My men will be helping her to pick them up.'

He moved over to another part of the plan which dealt with the courtyard and gardens. 'When Karas gets to the bottom of the staircase he'll come out into a driveway where a car will be waiting. This car will carry the number plate of a high official of the World Health Organization. We have a forged pass to get him out of the Palais des Nations and then he'll be driven straight here. If all goes well he should be here between four o'clock and half-past.'

O'Keefe beamed round at the luncheon table, clipped the end of his cigar with a gold cutter, and rolled it between his lips to moisten it. The others remained silent. Weldon was impressed, despite himself, by the thoroughness and detail of his plan. At that moment, the doorbell rang. It was a loud, clamorous bell which reverberated through the empty hall. Then they heard the housekeeper's military steps moving across the hall and the creak of the door on its hinges, followed by the sound of voices. A moment later the door of the dining-room was opened and a man stood in the doorway. He was tall and large boned, with a long face and a slightly crooked nose. His clothes were baggy and unfashionable, his collar crumpled and his overcoat slightly frayed at the cuffs. Yet he looked around at the assembled company, not diffidently like an intruder, but with the sharp curiosity of a naturalist confronted with some new and exotic specimens. As his eyes came to Sarah they stopped for a moment in appreciation and a smile crossed his lips. He touched the heels of his clumsy black shoes together in a slightly caricatured gesture of formal greeting. Then he nodded his head to O'Keefe at the head of the table.

'My name is Karas,' he said. 'I believe you're expecting me.'

CHAPTER FIVE

THERE WAS quite a long silence. O'Keefe put down his pointer with a clatter on the table. He seemed, for once in his life, speechless. Weldon was the first to recover. He got up from the table and walked over to Karas. He gave him a smile of welcome and shook him by the hand.

'This is a wonderful surprise,' he said. 'We didn't expect you so early. It's a most exciting moment for us.' Karas nodded formally. He returned Weldon's smile, but in a guarded way. Weldon's sensitivity to atmosphere told him instantly that though Karas might give the impression of control, he was nevertheless a man under great strain. He visualized himself in Karas's position—confronted, after the harrowing experience of his escape, with a group of strangers in this outlandish house in a foreign country. He searched for some way of making contact, of breaking through the wariness and caution which he saw in Karas's eyes. 'My name's Weldon,' he said. 'You won't have heard of me but I know your work very well.' The expression on Karas's face showed no change. There must be some way, thought Weldon, of getting through to him. An idea came to him and he decided on impulse to take a chance. 'Max Bremer mentioned you when I met him at the Leipzig meeting.'

'Max?' The tension on Karas's face eased noticeably. He became a little less wary. 'You knew Max?' he asked eagerly.

Weldon nodded. It had obviously been a good idea. In fact he had never met Max Bremer in his life but he knew Max had been at the Leipzig meeting and he could bluff his way through. 'It was just an acquaintanceship really,' he said. He wasn't anxious to push it too far. 'We shared a table at the university restaurant one day. A very talented man. I was sorry to hear that he had died.'

Karas said, 'He spoke of me?'

'Just momentarily.' Weldon knew better than to over-elaborate. 'I asked him who else was working in his field at the Centre.' Weldon paused for a moment and then said, 'He spoke very well of you.'

Karas said with a faint smile, 'That was like Max. He spoke well of everybody.'

Weldon took Karas by the arm and led him towards the table. It had been a tiny but impressive demonstration of his skill. A stranger walked unexpectedly into the room and within less than a minute he had managed to create an atmosphere of something approaching old friendship. 'Let me introduce my colleagues. Sarah Manning. Miss Manning is a well-known American writer.' Weldon had a tendency to over-sell people slightly when introducing them. 'Sam O'Keefe. Mr. O'Keefe is responsible for the arrangements of your escape. And Mr. Walker—' Weldon couldn't quite think of an explanation for Walker.

Karas shook hands with them all. Weldon, still acting as host, said, 'Sit down and have a cup of coffee.'

At this point O'Keefe finally broke the silence. Frowning, he said, 'Dr. Karas, we're all very glad to see you, of course, but there's something I can't figure out.' There was a querulous, almost suspicious note in his voice. 'The time sequence is out of whack. How did you get here?'

Karas said casually, as if it were a matter of little importance, 'I took a taxi.'

'A taxi!' O'Keefe's voice rose in outrage.

'Yes,' said Karas. 'After all, why not? I received your note, which told me where you were. It seemed by far the quickest way to reach you.'

The explanation seemed to increase rather than allay O'Keefe's agitation. 'But if you got my note you knew what my arrangements were. I told you to go to the meeting at the Palais des Nations. Then, when you came out of the first session—'

Karas interrupted. He responded to the aggressive note in O'Keefe's voice with an increase of his own air of indifference. 'Yes, I know all that. But I could see no point in all those complications. It was much easier this way.'

O'Keefe said indignantly, 'But that was the arrangement! It was all fixed. I have half a dozen men down there now. They'll be looking everywhere for you. There's a special car, forged passes—'

'Well, I'm sorry—'

Karas's voice said plainly that he was not really sorry at all, that he regarded the original escape plan as a piece of childish melodrama and O'Keefe's manner as impertinent. O'Keefe began to lose his self-control. He said angrily, 'Can't you see you've ruined everything? Hell, we went to all this trouble to get you out. Why couldn't you follow instructions?' When Karas did not reply, he grumbled on, 'My boys won't know what the hell to do. They might easily get caught.'

Sarah said, 'Forget it, Sam. We wanted him here and we've got him. What does it matter how he came?'

O'Keefe turned on her. 'With all due respect to you, Sarah, you don't understand a goddam thing about security.' He brooded for a moment and then said to Karas, 'How did you get away from the guard?'

'There was no guard.'

Walker's cold, nasal voice cut in with startling clarity. 'Our information was that you would be accompanied everywhere by the man who shared your room. Someone called Varkany.'

'He wasn't a guard, he was a friend of mine. A fellow scientist.'

'He wasn't there to keep watch over you?'

'How do I know? Can you ask a friend a thing like that?' Karas said reluctantly. 'I suppose he probably was asked to keep an eye on me. It was my first trip to the West.'

'How did you get away from him?'

'I just told him I'd forgotten something and had to go back for it. Then I slipped out the side way.'

O'Keefe was incredulous. 'And he fell for a trick like that?'

Karas took a sip of coffee and then put down the cup as if it tasted cold and sour in his mouth. 'I suppose he trusted me.'

Suddenly all Weldon's instincts warned him of the presence of danger. A little more conversation with O'Keefe and Karas would be regretting his decision to defect. Already, Weldon could see, Karas was being troubled by thoughts of the friends and colleagues he had left behind him in the Schwartzwald Hotel—whatever their political views, they at least spoke his cultural and scientific language in a way O'Keefe never could. Weldon saw himself in Karas's position, at the culminating point of months of tension, fear and self-doubt. In such a frame of mind a man could be panicked by any little thing. He needed gentle, careful handling. Instead of which, within minutes of entering the house, he was involved in a petty squabble about the arrangements for his escape. It was his urgent duty to break it up.

Weldon said to O'Keefe, with an unusual air of command, 'I don't think these details are of any importance. The main thing is that Dr. Karas is here. This must have been a most exhausting experience for him and we ought to give him a chance to rest. We can talk at our leisure later this evening.' He looked at Karas and was rewarded with a glance of gratitude. His intervention had come just in time. He smiled reassuringly. 'Perhaps you'd like me to show you to your room.'

When they were going up the staircase, he said, 'You must excuse O'Keefe. He spent weeks planning a very elaborate escape for you. I'm afraid you made him look rather foolish.'

Karas laughed and Weldon realized with relief that the crisis was over. Plainly he was a man of some resilience. 'I think he must have been reading too many spy stories.'

'I shouldn't be surprised.' Weldon felt an instant liking for the other man. Then he felt ashamed as Karas said warmly, 'It's good to meet someone who knew Max. I don't feel quite so much of a stranger.'

Weldon instinctively tried to move the conversation away

from Bremer. 'Oh you'll soon get to know us all very well.' He took Karas into the bedroom on the first floor which had been prepared for him. It was, like all the main rooms of the villa, spacious and rather grandiose, with elaborately patterned wallpaper and a chandelier of Venetian glass. Two full-length windows gave out on to a balcony looking over the garden. 'I hope you'll be comfortable. We've tried to provide everything you might need. If there's anything else, you have only to ask.'

Karas glanced around the room. He said with faint irony, 'It looks quite palatial.' Weldon had the impression that physical comfort was of relatively minor importance to him. Karas said, 'You are a scientist yourself?'

'I trained as a biologist. But I'm not in active research any more.'

Karas did not, to his relief, ask him how long it was since he had done any laboratory work, or what his publications were. Instead he said, 'Where did you train?'

'In London. University College.'

Karas looked at him with sudden interest. 'You're not American?'

'No. All the others are, as you probably realized. But I'm English.'

The next question surprised him. 'Tell me,' said Karas, 'are you familiar with Kensington Gardens?'

'Yes.' He was a little puzzled. 'Everyone in London knows it.'

'My father was there many years ago. He stayed in a little hotel in—what is it now? The Bayswater Road.'

'Yes. That would be it.'

Karas said, 'Are they much changed, those gardens? Does the band play on Sunday afternoons, the way he described it to me?'

'Yes. I suppose it does. Of course, it's a little while since I've been there.' He watched Karas walk over to the window and look out on to the garden. 'I hope you won't mind staying here for a week or so,' he said. 'We have to organize your passport. I take it you didn't bring one with you?'

'No. They are kept by the head of the delegation.'

'That was what we anticipated. We shall have to get photographs and a specimen signature.' He tried to sound as casual as possible. 'To avoid publicity we've arranged for you to travel under the name of Paul Stratton. I hope you don't mind that.'

Karas, to his relief, seemed unconcerned. 'If you think it necessary—'

'I'm afraid it is. Your people might well raise something of a hue and cry. And the other thing is that while you're waiting here for the formalities to be fixed, Miss Manning —you remember meeting her downstairs?'

'Yes, of course.'

'She's a journalist and if you agree she'd like to ask you some questions. But that can wait until tomorrow. Meanwhile,' he said, 'I'm sure you'd like to be left alone. If there's anything you want, just let me know when you come down and join us later.'

Before he left the room he looked once again at Karas's dark angular figure as he stood pensively looking out of the window. This, he knew, was the most important job of his career—to understand this man, to gain his confidence, to anticipate his every thought and desire. He must be constantly with him as a reassuring presence, yet never be so obtrusive as to get on his nerves. Always, in all circumstances, he must steer him gently in the direction which Henderson had laid down for him.

He had never thought it would be easy. Now, in a moment of insight, he realized that the whole project was hopelessly unreal. He knew little of Karas as a person, he had no knowledge of the circumstances which had brought him to this present place at this particular time, but even a short conversation was sufficient to reveal how unfitted he was for the passive role planned for him by Henderson. For a little while, perhaps, under the influence of an environment completely strange to him, he might be malleable and ready to fall in with the plans which had been made for him. But it would be a mistake to rely on that for long.

Meanwhile he was to be Karas's friend. It was his job. The friendship had been bought and paid for; it must be supplied according to contract. And if the occasion so demanded, it would have to be withdrawn as easily and quickly as it had been given, or used as a disguise for deception or betrayal. The contract covered that too. Weldon was overcome with a sudden pity for Karas; or indeed for any man who had to face the world with no better friend than himself.

CHAPTER SIX

THE NEXT DAY Karas was awakened by the sun forcing its way through a gap in the heavy velvet curtains. For a moment he lay half-asleep in the unfamiliar bed, wondering where he was. He blinked and looked around him, expecting to see the familiar outline of the wooden walls of his own bedroom at home, with the picture of the bearded political demi-god on the wall to his right. Instead, there was an elaborate Italian chandelier and a dressing-table mirror surrounded with gilt cupids. In a moment, he realized where he was.

He got up and opened the windows. There was frost on the glass, but when he opened the casement the air was crystalline. He could see across the garden over the thick copse to the ice-blue lake. Beyond this the mountains rose like painted scenery. They were not remote or shadowy, like the mountains he remembered looming over the vast plain at home, carrying within them all the remoteness of Asia itself. They were blue and familiar and approachable, mountains for climbing, and ski-ing, a background for pictures in a fashionable magazine. To the left lay the town of Geneva—and the Schwartzwald Hotel, in which slept the colleagues who trusted him and whom he would never see again.

He looked at the chair where he had left his clothes the previous night. It was empty. The pyjamas he wore had been provided for him. They were the correct size but with a design rather too colourful for his taste. On exploring the bedroom, he found a pair of slippers and a silk dressing-gown. The wardrobe contained a row of suits on rails, as light in weight as if they were to be worn in the tropics, but of dark material and discreetly cut in the American fashion. The chest of drawers was filled with socks and underclothes, handkerchiefs, and white shirts with soft collars. There was a row of sombre ties hanging on a brass rail, and three pairs of black shoes. On the table in the centre of the room were three packets of cigarettes, one European, one American plain, and one American with filter tips; there were also several books of matches and a packet of chewing-gum.

The private bathroom which adjoined the bedroom was

dominated by a vast white tub with claw and ball feet and a mighty pair of brass taps at one end. Arrayed on the shelves and dressing-table were soap and toothbrush, shaving tackle and an electric razor, talcum powder, deodorant and after-shave lotion. Enormous white towels hung on racks, warmed by the hot pipes. Karas turned on the bath taps and watched the water thundering into the bath. Then he stripped off his pyjamas and regarded himself in the mirror. He looked first at the tough muscular body, then at the face, already at thirty-five prematurely lined. It occurred to him that the naked body he saw in front of him represented the sum total of everything he had brought with him into this new world. At the half-way point in his life, he was like a child born again. He had no money or friends or influence. He had no real knowledge of the tasks confronting him. He was completely penniless and alone.

Yet at least he knew what to expect of himself. The real unknown factor lay in the other occupants of the house, these strangers he had come so far to meet. As Karas lay in the bath, he cast his mind back to the previous day. He had spent the rest of the afternoon with Weldon, talking about his escape and the details of his life at the Centre. He had taken an instant liking to the Englishman. He had no illusions about Weldon's strength or importance or even about his quality as a scientist, but these things seemed to him of minor importance. What he needed most of all at this stage was a little warmth and understanding, a touch of elegance and civilization—and these he had found in Weldon. It occurred to Karas that the organizers of the escape could not be entirely stupid, if they had managed to guess his mood so accurately.

Weldon had said to him at one stage, 'You were unhappy at the Centre?' He spoke like a man really anxious to understand. Karas found himself floundering in his answer. He had found his mind going back to that strange period of just over a month after he had taken his decision to defect. On Sophia's advice he had rewritten his report, inventing some plausible nonsense which poor Pilic was at this moment fruitlessly trying to confirm. And from that moment the clouds which had hung over him were immediately dispersed. Suvorin had beamed upon him. Leskov had offered ponderous congratulations. Zabergan had completely forgiven the insults thrown at him. Pavlov had escorted him, with abject apologies, to the special dining-room. It was plain to him beyond possibility of doubt that the other scientists at the Centre were overjoyed that he had returned to favour. It was impossible not to be touched by their friendliness and to feel a sense of shame at the deception he was practising on them. He could not help but imagine their present disillusion at what they would certainly regard as his treachery, and their disgust when they discovered the truth about his report.

He lay in the bath for a long time. When he finally made his way down to breakfast it was after ten o'clock. The dining-room was empty, except for Sarah, who was sitting over a cup of coffee reading the Continental edition of the *New York Times*.

She smiled at him and pointed to the sideboard. 'There's bacon and egg on the hot-plate,' she said. 'Did you sleep well?'

'Very well.' He helped himself to food and poured out a cup of coffee and brought it to the table.

'I hope that's what you like to eat,' she said. 'We didn't know if you were used to something a bit different.'

He laughed. 'Caviare? Blinis? Sweet champagne? Not for breakfast, I think. Anyway,' he said, looking down at the lightweight charcoal-grey business suit, 'they would hardly go with my new clothes.'

'Yes, I see what you mean. I must say I think the button-down collar is going a little far. O'Keefe might have let you work up to that.'

'He's a very thorough man.'

'He tries.' She sighed. 'God knows he tries.' She lit a cigarette. Incidentally, I hope you won't imagine all Americans are like O'Keefe.'

'No?' He looked up from his breakfast with interest. 'He's really much what I expected.'

'That's just cold-war propaganda. At least I hope it is. I wouldn't like to think it were true.'

He buttered a piece of toast. 'This is a very beautiful house.'

'Well, it has something, I suppose. But you wouldn't call it exactly homey.'

'You have been living here long?'

'No,' she said. 'Not very long.'

'I find it extremely comfortable.' He smiled. 'The United States Government is generous with its employees.'

'Well—' she said awkwardly. It was going to sound like a pretty weird story to a man who had spent his life behind the Curtain. Still, it had to be explained sooner or later. 'We're not exactly employed by the U.S. Government. This house belongs to my uncle. He's a very rich and influential man. He heard your story from one of his agents—'

'My story?' asked Karas sharply. 'What story?'

'Well, I don't know exactly. Just that you wanted to get away, I guess. So he decided to help you.'

Karas frowned. 'This is a little difficult for me to understand. Why should he want to help me? He knows nothing about me.'

'Why should our Government help you, if it comes to that?'

'I could understand that,' he said. 'They'd do it for politics. Propaganda, to show that people wished to escape from the socialist system.'

'Yes. Well, I suppose my uncle's motivation's pretty much the same when you come down to it.' She looked at him carefully. 'I hope that doesn't offend you.'

'No. Why should it? I hate the socialist system. And I'm most grateful to you all.'

'Fine.' She felt a sense of relief. She realized now that all the time she had been a little scared of Karas, fearing that he might be difficult and suspicious and might resent being written up for *Planet Magazine*. Now it looked as if the whole thing might go smoothly after all. 'We'd certainly like to have your confidence, because we want to help you all we can. As I'm sure you understand, getting away is just the beginning. You're here without a passport in a neutral country. The Swiss don't much like these escapes—they find them embarrassing diplomatically—so we have to lie pretty low. As soon as we can, we'll get you to the United States.'

She saw a slight frown pass across Karas's face. Had she said something wrong? She pressed on quickly. 'But I'd like to talk to you about my own part. I work for one of the big international magazines—*Planet*. You may have heard of it.'

'The name is familiar,' said Karas.

'What I'm hoping,' she said, 'is that you'll give me a series of interviews so that I can write a story about you.' She had rehearsed the approach—articulate but sincere, not too slick or she would put him off. 'I don't mean an ordinary newspaper story. What I would like to do is something in the nature of a biographical study. We'd go into your general

142

background, the life you led at the Centre, your reason for coming here, what you think about science and the cold war and so on.' She said, trying not to sound too anxious, 'How would you react to that?'

Karas thought for a moment. He had the feeling that matters were moving rather more quickly than he would have wished. From the very beginning he had been aware of the danger that if these people organized his escape they might assume that he was their property, to use as they wished. He had no desire to antagonize anyone, but he was cautious.

'It's very kind of you but—I feel I'm hardly the person for this. I'm not at all important, you know. My life and opinions are really of no significance.'

For a moment she wondered if he was indulging in mock modesty. Then she realized he was quite sincere. She laughed. 'I can see you don't understand about Western journalism. You don't have to be eminent. If you're reasonably young and photogenic and you have done something unusual, that's quite enough. You may not realize it, but your story is an absolute natural. Ten million people will fight each other to read it. If you're not famous now, you will be afterwards.'

He thought for a moment. 'Is that good?'

'If one's going to be realistic, yes of course it's good. I don't know how it is where you come from, but in the West the thing that beats most people is that nobody's ever heard of them. A name that rings a bell in the public mind is the most convenient marketable asset there is. I can turn you from an anonymous laboratory worker without a penny in his pocket or a suit of clothes to his back into a man the whole world wants to meet.'

She paused, slightly disgusted with herself. It was the kind of approach that they taught you at *Planet* for dealing with a difficult subject, and practically speaking it always worked. Ordinarily speaking, she found it fair enough. The subjects were usually seeking reassurance and you gave it to them. What you didn't bargain for was somebody who sat and listened to you the way Karas was doing now, not discounting the sales talk at all but studying your words as if they could be nothing but the honest truth. She said hurriedly, 'But don't let me talk you into it. If the idea doesn't appeal to you—'

He said, 'What would it mean exactly?'

143

'You just sit and talk to me. I ask you questions about one thing and another, and if you want to answer them you do; if you don't, you don't. We have a tape-recorder going, and later I transcribe the tape and use it as the basis for my articles. I show you the rough draft for comment and criticism. If there's anything you don't like, we can cut it out then.' She smiled at him. 'How about it? Is it a deal?'

He thought for a moment. It would really be unreasonable to refuse, after everything that had been done for him. 'All right. When would you like to start?'

She had been about to suggest that same day, but she realized in time the danger of giving him the feeling of being rushed. 'You're entitled to a day off,' she said. 'How about tomorrow morning?'

She spent most of the rest of the day with him, trying to put him at his ease so that he would feel less inhibited when the interview began. He asked questions about life in the West, about herself and her own background, but it was plain to her that his knowledge of the world outside his own country was far wider than any of them had expected. Certainly O'Keefe's picture of him as a man liberated with an almost virgin mind from a prison camp was ludicrously far from the mark. In many ways he seemed little different from any man of his age in the West who had spent the last fifteen years in the cloistered atmosphere of an academic research centre. Yet the resemblance was not complete. Behind the easy breadth of culture, the humour, the rather formal courtesy, there was a toughness she had not encountered before, an ever-present acceptance of the world as a dangerous and potentially hostile place. He lacked the insipid, theoretical approach which had always made her impatient with American and European academics. He had the inherent dignity conferred by hard practical experience. As his character began to emerge in conversation she felt a sense of excitement at the possibilities offered to her for her article. Here at least was no pompous tycoon or promiscuous ballerina. Perhaps Henderson had been right —at last there was something important for her to do.

The next morning after breakfast she took him into the morning-room, where she had set up the tape-recorder. When they were seated on opposite sides of the table, she took out a few notes she had already made and put them down in front of her.

144

'Now, I want you to relax. Remember this isn't a formal interview. Nobody's going to hold you to anything you say. To start with it's really a question of filling in background.' She glanced at her notes. 'I have a few biographical details about you but not many. You were born in Budapest?'

'No. In Györ. It's a small town about fifty miles west of Budapest. My father was a schoolmaster there.'

'What did he teach?'

'Modern languages.'

'You speak excellent English. Did you learn it from him?'

'Yes. And German also. He would talk to me all the time in foreign languages. It was a kind of game. Also my mother spoke German. She was half-Austrian.'

'You lived later in Budapest?'

'Oh, yes. We moved there when I was five. That was a few years before the war.'

'Why did you move?'

'My father got a better job.' A shadow passed across his face. 'At least he said it was better. Now I think it was just that he wanted to get to the capital.'

'Why?'

He said wearily, 'Politics. Everything was politics in those days.' He looked at her and said, 'How old are you. Twenty-five?'

'Twenty-six.'

'You were born in 1941—in America. You don't know how lucky you are. It's really impossible for you to understand how things were then.'

'I've read about it, of course.'

'Reading about it is one thing—' He sighed. 'Politics destroyed everything. Your friendships, your love of your country, your feelings for members of your family. You take my father, for instance. He wasn't a very effectual man. But that didn't matter when I was small. He was kind to me, he gave me sweets and played with me. In those days we were just two individuals who accepted each other. But then, after we went to Budapest—' In his memory he saw his father, small, pedantic, not very successful, trying to face up to the big city. He was ashamed of his own intolerance. 'Looking back, it was partly my fault. Children expect too much. I began to see him in the context of other people. It was obvious to everyone that what he was trying to do was hopeless. I suppose he suspected it himself. But it was hard for him to realize that I knew it too.'

'What was he trying to do?'

'I don't think he really knew. He was one of those vague idealistic Social Democrats. He and his friends used to hold meetings and pass resolutions, but nothing ever really happened. My mother used to laugh at him and tell him he was wasting his time.'

'She wasn't interested in politics?'

'Good heavens, no. She was a plump, cheerful, rather extravagant woman. At the beginning that is. My father used to worry about everything but she would tell him that life was short and that he ought to make the most of it. It didn't have much effect on him because, as things were in those days, everything always turned out even worse than he thought it would. So gradually she became quieter and quieter and I could see that she was beginning to worry too. Even when I was a small boy and didn't really understand anything, you could feel in the atmosphere that things weren't right in Hungary. Then my father began to get into trouble.'

'For what?'

'For nothing very specific. As I gather, the Government didn't bother people like him too much at first, but as the Nazis became more influential, they turned the screws a bit. I remember whispered arguments between my mother and my father about what he ought to do. He was a member of various committees. You know the kind of thing—preservation of civil liberties, protests against anti-semitism and all that. They didn't do any good, of course. My mother wanted him to resign and play in with the school authorities. Part of him agreed with her, but on the other hand he felt he'd be selling out. I remember him saying, in that anxious way of his, "But, Magda, could I go on respecting myself?" She got a little tired of it after a while. After all, he wasn't very important—one had to face that. He wasn't hurting the Government—only himself. He got the message in the end and did what she suggested.'

'Did he regret it?'

'I don't know. He didn't talk about it to me. Maybe not even to my mother either, after he had done it. And soon after that, Hitler attacked Russia and he was called up for the army.' He paused, and then said, 'And the ridiculous thing was this. He had a murmur in his heart and he could have got out of it—but he wouldn't tell them. Can you understand that?' His voice rose in something like outrage, and then with an effort he controlled himself. 'He was killed in the Ukraine in 1943.'

There seemed little to say, and she remained silent. Karas went on. 'He was a loser, you see, that was the point. It was something within him, I suppose. Even when he died, he was killed fighting for something he didn't believe in.'

The uselessness, the absurdity of it came back to him as he spoke. It had not been so much a tragedy as a ghastly practical joke which fate and the forces at work in their lives had played on them. Surely, in death at least, a man should have a little dignity. He tried to explain. 'If he'd decided not to be a hero, the least he could do was to survive. Survival may not be heroic. But it has a kind of meaning in itself.'

'Does it?' she said.

There was, he fancied, a slightly doubtful tone in the well-bred voice. She had a way, he noticed, when anything was said which disturbed her, of leaning her head back a little and half-closing her eyes which gave her a withdrawn, supercilious expression. He felt a flash of resentment. He would not be judged and patronized. His voice took on the harsh, dogmatic tone that he used when he was angry. 'Yes, of course it does. Survival shapes the future. What no longer exists, no longer matters. That's a biological principle.'

He thought of Max, who in destroying himself had denied his own creed; who had, like his father, abdicated responsibility and left the future to others. Then he looked at the girl, who in her silence seemed to criticize him for what he was saying. He was overcome with impatience for her American romanticism, founded on money and privilege and a world in which the individual, if he was rich enough and the right colour, was sacrosanct. What did she know of the hard, hungry years, when men lived and fought like wolves; of the cold, alien life in the Centre, when a single false step meant the end of a lifetime of work and struggle? It was a tame world she had lived in. The fight for existence had no meaning for her. He wondered now why he had agreed to the interview. It was impossible for them to understand each other. He passed a hand across his forehead. 'I feel a little tired,' he said. 'Would you mind if we stopped for a while?'

'Of course.' Her voice was sympathetic and he wondered if perhaps her disapproval had been a product of his imagination. She turned off the recording machine. 'That's enough for today. We can start again tomorrow.'

The next day he felt better. He said as they sat down together at the table, 'I'm sorry if I was a little curt yesterday. I somehow formed the idea—' He found it difficult to go on. 'It's hard to explain. But in my kind of life nothing has been very easy. One has to improvise, to do the best one can. Theoretical considerations become difficult to apply. It tends to make you sensitive to criticism.'

'Yes. I do see that,' she said seriously. 'Truly, I understand.'

He looked at her, at the soft, groomed skin, the fashionable clothes, the manicured hands. But in her face there was a serious childlike expression which touched him. She badly wanted to understand, she genuinely thought it was possible. It would be cruel to destroy her belief. 'What shall we talk about now?' he said.

'Well, if you don't mind—' She said tentatively, as if fearing a rebuff, 'After your father died . . .'

'All right.' He paused, casting his mind back. 'Well, after that it was pretty hard. We didn't have much money. My mother had to go out to work. They took her on as a clerk in a Government office. She hated it. She was always saying she hadn't been brought up to work. And as the war went on, everyone got very scared. Because we knew that if the Germans lost we were going to have the Russians and we'd heard about them in Poland. Then they came—in the winter of 1944. That was a terrible time.'

He stopped for a moment, remembering. It had been the kind of thing you had never believed could happen—and it had happened. Then once it had begun, you had thought it would never stop—but it had stopped. That was the lesson time taught you—that time was always the victor in the end. But always, before the end came, there were casualties.

He said, 'My mother died that winter. We were short of food. The flat was miserably cold. It was funny—she had always been rather a soft woman. She wanted fun and pleasure and clothes and she used to feel very sorry for herself at the way things had turned out. But that winter she stopped complaining altogether. She went out and worked and begged for food and fuel and patched my clothes and kept me alive. She was scared stiff, of course. But it was as if things were easier for her, now she knew the old world would never come back and that there was nothing to hope for really, except to keep alive from day to day. There was a sort of simplicity about it. In a kind of way we had happiness we hadn't had before. Then the influenza epidemic came and she caught pneumonia. There wasn't any penicillin in those days.'

'How old were you then?'

'Fourteen. Luckily I was a clever boy, and the new director of my school had known my father. They put me in a hostel. That was quite a privilege. We had hot soup and bread and sometimes potatoes—you could live on it. And whatever one might think about the Communists, at least they were interested in education. So I was lucky really. I did well in my examinations and got a place in the University. I graduated as a biochemist in 1951 and then I went to work under Krassner. He was interested in cell structure, particularly from the biochemical point of view. So I started to work on that.'

He began to speak more quickly and confidently. The weight which had been pressing on his mind throughout the discussion of his personal life was lifting. Once he could confine the conversation to his work, and matters relating to it, he felt more at ease. He started to describe his various research projects under Krassner, simplifying them a little to make them more comprehensible to someone unfamiliar with the technicalities of science. She listened to him attentively. At the end she said, 'And did this all lead on to your present research?'

'Indirectly. It was over ten years ago, of course, and the emphasis of this kind of work has changed a lot since then. As we got to know more about the detailed structure of the cell, chemistry became more and more important, and that was very lucky for people like me. We were in a good position to understand the implications of the new developments. There weren't many of us available and so all the big units were looking for us. And, of course, we needed the kind of facilities that only they could supply.'

'That was how you got to the Centre?'

'Yes. I had become known in my own particular field and Krassner thought well of me. My published work had attracted some attention. And at this time Suvorin came on a visit to Budapest. You know about Suvorin?'

'The director of the Centre?'

'That's right.' He tried to describe Suvorin in the way a stranger might describe him, a man whose life had not been irrevocably changed by the vagaries of that brilliant, suspicious mind. 'He's a remarkable man in his way. He's always fallen short of really important creative work himself, but he has an unusual talent for bringing out the best in others.' And the worst too, thought Karas regretfully, but he did not say it. 'He took over the Centre when it was nothing at all and built it up so that the whole world knew about it. When we met, he took to me straight away—he was always impulsive in his dealings with people. So he tried to persuade me to come to the Centre. Krassner was almost ready to retire and he recommended me to accept the offer. So I went.'

He spoke casually, as if describing any ordinary situation in which a young man was offered a job and decided to take it. That, he had almost succeeded in persuading himself, was all there was to it. Now they could go on. She could ask him about the Centre, the people, the work he did there. He could give her the story he had prepared about why he left—nothing to do with Max or the letter, of course, or Sophia. Just a general dissatisfaction, a desire for a freer atmosphere, a rebellion against restraint. He had it ready for her, just as he had had his reason for leaving Budapest ready. This was an article for a newspaper, it was not an inquisition, he did not have to defend or explain himself to anybody . . . But the next question was not what he had expected. She glanced at her notes and looked up, frowning a little. 'You didn't mind leaving Hungary?'

He shook his head. 'There was nothing much to leave. I had no relatives. My parents were dead—'

'No, I didn't mean that.' She seemed reluctant to go any further and yet unable to stop herself. 'You went to the Centre in 1957?'

'Yes.'

'You were in Budapest the year before?'

He felt his heart thumping within his chest. He knew what was coming now. He realized that it had been stupid to hope he could avoid it. 'Yes, I was there.'

'During the uprising?'

'Yes.'

Her head was slightly tilted back, in that critical way that had angered him the day before. The cool, detached voice asked, 'Did you take part in it?'

'No. Not at all.' He spoke firmly, almost angrily. What did a girl like this know about anything? He would not excuse himself to her. 'You must understand that I'm not a political person. Not in any way.' His voice rose. 'I'm a scientific worker—'

'Yes, I understand that.' The change in his manner alarmed her, yet something drove her on. 'But you must have had some feelings about it.'

He shrugged his shoulders. 'I thought they were foolish. I did not believe it was possible to win against the Russians. Only fools fight when it is impossible to win.'

'Were any of your friends involved in the uprising?'

'Of course,' he said shortly.

She asked, 'Were they killed?'

'Many of them, yes. Some in the fighting, some executed. Others escaped into Austria.'

She said, in a voice filled not so much with censure as with disappointment, 'And you took no part at all?'

'No.' There was a short silence then he asked harshly, 'You're waiting for me to explain—to apologize?'

Perhaps, in some way, this had been what she was hoping for. But she said, 'No.'

'Good.' He added defiantly, 'I've no intention of excusing myself.'

'Please,' she said, 'don't think I'm blaming you. I can sympathize with what you all went through. I didn't say you ought to have done anything. I just wondered what you felt—'

'About what?'

'Oh, about the Communist Party—your Government—'

He sighed impatiently. 'I keep telling you I'm non-political. The Government was there. It was a fact. It was also stupid, inefficient and tyrannical—like every other Government anyone could remember in Hungary. Was I expected to do something about that?'

'No. No. I suppose not.'

He felt a sudden nostalgia for the Centre, where at least everyone understood about matters of this kind. It was part of their common knowledge, their common fear—they had developed a kind of tact which prevented them touching the delicate points of one another's shame. He said bitterly, 'They wasted their lives, those young men. They are dead and they changed nothing. This is not a world for heroes, believe me.'

'Yes,' she said sadly, looking away from him out into the garden. 'Yes, I've been told that before.'

CHAPTER SEVEN

EACH MORNING they sat at the table with the tape-recorder between them, picking up the threads of his life, unwinding them a little, dropping them when she felt resistance arising in him, but coming back to the loose ends when the opportunity offered. The longer they talked together, the more difficult he found it to keep any part of his life to himself. Each event they discussed led either forward or backward to another; an area that he had sealed off from one direction was approached by some other avenue which he had failed to anticipate. He became increasingly reluctant to talk about himself. He formed the habit of terminating the interviews after a fairly short time and going off by himself for walks in the grounds of the villa.

He began to resent all the trappings of his new way of life. He discarded the fur-lined suède jacket with the beaver collar which had been put out for him on arrival and retrieved from the housekeeper his own overcoat, a long dark grey double-breasted military looking garment with a high collar and sleeves that came half-way down to his knuckles. He was aware that it looked antiquated and rather absurd in his present context. And yet he found a kind of comfort in it which was missing from any of his new possessions. It had been bought with money he had himself earned, it had warmed to his body in past winters, it held memories, it was his own. He clung to it as if it were the only aspect of reality which remained to him.

The days passed slowly. Each evening they sat down to dinner in the great dining-room. The first euphoria of the escape had left them all now and they waited impatiently for Karas's passport to come through. As he became increasingly taciturn, conversation became more difficult. On O'Keefe in particular, the strain began to tell. He had begun by treating Karas with a kind of determined good-fellowship. He had told him jokes and stories, he had tried to bring him out of his shell by kidding him along a little. When none of these devices had met with any response, he had turned morose and sulky. Each night he drank a little more than the last. He began to brood over his grievance about the escape, and blame Karas for the fact that one of his men, in the confusion caused by the non-arrival of Karas at the Palais des Nations, had insulted a U.N. official and got himself arrested.

They were sitting over the remains of dinner one night after Sarah had left to go to her room. O'Keefe suddenly said, 'We still haven't been able to get Rieber out of jail.' He made the statement like an accusation. 'It's a hell of a business, I can tell you.'

'It was his own fault,' said Weldon.

'It wouldn't have happened if everyone had followed instructions.' O'Keefe looked round, as if hoping for an argument. When nobody spoke, he seemed to give up the idea. He swilled the brandy round in his balloon glass and sniffed it noisily. 'This is the real stuff all right.' He turned to Karas and said, 'You like it?'

Karas gave a polite nod. 'Excellent.'

For some reason O'Keefe seemed to find a disparaging overtone in the word. 'I should damn' well think it is,' he said aggressively. 'This is Armagnac, boy—the real stuff.'

Weldon was momentarily exasperated. 'As a matter of fact,' he said, in a small cold voice, 'it's not Armagnac. It's Cognac.'

O'Keefe's small eyes opened a little wider. He almost seemed to be pleased at the challenge. Were the troops planning mutiny? If so, he was in the mood to deal with it. 'Cognac be damned,' he said. 'Do you think I don't know the difference?'

'I wasn't talking about you,' said Weldon. 'I was talking about the brandy. I'm certain it's Cognac.' Exasperated by the scornful look on O'Keefe's face, he said, 'If you don't believe me, let's look at the bottle there on the sideboard.'

He was about to get up but O'Keefe waved him back. 'No, wait a moment. Let's have some fun. You say it's Cognac.' He took out his wallet. 'I have fifty dollars here says it isn't. How about it, Art?'

Weldon looked at him with the special kind of loathing he reserved for men who addressed him as Art. Nevertheless, he hesitated. He was not afraid of losing, but he could imagine the rage O'Keefe would be in if he lost. Then he noticed O'Keefe grinning triumphantly at his hesitation. 'All right,' he said, 'if you insist.'

O'Keefe took a fifty dollar bill from his wallet and tossed it on the table. 'Cover it, fella.' Weldon took a bill from his own wallet and covered it. 'Now we'll go and see who's correct.' O'Keefe pushed his chair clumsily back, scraping it on the marble floor. As he did so, Karas spoke for the first time. He said, 'You lose, Mr. O'Keefe. It is Cognac.'

It was like a challenge. O'Keefe turned on him. 'What the hell do you know about it?' He pointed to Karas's glass. 'Don't tell me you're used to drinking this kind of stuff.'

'Of course not. The brandy in my country is terrible. I do not pretend to be a connoisseur.'

'Okay then—'

O'Keefe spoke with the air of a man who has scored an easy victory. Just as he was about to turn back to the side-board Karas said, 'But I'm sober enough to read a label on a bottle. It's Cognac.'

There was an appreciable silence. Then O'Keefe turned back to the table and moved menacingly towards Karas. Weldon got up rapidly. 'Look, Sam, let's call this thing off. It's not important—'

O'Keefe shouted, 'Is he trying to say I'm drunk?'

'Of course not.' Weldon looked pleadingly at Karas. 'That wasn't what you meant, was it?'

'No. I simply said—'

'I know what you said,' bellowed O'Keefe. Another thought struck his mind. 'You saw the label when I poured out the brandy?'

'Yes.'

'And you let me go ahead and take a bet with Art, knowing I was bound to lose?' He was overcome with a sense of genuine outrage. 'Is that your idea of a straight deal?'

Karas said, 'You never asked my opinion.'

O'Keefe looked at him with disgust. 'Jesus!' By his standards, evidently, an unforgivable piece of deception had been committed. He said to Weldon, 'Okay, take your lousy fifty dollars. If you need it that badly—' There seemed to be an inference somewhere that the whole episode had been a plot between Weldon and Karas to humiliate him. 'I suppose it's the kind of thing one has to expect—'

So far, Karas had managed to preserve a certain detachment from the situation. But now he felt an anger rising within him which he could not restrain. The strains of the last few months had almost exhausted his capacity for self-control and the interviews with Sarah had brought to the surface emotions which had upset him more than he cared to think. At the back of his mind was an increasing fear that he might have made an appalling mistake. What was he doing in this ridiculous villa, utterly at the mercy of a group of strangers, and subjected to the taunts of a drunken buffoon? He said coldly to O'Keefe, 'What exactly do you mean by that?'

O'Keefe shrugged off the question. 'Forget it,' he said. 'You wouldn't understand.'

'I'm afraid that's not good enough,' said Karas. 'When I came here, it was under the assumption that I should be treated with courtesy and respect. I put myself in a position of dependence. I must ask you not to exploit it by insulting me.'

'Hey, wait a minute!' O'Keefe's voice rose in outrage. 'I want to remind you of one or two things. This whole operation has been laid on especially for your benefit. It's costing Mr. Henderson maybe a hundred thousand dollars. Perhaps it's too much to expect gratitude but at least I think we're entitled to a little co-operation. And what do we get? You won't follow instructions. You screw up our whole plan—'

'It was a ridiculous plan,' retorted Karas. 'Nobody who knew his job would have made it. It was dangerous and unnecessary. If I had followed your instructions I should have been arrested too, as well as your friend Rieber. You should be pleased that I had sufficient sense to avoid that.' He said with disgust, 'I had no idea, when I agreed to come here, that I should be putting myself in the hands of amateurs.'

'Amateurs!' cried O'Keefe. Plainly Karas had struck him on his tenderest spot.

Before he could say anything further Weldon intervened. 'I don't think that's really fair—'

At the sound of his gentle, reasonable voice, Karas's anger subsided. 'I wasn't referring to you—or Miss Manning. You've been very kind and I appreciate it. But I have to make something absolutely clear. There's been talk of gratitude. Well, of course, I'm grateful to you—you've been a great help to me. But so was Suvorin in his time. Generosity means nothing if it's just an effort to possess somebody. I thank you very sincerely for what you've done. But I don't belong to any of you. Or to your Mr. Henderson with his hundred thousand dollar investment.' He stood up from the table and walked towards the door. 'Perhaps you'd better tell him that.'

After the door had closed behind him, O'Keefe said bitterly, 'The bastard.'

'He's not really, you know,' said Weldon. 'I admit he has his difficult side—'

'The trouble with you, Art,' said O'Keefe, 'is that you're a nice guy.' There was a trace of contempt in his voice. 'You want to think well of everyone.'

'No, it's not that.' Weldon was wondering how to handle the situation. Somehow he had to prevent O'Keefe from losing his head. He was fairly confident of his ability to make Karas see reason, so long as he was left alone to do so. He said carefully, 'We've got to try to understand him. We have to remember the strain he's under, the background he comes from—'

'Background hell,' said O'Keefe. 'He doesn't give a damn for us and never has. It's been like this ever since he came here.' He brooded over his grievances. 'That screwy business of arriving here in the cab. Ignoring orders. Breaking all our security. Looking down on us. Acting as if he owned the joint.' He said fiercely, 'I tell you, Art, I know this kind of guy. He's nothing but trouble.'

'I've spoken with him a lot. I think you misunderstand him.'

'Oh sure, he plays up to you. Plays you off against me.' His resentment seemed now to be taking in Weldon himself as well as Karas. 'Listen, Art, I know you think this is a personal thing between him and me, but it's not just that.' He made an obvious effort to sound calm and judicious. 'One of the things I'm supposed to study here is this man's general attitude. And I'm telling you right now that I don't like it. I don't like it at all. Look what we've done for the guy. The trouble we've gone to. The dough we've spent. And what do we get for it?'

Weldon said delicately, 'I think it's a question of handling. You see, Sam, Eastern Europeans, particularly Hungarians like Karas, are very different from us.' He tried to think of a flattering way to put it. 'They're not so direct. They're very proud and sensitive. What you may regard as good-natured ribbing they're liable to take the wrong way.'

'What, for instance?'

'Well, when you keep asking him how it feels to be a free man again, and telling him how much more money everyone earns in the West—all that kind of thing. I know you don't mean any harm by it—'

'Christ, it's the truth, isn't it?'

'Yes, but just the same—'

'I'll tell you something, Art,' said O'Keefe earnestly. 'You're a smart fellow, but you're off-beam here. This guy isn't sensitive—he just doesn't like us.'

'I don't think so.'

'Believe me,' said O'Keefe with confidence. He thought for a moment. 'And there's something else that bothers me. Do you know the Russians have never let out a word about this escape. It might never have happened.' He looked suspiciously at Weldon. 'Doesn't that seem odd to you?'

'Not particularly.'

'Well, it does to me.' He was about to say something further and then stopped himself. 'How about all this stuff he was giving us just now? What do you think he's really getting at?'

Weldon tried to think his way into Karas's mind. He thought of the things Sarah had told him about his reactions to the questions in the interview, the hints Karas had dropped to him in the conversation. He remembered the odd little inquiry Karas had made when he had first shown him to his room, about Kensington Gardens and the band playing on a Sunday afternoon. He tried to picture himself in Karas's position, a man with a dream of peace and ease and non-involvement, trapped in this gloomy villa with a group of strangers, cross-questioned about his past life, confronted with a man like O'Keefe. It was hardly surprising that he had taken fright for a moment.

'I can't be sure,' he said. 'The fact is, we haven't handled him properly—none of us. We all took it for granted that he'd be so grateful for what we were doing that he'd fit in with everything we had planned for him. But after all, he doesn't want to escape from one prison to another. We need to stop hustling him. Take it easy. Regain his confidence.'

O'Keefe looked dubious. Then he gave in. 'Okay, play it your way and see how it goes.' He cheered up a little. 'In the meantime, he still hasn't got a passport. He can't move far without that.'

CHAPTER EIGHT

WELDON drummed his fingers nervously on the window-pane. 'Look at him now,' he said.

Sarah came to the window and looked out. Karas was walking in the garden alone, as he often did in the afternoon. He was wearing his old grey overcoat with the collar turned up against the wind. His hands were crammed deep into his pockets and he did not look up at the house or at anything around him. He might have been alone in the middle of a vast, desolate plain.

'You see what I mean?' said Weldon. 'A happy man doesn't walk like that.'

'It hasn't been easy for him,' she said.

'I know. I know.' His sympathies, like hers, were with Karas. Yet the dominant impulse in his mind was self-preservation. Somehow Karas must be prevented from ruining them all.

The responsibility for coping with the present crisis was, he knew, his and his alone. He had been chosen to get close to Karas, to befriend him and give him confidence, and he had so far failed in his task. Karas's sense of isolation was now only too evident. He had kept to his room all morning and taken his breakfast and lunch on a tray. Now at last he had ventured out, but in such a way as to discourage all human contact. Ought one to leave him alone for a while, to grapple with his own problems? Or would it be better to approach him and have the whole thing out? He could not make up his mind.

'We've got to get in touch with him again,' he said, talking as much to himself as to Sarah. 'Just now he seems to have a plate-glass barrier around himself.' He pondered for a while. 'It's a question of the best way to do it. I was wondering'—he looked at her diffidently—'if perhaps you might be the best person to make the first approach.'

'Well—I don't know. If you really think so—' Weldon relaxed a little. From her tone he knew that she would try. Between them they might be able to manage it. If they could only keep him away from O'Keefe . . . He looked again at the gaunt figure in the shabby overcoat, passing along the gravel path under the window of the great drawing-room where they stood. It was curious how the coat seemed to draw Karas back into another world, to remove him almost physically from their grasp. For a few days it had seemed that they had been near to an understanding with him. Now he was a stranger again.

At the end of his circuit of the garden, Karas's pace quickened, as if he had taken some kind of decision; abruptly he turned to the left and walked past the side of the house. Weldon said, 'Where do you think he's going?'

'What does it matter?' she exclaimed impatiently. 'He's not a prisoner, is he?'

'No. No—of course not.'

Weldon did not sound too confident. She watched him twisting the signet ring on his white, delicate finger. There was a frowning, worried look on his face, which always irritated her a little—it was surely wrong that a man should live his life in a state of such anxiety. She said, 'What he said was right. We don't own him. He's a free agent.'

Weldon shook his head despondently. 'I don't think you really understand.'

'Yes I do,' she said. 'But really, you mustn't be too afraid of my uncle, you know. Apart from anything else, it only provokes him to behave badly.'

It was his turn to be impatient. 'That's the sort of talk one always hears from people who aren't really involved.' He spoke with an unusual degree of authority. This was a subject on which he had no doubts, no uncertainties. 'It's no use a person like myself trying to stand up to Henderson. I have no weapons. He uses me to do something, and if for one reason or another I don't do it he'd break me without a thought.'

'You're exaggerating. He's not like that at all. He may sound ruthless at times—'

He was angry with himself. How had he become involved in this humiliating discussion? Yet like the courtier he was, he kept his anger within him. 'Perhaps you're right,' he said. He forced a smile, to terminate the conversation, but it was a tense, sad smile, a smile which confessed his impotence more than anything he might ever say. Sarah tried to think of some way to encourage him, but she could find no words that would not have sounded insufferably patronizing. Then she saw that Weldon's attention had left her, that he was looking over her shoulder. She turned round and saw O'Keefe standing in the doorway. He wore an angry, yet at the same time a triumphant expression, in the way of a man who has predicted disaster and seen his fears fully realized.

'What did I tell you?' he said. 'What did I tell you? I knew we couldn't trust that guy.'

Sarah felt herself stiffening with instinctive resistance. 'What are you talking about?' she said.

'Karas.' In some way he seemed to consider he was scoring over the pair of them. 'You know what he's done? Just now they phoned in from the lodge. They caught him trying to get away.'

Weldon was incredulous. 'Get away?' he said. 'Where to?'

'I don't know yet. Naturally they held him there and got in touch with me. I told them to bring him back to the house.'

Weldon was about to speak but Sarah broke in to forestall him. She said coldly, 'On whose authority?'

He regarded her for a moment like a boxer assessing the fitness and capacity of a future opponent. He said deliberately, 'Listen, I hold the responsibility here. Henderson told me—'

She said icily, '*Mr.* Henderson.' She was pleased to see a shadow of indecision pass across O'Keefe's face. She went on, 'As I heard it from my uncle, you were instructed to arrange the escape. Did anyone tell you to keep him a prisoner?'

Uncertain of himself, O'Keefe blustered a little. 'This is crazy. You don't understand the problem. If he walks outside this garden the Reds could get him. Or he could be picked up by the police.'

'That's his affair. He's old enough to know what he's doing—'

'Oh, sure,' said O'Keefe sourly. 'Sure, he knows all right. He knows plenty.'

'What do you mean by that?'

'He's a real smart cookie. He didn't need any help to get away from that delegation. All he had to do was to walk out and nobody took any notice.' He said contemptuously, 'Do you believe that?'

'Why not?'

'They may be stupid on the other side, but they're not that stupid. If you want my opinion, the whole thing smells. Why haven't they announced that he's defected?' His voice rose. 'If you ask me, he's a double agent.'

'Don't be absurd, Sam,' said Weldon. 'You've been seeing too many movies.' Yet the doubt, once suggested, sapped a little of his self-confidence. Less certainly, he said, 'We're not dealing in secret information here. It doesn't make sense.'

O'Keefe too seemed to feel the necessity to retreat from an extreme position. 'Well, I can't claim to be an expert on the scientific side. I'm only a layman—'

'Your job was to arrange the escape,' said Sarah. 'You've done that. Now it's Arthur's responsibility. Isn't that so?'

160

Weldon shifted uneasily. He knew it was true, but it was frightening to hear it put so bluntly. 'Well, I suppose, technically.'

'That was my understanding.' She said to O'Keefe, 'If you want to check with my uncle—'

She left the sentence unfinished, like a threat. She could feel O'Keefe's hatred like something physical in the room. Her pity for Weldon increased. She knew that this was the kind of situation he had struggled all his life to avoid. But surely he must realize there was no way of escape? There were obvious risks in accepting responsibility. But he would certainly be damned for evading it.

There was the sound of footsteps in the hall and a moment later Karas threw the door open and entered the room. He stood there for a moment, wary, savage and alert. He closed the door and said coldly, 'It's time we settled a few things.' He walked to a chair and sat down. 'Firstly I want some information. Am I to understand that I'm imprisoned here?'

Sarah started forward apologetically. 'It's all been a mistake,' she said. 'Those men at the lodge exceeded their instructions. We'd like to apologize—'

'Apologize hell!' broke in O'Keefe. He glared at Karas. 'It was I who gave the order that you shouldn't be allowed out of the gate. I did it in your own interests.'

'It is for me to decide my own interests,' said Karas.

Weldon intervened. 'There is a certain danger, you know,' he said in his slow, reasonable, gentle voice. 'I don't suppose the other side have taken very kindly to your escape. They might well be waiting for you.'

'Out in the road?' said Karas contemptuously.

'It's possible. Just because they're lying low it doesn't mean they've accepted the situation. They may well know that you haven't left Switzerland. They may even have discovered where you are. Surely it makes sense to be careful?'

Karas thought for a moment. Then he said decisively, 'What you're saying doesn't make sense to me. I have to come out in the open some time. I can't hide all my life.'

'No, obviously not,' agreed Weldon. 'We're not suggesting that. It's just for a week or two, while you're here. Once you get to America—'

Karas interrupted him. 'That's another thing,' he said. 'I've been thinking it over. I don't think I want to go to America.'

As soon as he said the words, Weldon knew that this was
what he had been secretly dreading from his first meeting
with Karas. This was the crisis of the whole affair. If he
failed to keep his head now he was finished. He heard
O'Keefe's cry of rage and spoke quickly to keep control of
the conversation.

'What's the trouble?' he said. 'Why have you changed
your mind?'

'I haven't,' said Karas. 'It was an assumption of yours
that I wanted to go to America. Nobody ever asked me.'

'But hell!' said O'Keefe. 'The whole arrangement—'

'It was your arrangement, not mine. I'm very grateful for
it, of course, but I'm sure,' he said, with a trace of irony,
'that you wouldn't want to bind me to anything in return.
I gathered from Miss Manning that the whole thing was
done out of pure generosity on Mr. Henderson's part. Isn't
that true?'

'Yes, of course,' said Weldon quickly. If only O'Keefe
would keep quiet, the situation might still be saved. 'Perhaps this was an error on my part. I should have discussed
it with you.' He said sympathetically, 'I see your point.
But I'm afraid that it isn't really possible.'

'Why not?' said Karas. 'You're always telling me how free
I am, now I'm in the West. Well then, I'm free to stay in
Europe.'

'But why? What have you got against America?'

'Nothing in particular. But after all, I'm a European. Is
it so strange that I should wish to stay in my own
continent?'

'But—' Weldon had a vision of Henderson's reaction to
the news that Karas had decided not to come to America
after all. It was too dreadful to contemplate. He shook his
head helplessly.

'Why are you so distressed?' said Karas. 'You tell me you
want nothing from me. Mr. Henderson wanted to help me,
that was all. Why should you care whether I come to
America or not?'

The only thing to do was to give way, at least temporarily.
Weldon said, 'Of course, it's entirely your own choice—'

'Is it hell!' O'Keefe could contain himself no longer. He
turned on Weldon. 'Listen, Art, I'm not agreeing to this.
We've done everything for this guy. We've fixed an escape
for him, we've looked after him, given him food and
clothing. And now that he's made use of us he wants to walk

162

out on us. If you think Henderson's going to stand for that—'

'Mr. Henderson has no alternative,' said Karas. 'He can hardly wish to imprison me indefinitely. And if he doesn't—' He shrugged his shoulders.

'That's just a load of bluff,' said O'Keefe. 'How far could you get without us? Not a dollar in your pocket, not a spare suit of clothes, no passport. All you've got is that god-damned overcoat, and that's ready for the incinerator—'

Karas said to Weldon, 'Who is in charge here?'

'I am.'

Karas said tightly, 'Then tell this fool to shut up.'

O'Keefe moved towards Karas, balancing slightly on the balls of his toes. He looked very large and very dangerous. He clenched his hands and said, 'Stand up and say that again.'

Karas remained in his chair, his coat lying open, his legs crossed, the toe of his right shoe tapping up and down very slowly. He seemed completely unmoved. He said to Weldon, 'I mean it. I'll talk to you. I'll talk to Henderson if you like.' He waved a hand at O'Keefe. 'But get him out of here.'

Without haste he uncoiled himself from the chair and stood for a moment in front of O'Keefe, regarding him without obvious emotion. Then he smiled at Sarah and walked out of the room.

There was a short silence. Then O'Keefe said, 'The lousy little Red.'

'It was your own fault,' said Sarah. 'You provoked him.'

'I provoked *him*! Jesus, that's good. He's been needling me since the moment he walked in this house. If I ever saw a guy who's looking for trouble—' He clenched his jaws together. 'Okay, if he wants trouble I can give it to him. If he thinks he can push us all around—'

Weldon frowned and put his hand to his forehead. 'Just stop talking for a moment, Sam. I've got to think.' He sat down and stared out of the window at the gathering dusk. 'I understand how you feel, but when it comes down to it, personal issues aren't important. We have to consider what Henderson wants.'

'Well,' said O'Keefe, 'there's an easy way to find out.' He walked to the telephone. 'I'm going to ring Henderson now and tell him what's going on here.'

A sudden note of command came into Weldon's voice. 'I wouldn't do that, Sam.'

O'Keefe stopped on his way to the telephone. 'Why the hell not?'

'For your own sake,' said Weldon. 'Believe me, it would be very dangerous for you.'

O'Keefe wavered. Despite himself he was impressed by the confidence in Weldon's manner. 'Why?'

'Try to put yourself in Henderson's place.' Weldon spoke with the easy command of the expert. When it came to assessing the psychology of power he had no doubts about his own judgement. 'He doesn't care a damn about any of us personally. Whether we're nice or bad guys, right or wrong, it means nothing to him. He has no interest in Karas personally either. But Karas is important to him, he needs him. He can't do without him. You—' He made an apologetic gesture. 'He can replace you any time he cares to snap his fingers. Who do you think is going to win the argument?'

He could see that his words had carried conviction. The rage died out of O'Keefe's eyes, to be replaced by a kind of primitive caution. 'Okay,' he said. 'So what do we do then?'

'Well,' said Weldon slowly, 'let's look at it this way. If Karas refuses to go to the States, he's cutting off his nose to spite his face. We can't force him to go, it's true. On the other hand he's in an impossible position without us. He can only wreck our plan if he's prepared to ruin himself as well—'

'That's what I told you,' said O'Keefe impatiently. 'He's bluffing.'

Sarah shook her head. 'He's not bluffing. He's not that kind of man.'

'How do you know?'

'I know,' she said.

Weldon frowned. He was always distrustful of these simple explanations of human motives. 'I couldn't be sure myself,' he said. 'But anyway it's a mistake to go by guess-work in a matter like this. His attitude might change from hour to hour. The important thing is to keep in contact with him and find out what he's thinking.' He turned to Sarah. 'As I said earlier, I'm sure you're the one to do that. If anyone can persuade him to trust us, you can. Try to convince him that whatever he thinks, we're not against him, that we're really on his side and only trying to help him.' He was almost pleading. 'I'm sure he'd listen to you.'

She was still reluctant. 'Well, perhaps.'

'I'm sure this is the way to do it. Especially if you could somehow demonstrate—' He thought for a moment. 'I tell you what you could do. Why not take him out for a drive —you know, give him a feeling of freedom, showing him that he's not trapped. You wouldn't be in any danger in the car. You might even have dinner out, somewhere quiet round the other side of the lake. It might give him back his sense of proportion.' He gave her one of his gentle smiles. 'Would you do that for me?'

'All right. I don't see why not.'

'That would be wonderful.' As she got up to leave, he said, 'You can get the keys from Walker, and I'll tell them at the lodge to let you through.'

When she had gone, O'Keefe said menacingly, 'I suppose you realize the responsibility you're taking?'

Weldon nodded. 'I think so.'

'If you want my opinion, I think you're crazy. You're going to sit here for days without telling Henderson, just waiting for this guy to make up his mind? Is that what you're planning?'

'We've got to take it slowly,' said Weldon. 'Get him to relax. Show him the advantages of doing what we want. That's the only way to do it.'

He spoke with as much confidence as he could muster but he was aware that his words had failed to convince. O'Keefe shook his head sceptically. 'We'll see,' he said. 'We'll see.'

CHAPTER NINE

THE WHEELS of the big car kicked up the gravel from the drive as Sarah put it into gear and pressed her foot down on the accelerator. It roared down through the avenue of chestnuts to the end of the drive. When she drove up to the lodge, one of the two guards came out and opened the gates for her. He was a thickset young man in a dark blue suit, his jacket pushed out of shape by the guns strapped to his waist. He gave her no sign of recognition.

She turned the car to the right down the hill towards Geneva. She was still accelerating hard and she took the first corner with the speedometer touching eighty kilometres an hour, with the back wheels skidding on the dead leaves and just pulling back on to the asphalt a few inches short of the ditch. Karas was thrown sideways and gripped the door-handle in an attempt to steady himself.

'What are you afraid of?' he said, with a note of amusement in his voice.

'I don't know really.'

In the light and comfort of the villa, O'Keefe's stories of arrest or kidnapping had seemed absurd, but now she could not put them aside quite so easily. As the light of the headlights gave way to the darkness of the hedges which rimmed the road, she saw shadows behind every tree that could mean an ambush or a waiting assassin. She said, 'I'll be happier when we get on to the main road.'

At least, she thought as she looked through the driving mirror, there seemed to be nobody following her. The road, so busy with tourists in summer, was silent in the November dusk. Most of the villas were shuttered and silent, their gardens blanketed with mist. The lights of the town were only a mile or so away round the corner of the lake. A few minutes' fast driving would bring them to the main road leading from Geneva to the Mont Blanc tunnel.

When they reached the main road it was almost an anticlimax. She turned right, slowing her speed as she slipped into the traffic which poured over every afternoon from Northern Italy. Soon they were in Geneva. The neat, traffic-crammed streets were glistening with the wet, and the policemen were wearing mackintosh capes. A light rain was falling. She threaded her way through the traffic and took the road to Lausanne which skirted the northern border of the lake.

Karas sat in silence, huddled up in his overcoat. After a while his immobility began to oppress her. 'I suppose you're very angry with us,' she said.

'Not with all of you.'

'I think you are.' She paused for a moment to pass a small convoy of slow traffic. 'I've seen you like this before when you're angry. You put a barrier round yourself. It's as if you wanted to hold your anger inside yourself—to be alone with it.'

'Perhaps,' he admitted. He tried to explain. 'I've lived a very hard life, compared with yours. In dangerous situations silence is often a great help to survival. After a while it becomes a habit.'

'Do you think you're in a dangerous situation now?'

'I'm not sure,' he said. 'It's easy to make the mistake of

166

thinking people are working against you when in fact they're simply concerned with their own convenience.' He added, 'That was how it was with Suvorin. He saw enemies everywhere. In fact it was plain to all of us that these people he feared so much cared little about him one way or the other. They attacked him because he stood in their way. If he had moved out of their way, they would have forgotten him.' His mind returned to his present problems. 'What worried me this afternoon was that O'Keefe might be reacting emotionally towards me. You can't predict what a man will do under such circumstances.'

She said, 'You worry him to death. He's quite unable to understand you. He thinks you may be a Russian agent.'

He was suddenly shaken by robust laughter. 'I'm glad you told me that,' he said. 'That was very good for me.'

'Why?'

'Because it's so ludicrous. I was very angry about that business at the lodge, and now I can see it in proportion. It was just stupidity. One has to remember that,' he said. 'In every situation, no matter how tragic, however large or small, the most likely explanation of every human activity is simply stupidity.' He laughed again, softly and not unkindly. 'I believe in the stupidity theory of history.'

They drove for a while in silence. Then he said, 'This is a beautiful car. What is it?'

'A Mercedes 300. They're almost as fast as the Italians, and more reliable.'

'You drive it very well. Is it yours?'

'No. Sam hired three when we took the villa.'

'You live in great style.'

'I suppose so. Do you object?'

'Why should I?'

'I don't know.' She thought for a moment. 'I suppose it's with you coming from the other side. We have the idea that you are all rather puritanical.'

'You mustn't believe your enemy's propaganda,' he said. 'Most of us are much the same as you. Some of us crave for possessions—others for power. Some want adventure and freedom. Others prefer security. Of course, the opportunities are rather different over there.'

'And you?' she asked. 'What do you want?'

'That's a little complicated,' he replied. 'If I'm to be honest, I like possessions. I like good food and clothes, I like comfortable living. I'd like a car like this. But then so

167

would most people. The real question with all of us is how much we are prepared to pay for them.'

She knew that, in a roundabout way, he had introduced the subject which she was there to discuss. Yet she felt instinctively that it was too soon—it would be too crude to try to reassure him now that he would not be asked to pay an excessive price for anything he received. She drove on in silence. A few kilometres past Nyon she turned left off the road and began to zig-zag up the side of the mountain. With each hairpin bend the lake began to drop a little farther below them. 'Where are we going?' he asked.

'There's a restaurant up there on the mountainside. We can sit there and drink and watch the boats on the lake. Then have a little dinner if you like. I thought it would be good to get you away from the villa for a little while.'

He nodded agreement and she turned her attention back to the problem of steering the big car up the narrow twisting road. Eventually she rounded the last bend and the restaurant appeared in front of them—a building in chalet style with terraces cut in the hillside. As she parked the car she opened her bag and said, 'By the way, I forgot to give you this.'

She handed him a piece of plastic, the size of a visiting card, with his name and various other numbers and hieroglyphics stamped on it. He said, 'What is it?'

'It's an ISIS credit card. All you have to do is to present it and then sign any bills for anything you want to buy. The bill goes to ISIS. You can use it in the restaurant here, for instance.'

'Thank you.' He put the card in his pocket.

'Don't feel inhibited about using it,' she said. 'ISIS money isn't like real money. It's unlimited, it belongs to nobody, you can accept it without obligation and spend it without feeling extravagant. It's an entrance ticket to the affluent society.' He nodded his understanding. He seemed impressed neither by the easy invitation to luxurious living nor by the dependence on ISIS implied by the possession of the card. They went into the restaurant and were led by the *maître d'hôtel* to a closed-in terrace facing on to the lake. A tired, gnome-like waiter in a white jacket brought them glasses of vermouth. Karas looked out of the window. Far below them he could see the lights of Geneva and the moving dots of boats plying up and down the lake. She said, 'It's a beautiful view in the daylight.'

He nodded and then said, 'This is a strange country. So grand in some ways—yet so tame. It's as if man had built the mountains for his own convenience.' Unconsciously he turned his eyes towards the east. 'Where I come from we have mountains too. But not like this. There's a great plain, that stretches away for ever to the north. Lakes, forests, then a thousand miles away the hard frost and the nights that last for ever. You can feel the winds that blow down from there. The sky is huge above you, full of enormous white clouds, rolling away over the wilderness to God knows where. And to the east and south, the mountains. They're huge and heavy and not at all friendly like these. Nobody climbs them and nobody knows them. And over on the other side of them—' He shrugged. 'You just can't visualize what might be there. For all you know, you might drop off the edge of the earth.' He shook his head reminiscently. 'I didn't know what space meant until I went to live there. You feel like a fly on the desert floor. As if the whole country might roll over and crush you any minute. Do you know what I mean?'

She said, 'There are a few parts left like that in the States. Montana, Colorado. But they get less all the time.' She sipped her drink. 'And the life here? Is that very different from what you expected?'

'No, not really.' Seeing the surprise on her face, he explained. 'At a place like the Centre, everyone has a very good idea what goes on in the West. Many of them, like myself, came from Europe in the first place. Also, people are always visiting international conferences, meeting colleagues, and so on. They know very well that the West is rich, life is more comfortable, there is political freedom. They know all that.'

'Doesn't it make them discontented?'

'Not so much as you might think.' He pointed down at the chill, rain-swept valley. 'You know at this moment that the sun is shining in Florida. But you don't think about it very often. If life is tolerable . . .' He said, 'For ten years I was quite contented.'

'But you left in the end?'

'Yes.' He had been talking easily, but now she felt the caution coming back into his voice. 'Circumstances changed for me. And there was the opportunity to escape. So I decided to take it.'

She said, 'And now—do you regret it?'

'It's too soon to say.' He spoke dispassionately. 'I didn't expect it to be easy. I didn't think the people I would meet here would be so very different from those at the Centre.' There was a sardonic twist to his lips. 'So I'm not as disillusioned as you might think.'

'What do you want from the West? What are you hoping for?'

'Nothing spectacular. A career. To live like an ordinary person, freely, without fear, without interference. To do the kind of work I want. Perhaps, if things go well, to distinguish myself a little. Nothing more than that.'

He sat there looking down into the valley, talking as if to himself, twirling the stem of his glass between his fingers. She was fascinated by the power he had to make himself at ease in all circumstances, even the strangest and most menacing. In the space of under a week he had managed to mould his American clothes into something extraordinarily un-American. His suit was a little crumpled, the buttons on his collar were undone, his tie had drifted slightly over to one side. His shoes were scuffed and there was a gap of slightly hairy leg between his socks and his trouser bottoms. Yet he was not dilapidated. You could not feel sorry for him. He was in command of the situation. Without money, without friends or supporters, isolated in a foreign country, he nevertheless remained poised and unassailable. She thought of Maurice, with his careful stage-management of all occasions, the restaurant where the staff greeted him, the tips, the dress so carefully studied, the arrogance which, even at its most obtrusive, carried some thing tense and precarious at its heart. Beside Karas, Maurice seemed to her like a clever, precocious boy, nervously exhibiting a personality which would crumble to pieces at the first breath of danger. She said, almost resentfully. 'You have great self-assurance.'

'Have I?' He considered the matter. 'I suppose it's a matter of degree. We are all afraid sometimes, perhaps most of the time. It's simply a question of who is most afraid. And who has most to lose.' He smiled, and said without bitterness, 'I have very little to lose. It gives me a certain advantage.'

'It's not just that, is it?' she said. 'It's something inside you, nothing to do with circumstances. You don't have the kind of doubts some of us have.'

'Why do you say that?'

'It's the kind of thing a woman feels instinctively about a man. You can't easily express it.' She looked out of the window without meeting his eyes. 'I imagine you have had great success with women.'

'Variable,' he said, precise as ever. 'Some women like me very much. Others detest me.'

'Why?' she asked.

'I don't know. I think,' he said equably, 'that it's because I have no charm.' He explained, 'As I see it, charm is the quality which leads people to forgive you, to make excuses for your behaviour and give you the benefit of the doubt. Certain people have it, Weldon for example. People say he's a nice fellow, he means no harm.' He laughed, the easy laugh of a man who envies nobody. 'Nobody ever said that about me.'

They sat in silence for a while. Then the restaurant began to fill up and the two waiters laid the table for dinner. He ordered an expensive meal and a bottle of excellent claret. He might have been dining in such places all his life. When the food came he ate rapidly and with gusto; without paying much attention he managed to drink by far the larger part of the bottle of wine. At the end he ordered brandy for both of them and a Havana cigar for himself. As the waiter snipped the end of it, he said cheerfully, 'You think I can learn to live like a capitalist?'

'Without any difficulty at all.'

He laughed. 'The way you live is nothing to do with politics really. It's here.' He banged his fist against his upper abdomen. 'There is something here that makes you enjoy the sensual things of life. Or prevents it,' he added. His gaiety faded a little at the touch of memory. 'Like poor Max.'

'Max?'

'My friend, Max Bremer. I must have spoken to you of him.'

Of course, Bremer was the one who had died. 'Yes, I remember now.'

'He was the finest man I ever knew. The kindest, the most intelligent.' He shook his head sadly. 'But he had no talent for sensual enjoyment.'

'Does that matter so much?'

'I think it destroyed him,' said Karas simply. He was silent for a moment, then he said, 'Max gave me something no woman ever gave me, a knowledge of myself. When I

171

compared myself with him, I saw myself as I was. I saw my own strength in his gentleness, my own crudeness in his sensitivity. He made me realize that as a scientist, my mind was good but something a little short of first-rate. I found out—' He stopped suddenly. 'Oh, many things.'

She would have liked to have pressed the matter but felt instinctively that it would be a mistake. She said, 'He died, I believe?'

'He killed himself.' He added, 'That's why I'm here now. The escape was arranged for him. I took his place.'

'How did you know—about the escape, I mean?'

He hesitated for a moment. 'From Max's wife.' He became awkward and abrupt. 'She told me that, if I wished to go in his place—' His face was shadowed. 'If you don't mind, I'd sooner not talk about that. This is my first really happy evening for—oh, a long time.' He smiled with determination. 'I think we should keep it happy. Perhaps we should talk about you.'

More from a desire to help him than because she wished to do so, she spoke of her own life. She described the childhood spent in the world of a career diplomat, moving between one capital city and another, in large barren, unfriendly houses, filled with the endless tedium of adult conversation. She told of her father's death when she was eighteen, of a few years spent living with her mother, of her tenuous relationship with Henderson. She described her mother's wanderings about the world with a succession of lovers, each one a little less dignified than the last. She told him of Paris and New York, of *Planet Magazine*, of Falkenburg and Jennet. At the end he said, more as a statement than a question, 'You don't really like your life?'

'No, not really.' She said, 'Perhaps I'm like your friend— I haven't the capacity for sensual enjoyment.'

'I don't think that's true,' he said. 'Do you?'

'I don't know,' she replied. 'It's difficult, isn't it? People tell you things about yourself—' People like Maurice, for instance. They told you that you were cold, arrogant, impossibly demanding. You didn't feel like that, but then we were blind to our faults. 'Perhaps they're right.'

'What kind of things?' he said.

She smiled thinly. 'I'm said to be difficult to please.'

'By whom?'

'Oh—' She shrugged her shoulders. 'Men.'

'And are you?'

'Perhaps. But then,' she said defensively, 'I can't help that, can I? It's the way I am. There's nothing I can do about it.'

He regarded her for a moment and then said, 'Why are you so difficult to please? What are you looking for?'

'I don't know exactly. I suppose I always had the idea that I should recognize it when I found it.'

His voice softened a little. 'It may not exist. Have you thought of that?'

'Yes,' she said. 'Naturally I worry about that all the time. Sometimes I think I ought to settle for less. At other times I've tried to persuade myself that I'd found it when I hadn't really. But in the end I couldn't fool myself any longer.'

He took a sip of his brandy. 'What was it that they lacked —these young men who failed you?'

'I don't know. It was a little different in all of them.' She tried to analyse it for herself. 'I suppose if I were to try to find the common factor I'd say—courage.' Instantly she thought, no, that wasn't quite right. 'I don't mean just going into a lion's cage or something. I don't think I even mean one of those men with ideals who like marching through the South in support of the Negroes. No, it's something private, inside a man, something that makes him say, whenever the world hands him something—what does this really mean? What do I personally think about it? He won't accept what the world brings, he won't be conned by it, he won't play in. Whatever coin it hands him he bites it to see if it's a fake. And if it's a fake he throws it back—' She stopped. 'I don't know, this probably means nothing to you. I'm really very confused about it.'

He laughed. 'Now I've embarrassed you.' She looked younger and much less self-assured. He said, 'You're a nice girl. I see that now.'

'You didn't think I was nice before?'

'A little disconcerting perhaps. During the interviews—'

He stopped, as if afraid of saying something to offend her. She said, 'I annoyed you, didn't I?'

'On one or two occasions,' he admitted. 'You have, if I may say so, a slightly supercilious way of looking at people, as if they were failing you in some way.' On an impulse, he mimicked the expression that had angered him during the interviews, tilting his head back, with his face expressionless and his eyes half-closed. 'This kind of thing.'

He ceased his imitation and looked at her. To his astonishment she had blushed a fiery red. 'What is it?' he asked.

'But that—' She was stammering in her embarrassment. 'That's nothing to do with the way I feel.' In her voice confusion was struggling with relief. She said shyly, 'I suppose I'd better tell you. I wear contact lenses. They make you do that sometimes.'

He laughed, but it was a laugh not of scorn but of affection. 'I'm so pleased,' he said. 'So pleased. Now I feel I know so much more about you.' It was as if he had been given a secret clue, not only to her facial expression but to her whole personality. He said, 'To make you feel more at ease I will confess something too. I was a little intimidated by you at first. Did you know that?'

She was genuinely surprised. 'No.'

'It's true. To a person like myself, coming in from the outside, you seemed very strange and unapproachable. It was not simply that you were very attractive. We have beautiful girls where I come from. It was not simply that you were rich and well-dressed, though that came into it. It was also, I think, that you had lived your life in a society where beauty in a woman is really valued and regarded as something significant in its own right. That gave you a sort of power which I had not encountered before. I was impressed, and yet at the same time you weren't really a person to me. I couldn't see you as the sort of woman I could ever know or like. There was no basis for intimacy. But now I see that behind that elegant façade you are emotional and idealistic, more than a little vulnerable. In other words—a nice girl.'

He looked at her in a way no woman could ever mistake. In that moment she knew without question that for him she had ceased to be a phenomenon of his new life, a symbol of feminine privilege and an asker of tiresome and intrusive questions—she had become a woman to be desired and possibly even loved. It was at this stage that irreparable misunderstandings occurred. The man knew what he wanted at a time when you were still undecided. It was so easy at the beginning to be either too compliant or too discouraging—and in either case you might regret it afterwards. It was difficult enough with a man from your own world, who fitted into a pattern you felt you understood. But with a stranger such as Karas there was no guideline. The language would have to be learnt as they went along.

The idea that he might want to make love to her was exciting yet frightening in its implications. If only the moment could be put off, if he would leave it until she felt more sure of herself . . . But, looking at him, she knew he would not. It occurred to her, too, that if he were to feel rejected by her, he would certainly refuse to come to America. The whole enterprise would be destroyed. Her uncle would be made ridiculous, Weldon would certainly be ruined. She realized now that Weldon must have guessed what would happen when he suggested that they go out alone together—he had gambled on her to save his career. She felt oppressed by the responsibility placed upon her.

She had been looking out over the lake as she thought. As she turned back towards Karas she saw that he had been watching her intently and she was overcome with an unreasonable panic that he had been reading her thoughts. She looked at her watch and said abruptly, 'I think it's time we were getting back to the villa.'

He paid the bill and they walked out to the car. A cold wind full of sleet was blowing off the mountain behind them. Inside the car it was silent and remote; the windows had been misted by the damp snowflakes on the outside. As she put out her hand to switch on the engine, he caught it gently in his own and held it.

'Wait,' he said. 'Just for a few minutes. For a little while we're safe. There's no world outside, no villa, no O'Keefe. Even the restaurant's gone. We're safe here.'

His hand was strong and slightly rough, chapped by the cold. They sat without speaking for a while, watching the sleet build up on the windscreen. She was overcome by a fear that if he made a move towards her she might jump out of the car and run for the restaurant, for the shelter of her own familiar world. It was absurd. She was twenty-six. He was a man like all other men. There was nothing to be afraid of. She waited for him to say or do something, but he made no move. Gradually she relaxed, and they sat in silence for a little while. She felt somehow helpless in her lack of knowledge of him. She searched for something that would make him real to her as a man, as somebody that a woman might consider as a lover. A memory came into her mind of a change in the tone of his voice during the interview, a momentary embarrassment at the mention of a name. She said, 'I've told you a lot about myself this evening. Can I ask you something?'

'Of course.'

'It's about Bremer's wife.' She felt the muscles of his hand tighten a little. 'What did you say her name was?'

'Sophia.' Again there was a slight awkwardness in the way he spoke the name. She might have imagined it before, but in this intimate darkness it was unmistakable to her ear.

She asked, 'Was she your mistress?'

'Why should you think that?'

'Was she?'

For the first time since she had known him he seemed evasive. 'Never while Max was alive.' His voice was unhappy. 'I hardly noticed her in those days. She was just—someone in the background. Then, afterwards—'

'Yes?'

'She was lonely. She wanted me. It seems she always had. And we were drawn together—' He hesitated. 'It's hard to explain to someone like you. Unless you have lived that kind of life—' He repeated, 'It's really impossible to explain.'

'Were you in love with her?'

'No. Not at all. She knew that.' He said seriously, 'I did not betray Max. I want you to believe that.'

She laughed, but without any real amusement. The sound echoed through the confined space of the car. 'That's all it means to you, isn't it? Whether you might have done something against Max?'

He was puzzled. 'Of course. What else?'

For some reason the tension had left her. She said, mocking him a little, 'You don't understand women very well, do you?'

He was not at all disconcerted. 'Perhaps not,' he said.

'And you don't much care?'

'One cannot have a talent for everything,' he said, reasonably. 'I like women and I want them to like me. But if they don't like me I don't cry about it—there are always others. I don't think understanding has much to do with it.' He paused. When he spoke again, his voice held a challenge. 'Do you?'

'I don't know.' After she had spoken the words she realized that her voice did not sound like hers at all, it sounded lost and rather helpless, as if asking for reassurance. She tried to think of something to say which would seem strong and confident and assured, that would regain for her the ascendancy that she felt she was beginning to lose. His hand moved away from hers and in the darkness she felt it touching the side of her cheek. He had not moved any nearer to her. Yet through the stroking of the tips of his fingers against her face he transmitted a sensuality which was almost suffocating. She waited for him to act like any other man and to move closer to her, but he showed no signs of doing so. It came to her that he had no intention of doing so, that he could say everything he wished to say through this soft, repeated touch of his fingers on her cheek. He would wait for her to respond, and her response would imply an acceptance of everything the fingers were saying, everything he would do to her and demand from her. The move on her part would be the signature of a contract which would have to be honoured, a contract without limitation.

She touched his wrist and drew his hand away from her face. 'Not yet,' she whispered.

'Not yet?'

You could sign the contract by implication. She saw the danger and retreated. 'Perhaps not ever. I can't promise anything.' Yet there was something within her which cried out against the thought of allowing the affair to stop at this early point—she could not bear the thought that he might leave and that she would never see him again. And because of this, the promise which she had denied in words was present in the tone of her voice. She knew it was there and that he heard it too and was satisfied.

She leaned forward in her seat and twisted the self-starter. The engine coughed, like an animal resenting the cold in its bones, and then took hold. The windscreen wipers pushed away the sleet and the lake appeared again in front of them. They were back in the world again.

She turned the car carefully on to the narrow mountain road and made her way down towards the lake. The sleet turned to rain as they descended. Neither of them spoke, but it was a warm, companionable silence. There was something comforting to her in the way he found it unnecessary to prolong their conversation any further. She felt that he had understood her position and accepted it without resentment. She thought of Maurice, who would have argued and persuaded and flattered and charmed her in a reflex attempt to obtain something more out of her than she was prepared to give. Out of weariness she would probably have given in and then despised herself afterwards for her weakness. That had been the pattern of their whole relationship; a struggle for transient domination, for minor advantage.

With Karas, she knew instinctively, it would be different. He was stronger than Maurice and in the end he would want more. There would be no bargaining with him. The terms he offered would not be negotiable. Yet there was a hope in her heart that they might be the kind of terms she would be happy to accept without reservation.

There was less traffic along the lakeside, and the streets of Geneva were almost empty. They drove out to the south and then turned left off the main road. The vague apprehension which had caused her to drive fast and dangerously when she had first left the villa had now left her completely. She reflected how curious it was that the very fact of being confined to the house and grounds had in itself created an unreasonable fear of what might be outside. Now she drove easily and rather slowly, reluctant to end this quiet, undemanding intimacy.

It was after ten o'clock when they drew up in front of the villa. As soon as they rounded the end of the drive it was obvious to her that something had gone wrong. There was a strange car in the driveway and the windows of the house were ablaze with light. Sarah was overcome with a sudden fear. She said, 'There's something unusual going on. Perhaps you'd better stay in the car.'

'No. That wouldn't help.' He got out and they walked together to the door. When they entered the hall they were immediately met by Walker. He took Karas by the sleeve and whispered to him, 'It's the police. Just keep your head. Remember your new name.' Karas felt something being slipped into his pocket, but before he could examine it the door of the main living-room opened. He was confronted by a tall man in a grey suit with a sallow face and a melancholy expression.

'If you'd come in here immediately, please,' he said. It was an order rather than a request. When the three of them were in the room he closed the door carefully behind them and motioned them to sit down. Karas looked round and saw that Weldon and O'Keefe were already there. Weldon gave him a reassuring smile. Sitting unobtrusively — by a table in the window was a young man with a notepad and a ballpoint pencil.

'My name is Roux. I'm from the Geneva Police,' said the tall man. He pointed to the other stranger. 'This is my colleague, Monsieur Lamotte. We have one or two questions we'd like to ask.' He took a seat himself, directly facing Karas. 'It's on a diplomatic matter. I've just been telling your friends here that we've received a disturbing piece of news. It seems that during the recent international scientific meeting at the Palais des Nations, a member of a certain delegation disappeared. The Government concerned did not notify us at the time—they say the reason for this is that they assumed he had left of his own accord and would probably present himself at their Embassy in due course. They now say they believe him to be kidnapped and to be living without a passport, in Geneva itself. This, of course, presents us with a very serious situation.'

Sarah said, 'Supposing he hadn't been kidnapped. Supposing he left of his own free will—'

Roux turned momentarily to her and shook his head. 'That would not necessarily give him the right to stay here. Switzerland is a neutral country. She is very sensitive about getting involved in matters of this kind. We have no wish to be involved in international incidents.' Before she could speak again, he went on, 'But I'm informed by Dr. Weldon and Mr. O'Keefe that this has no significance for any of you, since you all have valid American passports. Is that so?'

'Yes,' she said helplessly. 'Yes, of course.'

'Good.' He turned back to Karas. 'You, monsieur, could I have your name?'

The short delay while Roux had been speaking to Sarah had given Karas time to think. If he really meant to destroy Henderson's plan to refuse to go to the United States, he must do so now or not at all. It would mean abandoning his only support and throwing himself on the mercy of a neutral government which plainly had no desire to antagonize a great power for his sake. He would be destitute and friendless. His own government would be pressing for his deportation. He was in a trap from which there was only one possible exit. In a calm, almost indifferent voice he replied, 'My name is Paul Stratton. I'm an American citizen.'

'Your address?'

Karas hesitated only a fraction of a second as he visualized the passport form which Weldon had instructed him to fill in. 'Twenty-four, Forest Drive, Tenafly, New Jersey.'

'Occupation?'

'I'm a chemical engineer for ISIS.'

'Ah.' Roux inclined his head respectfully at the name of ISIS. 'You have proof of this?'

'Of course.' Karas took out the credit card from his pocket. Roux scrutinized it and handed it to Lamotte who copied out the details and handed it back to Karas. It almost seemed as if he might be satisfied. But, then, as if as an afterthought, he said, 'Perhaps I could also see your passport.'

Without hesitation Karas put his hand in his overcoat pocket and drew out the cardboard folder which Walker had dropped into it at the door. It was, as he had hoped, a passport. He handed it across to Roux. Roux opened it and went through the details with some care, finally stopping at the photograph. He looked up at Karas and compared him with the photograph, then he took another snapshot out of his pocket and compared him with that. After quite a long silence he said, 'And how long are you planning to stay in Geneva?'

Weldon cut in quickly, 'We're proposing to leave almost right away. Doctor Stratton and I have a meeting in New York on Thursday. We were thinking of taking a plane on Wednesday.' A dubious expression came on to Roux's face. He looked again at the snapshot and pursed his lips. Weldon said, hurriedly, 'Or even perhaps tomorrow—'

Roux continued to look at the snapshot. The silence was oppressive. Finally he said, 'Tomorrow, you said?'

'Yes.'

'I think that would be the best thing.'

'If we can get reservations—' said Weldon.

'I will see that you get reservations.' Roux put the snapshot back in his wallet and handed the passport back to Karas. 'I wish you a safe journey, Doctor Stratton.'

'Thank you.'

'Switzerland is neutral,' he said, like a man repeating a lesson. 'We are friends to everyone. We want no problems here.' He made a gesture to the young policeman, who put his notebook in his pocket and prepared to leave. Roux nodded solemnly at the assembled company and the two policemen walked out to their car.

When they had driven away Weldon looked apologetically at Karas. 'I'm sorry about this,' he said. 'They've been here for the last hour or two. They searched the villa from top to bottom. Obviously, they must have had some tip-off from your Embassy—'

Karas looked at him for quite a long time. In the end he said, 'It was unnecessary. I had decided to come to America anyway.'

PART THREE

CHAPTER ONE

THE BOEING BANKED SLIGHTLY. There was a cascade of golden lights through the cabin as the windows on the right-hand side tilted up towards the afternoon sun. Down below, the clouds parted to show a vast, barren, white landscape, wrinkled with ridges of mountains and pitted with ice-bound lakes. 'Newfoundland,' said Weldon. 'Not very far to go now.'

Karas acknowledged the information with a nod. He glanced down at the frozen, deserted hills, his first glimpse of the Western Hemisphere. It was like looking at a contour map in an atlas. The rivers did not move, there were no men to be seen, a town was no more than a cluster of dots on an architect's drawing. This might be anywhere—Scandinavia, Siberia, Japan. There was nothing here to symbolize his entry into a new world.

If he was looking for a symbol of the West he would do better to turn back to the magazine which the stewardess had pressed on him. This was exotic enough, in all conscience. One could not fail to be impressed by the lavishness of the colour, the startling advertisements, the glossy, opulent paper on which it was printed. It should have invited him to read, but somehow it had the opposite effect. He found his attention wandering after the first few paragraphs of each story. An inquiry into the health of astronauts, an analysis of the Kennedy assassination, some sensational pictures of half-naked women with the heading *Is There Really Anything in Witchcraft?* . . . The subjects seemed attractive enough. Why did they arouse so little interest in him?

'Well,' said Sarah. 'What do you think of *Planet*?'

'This is where you propose to print my life story?'

'Yes.'

He shook his head in bewilderment. It seemed absurd that the details of his life should be strung in columns between advertisements for whisky and deodorants, to be glanced at casually by middle-aged matrons trying to while away the hours of a tedious journey. So much money, so much effort, so much technique—for a glance and a yawn and a quick turn of the head towards beauty hints or the theatre section. It was a strange way to become famous.

He flicked the pages over, reading here and there a headline, the caption to a picture. It annoyed him to notice his own restlessness—for the first time in years he found it difficult to concentrate. In the past he had always prided himself on being able to sit in front of a book or a chessboard or a laboratory bench and shut out everything but the matter to which he had decided to give his attention. Now his mind was easily distracted by trivialities. He found himself engaged in futile conversations that led nowhere, ordering food and drink which he realized afterwards he did not really want.

He tried to tell himself that this was a temporary reaction to the anxieties which had preceded and followed his escape. Certainly it had grown much worse since the night when the police had called at the villa. When he looked back on it, the whole episode had a curiously unreal, theatrical quality about it. And the false passport, which had not seemed important to him earlier on, was beginning to worry him now. When he had expressed his disquiet, O'Keefe had brushed him aside. 'Don't worry,' he had said with confidence. 'This is just a temporary thing. We'll get you a proper passport when you get over there.' Anticipating Karas's next question, he had said, 'Everything's fixed at Kennedy Airport. Nobody's going to ask you any questions.'

Karas had left it at that. Now that he had decided to go, he was in their hands. He had no alternative but to accept their arrangements. Yet he was uneasy. There had been little opportunity to talk to Sarah since their conversation in the restaurant on the top of the mountain. He was disturbed to realize how much he had abandoned his natural caution in his desire for her and his longing to trust her.

He came to the last page of the magazine and tossed it impatiently on the table before him. Sarah, who was in the seat next to him, said, 'You don't much like it?'

'It's like the food you get on these planes,' he said, indicating the plastic trays of half-eaten delicacies which the air hostess was busily removing. 'It's a brilliant feat to serve such elaborate meals in an aircraft at 10,000 metres. The food looks marvellous, it's perfectly presented. But somehow, I don't know why—you end up by leaving most of it.'

She said, 'I'm afraid you'll find a number of things in

the West a bit like that. A mixture of something quite remarkable with something else that's pretty awful. The trick is to take what you like and throw away the rest.'

Karas smiled without replying. Sarah looked away from him and caught the eye of O'Keefe, who was sitting with Weldon opposite to them. There was a frown of disapproval on O'Keefe's face. But he said nothing. Ever since they had left Geneva his attitude had been increasingly subdued, perhaps a reaction to the increasing proximity of Henderson. Catching her eye on him, he buried his face in the *New York Times*. The icy landscape moved gradually away to the north.

The plane circled out over the sea, dropping swiftly, until they could see the white chopping waves and the ships jerking up and down on the swell. The engines changed and they came tearing in towards the land. There was the inevitable moment for Sarah when she was overcome with fear that they had dropped short and were going to hit the water; then the rumble of the wheels on the runway, the scream of engines going into reverse, and they were down.

As Karas stood up to collect his luggage, O'Keefe stopped him. 'We stay here for a moment.' He nodded to Walker, who left with the other first-class passengers. The rest of them waited in their seats. About ten minutes later, Walker returned with an official of the airport. They left the plane and were led to a special entrance, where an impassive immigration official scrutinized their passports. He looked at Karas with considerable curiosity and then stamped his passport with the rest.

As they passed through customs Karas could see the other passengers scrambling for their suitcases and wheeling them in little trolleys towards the outlets. In the gallery of the customs hall crowds of friends and relatives waited, waving and shouting greetings. There was a festive quality about the scene which he found engaging. In his country travel was a serious, determined business, a battle with elbowing crowds, a struggle for survival. Here a gayer atmosphere seemed to prevail. Groups of individuals stood around in strange hats, with large buttons on their jacket proclaiming Alabama Goodwill Mission to the World. One group carried a banner which said Welcome Home Uncle Willie.

He was led quickly past the barrier. Their own luggage was not examined. Outside the building a large black

Cadillac limousine was drawn up waiting for them. They piled into the back while Walker supervised a group of Negro porters in packing away the luggage. When it had all been stowed in the boot, he handed out bundles of dollar bills and sat down beside the driver.

It was a cold, sparkling afternoon. The big car joined the stream of traffic surging towards the city. Karas watched it with fascination. The traffic here had a quality quite different from anything he had previously seen. On the long, straight roads of Eastern Europe, the rare, sturdy little cars buzzed along between vast deserted fields, or ploughed their way along primitive tracks between forests of birch and pine. In Switzerland the small European cars were like children breaking out of school—jostling, overtaking, stopping and accelerating; driving was a violent, noisy, competitive activity. But here the huge, silent vehicles moved forward without apparent effort, like a great school of fish impelled forward at constant speed by some irresistible instinctive drive.

They passed the grounds of the old World's Fair, and in front of them rose up the silhouette of Manhattan Island. They crossed the Triborough Bridge and drove along by the East River, turning right up 72nd Street, between the tall cliff-like blocks. The limousine drew up at the entrance of a large apartment block in the east sixties. Two porters came immediately out of the entrance and began to unload their luggage. The doorman saluted and opened the door of the limousine.

'Okay, we're here,' said O'Keefe. There seemed, Karas thought, to be a slightly military atmosphere to the whole operation. As he found himself being led to the door by the doorman, he wondered why it was necessary to have so much advance planning. Perhaps it was the American passion for slickness for its own sake. Then, just as he was about to enter the building, a car drew up with a scream of tyres just behind the Cadillac. Two men jumped out. One of them shouted, 'Get him, Joe!' The other raised a small black object to his face, and Karas was momentarily struck with horror. Was he safe nowhere? Was he to be shot down in cold blood in a New York street? He waited helplessly for the man to open fire but nothing happened. O'Keefe and Walker rushed at the men and he heard voices raised in anger. Then he was hustled into the elevator with Weldon and Sarah. 'What was that?' he said.

Weldon frowned. 'Newspapers,' he said. 'It looks as if the other side have finally blown the news of your defection. They must have been watching the airport.' He added reassuringly, 'Don't worry. O'Keefe knows how to handle them. We'll try and see you're pestered as little as possible, though they're bound to be a problem just at first.' His face twisted into a half-smiling, half-melancholy expression. 'I'm afraid you'll have to face the fact that your famous.'

The apartment was on the twenty-fifth floor. At first sight it seemed to Karas almost as large in area as the villa itself. The main living-room occupied a corner of the building, with a magnificent view which took in a vista stretching from Rockefeller Center to the huge rectangle of Central Park. Down below the same schools of mechanical fish slid along the crevices between the man-made cliffs, sometimes stopping, sometimes separating and joining other streams. It was growing dark and the lights were beginning to come on all over the city. Sarah was standing beside him at the great window. 'So this is it,' he said.

'Yes, this is it.' She looked up at him in an effort to gain some clue to his reaction, but his face was impassive. 'It scared me the first time I saw it,' she said. 'I suppose as a man, you can't admit that.'

'Fear is a physiological reaction,' he said. 'As a biologist I have no choice but to admit it. Size is always intimidating at first sight.' He smiled. 'But I try to remind myself that inside those very tall buildings the men are no bigger than I am.'

She was silent for a moment. Then she said, 'Would you mind if I gave you some advice?'

'Of course not.'

'I want you to understand what things are like here. As you look down on it all now, it looks so enormous, so indifferent. Isn't that so?'

'Yes.'

'You can't think now how it could ever take notice of anything so small as you are. But you'll find, when the story breaks tomorrow, that it does care. It will be fascinated by you. It will want to know everything about you. Every silly detail. At first you'll be astonished, then embarrassed, and perhaps a little flattered. I've seen it before in people who have suddenly become celebrities. After a while they get used to being an object of interest—it's rather habit-forming.' She paused and looked out of the window. 'What

I really wanted to say is—don't expect it to last. Your first impression—the one you have now—that's the right one.'

'Don't worry,' he assured her. 'I shan't become addicted to reading about myself in the newspapers.'

She turned away from him in slight embarrassment. 'It's not just the newspapers. It's people too. Americans like new faces—new experiences—'

'Not all of them, surely,' he said. 'You're not like that. Or Weldon—'

'Weldon's an Englishman. Englishmen aren't really interested in strangers. If they do care about you—which they usually don't—they care about you as an individual. So he doesn't count. And as for me—' She halted and then said awkwardly, 'Well, it's different with me.'

They were both momentarily silenced by the implication of what she had said. It was as if they were back on the mountainside, sitting close together in the darkness of the car, where thoughts passed without words and powerful emotions could be felt through the delicate touch of a hand. She had closed the conversation then with the words, 'Not now. Perhaps not ever.' Now, they both knew, the subject had been opened again. Embarrassed by her own revelation, she moved away from him, and the tension was broken. She said, 'If you'd like a drink—'

'No, thank you.' His mind returned to her warning. Somewhere, it seemed to him, there had been a false note in it. 'I can't believe you're really afraid my head might be turned by reporters or society women at cocktail parties. You know me better than that.'

'Well, it was just a warning—'

'Yes. But against something more specific.' Then the answer occurred to him. 'It was your uncle, wasn't it?'

She flushed. 'Yes, I suppose it was, really.' She spoke with a sudden urgency. 'I don't want you to misunderstand me. I love him and I think he's a great man. But he has certain limitations. His life has been a series of melodramas. While you're playing with him in one of them, you're terribly important to him. He cares about you, he charms you, he laughs and cries with you. It's as if your whole life had always been bound up with his. But the play doesn't last for ever. The cast changes. You may not have a part in the next one. Believe me,' she said ruefully, 'I know this. I want you to remember it.' She moved back into the room and nervously lit a cigarette. Her anxiety was apparent.

He said, with gratitude in his voice, 'You're afraid for me. That's very sweet of you.'

'It's just that I feel responsible for you. After all, we brought you here—'

He shook his head. 'Nobody brings me anywhere,' he said decisively. 'I came of my own free will. I wanted to come.' He passed lightly behind her and touched her on the shoulder. For a moment she felt his hand gripping her through the thin silk of her blouse. Then he moved away. 'Perhaps it would be nice to have a drink after all.'

CHAPTER TWO

THE NEXT MORNING they went to Henderson's office. They left the apartment block by a small side entrance to avoid photographers, and took a taxi down Park Avenue. The office was on the top of a building near Grand Central Station, some distance from the main ISIS headquarters, which was located in a block farther West between 5th and 6th. As the car crawled through the traffic Weldon kept looking at his watch. 'It's impossible to be punctual in this city,' he said fretfully.

'Take it easy,' said O'Keefe. 'Stop worrying.'

'I'm not worrying,' snapped Weldon. He nibbled his left thumbnail. 'It's just—one tries to make arrangements—'

His anxiety at the thought of his coming encounter with Henderson was almost embarrassing. He was like a man, thought Karas, who was afraid of heights. He knew it was foolish and illogical, he resented it and tried to ignore it. Perhaps in the last resort there was nothing he could do about it. Perhaps he should have chosen to cut his losses and spend his life on the ground.

They were kept waiting for a little while in Henderson's outer office. Then there was a buzz on the intercom and they were shown in. It was an enormous office looking out on to the East River. Two of the walls were taken up by windows. The other two were covered by bookshelves and by portraits of horses. There was a table in the middle of the room but no desk. Henderson himself sat in a huge old leather club armchair; to his right was a telephone table, to his left another table containing papers. This latter was on a hinge so that it could be swung round in front of him to enable him to write if he felt so inclined. As they were shown in, he lumbered up from his chair and advanced towards them.

'Hallo, good to see you.' He kissed Sarah on the cheek. 'How are you, baby, all right?' Without waiting for an answer he turned to Weldon and O'Keefe and patted each of them on the shoulder. Then he directed all his attention to Karas. Karas found himself shaking a huge bony hand, looking up at a magnificent living ruin of a face. Above the face was a thick mat of hair, almost theatrically white. The brown leathery skin was sagging on the great bones of the head, and there were sacs underneath the blue, slightly bloodshot eyes. The very size and physical decay of the man were sufficient to strike awe into anyone meeting him for the first time. It was as if he carried written on his face an account of a life which, measured in terms of conflict and incident, was the equivalent of several normal lives. Only an organism of superhuman strength, one felt, could have survived the battering of such storms, could have remained dominant in the midst of the strains to which it had been subjected. And yet together with the signs of survival were the signs of irreparable damage, the heralds of eventual capitulation. They were there in the uncontrolled twitch of an eyelid and the lack of steadiness in the grip of his hand. The voice, mighty as it still was, carried in it a tiny crack, a loss of resonance. Surely, thought Karas, these delicate signs of decay must be evident to those around who served Henderson, who watched him every minute of the day. They must already have begun to wonder what would happen to them when the sap ran dry and the great tree cracked under the next big storm . . .

'I'm very glad to meet you, Dr. Karas. Very glad indeed.' Henderson looked down at Karas in a proprietary way. It was as if he were examining a rare and expensive new addition to his racing stable. 'I've heard a lot about you and it's a great honour to have you with us. We're proud to have been able to assist you in making your way to the United States.' He waved a hand towards Weldon and O'Keefe. 'These fellows been treating you all right?'

Karas replied conventionally. 'They've been very kind.'

'Don't think of it. It was our privilege.' Henderson's voice rolled over the others like a ground-swell. There was no possibility of fighting against it. 'I wish I'd been there with you all in Geneva, but I'm not a young man any more and I have to get a little bit of sun at this time of year. Otherwise my joints begin to seize up. But I was following what happened, believe me. This is a great achievement and it's going to be a great story for *Planet*. Isn't that right, Sarah?' Sarah nodded briefly. He said to Karas, 'She's a brilliant writer. I can say it even though she is my favourite niece.' Turning back to Sarah, he asked, 'How did you make out? Did you get some good tapes?'

'Very good.'

'Fine. Fine. I want to hear them all. Remind me, now. I mean that. I want to hear them.' It was apparent from his tone that he never would. He said to the room at large, 'This is really something big. This is history. We're privileged to take part in it. Now, why don't you all sit down?'

They arranged themselves about the room. Henderson lowered his large frame into his club armchair. As he did so he said to Karas, 'This is the first chair I had in the first office I ever had, forty-five years ago. I've had new covers put on it six times. I sit here rather than behind a desk because my doctor tells me to relax. It reminds me all the time that I have younger guys like Arthur and Sam here to do the hard work. I'm around to have a few ideas and look at a situation in a way they don't have time for.'

There was a faint buzz from the telephone and an orange light came on. He reached automatically for the instrument. 'Excuse me.' He listened. 'Okay, I'll speak to him.' A pause. 'Hallo, Jack. I know what you want, don't tell me. Yes, it's a great shame. I'm sorry for you. But that's how it is with a big organization. You know how it is in ISIS. You want to scratch your ass, you've got to ask the ISIS lawyers first. If there's a delay I can't help it. It's not the way it was in the old days. We could do it over a drink then—' He listened again for a moment and his voice turned suddenly harsh. 'Jack, you had the chance of a straight deal with me but you didn't want it. You thought I was dead and buried or something. Right, now you're stuck with it, so be happy.' He guffawed. 'Okay, then go to hell.' He turned jovially to O'Keefe. 'That was Jack Anders. You remember him? He's got a patent on some plastic wrapping material. He wants to do a licence deal. He'll get it in the end but they'll tease him for a few months. Those ISIS executives have to show they're earning their dough.' He wiped the matter from his mind. 'Now, Dr. Karas, I want to hear all about your experiences. This Centre you came from over on the other side. I gather it's a pretty big, well-equipped place?'

'That's true. I would say—'

'I guess you'd like to compare it with what we've got over here. I make some cracks about ISIS, but up at Falls Ridge we've got one of the greatest damned research outfits you ever saw. I know you're going to be very interested to see it—' He picked up the telephone and pressed the button. 'Mrs. Schroeder, has Dr. Forsyth arrived? He has?—Good, ask him to come in here, will you?' He put the telephone down. 'I had him come in here this morning especially to meet you. You're going to like him, I know that. He's a great guy—and a great scientist. Right, Arthur?'

'First-rate,' said Weldon.

'You and he can talk together in your own language. Personally I don't understand a goddamned thing he says most of the time, but they've done some wonderful work out there. Wonderful.' A reverent look came on to his face. 'If I'd had a formal education nothing would have made me happier than to be a scientist.' He said to O'Keefe, 'Did you know that, Sam?'

'No, sir, I never knew that.'

'That would have been my ambition. A really satisfying life. But I didn't have the opportunity. So I became what I still am today—a dealer. A man with a finger in a hundred things, who doesn't really know a bloody thing about anything. Don't let me fool you, Dr. Karas. I'm just an ignoramus. These young fellows here know it. My niece knows it. They're just too damn' polite to say it. Listen, I'll tell you something. When I was sixteen—' He broke off as the door opened. 'Ah, hallo, Dr. Forsyth. You'll excuse me if I don't get up. You know Sam and Arthur. This is my niece, Sarah Manning—she works for *Planet*. And Dr. Karas. You've heard of him.'

'Yes.' Forsyth was a thin, angular man with severe steel-framed spectacles and an accent which Karas found impossible to place but was in fact Australian. He shook hands and said, 'Very glad to meet you,' in a sharp, dismissive way. He managed to convey that he regarded himself as in no way involved in this particular enterprise, and was somewhat put out at having been summoned away from his laboratories to New York. He inspired in Karas an immediate, instinctive respect.

'Now that we're all here,' said Henderson, 'I want to get all your views. This is a delicate matter. It's got to be handled right. The newspapers, for instance.' He picked up a morning paper from the table by his side. 'Have any of you seen this?'

O'Keefe and Weldon nodded assent; Forsyth ignored the question. Karas said, 'I haven't.'

'Then maybe you'd better. It'll show you what we're up against.' Karas picked up the paper and took it back to his chair. On the front page was a blown-up picture of two men rushing furtively into an apartment building. One of them, he recognized with a sense of shock, was himself, the other was Weldon. It was a poor, blurred picture, and it made them look like fugitives from justice. There was a huge caption, IS THIS THE MISSING SCIENTIST?

'Somebody was pretty smart,' said Henderson. 'Fortunately he wasn't smart enough to watch the side entrance of the apartment building this morning. But we can't count on having much time to play with. They'll pick you up within the next twenty-four hours if we're not careful.'

The light flashed on again at his telephone. He picked up the receiver, still talking. 'And when the time comes we've got to have some kind of a story—Yeah, Nancy what is it? Look, baby, I'm in conference here. I just can't keep picking up the phone. All right then, tell Frank to fix it, what does he think I pay a lawyer for—'

Karas turned over the page of the newspaper. It was the first time he had read about himself in print and the experience was far from pleasant. The story was that a scientist, inevitably eminent, inevitably 'working on top secret research', had defected in mysterious circumstances to the West. Rumour had it that several attempts had already been made to kidnap or murder him, but that a last-minute escape had been arranged which brought him safely to the U.S.A. He might well carry information of the utmost importance in the cold war. Officials in Washington refused to comment. So far, no official request for asylum had been received. When it was . . .

Henderson was off the telephone again. 'Well, what do you think of it?' he said.

Karas looked up from the newspaper. 'It's rubbish, of course,' he said. 'They don't know what they're talking about.' Feeling that this sounded priggish, he added, 'I suppose that's to be expected.'

'Sure, but it's got to be handled. Washington are going to be as mad as hell. I don't mind making them mad, but we've got to do it so they can't easily get back at us. The thing is, there isn't a lot of time. We've got to decide what we're going to do and what we're going to say about you. That's what Dr. Forsyth's here about. I want—' The telephone buzzed. He yelled into it, 'Hell, what is it now?' His eyes narrowed. 'Okay then, put him through.' He put his hand over the mouthpiece and said to the room at large, 'Washington.' He took his hand off and listened. A nasal, querulous voice floated through the earpiece. Henderson broke in, 'No, Jim, I don't know where he is. Why should I? Sure, I've seen the papers. Like everyone else, I'm fascinated. I was hoping you might be able to tell me— No, I didn't recognize anyone in the photograph. It was just two guys in topcoats, turned away from the camera, as I recollect—Arthur Weldon? No, I don't know him.' He winked at Weldon. 'Should I? Listen, Jim, there must be a half-million people working for ISIS, in one way or another—well, certainly, I'll look into it. Sure I'll let you know if I hear anything. 'Bye, Jim.'

He put the telephone down and flashed at Karas an almost boyish smile. 'Well, you see how it is. You're hot. Evidently somebody recognized Arthur. Jim Froebel's an intelligent guy. He knows there's nobody else in ISIS with the guts to pull a stunt like this. We used to know each other in Mexico, before the war—' The telephone buzzed again. 'Listen, Mrs. Schroeder, I can't take this any more. Well, it's no use saying you're sorry. I've got business to do here—' A worried frown suddenly appeared on his face. 'I did? I don't remember that.' He listened to her voice with obvious anxiety. Then he rubbed his forehead with his hand. 'Well, if you say so. Hell, I can't remember everything. Oh, sure, if it's like that I'll have to go through with it.'

He put the telephone down. The animation had gone out of his voice. 'Evidently I fixed up another conference and forgot about it. So many damned things happening—' He left the sentence unfinished. 'I'll be through in an hour or so. Arthur, maybe you and Forsyth could entertain Dr. Karas for a little while. Then the three of you could join me for lunch.'

Weldon took Karas and Forsyth through to one of the guest offices on the next floor. Forsyth lit his pipe and said, 'Now that we have some peace and quiet, I'd be interested to hear something about your experimental work.'

Karas responded eagerly. He told Forsyth of Suvorin and Max and the work of the various sections of the Centre. He said, 'So far as molecular biology is concerned, I don't think we're any further advanced than similar units over here— in some ways not so far. We were working particularly on the synthesis of protein molecules, and it's possible that we had some useful leads about the methods of control of the various reactions. In regard to viruses, we were trying to work out in more detail the metabolic relationship between the particle and the cell it occupies.' He went on to describe the work in more detail. It was enjoyable to talk on his own subject with a man who obviously understood him. Forsyth listened attentively. He never interrupted except to ask a short question with the object of clarifying a technical point.

At the end he said, 'Well, that all sounds fairly conventional. Some of my own men are working from a fairly similar angle. Though it sounds as if you may have something to teach us on the technical level, at least.' He puffed for a moment at his pipe. 'And that's all you were doing?'

Karas hesitated only for a fraction of a second. 'Yes.'

Forsyth knocked his pipe out in the ash-tray beside him. Then he gave a keen glance at Karas and said dispassionately, 'That's the trouble with all this secrecy and competition in science. All kinds of silly rumours get about. Someone was saying they heard your laboratory was working on mutations. That they had some idea about producing wild strains of totally new viruses. That sounded to me like a damned dangerous thing to do.'

'I agree,' said Karas. He added firmly, 'But we weren't doing anything like that.'

'I didn't think it was likely myself. But you know how it is. Molecular genetics has gone to everyone's head nowadays. Not just science writers, but even the big boys themselves. Here's Edward Tatum going round talking about the possibility of altering existing genes in the human cells and Mac Burnet saying that if we're not careful we're going to make some new organism that might get loose and destroy us—'

'That's just talk.'

'Yes, I know. But there's some basis to it, as we're all aware. It happened more or less the same way with the atom, and there everyone's worst fears came true. So naturally it gets people nervous. But I could never believe it of a man like Bremer—'

Karas said, 'Max was one of the most responsible men I ever met. One only had to talk to him—' He turned to Weldon. 'As Arthur can tell you—'

Forsyth looked up at Weldon in surprise. 'You knew Bremer?'

Weldon said uneasily, 'I wouldn't say I knew him. I just met him in Leipzig.'

'You never told us that.'

Weldon shifted in his chair. 'It was just a casual conversation. Nothing of importance.'

Forsyth looked at him for a moment, frowning a little, and then shrugged his shoulders. 'Well, there we are.' He turned back to Karas and said abruptly, 'Would you like to come down to Falls Ridge and have a look at our laboratories?'

'Very much.'

'I'm going to Montreal tomorrow, but I'll be back next Monday. Will that do?' Karas nodded. Forsyth said to Weldon, 'Perhaps you could bring him down then.'

Henderson's club was an enormous dingy cavern of a place, its walls covered with bad oil paintings of defunct business men. Henderson led them up a marble staircase to the dining-room on the first floor. Here the tables were occupied by men almost indistinguishable from those in the portraits, portly, red-faced, and confident. Though the room was almost full, the tables were set so far apart and the ceiling was so high that only the lowest murmur of conversation could be heard. A white-haired Negro waiter showed them to a secluded table in an alcove.

'It's like eating your lunch in Lenin's tomb,' said Henderson cheerfully. He looked round at the other tables and guffawed. 'Look at them all. You know, there's a rule here that says you mustn't talk business. But you'll see more deals done here than any other place in town. Big stuff. You don't just buy companies nowadays, you buy politicians, you buy governments. One time, business was just business. Now it's all politics.' He said contemptuously, 'I don't hold with that myself. But that's the way it is.'

He ordered drinks from the waiter. 'You know what I have, John. Fetch these young fellows what they want.' When the waiter had gone, he said, 'But the great thing here is, we have privacy. No goddamned fellow's going to be popping up with a flashlight.' He turned to Karas. 'You don't know how it is in this country. The Press are everywhere. And you saw the papers this morning—they're really looking for you. So we've got to keep you under wraps for the moment until you know what you're going to say.'

'About what?'

'About your future. What you feel about things. What you're going to do from now on. You don't want to be pestered by these people. And the only way to avoid that is to say everything you've got to say, all at once, to the whole lot of them. Then it's over. See what I mean?' He popped an olive into his mouth. 'The way you do that is by a press conference. Now what I'm going to suggest to you is that O'Keefe fixes one up for you, say Tuesday next week, after you've had time to go out and visit with Forsyth here. Then you can tell them your story, answer a few questions and finish with it. How about that?'

Karas hesitated. He felt vaguely uneasy. There seemed to be nothing wrong with Henderson's proposition, but somehow it was a little too glib. The big voice, the easy, confident manner, bore the traces of hundreds of other propositions made during Henderson's business lifetime, not all of them entirely in the interests of the persons to whom he had made them. Karas had the sensation of being swept along towards an objective which was much clearer to Henderson than it was to himself. But it was difficult to oppose such force and confidence, particularly when he had no real alternative to suggest. He said, 'Well—'

'It's the only way,' said Henderson. 'Believe me.' He dismissed the subject, took out an enormous pair of black-rimmed spectacles and began to scrutinize the menu. 'Now, let's see what we're going to eat.'

He waited for the others to order and then said to the waiter, 'The usual, John.' This turned out to be a huge, complicated salad, made with fish and pineapples. 'I'm on a diet these days,' Henderson explained. 'I used to be a great eater once.' He slapped his stomach. 'I was the greediest bastard in the world. I ate too much, drank too much—in the end I got so goddamned fat I was disgusting.' It was somehow easy to visualize him as he had been then; the skin hung off his frame like a suit of clothes made for a fleshier man. 'Then I had a heart attack. My doctor said I had to cut it out or I could hand my chips in right then. Well, I had quite a few things I wanted to do, so I said to him, 'Doc, you tell me what to do, I'll take care of the rest.' In the end I took off thirty pounds in three months.' He said reminiscently, 'It was absolute bloody hell. I was so god-damned bad-tempered you'd never believe. I was an absolute son of a bitch. Made life a misery for everyone around me. My wife walked out, half my staff resigned, but I stuck it and I've kept to it ever since.'

He drained the last of his drink and began to pick at his salad in an unenthusiastic way. After a few mouthfuls a look of disgust passed over his face. 'Just the same, I still hate this crap, even after five years.' He turned suddenly melancholy. It was like the moment at the office when he realized that he had forgotten the conference. He said, 'Old age is a series of surrenders. You can't fight on all fronts any more. You've got to save yourself for the battle that matters. Why, when I was a young man I didn't know what it was to feel tired. I remember, when we started the Heavy Chemical Syndicate in 1948—'

He launched into a rambling series of reminiscences about the struggles of his earlier life. As story succeeded story Karas became lost in a maze of companies and associations, of battles between men he had never heard of, of millions of dollars lost here and gained there. The details meant nothing to him, yet there was a fascination in watching this old man unrolling the richly patterned carpet of his life. In so many ways he reminded Karas of Suvorin. It was strange that it should be so. Superficially the gigantic Henderson, with his huge physique, his bellowing rough good fellowship and amiability, was as unlike the academic, puritanical Suvorin as it was possible to imagine. He had none of Suvorin's intellectual subtlety or the bitter self-mockery that went with it. Henderson was not consumed by sensations of guilt or self-disgust. His picture of himself and of the world around him was simple, vivid, two-dimensional.

And yet the resemblances were greater than the differences. They lay in the vitality and aggressiveness, the egoism, the violent resentment of any authority but his own, the sense of outrage at any situation he failed to control. There was the paternal domination of subordinates, the absolute assumption that his life was not governed by the same rules as ordinary people. And beneath all his theatricality, as beneath Suvorin's acrid, blistering wit, there lay the same curious undercurrent of unhappiness and isolation, the fear of ultimate failure.

196

Karas was overcome with a feeling of unreality. What was he doing in this enormous, noisy, foreign city, in this expensive club, eating this lavish and tasteless meal? He was suddenly absurdly homesick for the world he had left —the cafeteria at the Centre with its slovenly, buxom waitresses, the stewed veal and the beetroot soup. He remembered with nostalgia the endless discussions about University politics, the technical problems of wayward centrifuges and temperamental electron microscopes. For a moment he forgot the claustrophobic boredom of it all. At least it had held the comfort of familiarity.

By contrast, Henderson's way of life seemed like a strange foreign game of which he was still ignorant of the rules. It was a gambling game, with money and influence for the prizes and with a Government which acted, not as a source of total power, but merely as a kind of referee—a referee who was sometimes difficult and stiffnecked, but who could be tricked or influenced by a man who knew the ropes.

To Henderson, it was plain, the game was everything— he had invested in it all his intellect, all his energy, all his interests. So far as Henderson was concerned, all the others who surrounded him were pieces to be moved here or there, cards in the hand he hoped to play. Karas was uneasily aware that Henderson's interest in him was based primarily on the fact that he represented, at least temporarily, an ace. But he would not be an ace for ever. Once the hand had been played, the cards would be thrown in and forgotten. What would his position be then?

He looked at Weldon and Forsyth. What rank of card did they represent? Weldon was a middle-rank workhorse of a card, a nine or a ten perhaps. Forsyth's position was a good deal less clear. Henderson, who tended to take control of everything he touched, who radiated possession the way some women radiated sex, did not seem quite to possess Forsyth. It was not that the Australian attempted any rivalry with the old man. He did not try to contradict or force his way into the conversation. On one or two occasions he expressed mild disagreement on some minor issue, but when Henderson brushed him aside, he shrugged indifferently and returned to his food. Now and then he looked around the room when Henderson was talking, as if he had heard that particular story before. On these occasions Karas noticed a frown of annoyance pass over Henderson's face. It was plain that he was not one of those talkers who was indifferent to the reaction of his audience. He required attention.

There was something reassuring to Karas in the realization that there was at least somebody in the organization who was not intimidated by Henderson. A scientist—somebody of his own kind. What, he wondered, was the source of Forsyth's independence? Was it rooted in abilities which made him indispensable? Or did he perhaps have some outside support which had not so far been disclosed?

Henderson grew suddenly irritable. Perhaps it was Forsyth's indifference, perhaps an accumulation of his disgust with his salad. He put down his fork and pushed away his plate. He said, 'I seem to have been doing all the talking.' He turned to Forsyth. 'You're the man we really want to hear. We don't often get a chance to talk to you. You hide away down there in those labs of yours.' Forsyth smiled. Henderson said provocatively, 'You spend a hell of a lot of money down there. Have you turned up anything recently?'

Forsyth finished eating and lit his pipe very deliberately. 'A few things.'

'Few is right.' Henderson said to Karas, 'Do you know, we spend over fifty million dollars a year on research, taking all the divisions together. And what do we get?' He recited scornfully, 'An emulsifying agent. So what? Everyone has one. An artificial fibre that turns out not to take dyes. A drug for some damned tropical disease—' He frowned as his memory failed him. 'What is it?'

'Trypanosomiasis.' Forsyth added, 'It's a very good drug. What's wrong with that?'

'Nothing,' said Henderson, 'except of course, nobody in Africa has the money to buy it. So we have to market it at a loss. Otherwise everyone says we're a lot of bastards. What kind of business is that?'

'If you look at our list of patents—'

'Sure, I know that one. You're going to say they bring me in a lot more than the fifty millions we spend. But most of those are old stuff. In five years' time half of them will be in the public domain. Then where will you be?'

Karas regarded them with bewilderment. It was only an hour or two ago that Henderson had been declaring his admiration for scientific research and wishing that he had had the opportunity of taking it up instead of going into business. Curiously, neither Weldon nor Forsyth seemed in the least surprised at this reversal of his attitude.

Forsyth said equably, 'What do you suggest we do?'

'I can't tell you what to do,' said Henderson irascibly. 'Hell, I'm not a research man. But I know one thing—you need some new blood up there.'

'Such as?'

Henderson waved grandiloquently at Karas. 'Such as this boy here. You say you have trouble getting the right people. I have to go out and get them for you.' A wolfish grin came on his face and he turned to Weldon. 'Isn't that right?'

Weldon smiled back, saying nothing. Karas felt like an article being sold across the table. Forsyth turned his horse-like face towards him. 'Do you think you'd be interested in a job at our laboratories?'

'Perhaps,' said Karas cautiously. 'We should have to talk about it.' He tried to think of a polite way of expressing his doubts. 'I'm not sure that I'd be of use to you.'

'Of course you'd be of use to him,' said Henderson. 'Hell, you were in charge of a whole research section—'

Karas cut in. 'I'm not interested in commercial work,' he said. Anxious to dispel any misunderstanding, and a little irritated at having spent so long as a listener, he had spoken more firmly than he had intended. He softened it a little. 'It's not that I have any prejudice against it. It's simply not my line.' He explained, 'My work is pure university stuff. You couldn't make money out of it.'

Forsyth said, 'I've been twenty-five years in this game. It's hard to know what you can make money out of. If we just looked where the businessmen told us to, we wouldn't find anything. Our policy is to be around at the growing points of research. Your work might well fall into that category.'

'I don't know,' said Karas. 'I'd visualized a university department—'

'We can give you everything there is in a university department,' said Henderson. 'You'll have all the assistance you want and all the money you want. How about that?'

'It's very generous of you,' said Karas cautiously. Now was the time, he knew, when he must raise the crucial question. His mind went back to the day when Suvorin had first visited his laboratory in Budapest. Karas had been very young then. He had been overcome at the thought of receiving a personal visit from such a famous, almost legendary figure. Suvorin too had praised his work, flattered him, made offers of money and facilities and assistance. He had made the Centre sound like a scientist's paradise. That was ten years ago—he had been a young man then and his naivety was perhaps forgivable. But no man should make the same mistake twice. He said, 'What about freedom?'

Forsyth cut in quickly before Henderson could speak, 'What kind of freedom do you mean?'

Karas had his answer ready. He had decided that the sincerity of everything that had been said to him could be judged on this one point. 'Freedom to work on what I want, to publish the results of any work where I want and in my own time. To disclose any results only if I wish to do so. Can you give me that?'

Forsyth rubbed his chin dubiously. 'Well—up to a point.'

'What do you mean—up to a point?'

Forsyth turned a worried face to Henderson. 'There's the question of his contract. He has to sign—'

'Ah hell, that's nothing,' said Henderson irritably. 'They all sign that, there's nothing in it—'

'What is it?' asked Karas sharply. The very casual way Henderson brushed the contract aside made him uneasy.

Weldon came in, soothing as ever. 'It's very much a formality. It's customary in any commercial organization. If by any chance there are commercial implications in your work, the contract stipulates that they are the property of the Company. That's quite normal. After all, the Company invests a great deal of money in research. It has to get it back, if only to finance further scientific work.'

Karas thought for a moment. 'So whatever I do becomes the property of the Company.'

'Yes,' said Weldon. 'In a sense.'

Karas shook his head. 'I don't like that.'

Weldon said, 'There's nothing to it. You can't really expect to own any patents yourself—'

'I'm not interested in patents,' said Karas. 'If there's money to be made out of my work, you're welcome to it. That's not the point at all.' Suddenly he saw himself sitting in the little car in the deserted road by the forest, photographing the sheets of Max's notes on the sensitive plate of his mind. Whatever the ultimate significance of those rows of figures, those neatly tabulated lists of instructions, they were a property held in trust, they were not his to sign away for a job and a secure position and a comfortable life in a new world. 'I must retain total control over my work and anything that comes out of it. I must decide whether to hand it over to you or not. That's definite.'

Forsyth shook his head. He said emphatically, 'No deal.'

'Very well,' said Karas. 'No deal it is.'

Henderson slammed his huge hand on the table. 'Shut up the lot of you and let me talk. It's always the same. If I leave two scientists together for fifteen minutes they start scratching each other's eyes out.' He turned on Forsyth. 'I'll tell you something, Bob. Twenty-five years in ISIS have filled you so full of bureaucratic crap that it's running out of your ears. And as for you—' He glared at Karas. 'You're getting steamed up over nothing. This is the most important deal anyone has done in ISIS over the last five years and I'm not letting the two of you foul it up because you don't understand negotiation. Now look, Dr. Karas—Arthur here assures me you told him you don't have any information of commercial, strategic, or political value whatsoever—'

'That's true,' said Karas steadily.

'And anything you may find out in the future—if this is offered to anybody, it's offered to us. Would you agree?'

'Certainly.'

'So the only thing you want to hold back is the decision whether to publish. Right?'

'Right.'

Henderson thought for a moment. Then he said, 'I'm an old horse-trader, Dr. Karas. That means I know when there's no use haggling any more. All right, I'll wear that. I'll accept your terms.'

Forsyth said, 'I said no deal. Everyone has to sign the standard contract.'

Henderson eyed him balefully. 'You'll do as I say, Bob. You've been getting too big for your breeches for some time. Time you realized who was boss here.' He raised his creaking bulk from the table. 'Make out the contract the way he says.'

He walked away from the table and out of the club like a king closing an audience. Automatically, Karas and Forsyth got up and walked out behind him. Only Weldon lingered behind to sign the bill.

CHAPTER THREE

'AT FIRST SIGHT, *there is little in his appearance which might give a clue as to the life he has led or the qualities which led him to take his present decision. He is a man of just under six feet in height, lean, dark and sharp-eyed. He speaks English with great fluency and only the faintest of accents. His face in repose—'*

Oh no, for God's sake, she thought—that wasn't any use. She slapped the typewriter carriage back and erased the last two sentences. This was really one hell of a job; every word written in blood. She was beginning to wonder miserably whether she wasn't much of a writer after all, that this would end up as just another failure to add to the others in her life. She felt the old impulse to pack up and run away from it, but where was there to run to? At least she must try to finish the job, no matter how bad it turned out to be.

She tried to force her mind back into the style which *Planet* demanded for this kind of story. The first rule was to be factual. Lots of hard information. It didn't matter how apparently trivial the details might be. You built up a main character on the basis of his height and his weight, his favourite breakfast food, his hobbies, the tiny likes and dislikes which made up the small change of his existence. The theory was that from the accumulation of all these tiny brush strokes a true picture of the man would finally begin to emerge. But of course, *Planet* readily agreed, there had to be something more than that, if the true dimensions of the character were ever to be carried across to the million readers. And the secret ingredient was warmth, sympathy, sincerity. Don't be scared of being corny. Let yourself go a little. Be human. Well, she would try.

'Behind a ready smile and an easy conversational manner lies a hard core of resolve, a total dedication—'

She stopped again. A dedication to what? He had to be dedicated to something, that was for sure. In *Planet* language, dedication was a must. In *Planet*'s world you were either a dedicated personality or a jerk—there was nothing in between. Yet somehow neither of these categories seemed to have any relevance to the true nature of Karas. The more she saw of him, the more he seemed to escape from the confines of *Planet*'s assumptions about the complexities of the human character.

Nor had Karas himself been very much help to her. Most Western celebrities had been interviewed so often that they had, consciously or unconsciously, developed a simplified, public-relations version of themselves which they supplied obligingly to the journalist on request. They went through their tricks, answered the old questions, turned on their opinions, their enthusiasms and their prejudices to order.

From the very first interview it had been apparent that in the way of predigested interview material, Karas had little to offer her. Her difficulty was not that he had told her too little about himself, but that he had told her too much. There had been something disconcerting from the very first about the way he had answered her questions—thinking very carefully about them first, then replying baldly and simply and to the point, as if he were speaking to her in confidence rather than through her to the world.

The result was a series of fascinating yet bewildering tapes, riddled with contradictions and the kind of facts which were not easy to present in a magazine article and yet were somehow impossible to ignore. It seemed to her, as she contemplated what she had learned about his character, that she knew him too well to write the article she had intended, but still not well enough for true understanding. It was simple to list individual characteristics, but the key to the pattern was missing. He had appeared so frank, and yet the information that really mattered had still escaped her.

'How are you getting on?'

He was standing in the doorway, watching her, a half-smile on his face. She wondered how long he had been standing there. She took the sheet of paper out of the typewriter and turned it face downwards on the table. It was like one of those occasions in her childhood when her mother had come into her room and found her writing poetry. She felt, quite illogically, ashamed of what she was doing. She stood up and said, 'It's not too good.'

'What's the trouble?'

'I don't know exactly.' She hesitated and then decided to tell him. 'I've come to the conclusion that I don't really understand you at all.' He showed no signs of surprise.

'You know enough for the purpose, surely.'

'I've made a first draft, but I shall have to tear it up. There's no real depth in it.'

'Perhaps they don't want that.'

He was right, of course. So far as *Planet* was concerned, she was probably worrying about nothing. 'I suppose I got too ambitious,' she said. 'I wanted to do you justice.'

'That sounds rather alarming.' There was a slight rasp in the 'r' of the word alarming. His English was almost perfect. Only occasionally, a slight roughening of certain consonants revealed that it was not his native tongue.

'Why?'

'Justice is a hard thing,' he explained. 'Few of us can stand up to it. I'm not particularly proud of some of the things I've done.'

She found herself springing to his defence. 'It hasn't been easy for you—'

'Oh, yes,' he said, 'I can make out quite a good case for myself. As I told you in the interview, it was a question of survival.' His face clouded momentarily. 'The risk of that is that survival can become a habit. It's possible to be too wise, too careful.' His voice was still as calm and judicial as ever. There was no self-pity in it—he was not crying to her for reassurance. It was as if he were recording a strategic error in a battle fought long ago. 'In those days I was alone and very much afraid. I was afraid all the time. I didn't have anything left over for other people. It seemed to me that if I didn't do them any harm, that was as much as could be expected of me. Even then I would be better than the great majority of people. That was what I thought then.'

'And now?'

'Now I don't know. In the last year or so I've begun to wonder—' He hesitated, searching his memory. 'I can't remember exactly when it started. It was towards the end, at the Centre. I was well placed there; I could manage Suvorin and I had a good future. It wasn't bad, all things considered. I had interesting work, there were plenty of girls—no great commitment, of course, but that wasn't what I wanted. Then—' He sighed irritably. 'Sometimes I think it all goes back to Max.'

She was conscious of a sudden spasm of jealousy. 'Why him, particularly?'

'I suppose, in a way, because he was the very opposite of what I was trying to be. I saw myself in relief against him. He was like the negative print to my positive. He was weak and indecisive and hopelessly vulnerable. He trusted everyone and expected them to trust him. He was soft and dependent. He had a better brain than I had, he was a far better scientist. Yet I could see myself gradually displacing him because I was the kind of man they really wanted at the Centre, not him. I didn't push for it but I could see it was one of those things that were bound to happen, and so could he. In the end he accepted it, without resentment, and without ever believing for a moment that I was intriguing against him. Then I began to realize that, so far from resenting me, he actually admired me, for being all the things he wasn't. That kind of generosity was something totally outside my experience. After a while, against all my principles, I began to feel'—he searched for the right word—'a kind of protective attitude towards him.'

She could see that he had begun to think of Bremer as an exceptional, almost saintly figure, yet to her there was something repellent about such a total lack of assertiveness. She found herself saying, with a cruelty she had not intended, 'You make him sound rather sickly.'

He was not disturbed by her lack of sympathy. 'Yes, I suppose I do. Sophia felt the same way as you. Perhaps it isn't the kind of personality that appeals to a woman.'

The exasperation she had felt when he had first spoken of Bremer was intensified by the mention of Sophia. She felt a desire to drag him back to the present, to remind him that the Centre and the Bremers were gone for ever. Reality was here. She shut her typewriter abruptly and said, 'How did you get on at lunch?'

He looked at her for a moment, noting that he had irritated her without being very clear why. Then he said, 'It was interesting.'

She forced a smile. 'You're being cautious again.'

'It's a little early to be anything else.'

'Did you like the old man?'

'He's a force of nature,' said Karas. 'I was suitably impressed.' He paused. 'I'm to go to the laboratories at Falls Ridge on Monday. Then there's a press conference on Tuesday.' He waited for her to comment but she said nothing. 'Is that a good idea?'

'It's necessary. I don't see any harm in it.'

He nodded, accepting her reassurance. Then he smiled, temporarily dismissing serious problems from his mind. 'In the meantime we have a little time on our hands. If you're not too busy working, you could perhaps show me something of New York.'

During the next few days she showed him round the sights of the city. They went to Rockefeller Center and the U.N. Building, took a ferry to Staten Island, went to a Broadway musical and a jazz club in the Village. They hardly saw the other inhabitants of the apartment—Weldon was visiting his wife in Westchester and O'Keefe was occupied with business of his own. They used the side entrance of the block and kept away from places where celebrities might be expected to go. They were not bothered by any more photographers.

As they sat over dinner in an East Side restaurant he said, 'This is the first time since I escaped that I've felt almost free.'

She did not ask him what he meant by 'almost'. 'I suppose we're none of us entirely free,' she said.

He looked at her in surprise. 'You are, surely.'

'Am I? Yes, I suppose in a way I am,' she admitted. She could do as she wished and go where she pleased. She was dependent on nobody. At one time it had seemed to her that no one with the liberty she now enjoyed could possibly be unhappy. Now she knew better. She said, 'Perhaps freedom's an illusion, like so many other things. I used to think, when I was a girl, that once I was twenty-one—that was the age I was due to come into my trust fund—everything would be all right.'

'And wasn't it?'

'It was wonderful for the first six months. And then—' She stopped. She felt herself moving on to dangerous ground. It had been like this before. You found yourself involved with a man and before you knew it you were pouring out your heart to him, hoping to trade your stale, useless liberty for something else—a little tenderness and support, the warmth of mutual dependence. But the man was always looking for something different from what you had to offer—and what he had to offer was never quite what you were looking for. There was disappointment and pain —and one day you knew you had failed again. You were back again with the freedom you had yearned so desperately to lose. 'It's probably my fault,' she said, as much to herself as to Karas. She saw he was perplexed and went on nervously, 'I'm afraid I'm not at all a stable, balanced person. Not the kind of person you admire.' It was really far better that he should have no illusions about her. If she could not trust herself to be cautious and prudent, at least she could trust him. He should be given the opportunity to see what kind of girl he was getting involved with. She said abruptly, 'I even had analysis at one time.'

'Why?'

'It's hard to explain. Probably all to do with my rotten childhood. My relationships with people are all wrong. The analyst said I expected too much of them. After all, what

206

have I to offer in return? I don't know. You see, I want desperately to give, and yet—' She suddenly stopped and said in an angry voice, 'All this is too boring for words. Why should you want to listen to my problems?'

'You listened for long enough to mine.'

'That's rather different.' She looked up at him and said earnestly, 'I want you to know that I don't talk to everyone like this. I'm not one of those women who go around looking for an opportunity—'

'Yes, I know.' His voice was reassuring. He said gently, 'Don't worry about what I think about you. I'm too old to imagine that the self-possessed façade you present bears any relationship to reality. You're afraid, just as I am, just as we all are. It's the human condition. Until you know what people are afraid of, you don't know anything about them.'

They sat in silence for a while. She felt the same sense of being trapped in a situation outside her control that she had experienced when they had sat together in the car outside the restaurant above the Lake of Geneva. This was not like Maurice or the others who had gone before him. She could not be sure how he felt about her or what he would ask from her. But she knew she no longer had strength to turn him away if he wanted her. She knew, too, that he must be aware of her helplessness. She glanced at his face for some clue to his thoughts, but there was nothing but the same grave, thoughtful expression which marked his approach to the other problems with which she had seen him confronted. She had a sudden picture of him poring over the chessboard, assessing the pattern of the game and the possible consequences of any move which might be made. Yet there was something reassuring rather than repellent about his calmness. It was as if the game he was playing was not directed against her, but a joint battle against the forces of the world in which he would move the pieces for both.

As they left the restaurant he said, 'I don't much feel like going back to that apartment. There's something about it—'

'Yes, I know what you mean.' She too had been increasingly oppressed by the apartment. It had seemed to take possession of them, reminding them constantly that while they lived there they were merely instruments of Henderson and the plans he had laid for them all. Once they entered the apartment it would be the end of their evening. The fragile intimacy which had been built up between them would be blown away in those vast impersonal rooms. She longed to hold on to it for a little longer. She hesitated and then said awkwardly, 'I have a little walk-up which I use when I visit New York. I share it with another girl but she's away just now. I could make you a cup of coffee.'

'What's a walk-up?' he said.

'Come along and I'll show you.'

They took a taxi uptown. The apartment was in the East Seventies, in a street of dingy brownstone houses. Sarah opened the outer door and they walked up several flights of stairs. It was the last apartment on the top floor. They passed through a narrow corridor, off which doors opened into two bedrooms, a bathroom and a kitchen. At the end of the corridor was the main room of the apartment. Karas had seen plenty of apartments as small as this but never one quite so crowded. Books crammed the shelves that lined the walls and spilled over on to tables and chairs. Every available surface was covered with framed photographs, phonograph records, and various forms of bric-à-brac. In the corners of the room were golf clubs and tennis rackets, skis and typewriters. There were potted plants, piles of old magazines, and a work basket from which various articles of underclothing spilled out on to the floor. Directly in Karas's path was a small stuffed alligator. Sarah said, 'Just kick it out of the way.'

At the far end of the room there was a pair of french doors. Karas opened them and walked out on to a small flat roof surrounded by trellis work. Far below he looked down on the deserted backyards of a row of houses. A huge ginger cat mewed at him from the top of a garden wall. 'I like this place,' he said.

'It has something, I'll admit. Though it gets a bit crowded when we're both at home. Fortunately that isn't often.' She joined him on the roof. 'It's fun out here on a spring evening. That's if you like the city, of course. Not everybody does. In New York it's usually too hot or too cold.' Karas was conscious of a bitter wind blowing in from the East River. She said, 'We'd better go back inside. Sit down and amuse yourself while I make the coffee.'

He took off his top-coat and sat on a large chintz-covered sofa which took up about a quarter of the available floor space. There was a book of Degas prints on the coffee table in front of him and he leafed through it abstractedly. He heard her movements in the kitchen as she prepared the tray. In a few moments she would return, they would sit together, they would be back to the intimacy they had known in the restaurant, in the car above Lake Geneva. And it would be for him to decide what happened then.

At another time, in another place, there would have been no doubt in his mind. He wanted her, more than he had wanted Anya or the others, far more than he had ever wanted Sophia. He could take her now, he knew. But he knew too that if he took her without love he would destroy something in her, and probably himself too. There was a commitment involved, far more than companionship, or a relief of mutual loneliness, or pleasure in bed. She would make the commitment totally. Unless he was prepared to meet her on those terms it would be far better for him not to become involved at all. It was still possible.

He tried to think of the future as he had always done since childhood, calculating the chances, planning for safety and survival, but now the calculations failed him—his intellect struggled to retain its dominance, and lost. He had a sudden overpowering picture of a world that might perhaps somewhere exist, in which caution could be abandoned, to be replaced by confidence and trust. There welled up within him a great longing for all the affection and loyalty which life had denied him. And in that moment he realized that without these things even survival was a worthless dream, a mere clinging to existence for its own sake.

She returned and put the tray down on the table. Then she hesitated. There was nowhere to sit except on the sofa. With the air of someone taking a difficult decision she sat down in the opposite corner of it, squeezing herself against the arm so as to leave the largest possible space between them. Then she leaned forward to pour out the coffee. On an impulse he put out his hand to touch her arm to stop her. 'Not just yet,' he said.

'Why not?' Her voice shook slightly.

'You know why not.' He moved across the sofa and kissed her. She did not resist, but her lips were tight shut against his and her body was rigid in his arms. She shivered slightly and he drew away frowning.

'Now have some coffee,' she said. Very deliberately she poured out two cups and handed one to him. He looked at her in surprise. He had felt sure that she had wanted him and was ready for him to make love to her. He had seen the moment of decision as entirely his own. He said, 'What's the trouble?' She swallowed nervously and lit a cigarette.

Fixing her gaze at a point on the opposite wall, she said, 'I really set this thing up, didn't I?'

'Set it up?' The expression was unfamiliar to him.

'I suppose you're quite accustomed to it. Girls inviting you to their apartments to make love to them—'

'Where I come from,' he said dryly, 'girls don't have apartments.'

'Oh, you know what I mean. After all, you were quite open about it. Those girls at the Centre. Bremer's wife—what was her name—?'

'Sophia.'

'Yes. Well—I can see that naturally you might think—' She left the sentence unfinished. 'I'm sorry if there was a misunderstanding. It was entirely my fault. It wasn't really meant to be that kind of an invitation.'

He moved back to the other end of the sofa. Gradually her body relaxed. She ran her hand distractedly, through her beautiful blonde hair. Her eyes were a little moist, her mouth tremulous. He said, 'Why are you so unhappy?'

'I told you I was no good to you, didn't I? I warned you. You must admit that.'

'You haven't answered my question.'

She hardly seemed to hear what he said. 'You don't want somebody like me,' she said. 'You want somebody easy and sensual. I know I look attractive but believe me I'm not worth the trouble. Lots of men have found that out.' She turned to face him and said intensely, 'And after all, you don't want any more problems. You have plenty as it is. If we stop here it's all right. We can carry on as friends—'

'And if we don't stop?'

'It will be impossible. I know it. I've been through it all before. I'm no good at casual affairs. I want too much, more than men want to give. And if they can't give me that,' she said helplessly, 'I find I can't give them anything either. It just doesn't work. So you can see how it is.'

This, for the sensible, detached man, was the moment to disengage. All his experience of women told him that. She was beautiful and exciting and she wanted him, but there would be no relationship with her that did not contain complexity and involvement.

The prudent man would play for time. He would talk to her about those other men, find out more about her before taking any irrevocable steps. That was the wise and sensible thing to do. Instead, Karas found himself saying, 'We can make it work.'

'No.' She said it almost painfully. 'It's a mistake. I don't want you to.' As he moved nearer to her, she said desperately, 'I'm hopeless. I shall make you miserable.' Her voice was trembling. 'If you must know there's something wrong with me. I'm frigid—'

'I don't believe it.'

He was touching her face now. He ran his hand gently down the side of her neck, over her shoulders, and on to the curve of her breast. She trembled and said, 'It's true. I've been told—not just by one person.' In her voice was something like panic. Her lips were parted and her breathing rapid. He made no attempt to kiss her but simply ran his hands down the side of her body towards the narrow waist. He felt the tingling of electricity from the thin silk of her dress. She said rapidly, 'I want you to know—I'm still a virgin—at twenty-six. I tried twice but I couldn't do it. I just seized up. I'm hopeless, hopeless. I just can't feel anything—' She suddenly took a deep sighing breath and fell into his arms, her hands clutching his shoulders. 'Oh, God, Peter, I want you so badly! Tell me it's going to be all right this time.'

He kissed her lips and felt her body give way in front of him. It was as if she were presenting it to him as an offering, a symbol of trust. 'Don't worry,' he said. 'It's going to be all right. I love you.' He realized as he said it that it was the first time he had ever used those actual words.

CHAPTER FOUR

THEY SPENT most of the week-end in the small apartment, returning to Park Avenue only late at night to sleep. Sarah went out shopping on Third Avenue and bought in food from which she made their own meals. Locked in the warmth and quiet of the tiny flat, it was possible to imagine, for a short while at least, that they were completely alone in the city, cut off from all conflicts and responsibilities. It was a delight to know that they had told nobody where they were —they were no longer the slaves of a knock on the door or a ring on the telephone. They idled the hours away, eating picnic meals, talking, reading, making love. They pushed together the two single beds in the small, feminine bedroom and lay between the sheets throughout the long grey Sunday afternoon. When the daylight faded, the neon signs flashed on in its place, casting a rose-tinted glow on the clouds which hung over the city. He said, 'It's all right now? You're not worried any more?'

'No. Not now,' she said. She clung to him, her face buried in his shoulder, her arms round his waist. 'With you it's all right.' Then, moving away, she said with a note of triumph in her voice, 'Maurice was wrong. He said I was asking for the impossible—looking for something that didn't exist. And I almost believed him.' She sat up and switched on the light. She looked down at him as he lay at her side. Her fair hair fell down across her naked shoulders; her eyes, without the contact lenses, were large and of a pale, translucent blue. She said, 'But you *are* here for good, aren't you? You're not going to disappear across the world again?'

'No,' he said. 'That's over now. I'll be staying here.'

'It doesn't have to be here,' she said. 'So long as you're with me, I don't care where it is.'

He smiled at her solemnity. 'Supposing I said I wanted you to come with me to the other side? Would you accept that too?'

She thought for a moment. Then she answered him quite seriously, 'Yes,' she said. 'Even that.'

The next morning the Cadillac called after breakfast to take Karas and Weldon to Falls Ridge. The big car crawled through the heavy traffic along the Henry Hudson Parkway and across the George Washington Bridge into New Jersey. As they drove along the Palisades Weldon said, 'You'll be startled by Falls Ridge. It's a really magnificent place. There's nothing like it in the world.'

In an irrational access of loyalty to his old employer, Karas said, 'The Centre was pretty good, you know.'

'Well, you'll see,' said Weldon with confidence. 'You can tell me afterwards how they compare.'

'Didn't you work there yourself at one time?'

'Yes. For a few years. Very routine stuff. Nothing on your level.' He spoke almost apologetically. 'Then they found out I spoke languages and asked me to do some travelling.'

Karas looked at the smooth, pink, over-handsome face, the Savile Row suit and highly polished shoes, the delicate hands and restless eyes. 'It must be very interesting—getting around the world as you do.'

'Yes,' said Weldon. There was a slight note of uncertainty in his voice, as if he were no longer sure if it was interesting. He said vaguely, 'It keeps me in touch. I meet people . . .'

There was a slight pause. Karas suddenly remembered the frown on Forsyth's face when he had heard about Weldon meeting Bremer at Leipzig. 'Like you met Max?' he said.

'Yes. That's right.' Weldon spoke shortly. Then he pointed out of the car window to the river below them. 'Just here you get rather a remarkable view of the Hudson.'

Karas gave the view a perfunctory glance. Then he said, 'What impression did he make on you?'

Weldon hesitated. He replied reluctantly, 'Bremer? Oh—' He shrugged his shoulders. 'It was only a short acquaintance, you know.'

'Even so,' Karas persisted. 'You remembered him several years later—'

'Yes, well—' There was an unusual note of impatience in Weldon's voice. 'He was obviously a very brilliant man.' He seemed to realize the inadequacy of this description. 'And a very warm, sympathetic personality.'

'What did he talk about?'

'Oh, his work, you know. The difficulties involved in handling bacteriophage. The quality of the other papers at the meeting.'

Karas said, 'He must have taken to you very much.'

'Oh, I don't know—'

'Oh, yes,' insisted Karas. 'He was ordinarily very shy with strangers.'

'Well, he wasn't shy on this occasion,' snapped Weldon. Karas looked at him in astonishment. It was the first time he had ever known Weldon to lose control of himself. He was particularly taken aback since there seemed to have been nothing in the previous conversation which could possibly have annoyed him. Why on earth should he be so edgy at any mention of the Leipzig meeting? Karas was trying to work it out when Weldon came in rapidly. 'I'm awfully sorry,' he said apologetically. He was obviously his old self again. 'I'm afraid I was irritable. It was nothing to do with anything you said. I have'—he sighed—'domestic problems. They make me a little tense sometimes.'

Karas nodded sympathetically. Presumably Weldon had encountered trouble at home over the week-end—a sick child perhaps, an unfaithful wife. The two men remained silent for a while. Eventually the car turned off the great highway and they passed through several small neat towns full of prosperous houses, modern schools and shops, and sedate little churches. 'Commuter country,' said Weldon. 'The husbands work in New York and come home by train each night.' He pointed to a group of women on the sidewalk, some wheeling prams. 'Those are the wives. They take the kids to school, clean the house, do the shopping at the supermarket. Then in the afternoon they play golf at the country club—or they attend classes on flower arrangement or something. In the evening they meet the husbands at the station. They drive them home, have martinis together, and put the kids to bed. Then they play bridge or watch television. Then they go to bed themselves.' He said sardonically at Karas, 'You chaps are always talking about the bourgeosie. Well, there it is.'

'You seem to know it very well,' said Karas.

'It's my own life,' replied Weldon. 'My wife and children live in a place just like this. The only difference is that I commute longer distances.'

Karas asked, with genuine curiosity, 'Do you like it?'

Weldon shrugged his shoulders. 'It's traditional to condemn it,' he said. 'The intellectuals say it's very suburban and stultifying. It is too, in many ways. But most of the wives like it, and it's the only way to bring up children if you work in the city. So everybody does it.'

A picture came into his mind of the trim, neat house in the select development in Westchester, of Blanche and the remote, foreign little children whose faces resembled his but whose voices were strange and whose interests he could not understand. He had spent the week-end with them. It had been the same as ever. The joy of the first meeting, then the gradual disenchantment, the conversation full of allusions that meant nothing to him. In the evening the children had insisted on watching television while he and Blanche had exchanged news. But the news had fallen flat —the two of them were like old acquaintances who had lost contact with each other's lives. His adventures round the world meant as little to her now as the P.T.A. and the bridge circle and Jan Sinclair's new baby meant to him. Conversation had gradually languished. In bed there had been the traditional love-making, perfunctory on both sides. He knew she suspected him of keeping a mistress in Europe.

Had she found someone to console her? Very probably— she was still attractive, even after the children. He could hardly blame her.

On the Sunday he had refused to go to church and pottered aimlessly around the house. There was nothing much to do. The atmosphere was not conducive to reading, and he had wandered restlessly from one room to another. After lunch they had spent the afternoon at the country club, but he did not play golf and the conversation of Blanche's friends bored him. He had found himself thinking of the England he had left fifteen years ago. He forgot the things that had so oppressed him then—the social rigidity, the lack of opportunity—and remembered only the bland tolerance, the politeness, the green, drowsy fields. He had been attacked by an agonizing loneliness. Oh, he had thought, for my own people. My own people . . .

To Karas he said, 'The truth is, I'm still a foreigner here.'

Karas knew instinctively that Weldon was a lost, rootless man, just as he himself had been all his life. He spoke with unusual gentleness. 'I understand.'

Weldon looked at him with gratitude. As he regarded the thin, battered, world-worn face, it seemed to him that he had suddenly grown near to something which he had always longed for, but had almost given up hope of ever attaining —a friendship with another man based on understanding and trust. He felt the need to say something to record the moment. But he was afraid that if he pressed it too hard, it would disappear. He said lightly, 'However, one must accept life as it it. There's no alternative.' As they stopped momentarily at an intersection he pointed to a giant supermarket surrounded by vast car-parks. 'You know they say the villages are the heart of Spain? Well, these are the heart of America.'

They left the town and moved into wooded country. The traffic had thinned out considerably. After a while they turned along a minor road which wove its way through a network of pine woods. They passed through a small village and then the car slowed down. On the right there was a wide gate from which a barbed-wire fence stretched away on both sides into the woods. As they stopped at the entry, two armed guards came out of a small building and approached the car.

'This is it,' said Weldon. They waited for a while as the driver produced their passes. The guards peered suspiciously inside the car and compared the photographs on the passes with the people inside. It was, thought Karas, a rather more thorough screening than the one at Kennedy Airport. Then the gate was opened and the car went through.

They drove for another half-mile before they saw the laboratories. It was a large complex of brick buildings, some of them as many as six stories high, set within a campus of lawns and flower beds. There was a great lake at one side, and behind it the wooded hills rolled away to merge into a range of mountains beyond. Karas was instantly reminded of the Centre. The mountains were lower, the lawns tidier, and the buildings somehow less rough and utilitarian, but otherwise it was much the same.

They got out of the car at the main entrance and went into the reception area, a large hall of marble and glass with another armed guard at the door and three reception-ists at desks facing it. One of them got up as they entered.

'Why hallo, Dr. Weldon.' Her voice was rich with an earnest, impersonal, and quite meaningless courtesy. It reminded Karas of the kind of greeting one got on boarding an aircraft. 'Dr. Karas? We're glad to welcome you to Falls Ridge. Dr. Forsyth will be down right away.'

A few minutes later Forsyth stepped out of one of the bank of elevators on the left side of the hall. He greeted them in his usual abrupt, laconic way.

'You're right on time,' he said approvingly. 'We've got a lot to show you. I've put the whole morning aside for it.' Without giving the remark undue emphasis, he nevertheless managed to make it plain that this was a considerable con-cession on his part. He said to Weldon, dismissively, 'Arthur, I know you want to talk to a whole stack of people, so we won't detain you. I'll take care of Dr. Karas and we'll meet again here at four o'clock. Right?' He turned to the receptionist without waiting for Weldon's reply. 'Linda, will you fix for the car to collect them then?'

He led Karas out of the entrance towards one of the other blocks. Karas was interested to see the change in his manner now that he was on home ground. In New York he had been formidable, but nevertheless slightly subdued and ill-at-ease. Here he was confident and authoritative, a man who gave orders and expected them to be obeyed.

For the next two hours they toured the laboratories. Despite himself, Karas was impressed. Weldon had been right in saying that they represented the ultimate in scientific luxury. The equipment at the Centre had been good, but it had been bought with some consideration of expense. Very complex and costly material, such as computers or electron microscopes, were available, but in nothing like the numbers and variety which ISIS was evidently willing to provide. The laboratory space had been limited, and rapidly expanding departments had suffered from overcrowding. Here the demand for expansion was met instantly with new and larger buildings, each fitted out with every facility which the scientist concerned could think of. The sophistication of the equipment was also noticeably in advance of anything which the Centre, with the best will in the world, had been able to buy. There were large, spacious offices, a multitude of technicians and secretaries, a vast library, and an animal house of a completely new, semi-automated design.

When they had finished the tour they went back to Forsyth's office in the Administration Block. Forsyth said, 'You like it?'

'It's magnificent.'

Forsyth accepted the compliment without surprise. 'We think so. ISIS has plenty of money and it's my job to screw it out of them for my people here. In my view, it's only what they deserve.' He turned on Karas as if refuting an argument. 'Believe me,' he said fiercely, 'this place isn't just equipment. We've got the finest bunch of workers you could wish to meet.' A secretary came in with two paper cups of coffee. Forsyth sipped his and grimaced. 'We can make any damn' thing except a decent cup of coffee.'

He pushed his coffee aside and began to talk. Deliberately and without haste, he painted for Karas a picture of life at the laboratories. He described the department heads and summarized the main lines of work in progress. He spoke of the generous vacations, the facilities for travel, and mentioned in passing the salary levels and the standard of life enjoyed by the staff. He described the large, comfortable homes, the fishing and the country club. He outlined his own career in ISIS, starting as an enzyme chemist twenty-five years before and working his way up through various departments before transferring to administration. He had done no laboratory work himself for ten years, but Karas could see that he had the gift, as Suvorin had, for keeping in touch with what was happening, and for smoothing the wheels of the various departments. He knew how to give encouragement when needed and to spot weaknesses as they arose. He could speak with understanding, if not with authority, of many different lines of research—in the way of a man who sat at the same table with research workers every day, puffing his pipe and saying little, but absorbing the atmosphere of science through the very pores of his skin.

All the time he spoke, Karas reminded himself that this was just another exercise in persuasion comparable to those he had experienced from Suvorin and Henderson. The homely atmosphere and the plain talk were just as much a part of an attempt to impress him as Henderson's vast office and incessant telephone calls. Yet because it was more subtly tuned in to his own personality he found himself being impressed. The picture Forsyth painted was an attractive one. This was the kind of world in which he could convincingly see himself taking a part.

Forsyth said, 'The operation divides across roughly into pure research on the one hand and applied on the other. You'd be in the pure research section. I might be able to swing you a separate independent group, with a staff of your own right from the beginning. I can't promise, but I'd certainly do my best. If we could arrange that, you'd be in a similar position to Waring, whom you met this morning. As you see it's a good life. Excellent facilities, freedom, a nice place to live.' He spoke casually, deliberately keeping all pressure out of his voice. 'isis is generous about travel. You'll have the opportunity of meeting all the big men in your own field. A sabbatical every seventh year. You could go over to Europe when you wanted, spend a bit of time with the boys in Cambridge. Visit Australia—I know some useful people over there—' He was silent for a moment, giving Karas time to think about it. Then he said, 'As you see, I'm selling this job to you. I want you here. We need people like you. You'd earn between thirty and forty thousand dollars a year. Not bad, I think you'll agree.'

Karas nodded agreement. He had been earning the equivalent of about five thousand dollars at the Centre. But he allowed no change of expression to cross his face.

'You'll see my house when we go to lunch. You could afford one like it if you wanted. There's a retirement pension scheme. It's all worth considering. A scientist has a good life in this country.'

'Yes. I can see that.' It all sounded perfect apart from one thing. But without that one thing it was valueless.

Karas said, 'What about the contract? I meant what I said at lunch the other day. I must have complete freedom.'

Forsyth thought for a while. Then he said, 'I've been giving it a lot of thought. It's against my principles. It would mean putting you on a different footing from the other workers. But well—' He made a gesture of resignation. 'I think I could swing it. And supposing I can, would you come?'

Karas was tempted to accept there and then. But inherent caution prevented him making an immediate commitment. He said, 'May I have a day or two to think it over?'

'By all means,' said Forsyth easily. He gave Karas a speculative look. 'Of course the alternative is a university. You could get into one all right—plenty of the colleges would be glad to have you. But you wouldn't do as well as here either for salary or facilities.' He grinned. 'And after all, it *was* ISIS that got you out, wasn't it?'

Karas corrected him. 'It was Henderson.'

Forsyth's mouth tightened a little. 'Henderson . . .' He seemed about to say something further and then to decide against it. He stood up abruptly. 'Perhaps it's time we went for lunch. We can talk about Henderson afterwards.'

Forsyth's house was a few miles from the laboratories. It was large and sprawling, set among birch woods, with a good deal of ground to it which stretched right up to the foothills of the mountains. 'The Appalachians,' said Forsyth. 'The range runs north right up to Canada and south down to Tennessee.' He drove the Buick station wagon into the three-car garage and led the way into the house. Despite its size, the house was simply furnished with chintzes and reproduction furniture in the American style. There was a good deal of pine panelling. Forsyth's wife was a plump woman with snow-white hair and a hard mid-Western voice. She produced a simple meal of cold ham, salad, and beer, and then left them alone.

Forsyth lit his pipe and puffed at it silently for a while. He seemed to be considering what would be the best way to introduce the subject that was on his mind. Finally he said, 'How are you managing to settle down in New York?'

'Not bad. Naturally, it's a little strange at first.'

Forsyth nodded understandingly. 'You must find certain things very confusing.'

'Just at times.'

'Sometimes they may be even more confusing than you realize.' He paused, and then said with an expression of distaste, 'That lunch last week, for instance.'

The intensity in his voice surprised Karas. It occurred to him that, in spite of his pretence of indifference, Forsyth had deeply resented his treatment by Henderson. He was taking up the classic defensive attitude of the intellectual who had been bruised by his contact with power. Karas became wary. He had no desire to be involved in any organizational battles. 'He's a very remarkable old man,' he said non-committally.

Forsyth grimaced. 'He's a salesman,' he said without trying to conceal his contempt. 'You probably haven't been exposed to salesmen before. They're like actors—what they really sell is themselves. They can believe what it suits them to believe.' He paused, waiting for some reaction. But Karas said nothing. 'He started as a young man selling mining stock. Then he worked his way into the chemical business and managed to get hold of a few licences for South America. Out there he got himself tipped off about mining deposits. He was known to be generous to those who helped him—civil servants and so on. Do you follow?'

'Of course.' Karas was surprised that Forsyth should think that he would not. After all, it was the standard Marxist picture of an entrepreneur. He had never expected Henderson to be anything else.

'He got bigger and bigger. Eventually he was in all kinds of things. Then he ran into trouble in Costa Rica. Somebody found out what was going on—somebody who hadn't been paid off. There was a scandal. The Federal Government got scared. The Good Neighbour Policy and all that. The Costa Ricans were threatening to nationalize all American property. So Washington stepped in and forced him to make a deal. It was similar to the Persian oil thing. A consortium. ISIS took over Henderson, made a new contract on more generous terms, took a few local vice-presidents into the subsidiary—you know the sort of thing. Everyone's face was saved. The only trouble was—we got stuck with Henderson.'

'You?' said Karas.

'ISIS.' Forsyth leaned forward. 'I'm an ISIS man, Dr. Karas, have been for twenty-five years. That's where my loyalties are. Henderson's the second biggest shareholder in the corporation, but he's not an ISIS man—not in my sense of the word.' He spoke with the pride of a man who feels himself the member of an exclusive society, to which wealth alone could never give admittance. 'You may think that because he's a very rich man and occupies most of a building on Park Avenue, that he can do as he likes within the organization. It would be very understandable if you thought that.'

Karas said cautiously, 'He certainly acts that way.'

'I told you,' said Forsyth. 'He's a salesman.' Realizing the explanation was inadequate, he went on, 'Let me explain. Being unfamiliar with the modern capitalist state, you may fall into the trap of thinking that money represents power. In a small organization that's so. But not in ISIS. ISIS is like a small state in itself. It doesn't operate on ordinary commercial principles. It likes to make money, but not too much at a time for fear it may attract the envy of Governments. It's scared of looking like a monopoly, so it cossets its competitors as if they were its children. It's generous with its employees and helpful to the civil servants wherever it operates. It doesn't like to wield too much power or to attract too much attention. It has no fear of commercial competition, but it's desperately afraid of nationalization, or anti-trust legislation. Its main preoccupation isn't money or power, but simply keeping itself in existence. Does that surprise you?'

Karas had a sudden picture of ISIS, like some great prehistoric animal, lumbering through the world in perpetual fear of being destroyed by the process of evolution. 'It sounds logical,' he said.

'Of course it's logical.' Forsyth looked at Karas intently, to make sure his words were going home. Then he leaned back in his chair, apparently satisfied. 'When Henderson shouted me down in his club the other day, he was playing games, Dr. Karas. He was pretending he was back in the old days, before Costa Rica. I let it go—he's an old man, after all. But I wouldn't like you to be misled.'

'Misled?' said Karas. 'About what?'

Forsyth said with unusual intensity, 'About who really counts in this outfit. Where the real power lies. For example, you remember the way he was riding me about how much we spend here, and how little we find?' Karas nodded. Forsyth went on contemptuously, 'Well, I have to listen to that once in a while from marketing men like Henderson —it's one of the things I'm paid a lot of money for. They like to think they're in charge of us. But that's been out of date for years. Nowadays, in ISIS, research doesn't exist simply to produce products. It exists for its own sake. We can't afford to stop doing research, just as we can't afford to over-exploit natural resources or be too rough with competition. We can't, in fact, afford to do anything which would look greedy or irresponsible. The whole of ISIS is one vast public relations exercise. And there's no better public relations than science.' He showed his teeth in a humourless smile. 'It's true what Henderson says, that the Research Division spends a large proportion of its money on projects which are of no commercial significance at all. But what can the corporation do about it? They can't wrap the division up. They could fire me, but they're scared to do that. It would look bad, and they can't afford to look bad. Anyway, there are three vice-presidents who came up through Research, and they would always support me. In the end, you'll find I do pretty much as I please.' He paused for a moment. 'Fortunately what pleases me is what you want too.' When Karas made no reply, he said, 'Listen, Dr. Karas, you're one of us. You don't belong with those salesmen on Park Avenue.'

It seemed to Karas that he was being invited to betray Henderson by implication. He said, 'It was Henderson who fought for me about the contract.'

The impatience came back into Forsyth's voice at the mention of Henderson. 'He doesn't know what it's all about. He just wanted to oblige you because he needs you.'

'Why should he need me?'

'To get himself on the cover of *Time Magazine*. To show ISIS that he's someone to be reckoned with. To show the United States, if it comes to that. Do you think ISIS doesn't really know what's going on?' he said violently. 'You think they like it? Do you think the Federal Government doesn't know? Do you think *they* like it?'

Karas shifted uneasily. The same doubts had occurred to him. He had put them down to his ignorance of Western life. Raised by Forsyth, they suddenly assumed a new and alarming character. He asked, 'Then why don't they stop it?'

Forsyth drummed his fingers on the table. He searched around for a way of explaining the situation. 'Life's very complicated in a free society,' he said. 'It's too early for ISIS to interfere. Henderson may have friends in Washington. They may not know quite how to handle the situation. He's a tough, dangerous old man, you know. And they have to think of the Press. He knows that and he's using it. Why do you think he's laid on this press conference?'

Karas said, 'It was forced on him. Some newspaper had already found out about me. There was that photograph taken outside the apartment house—'

Forsyth grinned sceptically. 'Yes, I know—I saw it. Our newspaper men are brilliant. They can figure out just when you're likely to be coming through Kennedy Airport and lie in wait for you . . .' His disbelief hung heavily in the air. 'Have you been troubled by the Press much since?' he asked.

'No,' said Karas. 'Arthur Weldon found a side entrance to the apartment house—'

'Oh, I see.' Forsyth was mocking. 'And the newspapers didn't. They suddenly turned very stupid, didn't they, after being so brilliant?' He laughed suddenly, almost affectionately. 'The old bastard.' Then he terminated the conversation. He stood up, looked at his watch. 'But we can't stay here talking all day. It's time you were leaving for New York.'

CHAPTER FIVE

As HE SAT with Weldon in the back of the limousine, Karas was overcome with a sense of utter weariness and disgust. It was impossible to mistake the inference behind Forsyth's last words, or to doubt the truth behind it. The whole business of the photographers had been an elaborate charade to force him to do what Henderson had planned for him. And as he thought of it in these terms, he remembered other things which had vaguely disturbed him at the time but which he had forced into the background of consciousness as they began to trouble his peace of mind. He remembered Forsyth's surprise that Weldon had met Max and Weldon's uncharacteristic flash of irritation in the car that morning at the mention of Max's name. He thought back over all the things that had happened to him since he had first walked through the door of the villa, and all the things he had been told. He thought of the dinner on the mountain overlooking the lake, and the visit of the police to the villa in Geneva. He felt very tired.

Weldon broke the silence at last. He said, 'What did you think of the laboratories?'

'They were the finest I've ever seen.'

'And Forsyth? You got on all right with him?'

'Yes, I think so.'

'He's a little cold. Hasn't much sense of humour and no outside interests at all. Rather a boring man personally. But a fine administrator. He's done a wonderful job there.'

'Would you say he was honest—trustworthy?'

Weldon looked at him uneasily, as if wondering what was behind the question. 'Oh, yes, I think so.' He paused. 'Mind you he's not everybody's dish. He and Henderson don't exactly see eye to eye—' He moved quickly away from the subject of Henderson. 'I imagine he offered you a job?'

'Yes.'

'Do you think you'll take it?'

'I don't know.'

Weldon gave him another solicitous glance. It was plain to Karas that Weldon's job was to peddle reassurance and to keep him in a relaxed frame of mind. Any form of abnormal or preoccupied behaviour was a source of anxiety to him. He felt almost sorry for what he was about to do to Weldon. He said suddenly, 'Arthur—do you enjoy your job?'

Weldon was a little taken aback. 'Well, I suppose it's like every other job. It has its good and bad points.' A shadow fell across his smooth, handsome face. 'I don't suppose any of us get exactly what we want. We have to make compromises.' He added, almost defiantly, 'I've got nothing to complain about.'

Karas said, 'Even when it involves telling lies to people who trust you?'

A flush started on Weldon's neck and spread up over the whole of his face and temples. 'Lies?' he said. His voice shook slightly.

'Yes.' Karas spoke in his usual calm, dispassionate voice. 'You never met Bremer in your life—in Leipzig or anywhere else. Did you?' He went on hurriedly, anxious to save Weldon the humiliation of answering. 'You lied about that photographer too, outside the apartment block. You knew he was going to be there, it was all arranged beforehand. And the Swiss policemen who called at the villa. I wondered about that at the time, it seemed so very convenient, but I couldn't be sure then. Now I am. It was faked, wasn't it?'

Weldon's lips were held tight shut, as if he were afraid of their trembling. His handsome baby face had crumpled, his expression was almost tearful in his distress. Karas looked away in embarrassment.

After a while Weldon spoke in a small, timid voice. 'You have to realize, Peter,' he said, 'that there are considerable limitations to my control over events. In my position—'

Karas was suddenly outraged by Weldon's lack of spirit. 'Yes, I know your position.' He spoke angrily. 'You're a messenger boy. You do as you're told.' He saw the look of agony on Weldon's face and was disgusted with his own cruelty. 'No, Arthur, that's not true. I didn't mean that.'

'You've every right to say it,' said Weldon gloomily. 'I'm very ashamed of the whole affair. The fact is that it never occurred to any of us that you might not want to come to America. When you said you'd sooner stay in Europe, we rather lost our heads.' He said urgently, 'But I didn't have anything to do with that business of the police. I want you to believe that. O'Keefe did it on his own. He didn't even tell me beforehand.'

'And the newspaper photograph?'

'That was Henderson's idea. He thought it would help to reconcile you to the necessity of the press conference.'

'I see.'

There was a long silence. Then Weldon said, 'I can quite see you're thoroughly disgusted with me. You trusted me and I let you down.'

The curious thing was, thought Karas, that instead of any real resentment against Weldon he felt a certain disgust with himself. The trouble was that it was too easy to humiliate Weldon. It was like punishing a child. 'Never mind,' he said wearily. 'It's not important.'

'Yes it is—for me at any rate. You see,' said Weldon awkwardly, 'I valued your trust in me. I valued your friendship. The trouble was that I wasn't big enough or strong enough to be worthy of it.' Karas made a motion of embarrassment. It seemed to him that he detected a slightly complacent, masochistic note in this self-laceration. But Weldon went on, 'I know very well that I'm not a strong character. And I'm hopelessly dependent on my job. I'm not like Forsyth—I haven't any great qualifications, there isn't anybody interested in fighting for me if I get into trouble. You might as well know. Just before this assignment came up I was in pretty bad trouble. There are influential people in ISIS who want me out. It's no use pretending. I just can't afford to stand out against the organization.'

Something in his manner aroused a strange emotion in Karas, half-way between exasperation and a kind of protective affection. It occurred to him for the first time that what had attracted him to Weldon was that in a curious way he reminded him of Max. Beneath his slick, plausible manner and practised charm, there was the same helplessness, the same realization of his inability to battle against the Hendersons and Suvorins and Forsyths of the world.

Karas knew theoretically that aggression and the will to fight were a matter of physical make-up, a certain type of nervous system, a certain concentration of hormones. You could not despise a man for lacking them any more than you could blame a spaniel for lacking the virtues of a terrier. Yet there was still something outrageous to him in Weldon's easy acceptance of defeat. 'So you think we should all bow to the inevitable and give in?' he asked.

Weldon smiled at him in a way he remembered from Max. It was an admiring, submissive smile, like that of a woman. 'It's different for you,' he said. 'Anyone can see you don't give a damn for anybody.'

In Karas's mind came back a phrase from Max's last letter. 'I pass on my problems to you, to your ingenuity and courage and strength. It is yours now.' He said, with sudden resentment, 'Damn you, I won't have this! I won't fight all the battles of the world, while all the rest of you take refuge in your own weakness. What right have you to assume I should sacrifice myself if you're not prepared to?'

'It's not a question of right,' said Weldon. 'It's a question of what has to happen. You couldn't behave like me even if you wanted to.' There was a sad certainty in his voice. 'We all of us have to act in character. You'll find that out in the end.'

When they got back to the large apartment Sarah was waiting for them. After a little while Weldon left to catch the evening train home and the two of them were left alone. Karas poured himslf a glass of whisky and sat brooding silently in the huge living-room. Sarah looked at him with anxiety. 'What's the trouble?' she said. 'Did something happen down at the laboratories?'

He did not reply straight away. After a while he said, 'You lied to me, all of you. I know that now.' Before she could protest, he went on bitterly, 'It doesn't matter so much about Arthur. He's paid to tell lies. He'd be on the street if he didn't do as he was told. But you—' He looked at her in despair. 'How could you do such a thing? I can't understand it.'

She regarded him with frightened eyes. She began to speak, and then stopped and shook her head hopelessly. 'It's no use. I can't talk to you when you're as angry as this.'

'What do you expect of me?' he demanded. She was not Max or Weldon, one of the weaklings of the earth, for whom allowances must be made. She was one of his own kind—she must take responsibility. He told her briefly of his conversation with Weldon. Then he said, 'What are you going to tell me? That you knew nothing about it?'

She was pale and shaken but she replied with dignity. 'I knew Arthur hadn't met Bremer. I didn't think that mattered too much. I just saw it as the kind of unimportant lie lots of people tell at meetings or on social occasions. So far as the press photograph was concerned—' She hesitated. 'Well, I suppose I suspected something there too. It seemed odd the newspaper didn't follow it up, and it's the kind of trick one would associate with the old man, somehow—'

He said accusingly, 'And yet you say you love him. You admire him.'

She struggled to explain. 'It's his nature. He can't help it. There's nothing really evil about it. It's just part of the way he's lived. Can't you see?' She appealed to him.

He was reminded of Weldon's final defence of himself—'we all have to act in character in the end'. Yet surely a man had some choice within the limitations of that character? He might not be an angel but neither was he an ape, locked helplessly within a cage made up of his own habits and reflexes. There was always a choice—the kind of choice that he had made on that morning when he had first decided to lie to Suvorin about Max's letter, to place his loyalty to his dead friend above the interests of his adopted country and of his own career. If that choice was inevitable, then all his risks and sacrifices were meaningless, he was worth no more in the scheme of things than an amoeba which recoiled from a drop of acid and moved irresistibly towards a shaft of light. 'No,' he said. 'I can't accept that.'

She looked at him miserably. 'I can see now that I was wrong. I should have told you everything—even what I only suspected. But I didn't want to destroy your confidence—'

'My confidence!'

'Yes. Can't you understand—you were as strange to us as we were to you. We had no idea how you'd react to us personally, or to America, or to anything. We're not exactly proud of everything we have to show you here, you know. We may sound as if we are sometimes, but all the time we're wondering what you really think. We feel you sitting in judgement on us. We want desperately to impress you. We don't really know what you're like or what your standards are. Is it surprising that we make mistakes?'

He swallowed his whisky and put the empty glass down on the table. 'You want to know what I feel? I'll tell you. I feel like a zoological specimen. Always there's somebody watching me, studying me, worrying about me. Will I settle down? What do I like to eat? Will I breed in captivity? I'm provided with everything I might want—clothes, money, an apartment, a friend, a beautiful girl. Everyone tries to please me because if I escape or die it will mean the loss of their investment. I'm manipulated here and there, bribed, reassured, deceived if necessary Every one of you wants to use me. Henderson to make himself into a national figure, O'Keefe to get himself a better job, Weldon to save himself from being fired. Even you—'

She said miserably, 'You think that about me?'

'I don't know,' he said. With a perverse desire to hurt her he said, 'I haven't read your article for *Planet* yet.'

'You never will. I tore it up this morning.'

'Why?'

'Because it was slick and cheap. And anyway I couldn't write anything about you now—' She appealed to him. 'Surely you understand why?'

For the first time his manner softened towards her. He said, 'I'm sorry.'

'It's all right. I understand.'

'Do you?' He spoke with sudden weariness, 'Most of the time I can manage to hold out, but every now and then—' He ran a hand through his hair in desperation. For the first time since she had known him, he admitted to weakness. 'I feel utterly lost. I have no country. No true friends. Nobody I can trust. I belong nowhere. Even my passport's in another man's name . . .'

She came close to him. 'Are you still angry with me?'

His voice was tired. 'No.' Then he smiled at her. 'Not any more.'

She put her arms round him and kissed him. 'I love you,'

she said. 'I'm your friend—you can trust me. I'm your country now. You believe that?'

There had to be something in which he could believe. 'Yes,' he said. 'Yes, I do.'

CHAPTER SIX

KARAS AWOKE the next morning with a headache and a vague feeling of impending disaster. It was like one of those mornings in childhood when he had found himself dreading the coming day before he could remember the details of what his fear was about. Then, as his mind cleared, it came back to him. He recalled the events and conversations of the previous twenty-four hours, the deception which had been practised on him, the warnings of Forsyth, the impending decisions about his future. He felt tired and uncertain and out of sorts; for once he was doubtful of his capacity to meet the demands which might be made upon him. He remembered too that this was no ordinary day, in which he would be given time to think and arrange his forces in face of this new situation. It was the day of the press conference.

The previous night he had lain awake trying to work out a plan of action. He had considered breaking with Henderson and refusing to attend the conference on the grounds that he had been cheated and deceived. But caution had advised against it. Henderson, he knew, would be a dangerous enemy. If he quarrelled with the old man, who could he turn to? Forsyth? But Forsyth was an unknown quantity. Neither his honesty nor his power to carry out his promises was absolutely certain. It would be reckless to throw oneself absolutely on his protection.

Karas went over the situation in his mind again as he bathed and dressed, and came to the same conclusion. He must go through with it as planned, treading carefully, watching always for an opportunity to break away, to free himself from dependence on Henderson. Perhaps something would happen at the press conference itself which would give him some clue to a suitable line of action.

Weldon and Sarah were at breakfast when he went into the dining-room; O'Keefe had already left for the hotel where the conference was to be held. 'He's gone along to make advance preparations,' said Weldon. He added ironically, 'This is Sam's finest hour.' He looked at his watch. 'I suppose we ought to be moving along there ourselves pretty soon.'

The other two smoked cigarettes while Karas ate his breakfast. He made a leisurely meal, watching Weldon's impatience grow as the minutes ticked by. Finally he drained his second cup of coffee. 'I'm ready now.' As they all stood up he said to Sarah, 'Are you coming too?'

She shook her head. 'I'm afraid not. I just wanted to wish you good luck before you went. I have to go over to *Planet* this morning.'

'Oh.' He was suddenly downcast. He realized that he had been counting on her support. 'You couldn't get out of it?'

'I'm sorry. It's a royal command.' She stood up and squeezed his arm reassuringly. Weldon walked into the hall for his coat and she kissed Karas quickly on the cheek. 'Don't worry. It'll turn out all right. You'll see.'

She went back into her bedroom and he walked out of the apartment with Weldon. As they went down in the elevator Karas said, 'I think we can use the front door this time, don't you?'

Weldon laughed and looked up at him nervously. Karas smiled back and he was reassured. He said, 'I'll ask the doorman to get a taxi.'

When they got to the door the winter sun hit them full in the face. Karas said, 'It's a beautiful day. Let's walk.'

'Well—I don't know—' Weldon looked worried. Everything worried him, thought Karas, with a kind of impatient pity. Without waiting for Weldon's agreement he set off down the sidewalk. In front of him towered the hideous bulk of the Pan Am building. He strode ahead, saying, 'Do you know, I haven't taken a walk through the city since I left the Centre?'

It occurred to him that in a way it was even longer than that. He had not walked, as a free man, going where he wished, without thought of consequences, for many years—certainly not since he left Hungary. Perhaps not in all his life, if it came to that. Well, now he was supposed to be a free man, in the free world they were so proud of. It was time he tried it out. He would start in a small way, by walking down the street.

The exercise and the cold still air cheered him up. He was feeling more optimistic by the time he got to the hotel. But the hotel itself did something to dampen his spirits.

They walked out of the crispness of the morning into a vast baroque cavern. The marble steps led into an entrance hall hung with tapestries and embellished with gilt cupids. This in its turn led into another hall, equally huge but lit so dimly that the walls and ceilings were hardly discernible in the gloom. Here and there ghostly arrows indicated the way to the reception desk or the main restaurant. Weldon turned right into a further hall containing a bank of elevators. Noticing the expression on Karas's face he said, 'It's not exactly an intimate little place, is it? But they have the facilities we want.'

They went up to the twenty-fifth floor. Weldon said, 'We have a suite up here where we can wait until things are set up. Then we go along to one of the smaller ballrooms for the conference.' He walked about half a mile along various corridors until they came to the suite. The door was open and O'Keefe was giving instructions to a waiter.

He broke off when he saw them. 'Oh, here you are. I was getting worried about you.' He glanced at his watch and added fiercely, 'You're a quarter of an hour late.'

'There's plenty of time to go,' said Weldon.

O'Keefe was not appeased. 'A thing like this needs split-second timing. Believe me, I've plenty to worry about, without unpunctuality—' He broke off to dismiss the waiter and then said, 'I particularly wanted you here before Mr. Henderson arrived. We must all be absolutely clear about the plan.' He turned to Karas. It was plain from the expression on his face that the distrust of Karas which he had acquired in Switzerland had by no means been diminished by further experience. 'First I'd like to sketch out for you our objectives.'

Karas frowned. His doubts about the whole affair came suddenly to the surface when confronted with O'Keefe. Weldon stepped in quickly. 'He knows all that,' he said, with an unusual air of command. 'I told him about it.'

O'Keefe hesitated and then gave way. 'Okay, if you say so,' he said reluctantly. 'But he has to know the programme. Each one of us has to know exactly where he comes in. This thing has to be presented. Like a play, see.' He warmed to his theme. 'First we take the curtain up. Then we start our presentation slowly and lead gradually to the climax. We have a big story to tell and we're not going to throw any of it away.' It was plain that he saw himself in the character of an impresario. 'Now, like all dramatic productions, this one has its tricky moments. As I see it, our main problem is Mr. Henderson's speech.' A shadow passed over his face. 'We have to face up to the fact,' he said grudgingly, 'that it's Dr. Karas who represents the climax of the show. He's the one they want to listen to. I don't want Mr. Henderson to be submerged. There's a risk that, if he speaks first, they'll be waiting for Karas and they won't pay much attention. On the other hand, if he speaks afterwards—I know those boys. They'll be sneaking out of the room to file their copy.'

He sighed anxiously. Karas could see his dilemma. Henderson was unlikely to regard any conference as a success if his own vanity emerged bruised in the process. O'Keefe said, 'I've decided that on the whole it's less risky if he speaks before you.' Having disposed of that, he moved on to more congenial matters. 'I'll open the meeting myself. They all know me, you see,' he explained with satisfaction. 'I know how to handle them. I can strike the right note. Then we have Mr. Henderson. Just a short introductory speech. Then you, Karas. I think it'll be all right.' He said to Weldon, 'I've made copies of Mr. Henderson's speech for the Press.'

'I'd like to see that,' said Karas.

O'Keefe looked dubious. 'Well, I don't know. I mean, in a sense, it's still confidential—'

'Don't be ridiculous, Sam,' said Weldon. 'Of course he must see it.' He went over to a desk in the corner of the room and picked up some duplicated sheets. He handed one of them to Karas. 'There's nothing to worry you in it,' he said reassuringly. 'I helped to write it myself.'

Karas read through it rapidly. The others waited for his reactions. Finally he put down the sheets. 'It's a little over-dramatized, perhaps,' he said. 'I'm not nearly so important as you make me out to be.'

'Okay,' said O'Keefe irritably. 'So we know you're a modest guy.'

'Not especially,' said Karas. 'But it's necessary to be clear—'

Weldon broke in. 'Please, Peter,' he said. 'Try to understand. For this audience we have to dramatize a little. You must see that.'

'I'm not concerned with newspaper writers,' said Karas. 'I'm thinking of the men of my own profession, who know exactly the level of my achievement. I don't wish to look foolish in front of them.'

'Look, stop worrying,' said O'Keefe. 'After Mr. Henderson's made this speech, you'll be able to answer questions. You can get your point over then. Okay?'

Karas hesitated and then gave in. 'All right.'

'Right then,' said O'Keefe. It was plain that he was only just managing to keep his temper. 'Then, after the questions, I'll wind up. The small fry can get their drinks and go home. A few of the big boys have been invited to meet you socially. These are the top science writers—from *The Times, Time and Life, Scientific American*, and so on. And the guy from CBS.'

'CBS?'

'Yes, that's the TV network.' O'Keefe spoke with pride. 'We've got a nation-wide hook-up. Now they may want—'

Karas turned on Weldon. 'You didn't mention television.'

Weldon flushed. 'I'm sorry. I just took it for granted. There's really nothing to it.'

'I don't know,' said Karas dubiously. 'I'm not sure about this. I've never appeared on television.'

The tension in O'Keefe suddenly exploded. 'Oh, for Christ's sake—'

He stopped in mid-sentence. Henderson strolled into the room, his great head slightly down in a bull-like posture which Karas had already learnt to recognize as a sign of nervousness. His chauffeur was walking behind him in the unobtrusive fashion of a man hoping to avoid attracting the attention of a large and dangerous animal.

Henderson eyed them one by one, savouring the silence his entrance had produced. They were like schoolboys caught talking in class by the headmaster. 'What's the trouble?' he said, snarling a little. The tension which made Weldon agitated and O'Keefe fussy and officious expressed itself in Henderson in the form of pure aggression. He looked like a man who would welcome a fight as a form of release. 'You boys quarrelling again?'

He looked first at O'Keefe, then at Weldon. Each in turn looked sheepish and eventually turned his eyes away. Having satisfactorily intimidated his employees, Henderson turned to Karas. As if realizing that as the star performer Karas was entitled to special treatment, Henderson became jovial. He grinned and patted Karas on the shoulder. 'You don't have to worry, boy,' he said paternally. 'You'll be great—I know it. It's at my age you have to worry. There's nothing to television, believe me. Just forget the cameras and act naturally.' He evidently considered that he had done what was required of him in the way of reassurance. With a word from Olympus he had solved all their problems. He said to O'Keefe, 'Everything's fixed, I hope. No difficulties?'

The sharpness of the question led O'Keefe into a nervous qualification. 'I don't think so—'

It was disastrous. Like a boxer seeing his opponent's guard drop, like an animal scenting fear, Henderson moved in to the attack. 'What do you mean—you don't think so?'

O'Keefe realized his mistake immediately. He said, in the most positive voice he could muster, 'I mean no. No problems at all.'

'Then say what you mean. Never try to hedge your bets. You get no credit for that.'

O'Keefe flushed angrily. Karas was interested to see a new expression appear on his face, one that he had never dared to use in Henderson's presence before. His eyes were narrowed and the set of his mouth made his resentment plain to all. It was almost as if he were wondering whether he might not take the chance at talking back at Henderson. But habit was too strong. He accepted the rebuke in silence.

Henderson looked around the room as if searching for some other object for his spleen. 'Where's Forsyth?'

Weldon said shakily, 'I was going to tell you about that. He can't come.'

'What the hell does that mean?'

'I don't know. He just sent a message to say that he couldn't make it.'

'Did you ask him why?'

Weldon nodded quickly. 'I tried to get hold of him to ask him why, but they said he was tied up in conference and couldn't answer.'

'The bastard,' said Henderson with venom. He brooded for a moment while the others watched him in silence. Then, with an effort of will, he seemed to put the incident away in some compartment of his mind for future action. He said to Karas, 'I hear you and he still haven't agreed on the contract?'

'Not exactly.'

'Not exactly.' Henderson repeated the phrase with disgust. He was obviously tempted to make some acid remark but controlled himself. 'What's the matter, didn't you like the place?'

'Oh, yes, certainly I did. But—'

'You didn't like Forsyth? Maybe you didn't like me?' He grinned sourly. 'What is it?'

'It's nothing to do with that. But I must have time—'

'Time!' Henderson wagged his white locks in outrage. 'Everybody wants time. Nobody wants to go ahead and make a deal except me, and I'm just an old man.' He became mournful and self-pitying. 'I'd hoped to announce this morning that you'd joined our staff.' Karas was silent. 'I don't want to force you into anything, but can't you see that this is the time to say it if you're going to join us? If you say no, I'll forget it. No hard feelings. But it would be a big help if you'd make up your mind.' He used all the charm and softness of which he was capable. Karas was conscious of the enormous power of Henderson, the virtuosity and genius for persuasion which had brought him success in innumerable deals over the last half-century. 'As a favour to me?'

Henderson waited, like an evangelist hoping for a last-minute conversion. Again, Karas shook his head. Accepting defeat, Henderson switched his mind to another track. It was as if the incident had been totally forgotten. 'I've been reading my speech in the car,' he said. 'Seems pretty good.' He said to Karas, 'What did you think of it?'

Karas hesitated. He saw Weldon's eyes pleading at him, begging him not to start another argument. Obviously Weldon would be blamed if there was difficulty about the speech. Karas said, 'I thought it was fine.'

Henderson nodded in a perfunctory way. It had obviously not really occurred to him that Karas would do anything but agree. 'I don't want to speak for long. What they're here for is the questions.' He turned a benevolent eye on Karas. It was plain that by Henderson's standards he was still in favour, in spite of his tiresome obstinacy about the laboratory job. 'Now don't be nervous. These are nice guys and friends of ours.' A thought struck him. He said to O'Keefe, 'By the way, have you spoken to Jack Lewis?'

'Yes.'

Henderson did not elaborate. His voice took on the soft, encouraging, half-admonitory tone of a coach before a football match. 'Now remember, everyone, this has to go right. It's damned important for all of us. The whole country's going to be watching. The whole world, if it comes to that. I had Washington on the phone again this morning. Someone pretty high up—I can't tell you who.' His hand was trembling again, Karas noticed. His voice contained pride, but there was apprehension there too. He gave the impression of a professional gambler who knows he is playing near his limit. 'He wanted to know what was cooking. I said to him, "Take it easy, you'll know in a couple of hours".' He laughed sharply, without humour. There was defiance and confidence in that booming laugh, yet beneath it a slight undertone of bravado. He said contemptuously, 'Those monkeys, they can't do their own job, but they're wetting themselves the moment they hear of someone else doing it for them.' He paused and then said, 'If we'd left it to Washington, this fella here would still be back in Central Asia.' He turned to Karas. His grin was as jovial as ever, but there was strain beneath it. 'Eh, boy?'

The reminder to Karas of his debt to Henderson was made casually but effectively. Karas knew that it was a studied play to keep him in line during the conference. But the debt was there, after all. He nodded. Henderson looked him carefully in the face and seemed satisfied. Then the telephone rang.

O'Keefe answered it and listened for a minute. Then he said, 'Walker says they're all ready to run now. We can go down.'

The small ballroom was big enough to hold about a hundred and fifty people and there were well over a hundred present. O'Keefe's advance arrangements had been good, and there were reporters, not only from the East Coast and Washington, but from Chicago and the Mid-West. A few had even flown in from Los Angeles and San Francisco. In two corners of the room the television crews had set up their cameras and there were lights rigged round the platform. The room itself was decorated in the usual baroque style of the hotel, running heavily to gilt and chandeliers. Part of the elaborate moulding had been damaged by one of the lighting stands. O'Keefe grimaced. There would be a bill for dilapidations.

The newspaper men were clustered around the bar at the far end of the room, talking and gossiping together. Most of them were old friends and rivals, who met each other at this kind of function perhaps several times a month. Neither free liquor nor the prospect of a startling announcement made much impression on them as a rule, but this time they had the sense of something different. The buzz of conversation died away as the small party walked through a door on to the stage which was being used as a platform. It was hardly necessary for Walker to perform his duty of telling them that the conference had begun. They filed quickly to their seats.

There were five seats on the platform. Henderson sat in the centre, with Karas on his right and O'Keefe on his left. Weldon sat next to Karas. Henderson glared momentarily at the fifth seat, his lips tightening as he remembered Forsyth's defection. Then O'Keefe got up to speak.

'Well, boys,' he said cheerfully, surveying the packed seats with a pink smile, 'I hope you're comfortable and that you've got everything you want. If anyone finds he isn't being properly looked after, I'd take it as a favour if he'd just let me know.'

There was laughter and a few ironical claps. O'Keefe looked happily round the hall, savouring the occasion. 'Most of you have some idea about the reasons why we set up this conference. During the last week or two there have been a good many rumours flying around in regard to a certain missing scientist from the other side. We knew a little about this, but we couldn't say anything at the time. It's not that we wanted to keep anything secret from the American public for any longer than was necessary, but I'm sure you'll appreciate that this is a very delicate business. We didn't want to take any chances. We had to secure the personal safety of the individual concerned.'

Karas shifted irritably in his seat. Would there ever be any end to these trivial lies? They had delayed the press conference for the simple reason that they had hoped to sign him up on the staff at Falls Ridge. He was glad now that he had not agreed.

O'Keefe's voice took on the solemn note of a man making a historic announcement. 'Now at last,' he said, 'we feel justified in letting you into our confidence.' He paused and then said, with a certain reverence, 'But it's not for me to take up your time. The organizing brain—I may even say without exaggeration the genius—who conceived this whole daring scheme is a man known to you all by repute. He is a totally unique personality, one of the great original figures of American industry. I'm going to leave it to him to tell you the story of how this affair came about.' He paused dramatically. 'Ladies and gentlemen, Mr. John Henderson.'

There was a ripple of applause and Henderson rose to

his feet. He stood there for a moment surveying the audience. He looked very large and rather wild. With his white hair and brown, leathery face, his huge lanky body and his startling blue eyes, he did indeed look like an exceptional person. There was command in the set of his lips and the cold glitter of his eye. Yet Karas could see his hands gripping the desk hard to control their trembling. It was almost possible to sense the tension radiating from his body.

'Gentlemen,' he said. The word got scrambled in his throat and for a moment Karas, with the others, felt a tremor of anxiety. Then the old man recovered, cleared his throat and went on confidently, 'As Sam O'Keefe has just said, many of you know me.'

He spoke with faint irony, and there was a slight ripple of sympathetic laughter. It seemed to give Henderson the contact with his audience that he needed. He grinned back and went on, his momentary weakness forgotten. 'There was a time when I, and a few other fellows like me, made a good deal of news. We did quite a bit in our small way towards developing the natural resources of this country— and a great many other countries if it comes to that. We're pretty much a thing of the past now,' he said regretfully. 'Now it's the Federal Government and the big organizations that call the tune. What with restrictions of one kind and another, various types of interference, high taxes and so on, the individual who could strike out on his own, take risks, treat business as a personal adventure—that's all gone. Or pretty nearly anyway. We used to think we were public benefactors. Now it seems we're a public menace.'

His voice had taken on the querulous note of an old man on his hobby horse, and Karas felt a growing restiveness in the newspaper men. They had not come to be lectured. Fortunately Henderson was still acute enough to pick up the reaction and to halt himself in time. He broke into one of his boyish smiles. 'Still,' he said, 'they haven't quite finished us off completely. And maybe I can convince you this morning that public menaces like myself still have some kind of contribution to make.'

He turned his eyes momentarily to Karas and then back to the audience. 'Three months ago I heard through one of my contacts that one of the most brilliant young scientists on the other side was beginning to feel it was time he changed his job. Of course,' he said, gently ironical, 'that wouldn't be much news over here. He'd just go and work some other place and nobody would think any the worse of him for it. But when there's only one employer in a country, the only way you can leave him is to leave the country.'

He paused, feeling the heightened interest. He was very confident now. 'Well, when I heard this, it seemed to me that Dr. Karas had the right to be free to work where he wanted, the way any of us can. So I decided to make available to him the facilities to do just that. I can't tell you the details of how we arranged it, because this might endanger other people, and I'm sure that's the last thing any of us would want. It's already been revealed in the Press that Dr. Karas left a delegation of his countrymen in Geneva. All I feel justified in saying is that we assisted him then and that we've been looking after him ever since.'

Karas looked at the newspapermen. They were listening politely but with only minor interest, and none of them were writing anything down. This surprised him until he remembered that they already had the handout. So far, this speech was a repetition of something they already knew.

'There are a few things,' said Henderson, 'that I'd like to make clear. Firstly, I'm not a politician. As you may know, I don't think a lot of politicians.' There was a burst of laughter and some of the reporters scribbled something in their books. Evidently Henderson had departed from his script. He went on, 'And this wasn't a political act on our part. I want to emphasize that Dr. Karas doesn't possess any military secrets. None whatever.' He spoke emphatically and paused to let the point sink in. 'His work is essentially peaceful. He wants to carry it out in an atmosphere of freedom, without government interference. You all know that this is a cause which has always been very near to my heart. From the moment Dr. Karas left his delegation in Geneva he has been a free man, to come and go as he wishes. He has not belonged to me, or to the United States Government; he has belonged only to himself.'

Henderson spoke with great feeling and his sincerity communicated itself to his audience. There was a respectful silence. 'This, in my humble view, is the importance of this episode. It has not been a government affair. It has been the case of one free individual extending a helping hand to another.' He hesitated for a moment and then his voice boomed out. 'The great gift we have to offer the world is not technical or scientific advance. It isn't wealth or power or rockets or nuclear bombs. It is the gift of freedom.'

It would have been impossible not to applaud. There was a burst of clapping. When it had died down, Henderson said in a quieter voice, 'So, in my book, Dr. Karas has a degree of importance greater than if his work was significant from a strategic point of view. His free choice of our way of life is symbolic of the things we hold dearest. To him we represent a hope of a new deal and a new way of life.'

He smiled suddenly and attractively, his face a mass of deep brown wrinkles. He spread his hands out modestly. 'Now you didn't come here to listen to me—I know that. You came here to talk to Dr. Karas. Many of you, I know, have questions you'd like to ask him, and he'll be pleased to answer them for you. I'm glad to be able to tell you that he speaks rather better English than I do.'

Henderson sat down. When the applause had died away Karas rose to his feet. He felt the television lights hot on his face, and the cameras levelled at him like guns. He looked down at the faces in front of him and felt the force of their curiosity breaking over him like a wave. He had faced audiences before, but they had always been men of his own kind. These were strangers. He knew nothing of how they thought, or how they felt, or of their attitudes towards him. He was overcome for a moment by the fear of the unknown. And yet, as always at times of crisis, beneath his fear was a self-assurance, a confidence in the power of his own intelligence and resource to deal with any situation. He waited, with a faint, remote smile on his long face, for their questions.

The first came from a middle-aged man in spectacles sitting in the front row.

'Dr. Karas, can you tell us more details of your escape?'

'I was in a hotel in Geneva with a delegation. I slipped out when I saw an opportunity. After that, I made contact with agents of Mr. Henderson.'

'Can't you tell us a little more than that, sir?'

'I'm sorry. I'm afraid that would implicate those who assisted me.'

The first questioner retired baffled. Another man sitting near to him asked, 'Did anyone assist you on the other side?'

'I'm sorry. I can't talk about that.'

'Did you find it difficult to get away?'

'Mr. Henderson's arrangements made it fairly easy.'

There was a voice from another part of the hall. 'Is it definitely true that your work had no strategic importance?'

'Definitely. My work is pure science in the biological field. It has nothing to do with politics.'

'Can you tell us simply what it is?'

'It is connected with the chemical processes taking place within the living cell. Work of a similar kind is going on here—and, in fact, in almost every civilized country.'

'Why did you decide to leave your own country?'

'It wasn't my own country. My own country, as you know, is under occupation. I left because I wanted a freer atmosphere for my work.'

He had anticipated the kind of questions they would ask and prepared his answers. He delivered them in his fluent, slightly over-precise English. He could tell that they were impressed by him. Their questions were respectful and they took his evasions and refusals to disclose information with good humour. He had heard stories of aggressive American newsmen and he was surprised to find how courteous and deferential they were. Yet he could see, too, that they were a little disappointed. The questions were gaining nothing for them in the way of development of the story.

He was asked about the standard of work at the Centre. Was it more advanced than that of the U.S.A.? No, slightly less so if anything. Was he proposing to work at Falls Ridge? Possibly. He was certainly very impressed with the standard of research there. But nothing had been decided yet.

Had he gone to the Centre in the first place of his own free will? Yes. Was he a Communist? No, he never had been. He had no interest in politics.

Had he been in contact with the U.S. Government? No. There was a quiver of interest. Why not?

Why should he, said Karas calmly. This was not a political matter. Mr. Henderson had offered to bring him here and he had agreed. If the U.S. Government wished to contact him he would be happy to talk to them.

He was asked the conventional questions about his living conditions at the Centre, and his reaction to the U.S.A. He gave the answers he had prepared. Much of the questioning went over ground he had already covered in his first interview with Sarah. He began to feel they were running out of questions—that the whole thing would soon be at an end. It had really been nothing to worry about after all.

At this point a very tall man with a bald head and a cadaverous face stood up in the third row. He paused for a moment before speaking and the others fell silent. It came to Karas instantly that this was an important, possibly a dangerous man. Weldon leaned forward and whispered the word 'Lewis'. Lewis said, 'Dr. Karas, we've all been very impressed by your answers and I'd like to congratulate you on your magnificent command of our language. We recognize that this must be quite an ordeal for you and I don't want to prolong it unnecessarily. However'—he paused again and then said with great deliberation—'there are a few things which aren't clear to me and I wonder if you'd mind if I asked you about these.' His manner was deceptively mild. Karas said cautiously, 'I'll do my best.'

'Thank you. Now,' Lewis said slowly, 'at the Centre you were in a section under the general direction of Dr. Suvorin, I believe?' This was the first mention of Suvorin's name.

Karas said, 'Yes, that's true.'

'Were you the head of that section?'

'At the time I left, yes.'

'Had you been in that position for long?'

'No. Only a few months.'

Karas had the distinct impression that Lewis was asking questions to which he already knew the answers. 'Who was head of the section most of the time you were there?'

Karas hesitated. Then he said, 'Dr. Max Bremer. He was a great friend of mine—a colleague—'

'Yes, so I believe.' There was a dead silence now. It was as if the two of them were in the room alone. Lewis said, 'Is it true that Dr. Bremer died in somewhat mysterious circumstances?'

Karas suddenly felt danger pressing close to him. For the first time the faint smile left his face. He answered curtly, 'He committed suicide.'

Lewis nodded. 'That was the official report.'

There was scepticism in Lewis's voice. Karas said, 'It was true.' Lewis raised one eyebrow.

'Have you any idea why he killed himself?'

'No. None at all.'

'But he was your best friend, I believe?'

'Yes, he was.'

'Yet you still say you've no idea?'

Karas felt anger rising within him. 'I have already told you that.'

A collective tremor ran through the members of the platform. O'Keefe jumped up quickly. 'Jack,' he said plaintively, 'this is a very personal affair for Dr. Karas. I don't think we have a right to intrude on his private relationships—'

'Wait a minute!' Lewis turned momentarily to the other members of the Press, as if to enlist their support. 'We're supposed to be here to be given the truth about Dr. Karas. Some of us have travelled all the way across the country to attend. I'm afraid I have to say that to my personal knowledge you've told us a good deal less than the full story.' He turned back to Karas. 'Dr. Karas, you said you'd be prepared to answer questions. Are you going back on that?'

It was a challenge which could not be refused. Karas said, 'What do you want to know?'

O'Keefe sat down unhappily. Lewis said, 'You said that you had no secret information. I won't ask you about that now. But I'd like to ask you about Dr. Bremer. I have a report that he had access to some very secret information indeed. Is that true?'

Karas shook his head. 'No,' he said firmly.

'But it is true, isn't it, that the original escape was arranged not for you but for Dr. Bremer?'

Karas shook his head impatiently. 'I know nothing about that. I was offered the opportunity to escape and I took it.'

'Who offered it to you?'

'I've told you already. I can't speak of that.'

Lewis paused for a moment. Then, very slowly, he took a folded piece of paper out of his pocket, unfolded it and looked at the writing on it as if to be sure of confirming what it said. The room had fallen so silent that Karas could hear the sound of the paper crinkling in his hands. Then he looked up again at the platform. 'Dr. Karas,' he said, 'are you aware that Dr. Bremer's widow was arrested by your Government two days ago on a charge of espionage?'

In that moment Karas became unconscious of the men before him, of the whole packed, expectant room. The baroque gilded ballroom, the vast hotel, this strange world he now inhabited, became to him like the content of a dream. Instead he saw Sophia in the little threadbare apartment, crying over her broken ornament, caring lovingly for the few treasures she had preserved from an old life which had long since been destroyed. He remembered the evenings when he and Max had played chess and the slight dark woman brought them coffee and little cakes. He remembered her silence, her neatness, and the deep love for him which she had kept locked behind her austere, enigmatic face. He remembered how she had clung to him in the night, with a passion that had surprised and disconcerted him. That passion had now destroyed her, as in her heart she had always known it would. He could see her now, in the cold bedraggled park under the birch trees, as she said goodbye to him. She had known then how it would be.

What she had done had been by her own choice, it was true, yet the guilt remained within him and he knew it would never be lost. He had not even been able to give her love, only a few weeks of companionship and respect, before the shadows closed around her forever. He stood in silence as if before the grave of an old and trusted friend.

Vaguely he heard the confusion which broke out around him. He felt Weldon pulling him gently back into his seat, heard O'Keefe making a soothing speech, closing the proceedings hurriedly yet without giving the impression of total disaster. Then he walked with the others out of the door leading from the platform.

CHAPTER SEVEN

WHEN THEY WERE BACK in the suite, Henderson looked at him solicitously. 'Are you all right, boy?'

'Yes.'

'You don't look too good to me. Sit down and take it easy. We'll get you a glass of Scotch or something.' He shook his head. 'Christ, that was a hell of a thing to happen. I thought you were going to keel right over.'

'I'm fine,' said Karas. 'Don't worry about me.' He struggled to regain command of himself. 'I'm sorry I gave way there. It was a terrible shock. I never expected—'

'Of course you didn't,' said Henderson. 'It was an outrage. I've never heard of such behaviour.' He snarled to O'Keefe, 'Get Lewis up here right away. I want to talk to him.'

'I've fixed that already,' said O'Keefe. 'He should be up here any minute.' He added sulkily as if talking to himself, 'God knows what he thought he was doing—'

Henderson snapped, 'I thought you were supposed to have spoken to him beforehand?'

'I did,' said O'Keefe plaintively. 'But he didn't play square with me. He gave me the impression—'

'He gave you the impression!' Henderson looked at him with disgust. 'What are you—a school kid or something?'

Karas heard them quarrelling through the mist of his recollections. His first shock at the news about Sophia began to clear, to be succeeded by suspicion. He interrupted forcibly. 'Why did Lewis have to be spoken to beforehand?'

The tone of his voice stopped Henderson and O'Keefe in their tracks. With his customary sensitivity to imminent danger, Weldon said quickly, 'There was a rumour that Lewis had some special knowledge about your escape. The idea was that he should come up here and discuss it with us privately afterwards.'

'Why didn't you tell me about this?'

'We didn't want to bother you just before the meeting.' Weldon added rapidly, before Karas could speak again, 'It's incredible that he should have come out with it at the conference. It's public property now. He's damaged his own story. It was a crazy thing to do—'

'Crazy, hell!' said Henderson. 'Don't you fellows understand anything? He was playing for the TV cameras. He wants to make himself into a national hero, the bastard. At my expense. Well, okay, if he wants to play it that way, he can have it. I've fixed bigger guys than him.'

His voice was rising, his face turkey-red. Then the door opened and Lewis stood facing them, as if debating with himself whether it was safe to come in. Something like a minor convulsion shook Henderson's huge frame. It was impossible not to admire the act of self-control which lay behind it. His face softened, his whole body seemed to relax. His face creased in a huge benevolent smile and he shambled over to Lewis. He laid a great arm round the journalist's shoulders. 'Hi, Jack,' he said easily. 'Nice of you to come and see us. Have a drink.' He drew Lewis into the room as Weldon slipped noiselessly round to close the door behind him. 'Sam, let's have some drinks. What's it to be, Jack?'

Lewis hesitated, as if wondering whether the acceptance of a drink might in some way compromise him. Then he said, in his dry flat voice, 'Scotch on the rocks.'

'Scotch for Mr. Lewis—and you know what I have.' O'Keefe made the drinks. Henderson gripped his own glass in a huge paw. 'Campari soda,' he said to Lewis. 'Terrible stuff. But these days I've got to watch out for myself. At my age you've gotta be your own doctor. Eh, boy?'

He beamed at Lewis, who said cautiously, 'I guess that's right.' Henderson took a pull at his drink and grimaced. Then he looked at Lewis admiringly.

'Well,' he said, 'you really took us by surprise down there. It looks like you know more about this thing than we do.'

'I wouldn't exactly say that.'

'I mean it.' Henderson shook his head, as if fascinated by the spectacle of so much journalistic brilliance. 'But maybe we should have guessed that, from some of those big stories you've done these last few years. I remember particularly the one about the faulty instruments in the space capsule. You got a Pulitzer for that, didn't you?'

'Yes.' Lewis showed little sign of thawing, but Henderson was not deterred. He turned to Karas. 'I'm sorry, you two haven't been officially introduced yet. Jack Lewis is our top science writer. He's not just a writer, he's a Ph.D. as well, from Berkeley. He worked in a lab for some years. I might tell you I learned all I know about research from reading his column.' Lewis smiled dimly at Karas, who nodded back. Then Henderson said, still jocular but with a faint touch of acidity, 'I can't help thinking it's a pity you didn't tell us some of that stuff before the meeting, Jack.'

Lewis said, in mock surprise, 'Didn't you know it already?'

'Some of it,' admitted Henderson.

'Then why keep it back?'

'I explained that. We have certain obligations to individuals who helped us.'

'Phooey,' said Lewis disrespectfully. 'You were stringing us along.' He pointed to Karas. 'And him too, if I'm any judge.' He said, with calculated insolence, 'You know, Mr. Henderson, if you don't mind my saying so, I think you've been playing this a little too smart. It's usually a mistake.'

Karas saw Henderson's face turn pale. It occurred to him that it must have been many years now since the old man had been spoken to like that. The habit of a lifetime of power tempted him to lose his temper with Lewis, to shout and bluster and threaten, to demand respect and obedience. But there was an even older habit, born in those early years on the road, when humiliation had been a daily companion from one cheap hotel to another; it had followed him through deal after deal in his struggle to establish himself and vanquish his competitors. It was the law of the fighter, the climber, the hungry man. And that law said: The deal is everything—pride and dignity are luxuries which must be sacrificed when the deal demands it. And in accordance with that law he controlled himself. He spoke calmly, and with a kind of ancient dignity. 'Listen, Jack,' he said. 'What I said in that meeting was on the level. It was the truth. At my age I don't have to fool anybody. What I kept back, I kept back because I thought it was in everyone's interest. Will you believe me?'

There was a kind of magnificence in the way he had ignored Lewis's insult, and his voice carried a conviction far greater than any violent protestations could ever have given it. Lewis was placed on the defensive. 'Okay, if you say so,' he said. He paused and then added defiantly, 'But I still don't agree with what you're doing. You're on your own here. You don't know a goddam thing about science or scientists.' As Henderson was about to break in, he went on quickly, 'Oh, I know you've got your advisers. Arthur's a nice guy but—' He glanced apologetically at Weldon. 'I'm sorry, Arthur, I don't want to be offensive but it has to be said. You don't really have any standing on your own. As for you, Henderson, all you have is money. I might as well give it to you straight. The only reason those boys down there were prepared to take you seriously was because of your position with ISIS. They thought the organization was backing you. But when it came to the point, there was nobody up there on the platform but you.' There was a challenge in his voice which could not be ignored. 'What the hell happened to Forsyth?'

Weldon said, 'He couldn't get here.'

'Okay,' said Lewis sceptically. 'So he couldn't make it.' He spread out his hands and said to Henderson. 'You've got to visualize how it looks to people like me. Your own people won't tell you. I guess they must be scared of you. Maybe I would be if I worked for you, but, thank God, I don't. You may be smarter than the Government of this country, the way you were saying earlier on, but you're not going to prove it this way. It's time someone told you that this was a crazy idea from the beginning. The sooner you hand the whole thing over to Washington, the less trouble you'll be in.' He turned to Karas. 'I'd like to say right now, Dr. Karas, that I don't blame you for any of this. I know your work and respect you as a scientist. But you don't know this country and you haven't had any opportunity of meeting anyone outside Mr. Henderson's entourage. Naturally, you've been inclined to accept everything they told you. I hope I've managed to make it clear that there's another view to this affair.'

Karas was silent. In his mind he had a picture of how

the affair must seem to others. As an absurd fantasy, an old man's dream. Henderson had made a fool of him. Forsyth had tried to tell him the same thing, but he had been too cautious, too much a man of the organization, to say it point blank. Typically. Forsyth's most radical and significant gesture was the negative one of refusing to turn up to the meeting. Karas had a sick realization that he was in imminent danger of losing his most valuable possession, his status as a scientist. Without money, without family or country, that was the only thing he had to give him a place in the world. And so long as he stayed with Henderson it diminished day by day. Now Henderson no longer seemed to him like a king, but like a deluded, decaying old man, He felt a violent urge to fly to safety—to return to the world of responsible, thoughtful, serious people. Now even Suvorin and the Centre seemed like a haven to him. Whatever else, they had never made him a figure of ridicule.

Through his agony he heard the voice of Henderson. The old man had finally abandoned diplomacy. It was a fight now and he was hitting, with the violence of a man to whom combat was as natural as drawing breath. 'Okay, Lewis,' he said. 'So you've given your sermon and I've listened. I know your kind and I've fought them all my life. People like me have built up the wealth and liberties of this country in spite of socialists like you, and we'll continue to do so. I'll hand over my responsibilities to the State when I'm dead and not before. I didn't get this boy out of the dead hand of one government to hand him over to another. The reason I've put up with your impudence as long as this is because I've something to put to you which isn't just a matter of personal abuse like what you've just said to me. It's a straight question. You said down in that room that you had knowledge that Dr. Karas is in possession of secret information. What's your evidence for that?'

For the first time Karas saw Lewis disconcerted. He hesitated, then said, 'You know I can't reveal my sources.'

Henderson snorted contemptuously. 'Your sources! I had a bet with myself you'd say that.'

Lewis flushed. 'Look, you know how it is in journalism—'

'Piss or get off the pot, Lewis. We're not impressed.' He pressed his advantage. 'It was a lot of crap, wasn't it?'

'No.'

The old man's voice was charged with venom. 'You wanted

248

to make a show before the TV cameras. Okay, we understand. Just don't get so goddamned pure, that's all—'

Lewis was stung beyond endurance. He pointed to Karas. 'Ask him.'

'I've asked him, a dozen times. We've all asked him. It was our first question when we saw him. But if you like I'll ask him again.' He said to Karas, 'Tell the man, he won't believe me. Do you have any secret information?'

'No.'

Henderson turned impatiently to Lewis. 'Right? Now will you believe me?'

Lewis paused for quite a long time. Finally he came to a decision. 'Try asking Hoffman,' he said.

Henderson's eyes narrowed. 'Hoffman?' There was a startled note in his voice.

'You know who I'm talking about. Your man on the other side.' Nobody spoke. Eventually Lewis shrugged his shoulders. 'I don't suppose it matters if I tell you. He's leaving you anyway. This business scared the hell out of him and I don't wonder. He only just got out in time.'

Henderson spoke quietly. 'What did he tell you?'

'Everything he knew, I guess,' Lewis said. 'His story was that before Bremer died he destroyed everything. All his records. All the plans of his experiments. Naturally this aroused a certain amount of curiosity.'

'So?' said Henderson.

'Karas was Bremer's best friend. He appeared at Bremer's flat at 7.30 in the morning, the morning after Bremer took his sleeping tablets. It was at least half an hour sooner than he could have been expected to go there in any ordinary circumstances. He was never able to give a satisfactory explanation.' He said to Karas, 'Isn't that right?' When Karas did not reply he turned back to Henderson. 'It's thought that he received a letter.'

Henderson spoke to Karas in a voice he had never heard from him before. It contained neither the bluster nor the easy charm which he had always associated with the old man. It contained nothing but menace. 'Did you?' he asked.

Karas felt suddenly too tired to resist any longer. 'Yes, I did.'

'What was in it?'

'I can't tell you that.'

Henderson's voice rose angrily. 'Hell, what do you mean—'

'It was a private letter to me.'

With great intensity, Henderson said, 'Listen, boy, I'm not interested in your private correspondence. But this concerns me. I believed you when you said you didn't know anything secret or important. I went on record with that in public. And now I have to learn from Jack Lewis here all kinds of things you've been keeping from me.'

Karas lashed back violently. 'And what about the things you kept from me? How about those policemen in Geneva? And the fake photographers at the apartment building, to give you an excuse to keep me hidden?'

'I don't know who told you that—'

Karas ignored the protest. A suspicion that had been lingering at the back of his mind since they had first returned to the hotel suite, boiled over suddenly into speech. 'I think you knew Sophia Bremer had been arrested—that was why you wanted O'Keefe to talk to Lewis beforehand. You didn't tell me because you were afraid it might spoil your press conference.'

'That's not true! I swear to you—'

'I don't know whether it's true or not,' Karas said wearily. 'It doesn't really matter much, does it? The fact is that I can't trust you. You've lied to me before and you'll lie again if it suits you. I'm tired of you and your deals and your squabbles with Washington, and everything to do with you.' In that moment he made his final decision and he knew that it was right and inevitable. 'I'm leaving you. And I'm not going to Falls Ridge either. I've had enough. I'm finished with all of you.'

He waited for the violence of Henderson's reaction but even in defeat the old man retained the capacity to surprise. He said slowly, 'So you want to walk out on me. Okay.' There was an ancient pride in his voice. 'I can write you off like I've written off a lot of other lousy investments in my time. But before you go you've got to tell me something, because you owe it to me and you know you do. What was in that goddamned letter?'

Lewis said, 'It was the details of Bremer's experiments.' He challenged Karas. 'Isn't that true?'

'Not in the way you're thinking,' said Karas.

'What the hell do you mean by that?' said Henderson.

'You're taking it for granted that there was something very important there. Suvorin thought the same.' He said, 'But there wasn't. There was nothing.'

'Then why hide it?'

'Please,' said Karas desperately. 'Won't you accept my assurance—'

'That's not enough,' said Henderson. He walked over to the door of the suite and stood in front of it. 'Listen, I brought you here. I stood by your story. It's not just your good faith that's in question but mine too. You're not leaving this room till you give an explanation.'

Karas could no longer raise the energy to fight them all off. He said, 'All right, here it is. You're right in saying the letter contained notes on Bremer's experiments. And it's true he thought they were important and dangerous—that was why he killed himself. The responsibility was too much. He didn't know what to do, so passed his problem on to me.'

'Well then—' said Lewis.

'But when I looked at the notes they were just gibberish. They didn't make sense at all.' He said sadly, 'Poor Max, he'd gone out of his mind.' He looked around the room. They were all silenced. He walked towards the door and said to Henderson, 'Do you mind if I leave now?'

CHAPTER EIGHT

HE SLAMMED THE DOOR of the suite behind him and made his way through the maze of corridors towards the elevators. He moved rapidly and nervously, like a fugitive, though he had no idea what he was running from or where any refuge might be found. His sole idea was to get as far away as possible from Henderson, to remove himself from this dreadful hotel. He travelled down in the elevator with a wedding party and followed them to the Park Avenue entrance. When he walked down the steps into the street the winter wind struck knife-like through the thin grey suit and he remembered that he had left his topcoat upstairs in the suite. The doorman looked at him questioningly. Did he want a taxi? He shook his head. He had no notion where he wanted to go.

He set off down Park Avenue and then turned left, more with the idea of protecting himself from the wind than from any clear conception of direction. After a while he lost the irrational fear of being followed as he became swallowed up in the crowds that ebbed and flowed around Grand Central Station. His mind cleared and he began to consider more logically his next course of action.

One thing at least was plain—he could not stay out in the cold much longer without an overcoat. He saw a small hotel on the corner and went into it. As he hovered indecisively just inside the door a porter came up to him. Karas took a dollar bill out of his pocket and handed it to him.

'I'd like to put through a telephone call. To *Planet Magazine*. Could you get the number for me?'

The porter looked curiously at this tall, wild man with a slight foreign accent who didn't even know how to make a telephone call for himself. Then he shrugged his shoulders. A dollar was a dollar. He went to a pay phone-booth in the corner of the lobby, put in a slug and made the call. Then he handed the instrument to Karas.

'Is that *Planet*? I want to speak to Sarah Manning.' Karas closed the door of the booth behind him and waited impatiently for them to make the connection. It was several minutes before he heard her voice on the line. 'Sarah? It's Peter here,' he said.

Her voice was anxious, as if she could feel his agitation at the other end of the line. 'Is it all over? How did it go?'

There was no point in breaking it to her gently. 'A disaster,' he said bluntly. To forestall further questions he added, 'I can't tell you the details now. But everything's over. I've left Henderson.' He heard her faint gasp of astonishment. 'I've got to see you right away.'

'Of course.' There was no hesitation in her voice. 'Where are you?'

'I'm at a hotel near Grand Central.' He gave her the name. 'Do you know it?'

'I can find it.'

He said on impulse, 'I'd like to get out of New York. Just for a few hours while we talk. Is that possible?'

'Yes. I'll fix it.' She was cool and competent. He felt an enormous gratitude for her lack of questioning, her immediate assumption of responsibility. 'Just stay there. I'll take care of everything. I'll be round in half an hour.'

In just over half an hour she appeared through the door of the hotel. Her trim, striding figure, the neat blonde head and elegant green suit made the hotel look even smaller and shabbier than it had done before. Karas saw the porter glance at him with a new respect. He rose from his seat and gripped her by the hand. She kissed his cheek and said, 'I've got a Hertz car outside. We can talk as we drive.'

As he sat beside her in the car he was reminded of the first time they had driven together, in the Mercedes that night by the Lake of Geneva. Gradually he began to gain comfort, as he had done then, from being alone with her in a small world shut away from his enemies. She drove with confidence and determination; the navigation of the large car through the city's traffic was an activity as natural and automatic to her as walking. When they were away from the crowded midtown streets, she said, 'Now tell me about it.'

He recounted the happenings of the morning in as factual and unemotional a way as he could. She listened attentively, with only occasional questions. Only on one occasion, when he mentioned Sophia, did he see a frown cross her face. When he had finished, she was silent for a moment, and then said, 'I suppose I knew in my heart that something like this was bound to happen.' She paused. 'Oh, I don't mean precisely. Nothing I could really explain. I just had a feeling that somehow it wasn't real. It was a kind of dream.' She added, 'That's one of the dangers of being as rich as my uncle. You can populate your dreams, you can get other people to accept them. For a time anyway.'

In her voice there was a compassion for Henderson which he could not accept. 'He lied to me,' he said.

'Yes, I know he did. But I don't want you to think too badly of him.' She struggled to explain. 'He's like a child in many ways. He's aggressive and greedy and demanding in the way that children are. He's generous and emotional, too. If a child wants something badly, it doesn't consider truth or promises very much. Now if it were you—if you were to tell a lie or break a promise, that's different, that's very serious. Because you're a grown man, you'd be conscious of all the implications.'

Karas said bitterly, 'Only I have to carry the weight of all my actions. Is that fair?'

'Probably not. It's just the price you have to pay.'

'For what?'

'For being grown-up. For understanding what things are about.'

He shook his head. 'I'm not big enough to carry that,' he said. 'I'm tired. Everyone expects too much.' If only, he thought, he could get away to some place where there would be no lies or contrivances, where he would not have to test himself every day. He said, 'I can fight the world for a certain time—but not for ever. Nobody can.'

'What happens now?'

'I don't know. I can't think.'

She looked at him with obvious anxiety. He could feel that for the first time she was wondering about his strength and his capacity to survive. But he could not find the energy to reassure her. She said gently, 'Just forget all about it for a little while. What you need is some lunch.'

She drove in silence out of the city. She took the road leading north on the west bank of the Hudson. Every now and then she glanced at Karas as he sat huddled in the seat beside her. For the first time since she had met him, he looked like a man who might be beaten. The lines were deep on his pale face, his shoulders had dropped a little. He looked listlessly out of the car window like a man nearing the end of his endurance. At that moment she felt closer to him than at any previous time. It occurred to her how much she, and the others, had taken his strength for granted. It seemed strange to her now, not that he was showing signs of breaking, but that he had not broken long ago. Always there had been something about him which had led them to assume that his endurance was limitless. Now that she knew that it was not, it was as if the final clue to his character had been offered to her. In that moment of weakness, he seemed to reveal a depth of humanity which had always remained hidden from her before.

The place she had decided on for lunch was a country hotel on the bank of the Hudson, usually crammed with tourists in season but likely to be deserted on a bitter winter day such as this. The building was a mock-Gothic château poised on the side of a cliff with a parapet looking down over the great river. As she had hoped, they were practically alone. They drank two large martinis in the baronial cocktail lounge and she was relieved to see some colour return to Karas's cheeks. He began to talk again about the press conference and his final quarrel with Henderson. She said at one point. 'There's one thing I don't quite understand.'

'What's that?'

'Why you destroyed Max's letter. I mean, if you'd kept it you'd have had something—you could have convinced Suvorin there was nothing to worry about.'

'Max trusted me not to tell him.'

'Yes, I know. But if it was nonsense—surely that let you out, didn't it?'

Karas paused for a moment. 'He was my best friend,' he said. 'He was a brilliant, sensitive man. I didn't want to tell anyone that his mind had broken down.' Before she could speak, he went on rapidly. 'Yes, I know what you're going to say. I told Henderson in the end. And I wish to God I hadn't. I don't suppose for a moment he believed me.'

'Why shouldn't he?'

'Because he wants it the other way,' said Karas contemptuously. 'They all do. Governments, politicians, journalists, everyone. On both sides. They want science to be a matter of secrets and competition and military nonsense. They've driven themselves crazy with suspicion. It's impossible to talk sense to them any more.' He stood up quickly, terminating the conversation. 'That's enough about that. Let's go in and have something to eat.'

After lunch they sat in the lounge and drank brandy, talking of everything but the one problem which dominated their minds. Eventually the conversation died away and they sat in companionable silence, watching the daylight drain away in the winter air. He said, 'I feel better now. I can handle it.'

She smiled at him. 'You were just tired.'

'Perhaps.' He said, in a rather stilted, over-prepared manner, 'You've been very kind to me. Nobody was ever so kind. But from now on, it's my problem. You don't have to be involved.'

She looked at him in alarm. 'What do you mean?'

'I mean I have to go,' he said. 'I have to leave this country. I know how it'll be if I stay. After what happened at the meeting today—I shall be questioned by your Government. Nobody will believe what I say.' He said violently, 'It'll be impossible—impossible. I shall be tormented by policemen, by journalists. I can't stay here.'

'Don't you want me to go with you?'

'I couldn't ask that of you.'

'It depends whether you really want me.'

He said, almost angrily, 'You don't understand. You haven't thought it out. I have no country, no valid passport. If you go with me, you would be in exile, too. Your Government might not let you return.'

'Oh, for God's sake!' Tears of anger and mortification began to run down her cheeks. 'Do you think I want to hear all this stuff about governments and passports? I want to know whether you care for me enough to want me with you.

If you don't—well, that's that, I suppose. I haven't any rights over you. But you have to say it. Don't pretend you're thinking of my welfare, or anything like that—'

She could hardly believe the words which came from her own mouth. She remembered Maurice's bitter criticisms of her coldness and independence. Now, pride was a luxury she could no longer afford. She would implore him, if need be. But she would not let him go unless she knew it was inevitable.

He said, 'I have no money—'

Oh, if that were all they had to worry about! 'Money doesn't matter,' she said eagerly. 'A man like you could always make money.' Ideas flooded from her. 'You could write a book. There's all the material we recorded for *Planet*. We don't need to give it to them. We can publish it ourselves. I know a publisher in Paris—' She thought of Lapas, how eager he would be. It would be just his kind of book. 'In the meantime I have more than enough to keep us going. I'd make a loan to you—you needn't feel dependent—'

It is I who am dependent, she thought. But she was past caring what he thought of her. Either he loved her and he would understand—or he didn't love her and everything was over anyway. She waited anxiously, scanning his face for a sign of his decision. Then he smiled gravely and she knew it was all right, that it would always be all right between them. He kissed her and said, 'Then we've no time to lose. Let's get back to town.'

At Columbus Circle there was a newsboy on the corner shouting the evening papers. Sarah stopped the car momentarily and bought one. Karas looked at the main headline. It said, 'Riddle of Missing Scientist.' There was a picture of himself and an account of the morning's press conference. He read pieces of the story to Sarah as she drove. There were quotations from various people who had been interviewed by reporters. Mr. John Henderson had proved impossible to contact, but 'an executive of the ISIS organization' had quoted him as saying that he had nothing further to add to what he had said at the meeting. A spokesman from Washington had said, 'We have no official knowledge of Dr. Karas's whereabouts. Yes, certainly we should like to interrogate him. We hope to do so within the next twenty-four hours.'

Sarah drove down Central Park South and then up Fifth Avenue. They had decided to go to the small apartment; it was the only place where they had any chance of safety. She parked the Chevrolet in front of the brownstone and hurried up the steps to the front door. Karas pulled up the collar of his jacket and dived into the house after her. So far as he could see, there was nobody following them. They ran up the four flights of stairs of the walk-up as quickly and silently as possible, in terror that someone might come out of one of the other apartments and recognize them. But the house was quiet and apparently deserted.

Sarah opened the door of the apartment and turned on the light. Then she started back with a cry of alarm. A man was standing with his back to them, silhouetted against the window leading out on to the balcony. He turned round and they saw that it was Henderson.

The old man regarded them for a moment and then said in his harsh authoritative voice, 'Come in. Don't stand there in the doorway.' He closed the curtains and then stood looking down at them from his great height. He seemed far too big for the tiny room. 'Where the hell have you been?'

Karas moved to confront him. 'Does that matter to you?'

Henderson ignored the question. 'I've been waiting for a couple of hours,' he said querulously. 'I knew you'd be bound to end up here.'

Karas was about to ask him how he knew about the apartment, but what was the point? In any case, as soon as he thought about it, he knew the answer. It had been absurd to imagine that Henderson would ever have really let them wander around New York unobserved. When they had dined at the Village or gone to the theatre, or sat alone in the peace of this little apartment, there had always been someone, a man waiting round a corner, sitting at a table, watching a lighted window from across the street. If they stayed here this would be their future—a life without privacy or trust. If it was not Henderson who watched them it would be the Government, or ISIS, or the F.B.I. There was no chance that they would ever be able to live again simply and privately.

He waited for Henderson to declare himself. What did he want? Was he hoping to do some new deal, to put back the clock, to start the whole dreary process over again? 'Why did you come here?' he said.

'I want to help you.'

Karas said sourly, 'I think you've helped me enough.'

Henderson ignored the gibe. 'What are you intending to do?'

'I'm going away.'

'Easier said than done. They want to talk to you.'

'We'll manage,' said Sarah.

Henderson was halted for a moment by the implication of what she had said. 'You're going too?'

'Yes.'

The old man's surprise was only mild. It occurred to Karas that his spies would have told him about that side of things too. 'May I ask where?'

She was silent. They had discussed it in the car, but without coming to any firm conclusion. Henderson regarded her with the slightly patronizing expression of a professional in handling life's emergencies. He said, 'You won't find it easy. I don't know how hard they're looking for you, but there's a good chance of being picked up at the airport.'

The same possibility had been tormenting Karas ever since he had seen the evening paper. He said reluctantly, 'What do you suggest?'

'My own plane's ready to take off at Kennedy Airport. I came to offer you the use of it. The crew are standing by. They'll get you to Mexico in a few hours.'

Karas frowned. 'Why are you doing this?'

Henderson said, with an air of indifference, 'I feel a certain responsibility towards you. After all, I brought you here. I got you that passport, which could take some explaining. If you don't want to stay, I guess I have some obligation to get you away.'

That was true enough, thought Karas. It was also true that any investigation of the affair could be embarrassing to Henderson himself. He could be attacked by politicians and pilloried by the Press. If Karas escaped, the tendency would be for the affair to be forgotten in a week or two. It would be convenient for everyone if he got out of the country. No wonder Henderson had been waiting so impatiently.

Nevertheless, a favour was a favour. If one waited for favours which were made purely out of altruism, one might wait a very long time. He knew he must accept—there was no alternative. He said gravely, as his mother had told him years ago when accepting a gift from an adult, 'Thank you. That's very kind of you.'

'Forget it.' Henderson spoke with the ease of a man who

has given many favours in his time and is used to accepting gratitude without embarrassment. He clapped Karas on the shoulder and began to discuss the details of his plan. He seemed once more in command of the situation. Nobody would have imagined that only that morning he had received a crushing defeat. He made the organisation of the escape to Mexico sound like the triumphant culmination of the operation rather than a last desperate attempt to cut his losses. He was enjoying himself, dramatising the situation, crowing with delight at the thought of helping Karas to slip through the fingers of the Government. He gave the impression of a man who would sooner command a retreat than command nothing at all.

This, thought Karas as he listened to Henderson talking, was his last sight of the old man in action. He wondered, as he had wondered so often before, why it was so difficult to be angry with him for his egoism and his irresponsibility, hit utter lack of concern for others except in so far as they were involved in his aims of the moment. It was as Sarah had said. Some were forgiven. One had to leave it at that.

'Okay then, that's it.' Henderson looked at Karas. "All right, boy.' He noticed Karas's momentary frown of irritation. 'Perhaps I shouldn't call you that. But you must forgive me. I'm an old man. You're all kids to me.' He laid an arm round Sarah's shoulder and squeezed it with his huge hand. 'It's no use apologising to you—you know me too well. Since I don't intend to change myself at my time of life, why apologise?' He said with genuine affection, 'But I'm here when you want me. Always remember that.' He said to Karas, 'Look after this girl now, she's not so tough as she looks. But I know you will. I'm an egotistical old bastard and I talk all the time, but I see more than you think. I know what sort of guy you are. You gave me a kick in the teeth this morning, and I was mad for a while, but that's over now.' He said with a trace of sadness, 'I don't meet so many people I can respect these days.' Then he turned back to Sarah and kissed her on the cheek. 'Good luck, baby.' He shook Karas by the hand, crammed his hat on his head and was gone.

Henderson closed the door behind him and walked heavily down the stairs. When he appeared through the door of the house, his limousine pulled out of a parking space farther up the street and drew up in front of him. As he drove away, he thought: well, that was over. Another deal, another project. Not successful this time, but you couldn't win them all. The sign of a really first-class operator was his ability to get off the hook when things went against him. He had always been good at that. This would be a story to tell against himself. Though not entirely against himself, if it came to that. If the plane got away, as it almost certainly would, he could claim to have put one over on Washington right at the end.

He began to prepare the story as he would tell it to his cronies, when things had quietened down. It was admitted in the Club that he was a great raconteur, a fund of fascinating business folklore, a relic of the lost days when a man's life could still be a personal adventure. Even if it hadn't come off, it had been a grandiose idea in the great tradition. He could imagine them saying, 'Did you hear the inside dope about Henderson and the missing scientist? That was really something . . .'

And then, without warning, a spasm of depression overcame him and he saw another picture of himself. An old man talking of forgotten glories, his words only half-attended, his stories only half-believed. A man who hung round club corridors and smoking rooms, searching for an audience which every year would grow harder to find. A tedious relic of a forgotten age. For this, he knew with sudden clarity, was his last deal. ISIS and Washington between them would see to that. Now he would never make the cover of *Time Magazine*. He would sink into an obscurity which only his death would momentarily break.

The pain of the thought was more than he could bear. What was there now to justify his continued existence—to make sense of the exacting physical routine he had accepted to preserve his shattered decrepit old body? Searching for some small sensual pleasure to give him a moment of consolation in his agony, he saw the humidor built into the back seat of the limousine. It was always filled with Havanas but he had not touched one for years. He opened the box, took out a Romeo and lit it. But the taste was not the one he had held in his memories during the years of deprivation. There was something wrong with the cigar—or perhaps with him. The smoke was acrid and brittle on his tongue. He tried two or three puffs but it did not improve. Even in the smallest things, he thought, a man should cut his losses. He threw it out of the window.

PART FOUR

CHAPTER ONE

WELDON SWITCHED OFF the electric shaver and ran his hand over his chin. Then he looked at his face in the mirror of the hotel bathroom. Not bad, he thought, not bad at all. Skin still quite smooth and pink, no jowls or bags under his eyes. He hadn't gone bald, thank God, and those few white hairs around the temples were quite flattering, an expression of maturity rather than of age. Really, for a man of—his mind gave a little leap over the question of his exact age, as if it were unlucky to mention it, even to himself—for a man of his age he was holding up extraordinarily well.

Even so, one had to be careful. He ate and drank moderately and tried to get to bed in good time. That girl last night, for example. He could have had her almost certainly, if he had been prepared to go through all the rigmarole. But it was awkward here in the Savoy, where he was so well known. It would have meant going back to her flat in South Kensington. He knew it all so well. The quick, urgent love-making because you were new to each other and rather excited, then the strange room, the strange girl, the halting conversation, the realization that once sex was over they had nothing much in common. He would begin to feel tired and a little heavy from the wine, wondering when he could decently take his leave. And the girl would be touchy and deflated, made melancholy by the suspicion that once desire was satisfied he had no use for her any more. No, it had been better the way it was, to leave her fascinated and a little puzzled. Perhaps he might look her up again one day, but more likely he would lose her address and that would be that. His sexual urge was beginning to fade, like so many of the other impulses in his life. Fantasy was becoming increasingly more attractive than reality. With fantasy you could play it your own way, you were not disenchanted, you knew how things were going to turn out. Those drives of a man's youth, founded on hope and a desire to challenge the unknown in search of a great experience—you couldn't keep those up for ever. His life had gradually become a defensive operation.

261

He remembered the young Weldon, twenty years ago, who looked not so very different from the man he now saw in the mirror. The young Weldon had had great faith in the future. He had never laid claim to exceptional brilliance, but he had been conscious of a certain perceptiveness, a natural charm and a quick brain, a capacity for handling people. He had felt that with these he would not have too much trouble making a mark in the world. What would the young Weldon have thought of the man he had finally become? Weldon shrugged the thought from his mind. Perhaps it was the wine last night that was depressing him. He resolved to give up drinking altogether—he didn't really enjoy it. He concentrated on knotting his tie—a new one from Hardy Amies in an unusual shade of dark green. Then he went into the bedroom, put on his jacket and overcoat, tilted his hat to the correct angle, and let himself out into the hotel corridor. He had an appointment at the ISIS offices in a quarter of an hour's time.

As he walked along to the office, his self-confidence began to ebb. He had received a message from Mulholland to attend a conference with himself and O'Keefe. It had been worded in what could only be regarded as peremptory terms. A bad sign. The gossip in the Company was that since Henderson's spectacular decline after the Karas affair, both O'Keefe and Mulholland were on the way up. Well, he thought with resignation, he would have to learn to live with it. He had weathered a number of tricky situations in his time. Nothing was for ever. O'Keefe could lose favour as quickly as he gained it. Mulholland might drink himself to death. Either of them might get killed in an air crash. The main thing was still to be around when it happened.

Survival. Survival. That was what life was about. And then another part of him recoiled, asking: Survival for what? For fear and humiliation, for boredom and servitude? Was this really all he was worth? Was it too late to start again? Would he not actually be wiser to get out before his position became really intolerable?

His mind became possessed with a fantasy in which he stood up to O'Keefe and Mulholland and handed in his resignation. He had, after all, unusual qualifications. Languages, contacts, scientific knowledge—once it became known he was at liberty, all kinds of organizations, commercial and otherwise, would be queuing up for his services. ISIS had taken him too much for granted—they would find he could do far better without them. He would look back years later and wonder why he had stayed in the job so long. He saw himself as the head of some official scientific body. The executive chairman of a Foundation. Or perhaps—his mind changed gear into another of his dreams—he would disappear altogether. Another name, another identity. Blanche and the children might grieve for a while, but they would get over it soon enough. There was that numbered bank account in Zürich into which he had been paying small sums for years—it hadn't been as much as he would have liked, but there was enough to keep him going for a while. He saw a sunburnt man in a fishing village on the Mediterranean, or standing on the deck of a cargo boat heading for the South Pacific; or at a table in a night club in Casablanca, sipping a glass of vermouth, smiling enigmatically. . . .

When he was shown into the office, Mulholland didn't bother to get up and meet him. He simply waved him to a seat and went on talking to O'Keefe, who was lounging in an armchair smoking a cigarette. The pimples on Mulholland's face seemed to have increased a little, if anything, and his suit was an even more unfortunate shade of brown. The other man in the room was Walker, prim, enigmatic, and silent as ever, and yet curiously changed. Weldon wondered in what way for a moment, and then it occurred to him that this was the first time he had seen Walker occupying a position in the centre of the room instead of against the wall, effacing himself. He had noticeably gained stature since their last meeting in New York. In some indefinable way he had become larger and more formidable.

The atmosphere in the office confirmed Weldon's forebodings. The conversation between Mulholland and O'Keefe was quite a pointless one, and he knew that it was only being carried on to keep him waiting and make him feel inferior. He did his best to conceal his irritation by gazing indifferently out of the window at the grey London skyline. Finally O'Keefe seemed to decide that the necessary impression had been made. He terminated the conversation and turned his attention to Weldon.

'Hi, Art,' he said perfunctorily. 'Glad you could join us.' He spoke in the easy, confident manner of a man addressing a subordinate. Weldon remembered the time when O'Keefe had tried to bluster his way to an assumption of authority. Now, evidently, bluster was unnecessary. The game had been won. O'Keefe crushed out his cigarette and leaned forward. 'There's something we'd like you to help us with.'

'What is it?'

'It's about your friend Karas.'

He used the words 'your friend' like an accusation. Weldon was instinctively tempted to deny the implication, to say that Karas was not his friend and discount all responsibility for him. Then shame overcame him. The accusation of friendship remained unanswered. 'What about him?'

'As you know, when he bolted off to Mexico, our first reaction was to play it down, let the whole situation drop.' Weldon noted the easy use of the word 'our'. Obviously the Karas affair had not harmed O'Keefe, quite the reverse. Weldon began to wonder who O'Keefe had been reporting to, all the time he was supposed to be working for Henderson. 'Unfortunately,' O'Keefe went on, 'the way things are turning out, it looks as if we shan't be able to hold that position. It's now been decided that we can't just leave things as they are.'

Weldon thought quickly. It was important not to take all O'Keefe's claims at face value. It was likely enough that the rumours were correct and he was in a powerful position now that Henderson had gone, but there had been no official confirmation. 'Decided by whom?' he asked.

'By your employers,' said O'Keefe curtly. His boxer's face was set in an attitude of aggression, ready to deal with any challenge to his new position. 'By ISIS.'

'Not just ISIS,' said a dry clerk's voice.

Weldon swung round in surprise. He had almost forgotten Walker was in the room. Walker took off his glasses, carefully polished one of the lenses and put them back on again. He said to O'Keefe, 'I think it's important that Dr. Weldon should understand the situation.'

His manner was still quiet and rather formal, but the quality of subservience which had always characterized it in the days when they had lived together in the villa was completely gone. O'Keefe noticed the surprise on Weldon's face. He said, 'Perhaps I ought to explain something you don't know. Keith Walker has a special position here, in relation to the Karas affair. He has—' He searched for a phrase. Subtlety of expression did not come easily to him. '—official connections with Washington.'

Walker smiled, cat-like, and Weldon's mouth became suddenly dry. He remembered the morning they had all

264

gathered in Henderson's office, the old man shouting and joking, bullying, laughing, performing—and the men watching him. Each one had held his own concealed menace —O'Keefe the careerist, Forsyth the implacable enemy . . . and Walker, the spy. As Henderson had been deceiving Karas, so others had been deceiving Henderson. Disloyalty had fed on disloyalty, betrayal on betrayal. Every lie had carried another hidden in its core.

He remembered now the surprising ease with which they had procured the fake passport for Karas, the wait in the aircraft at Kennedy Airport while Walker had gone to make arrangements with the immigration officials. He said to Walker, 'It must have been a nasty surprise to you when they got away to Mexico.' Walker said nothing. Weldon went on, 'Did Henderson know who you were working for?'

'Let's forget about Henderson,' said O'Keefe. 'He doesn't matter any more.' The complacent brutality in his voice was a reply to a score of insults swallowed and contemptuous slights patiently endured. There was no longer any need for him to conceal his hatred for the old man. And not only for Henderson himself but for all those who had observed him in the days of his subordination. He fixed Weldon with a cold, triumphant stare. 'And there's something else we'd better clear up before we go any further. From now on, Art, you report to Mr. Mulholland, and Mr. Mulholland reports to me. You'll receive a cable from New York confirming that within the next twenty-four hours.'

For two years now, Weldon had lived in the constant fear that something like this might happen. He had fought against it, he had used whatever influence he could lay his hands on, he had struggled and intrigued ceaselessly, with the one object of retaining the independence which made his life tolerable. Now the struggle was over and he had lost. From now on he was a lackey to the pimpled vulgarian who sat grinning in triumph at him from the other side of the desk. He knew better than to expect any mercy from Mulholland. Now was the time, if ever, to present that dignified resignation he had so often rehearsed. But somehow he could not do it. The step was too enormous, too awesome. He had been with ISIS so long that the thought of abandoning its protection was suddenly terrifying to him. He must delay a little, give himself time to think. He stammered indecisively. 'I'm not very sure—' he began.

Mulholland interrupted, 'This isn't a question of what

you're very sure about,' he said brutally. 'This is a fact. I've been saying for years that this organization needed a proper chain of command and now at last we've got it.' He looked with unconcealed satisfaction at his new captive. 'For once we won't have a lot of argument about what you'll do and what you won't do. You'll be given an assignment like anyone else and do as you're told.'

'Just a moment.' Once again, Walker intervened. Though he did not raise his voice, it cut into the conference with a kind of effortless domination. 'This assignment is primarily my concern and I'm not prepared to accept that kind of approach to it.' He said icily to O'Keefe, 'I thought my superiors made it clear to you that I was to handle this in my own way.'

'Sure,' said O'Keefe. 'I accept that. But this is a question of principle—of internal organization—'

'I'm not interested in your internal organization,' said Walker with a kind of placid contempt. 'I have an important job to do and frankly you're not helping me to do it.' He regarded O'Keefe and Mulholland with prim distaste, like a tidy housewife confronted with a pile of dirty dishes. It occurred to Weldon that Walker found Mulholland and O'Keefe as detestable as he did. He had the sense of discovering, in the most unexpected place, a powerful ally. Perhaps all was not lost after all. Walker encouraged him still further by saying, 'As you know I have authority to deal with Dr. Weldon direct if necessary. I think I'd prefer to handle it that way.'

O'Keefe nibbled at his lower lip, as if considering the possibility of defiance. Then prudence won. 'Just as you like. You're the doctor on this one.' He turned a glance of pure hatred on Weldon. 'We'll talk about the organizational question later.'

Weldon and Walker left the office together and went to a small restaurant nearby for lunch. Walker ordered an omelette and a bottle of Vichy water. After a morning of O'Keefe and Mulholland, the atmosphere of quiet austerity which he generated was doubly impressive. Weldon felt an impulse to convey his sense of gratitude but could think of no way of doing it without sacrificing dignity. He too ordered a very light lunch.

'I hadn't met Mulholland,' said Walker with obvious distaste. 'Are there many like him in your organization?'

'Not too many. But one's more than enough.'

'Yes.' Walker fortified his agreement with a thin smile. 'I felt I had to intervene because I could see you were on the point of walking out. I didn't want you to do that.'

Weldon nodded gravely. He was greatly reassured by Walker's words. He himself could not be sure in recollection what he had been intending to do, but it was good to know that he had made the correct impression. He began to think he had indeed been on the point of walking out.

'Quite apart from that,' Walker went on, 'this matter has nothing to do with Mulholland at all. It's really far better that he shouldn't be involved in it.' He thought for a moment. 'Perhaps I'd better explain to you precisely what our problem is.'

He looked around the restaurant, as a reflex precaution to make sure they were not overheard. Then he went on, 'You see, nobody was very concerned at first when Karas went to Mexico. We were inclined to believe his story that he didn't know anything worth telling. We couldn't be sure but we thought it best to wait. We used our influence to prevent him selling himself to any other Western governments. That wasn't difficult because most of them had the feeling he was rather a hot potato anyway. Apart from that, we just kept an eye on him and waited to see what he would do. We were beginning to think he was pretty harmless.' He paused and took a sip of his mineral water. 'But unfortunately there's been a change in the situation.'

'In what way?'

'A few weeks ago he got in touch with a publisher in Paris called Lapas. It seems he wants to publish a book. Lapas has a reputation as a man who likes to publish sensational disclosures of one kind or another. Lapas has been interviewed by our people. Naturally he denies that the proposed book contains anything dangerous, but that means nothing. He claims to have met Miss Manning casually when he was in Paris, but he swears he doesn't know her very well. So why choose him? You can see it's rather alarming.'

'What do you want me to do?'

'We simply want to talk to him.' Walker's voice was easy and cultivated. Now that Weldon was getting used to regarding him as a person rather than as a vague figure in the background he saw that Walker was an intelligent, sensitive man. It was a pleasure to associate with him, after the others. He went on, in the same quiet, reasonable tone, 'It's fairly clear that Karas must have been pretty confused by every-thing that has happened. A man like Henderson takes a bit of understanding, even by people like us who are used to him. We can only imagine the effect he must have had on a man like Karas, who has spent all his life in academic circles, with no experience at all of business or American ways. Naturally he was thrown off balance. The whole atmosphere of the affair was too much for him. I think you or I would probably react in the same way.'

Weldon nodded agreement.

'I don't know what Henderson told Karas about the U.S. Government, but my guess is that it was something pretty lurid and inaccurate. After all, the old man's notoriously unbalanced on the subject. It wouldn't matter too much if Karas wasn't proposing to write this book, which is bound to get a great deal of publicity. We'd like to have the chance to straighten him out on a few factual matters. We'd like to make it clear to him how much harm he can do by hasty and ill-considered publication. I don't think Karas really wants to spend his life as a sensational figure, cut off from the scientific community. You know him better than any-body. Wouldn't you agree with me?'

'Yes. I think so.'

'He needs a chance of something better—a more stable, more dignified existence. We're in a position to offer it to him. If he doesn't want to take it, there's nothing we can do about it. He'll suffer and so will we, but we have no powers of compulsion. However, at least I think an effort should be made to explain the situation to him.'

'Why do you need me?'

'Because you're the man who really made personal contact with him on the right level. You and he speak the same language. An approach through you would have a much greater chance of success.' When Weldon was silent, he said, 'I know you feel a loyalty to him. But there's no conflict there. This is your chance to do something for him.'

Weldon felt a sense of relief. Ever since Karas had been mentioned he had been tormented by the thought that he might be driven into betraying Karas in some way. But evidently that particular test was not to be put to him. 'Well, if it's just a question of that—'

'Fine.' Walker smiled at him. 'I knew you'd be prepared to help if it was explained to you.' As if making a complete change of subject he said, 'Do you enjoy working for isis?'

'Well—' Weldon felt his way cautiously. 'In some ways, yes. But there are disadvantages.'

Walker said sympathetically, 'Like this morning?'

'Yes. That kind of thing.'

Walker said, 'That's one of the things about my particular group. We're very selective about the people we employ. I think we can claim a very high standard of personnel. College graduates and so on. It makes for pleasanter working conditions.' He gave the words extra significance. He was almost like a man feeling around in conversation with a girl before making a serious attempt at seduction. Weldon felt suddenly at ease with him. This world of inferences and suggestions and gently dropped hints was his world. He responded like an expert bridge player replying to a tentative bid by his partner.

'Do you have much problem in recruitment?' he said.

Walker made a rebid. 'Our problem,' he said slowly, 'is to get exactly the right people. Especially in highly technical fields.' He paused. 'Such as your own, for instance.'

He let the words hang in the air, and Weldon felt a sense of pleasurable excitement. There was surely no doubt about it now. Walker, in his circuitous way, was making an approach. He knew instinctively that it would not be followed up straight away. He would be given time to consider the possibilities of it, to show what he could do in his present task. Then perhaps the suggestion would be made in a more concrete form at a later date. Weldon's imagination swung into play. He saw a quiet, elegant man, unobtrusive yet knowing, a power hidden in the background, watchful and full of secrets. A beautiful girl would look at him across the dinner table and say, 'Tell me, Mr. Smith, what do you really do for a living?' And he would reply evasively, 'Import and Export . . .'

He caught Walker's eyes on him. Was there a glint of humour behind those all-concealing spectacles? He felt himself blushing. Walker said, 'Now, perhaps, I could tell you exactly what it is we'd like you to do.'

CHAPTER TWO

KARAS AWOKE EARLY, as always. Above him, as he opened his eyes, he saw the familiar dark blue silk canopy of the same four-poster bed that he had occupied on his first night of freedom. Beneath him was the same feather mattress, the down pillows, the lying half on and half off the bed was the gigantic flowered eiderdown. There was only one important difference. Now he was not alone.

Sarah was turned away from him in her sleep, her fair hair spread on the pillow. One arm was outside the bed-clothes, and the thin strap of her nightdress had fallen away to show a naked shoulder and the upper part of her right breast. She was breathing deeply. When she felt him move against her she wriggled slightly into the pillow as if fighting any attempt to drag herself back into wakefulness.

Carefully, so as not to disturb her, he got out of bed and walked on his bare feet towards the window. He parted the heavy velvet curtains and looked out on to the garden. It had snowed during the night. The snow formed a heavy carpet over the garden, weighing thickly like icing sugar on the hedges and bushes, and bending the branches of the big cedar tree in the centre of the lawn. The mountains towered above him across the lake, white now from summit to base, with here and there the black smudge of a pine wood. In the clear sharp air they looked near enough to touch.

It seemed to Karas like a great age since he had first set eyes on those mountains, yet it was only a matter of a few months. In the last six weeks they had moved from Mexico to Brazil, through Portugal and Spain and Italy, eternal fugitives from a danger they could hardly define, in search of a security which constantly eluded them. He had written innumerable letters—to governments and universities, to scientists working in his own field in various Western countries—but when he had received replies at all they had been cautious and noncommittal. His false passport gradually became an obsession with him. In Mexico they had tried to get married, but had panicked when the registrar had insisted on seeing his birth certificate. They had lived in fear of immigration officials, policemen, hotel clerks. Finally Sarah had thought of the villa.

'It was rented in my name,' she said. 'I have the lease for at least six months. We can live there on our own. Nobody will bother us.'

They had settled down there two weeks ago. The Dietrichs had greeted them without emotion. Sarah had reluctantly agreed to pretend that they were man and wife on the grounds that if the Dietrichs were scandalized they would be likely to gossip and attract attention. The melancholy impassive couple had taken the announcement with their usual phlegm—whether they believed it no one could say.

Karas heard an excited bark from down the garden. He looked down and saw Nico, the German shepherd dog, standing in the centre of the lawn, his tongue hanging out expectantly. They had bought Nico when they came to the villa, with the idea of using him as a guard dog. The Dietrichs, who had acquired him for them from some friends of theirs in one of the villages, had assured them that he had a reputation of great ferocity. In fact, he had turned out to be amiable and affectionate, happy to do nothing. They had grown hopelessly fond of him.

As Karas waved to him from the window, he barked again and rushed into the house. A moment later he thundered up the staircase and into the bedroom. The noise of his entry awakened Sarah. She sat up sleepily in bed, pulling the strap of her nightdress back on to her shoulder.

'What time is it?' she asked Karas.

'Seven o'clock.'

'Oh, Nico, you brute! Can't you give me a chance to sleep?' The dog pushed his muzzle into her hand.

'It was my fault really. He saw me at the window.'

'You ought to learn to sleep later.'

'I wish I could,' he said. There was so little to do nowadays that the days seemed endless. For the first time in his life he was searching for ways of wasting time. He drew back the curtains. 'It's been snowing. It's beautiful outside.'

She sat up in bed. 'I'll look at it later.'

He went back to the bed and sat down beside her. He kissed her and slipped his hand inside her nightdress, touching her breast. She suddenly moved away from him. 'No, darling, not just now.' She pointed to the dog. 'I really can't do it in front of him. He knows far too much as it is.'

'Shall I put him out?'

'No.' She was suddenly serious. 'I want to talk to you.'

'What about?'

She hesitated. 'I think I'm going to have a baby.'

He looked at her in surprise. It was something they had not planned—they had never even spoken of it. If she had asked him beforehand whether he wanted to have a child, he would have said that it was madness in their present predicament. He, of all men, was in no position to give hostages to fortune. All prudence and logic were against it. Yet prudence and logic were suddenly powerless before the thought of the new life growing within her body, a life for which he would be responsible. That responsibility was the signal for the final disappearance of a person it had taken him thirty-five years to create—Karas the chess-player, the opportunist, the carefree sensual man. The new Karas watched him go without regret. He had more important matters to attend to now.

She became anxious at his silence. 'You're not angry?'

'Angry? Good heavens no.' He kissed her again. 'It's wonderful. I'm absolutely delighted.'

'You really are?'

'Yes, of course.' It was strange, he thought, when he had struggled so long against possession, that he should welcome it so unreservedly. It was like moving across a frontier into a country where none of the old rules applied, when the opportunity to cherish and protect might mean more than anything a man could attain in his individual life. He realized the unreality of his old assumption that love was a relationship much the same as any other—a mere blending of sensuality and affection. Love was an identity—you could feel it for a child who had not yet been born, a woman you were only just beginning to know. He knew now that when he told Sarah in the New York apartment that he loved her, he had been speaking of something he did not understand. Only at this moment had it acquired a genuine significance.

Unreasonably, he felt regret that he himself had taken no part in the decision. He said, 'I'm sorry I was so taken aback, but it never occurred to me. I mean, I thought you were taking precautions—'

She shook her head. 'No. I decided not to.'

'You never told me.'

'Perhaps I should have done,' she said. 'But somehow—it was one of those very instinctive feelings.' She struggled to express herself. 'Perhaps it was because, in a way, when I found I'd broken through this awful thing that worried me for so long—you know, not being able to love anyone—I felt I had to go the whole way, everything. No reservations.' She said apologetically, 'I don't suppose that makes a lot of sense to you.'

'Why shouldn't it?'

'Because you're so competent and clever and analytical. It's hard for you to understand the silly things that go through women's heads. It makes you rather intimidating.'

'Even to you?'

'Yes,' she admitted. 'I was a little scared of you at the beginning. Not so much now I know you better.' She looked past him, out of the window. 'In marriage, it's not just taking off your clothes and going to bed. It's the mental clothes. They're the real disguise.' She smiled at him affectionately. 'You know what they say about there being a thin man inside every fat man? With you, it's the opposite way round.'

They dressed and went down to breakfast. The villa felt very still and empty. Beside Karas's plate there were three letters. Two of them were bills, the other was addressed to Sarah. As she read it the happiness left her face.

'What is it?' he asked.

'It's Maurice. He says he's very sorry. He won't be able to publish your book after all.'

'Why not?'

'Oh, there's a lot of stuff that means nothing,' she said wearily. 'He says he'd like to help you but he feels he was rather precipitate with his original offer. He says he doesn't usually commit himself so far before a manuscript's completed, and in any case this isn't really his sort of book. He suggests you try another publisher.'

'But he's already committed himself.'

'Oh yes. You could certainly sue him for damages. But of course he knows you're in no position to do so. After all,' she pointed out, 'you haven't even a valid passport to get into France with.'

'He wouldn't know that.'

'Wouldn't he? My guess is that the people who told him to write this letter told him it was pretty safe to do so.' She said, 'Poor Maurice. He never pretended to much integrity about money or anything like that. But he always prided himself on his independence as a publisher.'

He hardly heard what she said. He had no interest in Lapas. He searched his mind for an alternative approach. 'So what do we do now?' he said.

'I suppose we could try another publisher.'

'I don't know,' he said. His confidence in the whole project of the book, never very strong, had drained away with Lapas's refusal. 'I'm not a popular kind of writer. I can't dramatize things in the way you say people want. Perhaps the whole idea was hopeless."

She paused and then said tentatively, 'You don't have to write it, Peter, if you don't want to.'

'What else can I do?'

'We could just stay on here.' Her voice was eager, almost pleading. 'You've worked hard all your life. Surely you're entitled to play a little. We could have fun. Go up to the mountains and ski. We could buy a yacht. It's lovely here in spring and summer. We could wait until I have the baby.'

'And then?'

'Things will have calmed down. Something's bound to turn up.'

He considered it seriously, in the way he considered everything. Then he shook his head. 'It wouldn't work.'

'Why not?' He did not reply. 'Don't tell me you have scruples about living on my money.'

'No. It's not that.' He knew her plan was impracticable, but it was not easy to explain why. 'What you suggest sounds theoretically possible. But it isn't really. We can't cut ourselves off from the world totally. As it is we've spent over a month moving from one hotel room to another, seeing nobody, completely isolated. I can't spend the rest of this year taking walks round the mountains with Nico, doing no work, completely isolated from everything that matters to me. We can't live this way.'

'I could,' she said. 'I want no one but you. I'd be happy with that.'

'You think so now. Perhaps for a little while it might work. But soon you'd begin to pine for your own country and your own people. For friends. We're social animals. You have to face that fact.'

'The truth is,' she said unhappily, 'that I'm not enough for you. That's what you're really saying.'

He was gentle with her. 'No one person is enough for another person. Not exclusively.'

'You've never loved me in the way I've loved you.'

He evaded the impossible question. He said with sincerity, 'I've never loved anyone in my whole life as I love you.'

She was not consoled. 'That's what you say now. But you had Sophia, and all those other girls. You were never without somebody to make a fuss of you. And not just women. There was this Max you're so everlastingly on about—'

He looked surprised. 'Don't tell me you're jealous of Max.'

A flush spread over her face. 'Don't be absurd.'

Yet it was true, he thought. He had seen it gradually increasing over the time they had been together. She wished to possess him utterly. It was as if all the love and devotion

274

which had been dammed up in her during the years of her loveless childhood, all the bitter frustrations of her adult life, had exploded in the vast wave of emotion directed towards him. To her, love was a magnificent, all-obliterating discovery, the fact of sexual pleasure was a miracle almost beyond belief. And now there was the baby . . . That would be another object on which she could lavish the vast single-minded devotion of which she was capable. He could see that to her, at this time, it was totally impossible to think that he and the baby and her new-found capacity for love could not between them fill her life. But for him, deeply in love with her though he knew himself to be, it was out of the question to live within such narrow boundaries. Nor would it always be possible for her. The appetite for exclusive love would become sated in the end.

He said, 'You know I couldn't live without you. You're all I have—all I care about.' He saw the words of reassurance softening her anxiety. Yet the problem of his future had still to be faced. 'Just the same, I must do something. I must find some place in the world.'

'But what?'

'I don't know,' he said. 'I don't know.'

After breakfast he went out into the grounds with Nico. The snow had stopped now and the frost was already hardening it so that there was a thin white crust over the powder beneath. He could see the moving dots of holiday-makers on the ski slopes across the lake. Nico chased through the shrubbery after rabbits as he walked down the tree-lined drive. He went out into the road and walked for a long way around the southern border of the lake. It was good to get out into the fresh air. Nowadays he found the villa depressing; the emptiness of it, the huge rooms, the characterless furniture, all got on his nerves. The thought of staying there for the next nine months appalled him. The episode with Sarah that morning had not been the first sign of tension between them. Soon, unless something was done, even his love for Sarah, the only thing to which he could cling in a world which had rejected him, would be destroyed. Even that could not stand out against imprisonment.

In the afternoon he tried to write, but his concentration soon flagged. They played gin rummy together for a while and then watched the light beginning to fade across the lake. They were both startled when the telephone rang.

Karas answered it.

'Hallo, Peter, is that you?'

Karas instantly recognized Weldon's light, languid English voice. 'Yes.'

'It's Arthur speaking.' Rather fatuously, he asked, 'How are things with you?'

So they had found him at last. It was no surprise. He said, 'How did you know I was here?'

'Well—' Weldon paused and then said evasively, 'It wasn't too difficult really.' His voice took on a more urgent tone. 'Peter, I'd like to have a talk to you. Can I come up to the villa?'

Karas hesitated. But why not? They already knew where he was. At least it would be some form of human contact. 'All right. Where are you?'

'I'm in Geneva. I'll see you in about half an hour.' He rang off quickly, before Karas could change his mind. Karas put the instrument down and said to Sarah, 'It's Weldon. He wants to come and see us.'

Her face was set and angry. 'You shouldn't have agreed.'

'I can't seen any harm in it.'

'I don't want him here. You can't trust him.'

He laughed ruefully. 'Who said anything about trusting him?'

'He's just been sent here to talk you into something.'

'Of course.'

She came up to him and clung to him. 'Don't let him, Peter. Don't let him. It's dangerous. I know it.'

It was strange, he thought. Only a short time before, she had been one of them. Now that her loyalties had changed, they had changed totally. She was more suspicious and hostile than he could ever bring himself to be.

He comforted her. 'Don't worry. I shan't do anything rash.' He said, 'We can't hide for ever.'

It was just over half an hour later that they heard the sound of a taxi coming up the drive. Karas went to the back of the house and watched it through the window. Weldon was dressed for the cold weather in an overcoat with a beaver collar and a sealskin hat. After he had paid off his taxi he waited for a moment as it drove away. Like an actor preparing to go on stage, he seemed to make an unconscious inventory of his clothes, to straighten his posture and adjust his features into an appropriate expression. Then he went up to the portico and rang the bell. Karas let him in and they went together into the living room. Sarah was sitting in a chair beside the empty fireplace. 'Hallo, Arthur.'

There was hostility in her voice. Weldon picked it up immediately. He gave her a propitiatory smile. 'It seems a long time since we were all here together,' he said.

Neither of them replied. Karas said eventually, 'What was it you wanted to talk about?'

Weldon's voice was apologetic. 'Your future,' he said.

'I can look after my own future.'

'I don't think you can, you know.' He seemed to be begging Karas's pardon for disagreeing with him.

Karas said, 'Before we go any further, I think I'd like to know where you stand. I assume you're here on behalf of ISIS? What do they want?'

Weldon did not answer directly. He said, 'I suppose you know Henderson's out now?'

'I saw something about it in the papers.'

'He had to retire after that fiasco in New York.' Weldon glanced at Sarah to gauge her reaction but her face was expressionless. 'He was a great man, of course, but past his best. He made a lot of mistakes in his handling of the situation. That was fairly obvious.'

'None of you said anything at the time,' said Karas.

'What could we say?' Weldon replied quickly, as if it were an accusation he had met before. 'He wouldn't have listened. We should have ruined ourselves to no purpose. We had to wait until the right time came.'

'And then you all lent a hand in finishing him off, I suppose?'

For the first time it was possible for Karas to pity Henderson, the ageing lion finally pulled down by his enemies. In the end his strength had waned, his cunning had been blunted, his reflexes dulled. The day of the small man had arrived at last.

Weldon ignored the insult as he had ignored a multitude of others in his day. He said, 'It could be much easier for you, now that Henderson isn't there any more.'

'Why?'

'It makes it easier for us to co-operate with Washington. They really hated the old man, you know. On the other hand Forsyth is very well thought of, and he's on your side. We might be able to arrange something—'

'It's no good,' said Karas. 'I won't go back to America.'

Weldon was not discouraged. Presumably he had been expecting at least this degree of resistance. 'I think it would be a mistake to discuss details at the moment. I'm not empowered to do so anyway. I'm as much in the dark as you are about what's in their mind. I'm only here to find out if you're prepared to talk to them.'

'I don't know what I can offer them,' said Karas uncompromisingly. 'I won't go to America and I won't tell them anything about what Max wrote to me before he died. And that's all they really want, isn't it?'

'I can't tell you that. I don't know. But I can't see what you'd lose by talking to them.' Weldon abandoned his diplomatic manner. He spoke with obvious sincerity. 'Peter, you know how it is with me. I can't tell you much, I can't promise you anything. But I'm your friend, I really am, whatever you think. I know you can't go on living here. You haven't a chance of fixing anything up for yourself in any of the Western countries as things are at the moment. You need support from somewhere—a passport—'

His concern was plainly genuine and Karas was touched. Weldon went on, 'I know you won't give in to them, but they admire and respect you. You might well be able to do some kind of deal with them. Surely it's worth trying.'

Karas thought for a moment. Sarah said, 'Don't listen to him. He's lying.'

Karas shook his head. 'No, he's right, I must consider it.' He turned to Weldon. 'What exactly are you proposing?'

Weldon said eagerly, 'There's somebody very important in Geneva at the moment. He's staying down in the town and he's prepared to see you if you agree. I can make an appointment for you.'

'Who is he?'

'I don't know his name. But they told me this—he's bigger than Henderson.' He was almost pleading. 'I can't see that you could lose anything by just talking to him.'

Karas made a last desperate attempt to assess his sincerity. It occurred to him that Weldon was the only man in the world that he could call his friend. It was true that he had practised petty deceptions in the past, but all his knowledge of men told him that in his heart Weldon cared for him and respected him and would not in the end betray him. It was impossible to live without some kind of trust. And when all was said and done, why should Weldon lie to him? What was there to be gained? They could not force him to do anything against his will. For the sake of Sarah and the child, he had at least to give them a chance to make their proposition. 'All right,' he said. 'I'll see him.'

CHAPTER THREE

SARAH DROVE THE CAR slowly along the quay which looked out on to the tiny harbour. Across the road to her left lay a network of streets containing large, prim, residential houses. Karas peered out of the window at the street names. After about four or five streets he said, 'Rue Pasquier. It should be half-way along there.'

She stopped the car. 'I'll wait here for you.' But he made no move to get out of the car. Instead he took her hand, slipped off her glove, and stroked the long delicate fingers. 'You mustn't worry,' he said.

She was trembling a little. 'I'm afraid,' she said.

'It's nothing. They just want to talk. I can't lose anything by talking.'

'Yes, I know.'

'And just suppose anything did go wrong, you know the arrangements?'

'Yes.'

'But they won't be needed,' he said reassuringly. 'After all, this is Switzerland. And whatever you may think of ISIS, I doubt if they want my services enough to kidnap me—'

'Don't joke about it. Please don't.'

'All right, I won't.'

'Anything to do with losing you—I can't laugh at that.'

'I'll be back here in half an hour.'

'I'll be waiting. It doesn't matter how long you are.'

Her intensity of feeling moved him unbearably. He knew there would be times in the future when he would momentarily regret his freedom and resent the demands her devotion made on him. But it would be like the kind of nostalgia one had for a return to the simplicity and indifference of childhood. It was the desire to lose a dimension of life which was an enrichment and a complication at the same time. You might resent dependence, but in the end it was what life was about. No matter how you tried to avoid it, you were condemned to it when the time came.

Loyalty and dependence, he thought, were not so much virtues as the natural condition of man. They became perverted and exploited because men would sooner become loyal to something evil than to have no loyalties at all. It was important to seize on anything, however small, to which loyalty could decently be given—better to love the dog Nico than to be forced by the barrenness of your life to love the Organization, or the State.

'Don't worry,' he said. 'I'll be back.'

'You promise?'

There was something strangely childish about her demand for a promise, as if the expressing of his obligation in words could make a difference. 'Yes—I promise.'

He looked at his watch. It was time to go. He kissed her and she clung to him for a moment. Then he pushed her arms gently away from him and walked across the road.

It was a large house, set slightly back from the road, with a small, semi-circular driveway. Karas walked up the drive, his feet crunching noisily on the snow, and pressed the front door bell.

He heard the sound of footsteps on an uncarpeted floor and a moment later the door opened to him. He recognized without surprise the trim, discreetly dressed figure, the heavy spectacles and the forgettable, meaningless face. Walker said, 'Come in, Dr. Karas. It's nice to see you again.'

The hall was bare and poorly lit. What little furniture it contained was old and utilitarian, and there was a smell of floor-polish as in a school or a convent. Walker took his coat and led him along a corridor which led to the back of the house. He opened the door of a room and said, 'Perhaps you wouldn't mind waiting here for a moment.'

Walker closed the door and left. Karas looked around him. Plainly this had been either the dining-room or the breakfast-room when the house had been in private occupation. The centre of it was occupied by a thick-legged mahogany dining-table and there was a massive Victorian sideboard along one wall On the oatmeal-coloured wall-paper there were dingy oil paintings of mountain scenes.

It seemed a strange place for a senior executive of ISIS to receive a guest, and Karas felt the sweat of apprehension breaking out on his palms. He could not guess quite what was happening but he had a feeling that there was something wrong. The house was very silent. Then he heard a sound which was curiously familiar, though he could not place it for the moment. All he knew, from the reflex stirrings in his body, was that it was somehow associated with danger. It was a rhythmic soft muffled squeaking sound, which grew gradually louder with each repetition. He racked his brains to drag from his memory what it was. Then the door opened and he remembered.

Suvorin stood in the doorway, regarding him silently. Characteristically, he made no effort at a conventional greeting—his thoughts, as always, seemed to be turned inwards on problems and preoccupations of his own. His suit was crumpled and shabby, his scant, mousy hair dragged across his bald scalp. The corners of his mouth were turned down in his usual pessimistic expression. He was carrying a file of papers. He closed the door and his rubber soles squeaked their way to the table. He took a seat and put his file down in front of him.

Karas was the first to break the silence. It was obvious now that he had been tricked. He could not quite work out the details of the treachery. Obviously it involved Walker, probably Weldon too. He felt angry, humiliated, and also afraid. But it would be disastrous to give any sign of the fear which was rising in him. He looked coldly down at Suvorin. 'What are you doing here?'

'Can't you work it out? You used to be very intelligent.'

The first sound of that familiar, rasping voice seemed to dissolve the whole unreal world of the last few months. The dingy room, the poor light, the shabby furniture, were all reminders that wherever he might be geographically, he was back in Suvorin's world, under Suvorin's authority. Karas's mind raced over all the preceding events to try to find a meaning in what was now happening to him. Then Suvorin said, 'As you've probably grasped by this time, I'm here by agreement with the Americans.' He added, 'They thought I was the best person to speak to you.'

For a moment Karas was struck with panic. The bile rose in his throat. If he had felt naked before, it was nothing to the helplessness of his position now. For the first time he realized how much he had unconsciously relied on the Americans, even when he had rejected them. Now he had a sensation of total disaster, of being crushed irresistibly between two vast, ruthless, impersonal forces. What possible hope could there be for him now?

At the core of his despair one image dominated his mind —of Weldon begging him to come to this meeting, giving his promise of good faith on the word of a friend . . .

Suvorin looked at him sardonically. 'You seem a little shaken.' He walked over to the sideboard. 'Perhaps you'd like something to drink.' He looked over the bottles. 'A little English whisky? I believe you like that.'

Karas shook his head. He said, 'There's just one thing I'd like to ask you. About Weldon—'

He found it difficult to go on. There was something indecent in putting into words the suspicion in his mind. Something approaching compassion came into Suvorin's pale eyes. 'This is nothing to do with him,' he said. 'He doesn't know.'

Relief flooded over Karas. It was like feeling blood flowing back into a limb which had been momentarily paralysed. To be betrayed by strangers or by enemies seemed suddenly, by comparison, a small matter. It did not destroy the meaning of existence. He said curtly, 'I didn't come here to meet you. There's nothing for us to talk about.'

'I think there is.' As Karas turned towards the door Suvorin added, 'You won't be allowed to leave until you listen to what I have to say.'

Karas played with the idea of demanding his rights as the inhabitant of a free and neutral country. But it would be a waste of energy, he knew. He turned back to Suvorin. 'All right, then. I'll listen to you if that's what you want. What is it?'

Suvorin spoke like a schoolmaster dressing down a student for some piece of misbehaviour. 'It's necessary to educate you in your obligations. You seem to have acquired the idea that your skill and the knowledge you possess is your own property, to do with as you please. In fact, it was all acquired in my laboratory and belong to those who gave you the facilities to acquire it. You can't be allowed to go out and use it—or sell it—just as you please.'

Karas was reminded of Forsyth, defending the ISIS policy on publications and patents. The two economic systems were evidently agreed on one thing—whoever a scientist belonged to, it was certainly not himself.

'I think you ought to know something,' he said. 'If I'm not let out of this house very shortly, the police will be automatically notified.'

Suvorin was obviously unimpressed by the threat. This possibility had evidently been fully considered. 'You have a life to lead,' he said. 'You can't spend the whole of it under police protection.'

It was true, of course. Karas felt naked and exposed. He said bitterly, 'Why can't you leave me alone?'

Suvorin looked at him almost pityingly. 'Peter,' he said with a first touch of humanity, 'nobody is interested in you as a person. They're only interested in Max. When I asked you whether he had written to you before he died, you lied to me. Why did you do that?'

'It was a private letter. It was none of your business.'

Suvorin gave a grunt of impatience. 'You know better than that. When Max destroyed his notes, it was obvious he had something to conceal. When you realized I knew you had lied to me, you ran away.'

'I escaped,' said Karas. 'It's a little different.'

Suvorin ignored his intervention. 'The point is this. Neither we nor the Americans want exclusive use of the information. Those days are over. It is important for us to co-operate, not to fight each other, but we need to know what it is, for our own protection and for the benefit of the world in general. We can be trusted to use it responsibly —you might sell it to others who are less responsible or disclose it unwisely for the sake of sensation. Others might get hold of you and force you to disclose it. We can't allow that.'

His voice was flat and unemotional, and, as always, he looked slightly away from the person he was talking to. Karas knew Suvorin too well to imagine that this abstracted method of expressing himself indicated any lack of resolution. During the last few months, since he had left the Centre, Karas had begun to forget what total dedication to an objective could mean. In the men he had met in the West there was always some area of softness. With Henderson it was an old man's vanity, a dash of humour and generosity. With Forsyth it was his devotion to science and to his colleagues at the Research Institute. But in Suvorin there was no area to which humanity might appeal.

'I told them in New York,' said Karas. 'There was nothing in that letter. It was gibberish.'

Suvorin said dryly, 'We weren't inclined to believe that.'

'It's the truth.'

'It was a foolish explanation. I can't imagine what induced you to make it. It doesn't make sense.'

'Why not?'

'If it were true, why shouldn't you have told me in the first place? There was nothing to conceal.'

Karas said, 'Max was my best friend. I couldn't bring myself to tell everyone he had lost his mind.' It seemed unconvincing even to him. He said desperately, 'Can't you understand that?'

Suvorin pursed his lips, as if testing the explanation before rejecting it. 'Simply a matter of delicacy?' he said with a lift of his eyebrows. 'No, that's not convincing.'

'Why not?'

'Because I know you, Peter.' The grey eyes regarded him coldly. 'That might make sense for another kind of man—perhaps even for Max himself—but not for you. You were always a careful man, a careerist. You played up to me in the hope that I'd make you a section leader over Max's head. You exercised your brain on the chess-board and your body on those girls of yours from the University. After Max died you made love to his wife and used her to get you away to the West.' He paused. Karas said nothing. What was there to say? 'A man is the sum of the things he does,' said Suvorin. 'I don't see you as a romantic, ready to risk his career for a moment of delicacy about a dead friend.' He shook his head. 'No, I don't think that's the explanation.'

'All right, then, what *do* you think?'

Suvorin was silent for a moment. Finally he said, 'I think Max believed he had discovered something immensely important—probably to do with making very primitive living organisms which never existed before. After all, it's known to be a possibility. I think he was too frightened of its implications to go through with it and left the decision to you. As for whether his notes made sense or not—' He looked up at Karas and said shrewdly, 'I think you don't know. After all, how could you? He destroyed everything except those notes. You'd have to repeat the experiment.'

A great lassitude came over Karas. He could not summon up the energy to argue any further. He could tell by the confidence in the other man's voice that Suvorin knew he had arrived at the truth. He listened impassively as Suvorin went on. 'It was childish of you to think that the Americans would allow you to repeat it and then make your own decision whether to disclose your results or suppress them. They can't take risks like that any more than we can.' As if with an enormous effort of will, Suvorin managed to soften the harsh timbre of his voice. He spoke with gentleness and understanding, no longer like a schoolmaster, but like a father with an errant son whom he still loves. 'Peter, you were the best and the brightest of all my men. I wanted to do so much for you. If you rejected me in the end—well, perhaps that was my own fault. I wouldn't wish any harm to come to you. But you must understand that this is a very serious and important matter. We can't allow you to keep the information to yourself. We must know exactly what was in those notes. I know you destroyed them but I also know your memory. You must tell us.' When Karas said nothing, he took a pad of lined white paper out of the file in front of him and pushed it across the table. In a persistent, almost hypnotic voice, he said, 'You must write it down now.'

The threat was veiled, but it was clear enough. He could tell from the way Suvorin spoke that they had no doubt that in this last resort he would capitulate. The pieces had been moved, the game had been played. He had been bold and intelligent and skilful, but superior force had been mustered against him and he had lost. There was no shame in accepting defeat in such circumstances. They would not despise him. No man was called upon to sacrifice himself beyond the dictates of reason.

And yet . . . He looked at the piece of paper in front of him. Beyond all logic and common sense he knew that to write upon it would be an abandonment of his manhood, a capitulation which would destroy every vestige of pride he possessed. He would go on living afterwards but as a neutered animal, a man without a soul. He could not bring himself to do it.

Suvorin saw his hesitation. He said gently, 'This is not just a question of yourself. You have a duty to others.'

'Others?'

'Your dependents.' He gave a curious little grunt, as if he was doing something which was hurting him, deep inside. 'We shouldn't be able to guarantee the safety of anyone you—associated with.'

Far in the distance there was the melancholy sound of a foghorn on the lake. Apart from this the two men sat in silence. Eventually Karas said, 'We're scientists, civilised men. We're not barbarians. I can't believe you meant what you said then.'

'I'm acting under instructions,' said Suvorin.

Karas saw the look of suffering on Suvorin's face and knew that it had not been a bluff, that if he persisted in his defiance he was gambling not only with his own life but with that of Sarah and his child. He knew too that in agreeing to make the threat, Suvorin had destroyed his own self-respect for ever. Yet the object was attained. For such a matter as this, a man might sacrifice himself, but not those he loved. Slowly Karas drew the writing pad towards him and took the fountain pen out of his pocket. Suvorin said, 'If you do this, no harm will come to anyone. You have my word, Peter. After all, Max was my friend too, you know.'

The falseness of it struck Karas like a blow in the face. He remembered the cruelty Max had endured, the suspense and humiliation in which he had lived. If Suvorin could call himself Max's friend, then his word meant nothing. There was no use in pretending that what he was about to do now was anything less than a complete capitulation.

And yet he must do it. He turned back to the paper, thinking: so this is all there is, this is the end of it. Was he lost for ever? Was there no help anywhere? Suvorin sat at the other end of the long polished mahogany table, watching him intently. His podgy fingers were clasped together in front of him as if in prayer. Occasionally a faint, unpleasant crack would occur as he worked the knuckles against each other. Apart from that, the silence was intense.

Now the decision was made, there was nothing to be gained by delay. Karas felt an almost suffocating desire to finish the affair quickly, to start as soon as possible the process of setting the seal on his defeat. He looked down at the paper and made the usual effort with his mind which the process of memorization involved. It was a curious feat, which involved the elimination of everything else from consciousness and an intense attempt to visualize the particular item which he wanted to turn up from the files of memory. He had done it so often that it was an almost automatic process, a co-ordinated flick of the mind comparable to the actions of a practised athlete. Nothing ever went wrong with this automatic process, and he waited for the image of the page to appear on the screen of his mind.

He waited in vain. To his astonishment, no image appeared. He tried again, forcing it, concentrating, willing the memory to appear. But his mind was like a blank photographic plate. He could not remember a word of the letter, not a single word or figure of Max's notes.

His first reaction was a panic that his mind itself might have broken. He flashed quickly to other memories, an old experiment of his own, a chess problem he had read six months ago—they appeared as clearly as the day when he had first read them. But when he jerked himself back to Max's letter, the blank returned. It was as if the whole story had been burned away from the surface of his brain.

Suvorin's eyes were on him, anxiously seeking the reason for the delay. 'What's the matter?'

Karas put the pen down very deliberately on the sheet of paper. 'It's gone,' he said.

'Gone?' Suvorin was angry and incredulous.

'I've forgotten it.'

'Don't be a fool. We all know your memory.'

'It's as if—' he tried to express it in words. 'It's like finding yourself suddenly impotent. It's an automatic process that has nothing to do with consciousness. You always just assume you can do it. And until today I always could. Then—suddenly—'

Anger flashed across Suvorin's face. The thin lips tightened. 'You realize, don't you, that this wouldn't constitute an excuse—'

'Yes, of course,' said Karas wearily. He knew what Suvorin was about to say. They both knew the system. Only results counted. Reasons and excuses were irrelevant. To those who controlled events it would be a matter of no significance whether Karas was lying or was genuinely unable to remember. Only the facts mattered.

Karas looked at Suvorin and knew, as he saw the sweat of panic break out on the old man's forehead, that it would be the end of the line for him too. How many people had the gentle Max destroyed with that final letter of his? Suvorin said, pleading, 'Try, Peter—just once more—'

He made another attempt, but his mind remained opaque. He shook his head. 'It's no good.'

He pushed away the pen and the sheets of paper. Somewhere inside him, buried under the fear of what the future held, was a feeling of triumph. In the end he had not been defeated. If the victory had come from his unconscious or whatever power controlled it, well, perhaps courage came from there too. One could perhaps as reasonably claim credit for one as for the other.

He said, 'There's no point in my staying here any more.'

Suvorin seemed to consider the possibility of arguing and then to realize it was hopeless. Without saying anything further he got up from his seat and led Karas to a door at the opposite end of the room. The door led into a small hall with a side door leading on to the street. Karas's coat was lying on a chair. Suvorin watched him put it on and then unbolted the door.

'Goodbye, Peter,' he said.

He held out his hand. Karas hesitated for a fraction of a second. But, after all, why not? He shook hands. As he turned to leave, Suvorin delayed him for a moment. 'About the girl,' he said awkwardly. 'I don't know how much they really meant that. They don't always tell you everything.'

'No. I understand.'

'If she weren't with you, I doubt if any real harm would come to her.' He stepped away from the door. 'It's up to you. If you turn right it takes you into the town; left leads you back to the quay.'

Karas heard the door close behind him and he was left alone in the street. He paused, pondering over what Suvorin had said. Any part of it could either be the truth or a lie. The promises and the threats could be equally valid or equally empty. Only one thing was clear. If he went back to Sarah now, she would share the danger of his own life, whatever it might be. He had been offered the choice of saving her that.

But then he suddenly knew that the alternative was meaningless—there was no real choice at all. To give Sarah safety by abandoning her would mean nothing to her, since she cared everything for him, and for safety, practically speaking, nothing at all. To be abandoned was an infinitely worse fate than to run the risk of a shot in the night or a bullet through a car windscreen. He had made a promise and he must keep it. 'I'm your country now,' she had said. In all his travels and escapes he had never been more sure where his loyalty lay. To this at least he would never be a traitor.

God knows what will happen to her, he thought. If he went down, she would go down with him, and that was the way it should be. A man's disaster could never be sealed away. His future, for good or evil, belonged to her as much as it did to himself.

He turned left and saw her figure outlined against the gleaming water of the lake. She was standing by the quay waiting for him. He hurried down the street towards the car.